BUDDHA'S THUNDERBOLT:

The Uncredulous Tale of the Wizard Merlin

Jacob Asher Michael

A.V. Fistula Multimedia

New York

JACOB ASHER MICHAEL

This is a work of fiction. All of the characters and events portrayed in this novel are either fictitious or are used fictitiously.

BUDDHA'S THUNDERBOLT: THE UNCREDULOUS TALE OF THE WIZARD MERLIN

Copyright 2009 by John S. Michael

All right reserved, including the right to reproduce this book, or any portions thereof, in any form.

ISBN 978-0-557-25193-3

Published through www.lulu.com by:

A.V. Fistula Multimedia

720 Ft. Washington Ave. Suite 6K

New York, NY, 10040

jakemichaelmail@yahoo.com

Printed in the United States of America

Dedication

To my sister Ann who kept me writing,
and my sister Judith who kept on reading.

Acknowledgements

Thanks for many years of support from Tom and Bonnie Michael, Bill and Glo Delamar, Scott Stoddard, Juilene Osborn-McKnight, the Philadelphia Writers Conference, the Brandywine Valley Writers Group, the Chester County Writers Workshop, the Chester County Bookstore, Dennis Strain, Mark Bernstein, Deanna Kemler, Hugh Sutherland, Willow Branch Sangha, the Philadelphia Meditation Center, David Keys author of *Catastrophe: An Investigation into the Origins of the Modern World*, Andy Partridge of the band XTC composer of the song *Greenman* from the album *Apple Venus*, Venerable Ajahn Sumedho author of *The Four Noble Truths*, Venerable Thich Nhat Hanh author of *Living Buddha Living Christ*, and, of course, Matt, Jane, Steve, and Audra.

FOREWARD

Vis consili expers mole ruit sua.

Brute force bereft of wisdom falls to ruin by its own weight.

* * *

During the 5th Century CE, the ethnic identities and nation states that now make up the British Isles were not yet developed or differentiated. Geographic boundaries were still described using terms created by Roman provincial governments, regardless of the tribal societies who actually lived there. Thus, *Britannia* extended through most of present day England, while *Cambria* covered much of Wales. Scotland, north of Hadrian's Wall, was *Caledonia*. The entire island of Ireland was *Hibernia*. The countries in present day Europe simply did not exist.

This was an era of chaos and migration on a global scale. The Huns from the steppes of Central Asia swept down into Eastern Europe, forcing its Germanic tribes to flee south through the Balkans, and west into Spain, Britain, and North Africa. When Italy finally fell to the Germans, the well heeled citizens of Caesar's Eternal City fled east to Constantinople. They became part of a reduced empire that still called itself *Rome*, even thought its culture and language was Byzantine Greek. Those hapless Roman colonists left behind in the walled fortresses of northern Europe were suddenly minorities, surrounded by the very savages their fathers had subjugated for centuries.

In the Far East, the ancient dynasties of Southern China dissolved into a bloody collection of principalities. Meanwhile, the Northern Chinese were set upon by pillaging Siberian horseman, while Persia incurred raids by the so-called White Huns of the Caucasus. Strangely enough, with the empires of the East defending their northern flanks, south Asia flourished. The Gupta dynasty with their elephant armies, ushered in the Golden Age of India, delighting in literacy and the arts, while the rest of the world descended into disarray, barbarism and an ever deepening well of anarchy.

BOOK I: THE HERMIT

CHAPTER I: THE CORN MOON, AD 480

Ex oriente lux.

From the east, light.

* * *

"I could kill you," said Merthen to the black widow climbing one of the braids in his long white beard. "That would be the prudent course of action."

When he was a red-headed child in Constantinople, Merthen played a game with poisonous spiders. He and his fellow slave boys would catch a few black widows in a cup. Each of the boys would then place one of the toxic insects on his respective foot, and stand resolute while it crawled towards the warmth of his respective crotch. The first boy to flinch lost.

"This island will be the end of you," said Merthen to the eight-legged stranger.

Just offshore, near where Carmarthen Bay emptied into the Celtic Sea, an Iberian spice ship strained against her anchor lines. A few days earlier, this vessel had unloaded a shipment of Asian peppercorns. No doubt the spider was a stowaway from much warmer shores.

"You will not survive this evening's frost," said Merthen. He removed the feather writing quill tucked behind his ear, and pointed it at the tiny stranger. He inhaled, aware of the flow of his breath. "I recommend you return to your ship."

He flicked the black widow into air. It spiraled down, landing in a puddle by the sea wall. As if on cue, a sedge warbler swooped low and snapped it up in its beak. The bird flew off to its nest in a stand of bull rushes. Three fuzzy chicks poked up their gaping mouths.

Merthen was sliding his pen back in place when he felt something strike his left buttock. Whatever connected with him was a blunt object, soft like the head of a yearling ram not yet sprouting horns. Still, it was enough of a jolt to make him lose his balance. He fumbled to hold on to his ash wood walking stick.

From behind him, Merthen heard the voice of a young boy saying, "That hurt."

Merthen twisted backward to identify this child, and in so doing completely lost his footing. His lanky old body toppled over. The eighteen Indian rosewood beads strung around his left wrist smacked against the cobblestones, and his staff flew out of his hands.

The boy, a street urchin with shaggy brown hair and a snakelike fish in his hand, rubbed the top of his forehead, but he did not cry. Instead, he directed his hazelnut eyes at the trumpet swan carved onto the head of Merthen's walking stick and asked, "Is that a duck?"

"No," said Merthen, "it is a piece of wood."

During Merthen's fall, the four ponytails that hung down his back had wrapped around his face. He untangled them.

"Are you sure?" said the boy. He scratched at his bottom. "It looks like a duck to me."

Merthen, still lying on his back, popped the lid off the leather cylinder tied to his belt. From it, he pulled out a small vial of ink. He checked to make sure that the glass was not cracked. He snapped at the urchin. "You should be minding your step, boy. Where are your parents?"

Out from behind a stack of wool bundles, Widow Blodwen, the fishmonger, charged forward, with a meat cleaver in her fist. "Thief," she cried. "Stop him!" Her more than ample hips pounded across the marketplace. Her freckled face was furious red.

The boy broke into a sprint. Merthen reached over, and retrieved his walking stick. With a well-aimed flick of the wrist, he tossed it at the child's gangly legs. The boy glanced back. With all the grace of an acrobat, he leapt into the air. The long wooden staff spiraled under the child's dirty feet.

Widow Blodwen barreled onward.

The boy banked to the left. His shoulder bumped against a rickety table displaying used arms and cutlery. That was all it took to send a cacophony of knives and throwing hatchets scattering in all directions. The arms dealer was a wooden-shoed Frank with a huge handlebar mustache, two thick pigtails above his ears, and the back of his head shaved. He sprang from his stool and yelled, "Oh bugger!"

The boy zigzagged, first around the kettle at the tanner's stall, then up hill towards the castle. Widow Blodwen followed, huffing all the way.

The last sword left on the table teetered on the edge before it tipped, handle-down toward the earth. It ricocheted off a cobblestone that jutted up above the rest. Merthen, his face flush to the ground, observed the old weapon slide point-first toward his eyeballs. He jerked his head upward. Just below his earlobe, the tip of the freshly-honed blade slid to a stop.

Merthen's heart pounded against his ribcage, but not because of his brush with impalement. In his peripheral vision, he saw a dark figure, no bigger than a kitten. All the commotion had disturbed a black-eyed bilge rat, whose reaction was to scramble across the marketplace, terrified.

The rodent raced toward Merthen's belly, then changed course, scrambling down towards his feet. Merthen felt the slither of its tale brushing against his ankles. For a brief moment he shivered like an epileptic caught in the grips of palsy. And then the rat disappeared, employing the ancient talent for retreat all vermin possess.

Merthen closed his eyes. He jiggled the rosewood beads around his wrist. In a whispered tone he chanted, "*Gah-tay, gah-tay, para gah-tay, parasam gah-tay, bodhi svaha.*" A bead of sweat seeped into his eyes. His body stopped shaking. His mind stopped racing. He regained control, at least for now.

The sword that nearly skewered Merthen lay still, pointing at him like Dame Fortune's giant finger. Having been trained as a clerk, Merthen could not help but be drawn to the Latin words stamped on the weapon's blade. He read them out loud, since he was not one of those few literati who could read silently. "Made in Calabria," he said.

The Frankish arms dealer, who was down on his knees gathering up his knives, responded, "No, not Calabria. I bought that one from an old Roman Lady in Boulogne. Her grandfather brought it west from Constantinople. Pure wootz steel." He picked up a hatchet, and stood. "Just what I need, more dents."

Merthen hoisted himself up, using the weapon like a cane. He tapped his fingernail against the imprint. "I can read, Sir. According to this text, this sword was manufactured in Calabria. The style of the writing suggests it was forged by native Italians working under an Ostragoth. This is no antique. The lady misled to you."

"Ostragoths?" The Frank slapped his own head. "Those Germans make crap!"

With one well-practiced whirl, Merthen circled the sword above his head. "I suspect it is actually laminated iron. Excellent welding, though. It should clean up fine." He passed it over. "I am a freelance clerk, by the way. If you need any receipts, my fees are quite reasonable."

The Frank squeezed the handle of the sword. "That uppity hag! She sold me a two-bit butter knife! How am I supposed to sell this garbage?"

Merthen shook the dust from his cloak. "I really should not be spending money right now." He picked up his staff. "However, I might have a use for this piece. I harvest an apple orchard up in the hills. This could reach the fruit in the higher boughs. Would you be willing to part with it for fifteen denarii?"

The Frank shoved the blade back into its sheath. "Twenty denarii is as low as I can go. When my wife finds out about this, she is going to skin my testicles with a rusty razor."

"That would be distressing," said Merthen. He dug into his purse to gather all the cash he had, twenty denarii. "Twenty is reasonable price. Do we have a deal?"

The Frank gave him the sword and scabbard. "If any one asks, you did not buy this from me. I only sell Roman stock."

"We never met," said Merlin. He bowed, then felt a tug on one of his braids. The sun-burned face of the little street urchin was at the end of it.

"I dropped my kipper when you fell," said the boy. "Did you see where it went?"

Merthen scanned the square. He could not locate Widow Blodwen, but he did find the fish. It was half submerged in a puddle next to a wine crate. "That is a dead eel. Go away."

The boy stuck his finger up his nose. "I saw a piglet today. He had eyes like yours. Why are your eyes so blue?"

From upslope a ways, Widow Blodwen yelled, "There he is!" She jogged a few steps, leaned over and wheezed. The boy dashed off past the chandler's booth. He rolled under a cow's belly, and like the rat, disappeared into the maze of vendor's carts.

Merthen strolled over to Blodwen. He secured his new purchase to his belt.

Blodwen tucked an auburn-gray tendril back into her headscarf. "Quite a show, eh?" she said. "Why did you let him go?"

"Gentlemen in their dotage do not run." Merthen scooped up the limp fish from its puddle. He gave her a wink. "How is business, Missus B? I was hoping to purchase a baleen whale this morning, much like this specimen, but preferably more sanitary. Might you have one in stock?"

She shook her cleaver a halfheartedly. "Back in my day, I used to outrun all the lads." She hobbled back to her fish stand. "Are you getting any work?"

"Not lately. I sold some rabbits to Missus Myfany last week." He tossed the eel's carcass into the bay. "Have you heard any news about our neighbors?"

She plucked up a sea bass by the gills and slapped its skull onto the nail that stuck up from on her butcher's block. "I spoke with a skipper from Iberia this morning. He saw a couple keels crossing the channel. Saxons, I suppose." She rubbed her thigh.

"Did you injure yourself?"

"I took a spill the other day. My bum is all sore. And here I go chasing a sneak thief."

Merthen dug into his cloak pocket, and pulled out a strip of willow bark. "Chew on this. It should reduce the swelling. Unfortunately, I know of no poultice to protect you from thievery. I shall keep an eye out for your little crook."

"No point to that." She wiped some scales off her hands. "Some slaver will ship him off. I see those street orphans once, maybe twice, never three times."

"Excuse me?" said Merthen. A drop of sweat rolled down his face.

"Are you all right?"

Merthen sat down, with his legs forward like a child. He shuddered briefly, then closed his eyes. Tears streamed down his cheeks.

Widow Blodwen stumbled onto her knees. She shook him by the shoulders. "Merthen? Mister Ambrosius? Can you hear me?"

* * *

All he could hear was the creaking of a slave ship. He opened his eyes. A single clay lamp lit the galley. He tried to move his legs, but the cage that surrounded him was too confining. A rat arched its back in the corner.

He covered his face and screamed. More rats appeared. Their claws tapped against the wooden floor.

Through a dim haze, Merthen saw the figure of a street urchin with a splint of glowing sandalwood in his dirty little hands. The boy remained silent. The sweet figgy fragrance of blossoming bo trees wafted through the air.

Merthen called out, "There is nothing I can do! Can you not see this?"

Like a troupe of dancers, the rats paired off into four sets of two. Each couple paced around in a circle, one following the tail of the other. Merthen focused on the first pair. One of the creatures was emaciated. Its cohort was fat.

The second pair emitted noises. One hissed like a snake while the other cooed like a dove. The third set consisted of one contented individual, and one who was forever dissatisfied. The last two rats were mirror images; one exuded love under all conditions, the other perpetually withheld it.

Merthen cried, "I am trapped! Save me!"

Faster and faster the rats twirled. A whirlwind spiraled up from each pair. The flame in the clay lamp flickered, then went out.

Merthen extended his arm as far as he could. With his bare hand, he grabbed for the boy's burning incense. In so doing, Merthen snuffed out the ember, casting himself into total darkness.

"Enough," he screamed, "enough!" Although he could no longer see the rats, he could hear them crawling ever closer. The slither of their tales brushed against his ankles. He shivered. It all seemed oddly familiar.

And then he realized that he was repeating the events that had taken place earlier in the day. What he was experiencing was not reality, but a mental formation: a half-cocked hallucination cobbled together from jumbled memories. It had been a while since he had suffered one of these episodes. He was rather hoping he had seen the last of them.

One of the rats clasped its forepaws onto the soft skin below his toenail. Merthen wanted to remain dispassionate, to observe this pain as if he was an outsider. If he could only overcome the attachment to the self, none of this would concern him. He would be free.

But instead he wept. Was it just the harsh sting of the rat's sharpened teeth piercing the tips of his toes? Or was it the frustration that they had come back again, forcing him once more to bleed so they could lap up his warm wet blood.

His emotions swung between infantile terror and abject confusion. His thoughts were knotted together, like the rigging of a ship whose mast had been snapped off in a storm. He was unable to tell where one strand ended and the other began. When ropes get bollixed like that, all a sailor can do is find his sharpest knife and cut the lines.

Perhaps that was why there was only one thought that Merthen's exhausted consciousness could generate. It was, "Kill the rats. Kill them all."

* * *

Merthen's cheeks were bitter cold. Did someone slap his face? He opened his eyes. Widow Blodwen still held the wash bucket she had just emptied onto him. His hair was sopping wet.

"Where have I been?" he asked. "What did I say?"

Blodwen hoisted him onto a keg of salt and patted his cheeks dry with her kerchief. "You were right here. You said nothing. What happened?"

"I appear to have been struck by a mania." He took a swig from the water sack that hung from his belt. "I apologize for exposing you to my malady."

She gasped. "Mother of God! You had a vision. Did you see an angel? Did you see a fairy?"

"No." He massaged his temples with the flat of his hands.

Merthen put no stock in angels, fairies, or the charlatans who claimed to commune with them. Sorcerers and oracles were manipulative liars, reaping profit from broken souls desperate for answers. Even the Buddha, a man who would have gladly shared his dinner with a congress of demons, had no patience for those who, as he put it, *trafficked in miracles.*

"All I saw," said Merthen, "was a boy."

Blodwen inched closer. "What do you suppose that means?"

Merthen knew better than to affix meaning to the froth stirred up by his hallucinations. And yet, a vague concept congealed in his mind. The urchin boy he saw during his madness was holding incense like a monk. Could this boy be trained as a monastic? If that were true, then Merthen would not be the only one. Why, he might even start a monastery.

But then again, no. This was foolishness. Merthen was far too familiar with the dangers of expectation. Expectation led to craving and attachment. It enslaved the mind to the illusion that things are not impermanent. He would not tempt that, not again.

"It meant absolutely nothing," he finally said. A young woman was eyeing the brook trout on Blodwen's display table. "You have a customer."

"She can wait. Like it or not, you are not an average man, Mister Merthen. I may not be as worldly as you, but I know how many beans make five. This is a sign, old boy. Anyone can see that."

Merthen flung off his cloak. "You are far too superstitious." His flaxen blouse and orange silk neckerchief were drenched in perspiration. "Is there some place I can hang these?"

Chapter II: The Corn Moon, AD 480

Fallaces sunt rerum species.

The appearances of things are deceptive.

* * *

A savage's life is most precarious. Most children born to Saxon mothers succumb to illness or want before they take their first step. Few Germans live to see their grandchildren, but those who do have a fair chance of reaching sixty. Some even make it to ninety, an achievement almost unheard of, even among the Romans.

The longevity of the German has much to do with his habitat. As a creature of the woodlands, he must be always alert, physically fit, and able to adapt to the vagaries of the wild. And so it was with Merthen, whose life in the forest had exposed him to nature's harshest schooling.

Like the savages, he had learned how to survive, and did so to a very great age. Indeed, most of the merchants in Carmarthen had never seen him with anything but a crop of white hair. To them, he was like a feature on the landscape: a weathered boulder that had always just been there.

Thus, no one in the marketplace took much notice when Merthen rested on a crate by the docks. He bit into his apple and watched the clouds dissipate over Carmarthen Bay. Nearby, sandpipers dipped their oblong beaks into mudflats fringed with sea grass. If Merthen were to spend all of eternity re-living just this very moment, that would be acceptable.

* * *

And then, there was silence. A Carthaginian freighter anchored by the shoals stood still. Even its sails were motionless, like a ship in a cathedral mosaic showing Jonah being cast overboard.

Merthen observed Mister Hopcyn, the rag-and-bone-man, standing as if frozen, not even blinking. Even more unusual was the cracked frying pan Mister Hopcyn had just tossed into to his barrow. This piece of wrought iron refuse was now hanging in mid-air, not moving in any direction.

Merthen could not hear the crash of the waves, because the waves had ceased to crash. There was no wind, no motion of any stripe. As far as Merthen could tell, the only object in the universe which still possessed mobility was he himself. Was this some kind of dream?

A bird erupted in song. "*Sita Ram Ram Ram,*" it sang, "*Jay Jay, Sita Ram Ram Ram.*"

From behind the harbor master's house, a finch-sized songbird with a pink-orange belly flew through the stillness. It was a Kashmir flycatcher from the steamy forests of the Orient. How could this tiny creature have migrated all the way to Britannia's chilly shores? And why on earth would it want to?

The bird perched on the head of Merthen's walking stick. She clasped her claws into the tip of the wooden swan's beak.

"The boy," she said, "tell me about the boy."

Merthen did not try to shoo her away. Instead he jiggled the eighteen wooden beads on his bracelet. "Stay calm," he muttered to himself. "All dharmas are marked with emptiness."

She bowed, or came as close to it as her bird knees would allow. "Permit me to introduce myself, I am Lady Gopi from Lake Sambhar, haven of the pink flamingos. I have been retained as the investigator for your trial. Your defense attorney, Bright-eyed Athena, requested I compile a report regarding your relationship to the boy. I would like to ask you a few questions, Lord Wizard."

He breathed in. He permitted his eyelids to slide shut. When he reopened them, the bird was still there. "I am not a wizard," he said, but he did not say it to her. Rather he declared it as a kind of verbal reminder designed to keep himself on course. "And, you are not a bird. This is a hallucination."

She hopped onto his shoulder. "Have you ever had a hallucination like this before?"

He had, but he was not about to tell her. Over the years, he had trained his mind to deal with his untrustworthy perceptions. There was no point in arguing with the beings that arose from his warped imagination. No matter how he reasoned with them, they always claimed to be real. The proper course of action was to ignore them. Eventually, they would dissolve back into nothingness.

The bird chirped, "The gods just have a few questions, Lord Wizard."

Merthen snorted. "The gods? What rot."

As a youth, Merthen had been taught to associate polytheism with Huns, Germans, and other smelly brutes. But once he set eyes on the deity-packed temples of the Ganges Valley, he realized just how refined a pagan could be. As years went by, the Holy Trinity and the four heads of Brahma blurred together in his mind. Regardless of their number, they all seemed callous and aloof.

Lady Gopi jumped onto a hitching post. "It shall not take long."

"Lake Sambhar is located in India," said Merthen. "Why are you working for a Greek goddess? And what in Beelzebub's name are you doing here in Britannia?"

"I could ask you the same thing," she said, batting her eyes. "You are quite fortunate. When the gods try most men, they rarely conduct such a thorough investigation. Now then, about the boy."

Merthen scratched at his tonsure-like bald spot. "I have no idea what you are talking about. I suggest you return to that god-filled fairytale-land from which you emanate, and inform your employers that I do not care if they damn me. I should think they would wait till I was moldering in the grave before passing judgment on me."

"Not really. From their perspective, time does not work that way."

"Well in that case, you shall have to enlighten me. Tell me, little squab, how does time work?"

* * *

Gopi did not answer. Instead Merlin's ears were jolted by the crash of a pan landing in Mister Hopcyn's cart. A briny gust blew in from across the Celtic Sea, rippling the sails on the Carthaginian freighter. The hitching post upon which the talking bird had roosted, was now empty. Lady Gopi was gone.

Merthen used to feel tremendous shame that he suffered from delusions. But as he grew older, he became somewhat grateful that had survived so long despite his madness. At least he was not some senile old codger who could only see faces from his past. Given Merthen's personal history, such an illness would be more vicious than any torture the king's men could devise.

But these were dark thoughts, nothing but rumination. Merthen was aware that they, like the talking animals, were not to be believed. He breathed in, and compiled a mental listing of all those things for which he should be thankful: his good health, his education, the cool crisp air of his mountain home.

His positive contemplation was broken by a jovial voice.

"Well look what we have here!" it said with a Frankish accent thick as butter sauce with capers. "By Ajax's teats, could this be the Wizard of Britannia?"

This hearty hail issued forth from a raven-haired hunchback with one gray eye and one black. The stoop-shouldered fellow wore a yard-long stocking cap of red velvet, draped off to the left. Merthen followed its tassel down past the hunchback's twisted arm to a shriveled leg, tipped with a toeless foot.

The hunchback said, "It is none other than I, Thumbs." He gave a deep bow, well beyond the bounds of good taste. "I say, you look well, Ambrosius. We thought you were dead, old chum, but here you are tight as a tympanum."

Seeing Thumbs harkened Merthen back to when he performed sleight-of-hand in the squares of Paris. He recalled Lord Marcian, the proprietor of the Inn of the Fountain who had an unquenchable thirst for the ladies. And there was James, the street corner cithara player, who sang quaint little ditties laced with gems of wisdom. As Romans go, old James was a good salt. Too bad he drank so much.

"I am afraid, Sir," said Merthen, "that you have mistaken me for another. I am Merthen the Clerk, not Ambrosius the Wizard."

"Nice try," said Thumbs. "You are still wearing that girlish cravat. Besides, if you did not know it was me, why did you check my gimpy leg?"

Merthen tugged on the orange kerchief around his neck. He wore it out of dedication, a reminder of the monastic life he was forced to leave. If that piece of silk cost him a certain level of anonymity, so be it.

"What are you doing here?" said Merthen. "Did you run out of purses to snatch in Gaul?"

Thumbs exhaled. "Actually, I came into a modest windfall and determined it was due time I toured your sunny island. So, what brings you to this fine market? Still captivating the crowds with your stinging bowl?"

"Nowadays, I grow apples and bunnies." Merthen patted the bundle of rabbit pelts on his lap. "And I clerk a bit."

Thumbs chuckled. "What a waste of talent. You should come back to the continent. Did you hear? King Syagrius sent a petition to Emperor Zeno in Byzantium. Paris is going to rejoin the Roman Empire."

"What, again? Since when is Syagrius a king? Last I heard, he was still calling himself *governor*."

"He goes back and forth. Do you recall little Morgan, the beer wench with the wicked hind end? She was always fascinated with your shows."

"The redhead? I thought her name was *Faye*."

"Aye, that was her. She has become Syagrius's personal chambermaid, so to speak." Thumbs elbowed him in the ribs. "You know the Romans still talk about you. Remember that trick you did with the glass? How did you burn that paper?"

Merthen felt a tap on his shoulder. It was Mister Bedwyr the clothier, with a bolt of cambric under his arm. He aimed it at Thumbs. "Is this man with you?"

Merthen bowed. "Not really, no."

In one swift action, Bedwyr dropped the fabric and pulled out his linen shears. He pressed them against Thumb's neck. "Give me the thread!"

Thumbs swallowed hard.

Merthen considered making up a cockamamie story that would inspire the clothier to slash Thumbs to bits. But there would be no justice in that, and far too much blood. Instead, Merthen asked, "What did he take from you, Bedwyr?"

"A spool of silk. He was chatting it up with my wife. Once he left, the thread was gone."

Merthen motioned toward the shears with his walking stick. "Those are exceedingly sharp. I suggest you empty your pockets."

"Oh, I see," said Thumbs, "blame the cripple." He tipped open his purse and emptied its contents: a dozen coins and a bent silver pin. "Is this how you treat all your visitors?" He removed his cloak and shook it. Out fell a few chunks of hard tack and a sketch of a naked woman. She was licking a sweet plum.

"The hat," said Bedwyr. "Take it off."

Thumbs shook his claw-like hand. "No!"

Bedwyr yanked the cap off, exposing Thumbs's left ear, a pink oval hole with a half-inch long spike of skin above it. Bedwyr stepped back.

Through clenched teeth, the red-faced Thumbs muttered, "Satisfied?"

Merthen retrieved the hat from the ground, genuinely surprised that Thumbs had not nicked the thread. "It appears he is innocent, or at least less guilty than usual."

Bedwyr shook his makeshift dagger and scowled. "There is a Visigoth ship leaving at sun-up. Be on it." He rolled up his fabric and marched away.

Merthen handed over the hat. "You know they burn Hebrews here. If the knight constable learns you are a son of David, you shall find a spike up your colon before you can say *Ave Maria*."

Thumbs twisted his chin around, unimpressed. "That was just my stage persona. Besides, I only claimed to be half Jewish." He unrolled a loose flap of skin that covered where his collarbone met his hump. From underneath it, he retrieved a spool of purple thread.

Merthen snapped it out of Thumb's' one good hand. "I shall tell Mister Bedwyr that I found this lying about. The ship you will be boarding tomorrow is moored at Saint Catherine's dock."

Thumbs crouched low to gather his belongings. "You know old man, spending time with you *Welschmann* is making me think it might be nice to be cooped up on a ship full of Germans." He stood up. "If it is not too much bother, could you provide me with a place to bunk tonight?"

"I live up in the hills. You are much too lame to make the trip, and I am much too feeble to carry you. Go sleep on the Visigoth's ship."

"A barn would do. Might you have any friends who would take in a renter?"

"A few," said Merthen. "But if I directed you to them, they would no longer be my friends. You steal in your sleep, Thumbs." A misty rain began to fall. Merthen slipped his hood over his head. "Now, if you *were* my friend, I would strongly recommend that you locate a vessel pointed west and board it. You need to go home, and so do I."

"But you cannot just leave me here alone?"

Merthen wrapped his fingers around his walking stick. "Solitude can be an edification. I would like to say *go in peace*, Thumbs, but we both know you are far too lubricious for that. Instead I will simply say, find a boat and watch your back." He walked away.

From up north there was a lone clap of thunder. Thumbs scooted off to the whitesmith's stall. It had a roof.

Merthen plodded up the road. Above him the grey clouds glided by, until they came to a dead stop. The scant raindrops that were falling ceased to descend any further. Just as before, there was no wind, no sound, no movement.

* * *

Using her blunt black beak, Lady Gopi tugged on one of the long white hairs that sprouted from Merthen's earlobe. Her claws clung onto his collar. "If I may ask," she said, "when did you get so grumpy?"

Merthen rubbed his tired eyes. "Back again? I must be going potty. Did I eat a bad mushroom?"

Gopi asked, "What did the rats signify? The ones in you saw in your vision last week. Why were they in four pairs?"

"So… the talking bird wants to know about the spinning rats? How about this: you flitter off and ask the Goddess Athena about the rodents. Given her reputation for intellectual agility, I think she should be able to figure it out."

The bird shimmied her tail. "I am not one of your visions," she said.

"Well, in that case, let us examine your line of inquiry. If as you claim, Bright-eyed Athena is so *bright-eyed*, why is daughter of Zeus even bothering to pose the question? What could a simpleton such as I possibly tell the goddess of wisdom that she does not already know?"

"You raise a valid point. I will have to discuss this with my patron." Gopi flapped her wings and took to the air. "Good day, Wizard Merlin." She glided over the eastern highlands, deftly avoiding the glass-like drops of water that were, by all appearances, refusing to submit to the pull of Mother Earth.

Merthen pounded his staff onto the muddy turf. "Mer-*then*!" he cried, "My name is Mer-*then*, you bloody half-pint pigeon!"

Chapter III: The Harvest Moon, AD 480

Equo ne credite, Teucri.

Do not trust the horse, Trojans.

* * *

A three-legged stool is a tree-legged stool. Each leg of a stool is not a stool, but rather one part of a stool. Likewise, the top of a stool is just a fraction of the entire unit. All parts of the stool must be connected in order for the stool to function, and so exist as a stool. According to the Buddha, the universe is like a stool: an interconnected collection of parts that are but fragments of one entity.

Thus, each rabbit that Merthen raised in his woodland home was a fuzzy, button-nosed slice of the universe. The rabbit itself was also made of parts, such as muscles, bones, and soft white pelts. Merthen was hoping to sell some of these furs this afternoon. Unfortunately, no one was buying

Merthen pondered the concept of interconnectivity during his trip home from the market. He chewed on the sourdough roll he had earned reading a letter for Pryderi the baker. The correspondence informed the baker about the drowning of his brother in Brittany. It was horrible tragedy that ultimately resulted in Merthen getting a snack. And yet, the bread still tasted good.

Merthen heard the jingle of a horse-drawn wagon coming up the road. He gave a quick two-fingered wave to the driver, and the vehicle came to a halt. The wind ceased to blow as well. The leaves on the trees stopped quivering.

* * *

"I have raised your issue with the Goddess Athena," said the horse.

It appeared to Merthen that this question came from, well... the horse, which he knew to be impossible.

"I beg your pardon?" said Merthen to the driver, who may have been a human, but was at this moment little more than a shabbily dressed statue with cold unblinking eyes.

The mare arched her elongated neck as far back as her harness would permit. "Athena has given me a response. Would you like to hear it?"

Merthen jiggled his beaded rosewood bracelet. "Am I to assume you are a colleague of the Lady Gopi?"

"No. I am Lady Gopi. As you requested, I spoke with the Goddess Athena. She has directed me to continue my investigation. Although she is all-knowing, she wishes to discover what your perceptions are, as *you* experience them. She is not so much interested in conventional facts. Reality is so mundane. She would prefer to hear your intuitive reactions, as it were."

"Why should she care? And what if I refuse to cooperate? Will she turn me into a pillar of salt?"

The horse waved her auburn tail. "If you do not wish to provide your testimony, I cannot compel you by force. However, I can wait."

He crossed his arms. "I can wait as well."

"As long as I can? Come now, what harm would it do to answer a few questions?"

Merthen reared up his walking staff to thrash her, but then lowered it. "And if I answer your questions, will you leave me in peace?"

"That is my ultimate intention," said Gopi. "Now then, here is what I wish to know. Last week when you first met that brown-eyed boy, you had a vision. You saw four pairs of rats. What did they signify?"

Merthen studied her pitch black eyes. Through out his life, Merthen had experienced periods of madness. However, he had never generated a delusion quite so complex as this. And that fact that Gopi appeared on two consecutive episodes was unprecedented. Could this be a new, deeper form of insanity?

But then, Merthen harkened back to that late night discussion at Nalanda University when his fellow monk, Brother Tinh Tu, informed him that there is a mirror in the mind. With proper training, the mind could see itself. Could it be that Gopi was a simply a reflection of a process occurring within Merthen's own mind?

Merthen asked, "Who do *you* think the rats were, Miss Pony?"

"The rats were dancing in circles, chasing each others' tails. It was endless, pointless and endemic." Gopi stomped her front hoof. "I think they represent the extremes that keep an individual from experiencing interbeing."

Merthen tugged on his beard. "The eight mental agitations," he said. "One for each rat. I say Lady, are you some kind of Buddhist?"

"Not quite," Gopi replied. "The question is, are you?"

* * *

Merthen was startled by the noise of the rotating wagon wheel. The horse clopped off saying not a word. The driver bowed politely to Merthen, who nodded in reply, but mostly stared at Gopi, or at least the beast of burden she had most recently inhabited.

The cart rolled away, and Merthen focused himself on the road ahead. At the edge of the commons, he caught a glimpse of the street urchin who had so gleefully annoyed him nearly a fortnight ago.

As before, the brown-eyed boy approached, but this time he did not run. Instead he stepped, with a slow shuffle one might expect from an old crone or a cripple. The child was gaunt and sunburned, his britches stained with diarrhea. There was a scrape on his knee, not large, but pink and swollen.

"Spare some food, Mister?" said the boy in a mechanical monotone. His empty hands were cupped together.

Merthen did not intend to stop. Instead he paused, just long enough to make eye contact with the boy. Then the old man walked off briskly, which was the only way Merthen ever walked. So what if he saw the boy holding incense in his vision? Visions are bunk. No point to dwell on it.

Merthen's ankle buckled underneath him. His foot had slipped into a rut in the road. Odd that. He repositioned his other foot, and it slipped into the rut as well. It almost seemed as if the rut was slithering sideways, purposely trying to topple him. He tipped back, falling into the soft wet dirt.

The boy wiped his dripping nose. "You tripped," he said. "Do you always fall down?"

Merthen sat upright, face to face with the boy, and said, "I try not to make a habit of it."

"I saw you selling apples once. Can I get one?"

"That would be a possibility. Do you have any money?"

"No."

"Well then, what do you propose to give me for my apple?"

The boy leapt down and crawled on all fours like a bear cub. He snatched up every pebble within his reach.

Using his walking stick for a crutch, Merthen hoisted himself up to his full height, a towering two yards. He dusted off his brown wool cloak, and then observed the child standing at attention, clutching a pile of stones. The boy held them up, as high as he could, with an almost formal seriousness. As children go, he had rather big hands.

Merthen's heart fluttered, but not in a normal way. Was he hallucinating again? He usually perspired when he did. He ran his fingers across his brow. It was dry and cool.

Merthen recalled a fable Brother Tinh Tu told him decades ago. A beggar boy once saw noblemen giving alms to the Buddha, and decided to do likewise. But all the boy had to offer was a fist-full of gravel. Upon receiving this humble gift, the Buddha smiled. Because of that boy's noble actions, he was eventually reborn as Ashoka the Great, Emperor of all India.

Merthen jiggled the eighteen rosewood beads on his bracelet and considered the afternoon's events. Could this boy be a future emperor? Could he be a Buddha-to-be? But then again, what child lacks this potential? Perhaps, this boy was just a boy; this grey sky was just a grey sky; and this pile of stones was just a pile of stones.

"Be mindful," said Merthen, "you have too much to bear. I would recommend you lay your burden down. Tell me boy, what do they call you?"

"My name is Uther." Uther set the rubble down by the tip of Merthen's boot.

"And your parents? What are their names?"

"You mean mommy?" Uther pushed a lock of his hair from his eyes. His fingernails were filthy.

"Yes, what is her name? Where is she?"

"Her name is *Mommy*. She is in heaven with baby Jesus. She fell asleep on the floor, and Miss Gwenllian yelled at me. She hit me with a spoon."

"Do you have any other family? Is there anyone who cares for you or brings you food?"

A single tear rolled down Uther's cheek. It dripped down his chin and splattered onto his toes. They were caked in dry blood.

Merthen looked down at Uther's feet. "Rats," said the old man, "they bit you in your sleep, eh?"

The boy fidgeted. "Aye."

Merthen extracted an apple from his deep cloak pocket. "I am about to do something that may be potentially daft. Eat this."

The boy unceremoniously jammed the red-skinned fruit into his mouth.

"Now, when I was a sprout," said Merthen, "it was my misfortune to be imprisoned in a cage on board a Visigoth slave ship. Each night bilge rats would assemble to gnaw on my toes. My feet still bear the marks of their predation."

"Were you scared?"

"Apoplectic. And let me tell you, boy, that potent anxiety has scarred me deeper than any surgeon's blade. I have meditated on it for decades. Up until now, I was under the impression that I had become free from its harrowing grip. But perhaps simply freeing oneself from one's own suffering is not sufficient.

Perhaps, I need to do more." He stared at the boy. "I would wager you have been wounded as well."

Uther wiped away his tear. He showed off his devoured apple core. "I am finished."

Merthen stirred the end of his walking stick into the cluster of stones Uther had collected. "That rubble you swept up. Why did you offer it to me?"

"I was hungry."

Merthen breathed in, and then he breathed out; a simple action, which served as the foundation of all meditation. Indeed, this was the technique the Buddha used to achieve interbeing. When discussing the value of the breath, Brother Tinh Tu used to say, *As long as you have air in your lungs, you can meditate. And as long as you can meditate, you can become as fully awake as the Buddha.*

Merthen asked the boy, "Do you know who I am?"

"You draw with a feather."

"An apt description. I have been schooled as a monastic. Do you know what it means to be educated, boy?"

"No." A chuck of apple had fallen onto the ground. The boy snapped it up and popped it in his mouth.

Merthen knelt onto one knee. "Boy, my Christian name is Ambrosius. My friends call me Merthen. Can you say that? How is your diction?"

"Merthen. Mister Merthen."

"Excellent. Might I submit a proposal to you? I am in need of a domesticus to assist me in gleaning my orchards. Should you accept, I shall train you to be a monastic like me. You will be provided with suitable clothing, a dry chamber for sleeping, and an ample supply of victuals."

The boy scrunched up his nose.

"Food," said Merthen. "I will give you a cot and food if you work for me."

"Aye, I will do it." The boy licked some of the sweet juice still on his lips. "It is better than hay."

"Hay? Do you mean to tell me you have been eating hay?"

"No. I sleep in it. It stinks. I would rather sleep where it is dry."

"Well, there shall be no more of that. No domesticus of mine sleeps in hay."

"Who is he?"

"That is you. You shall be my domesticus." Merthen brushed a couple of lice from off Uther's scalp and crushed them underfoot.

"But my name is *Uther*, not *Domesticus*."

"You misunderstand me. *Domesticus* is your title. It means you are my helper. Here, take this." He gave the boy his furs to carry.

"You need my help?"

Merthen straightened his spine. "Evidently, the universe has deemed it so." He tapped his finger on the top of Uther's skull like a woodpecker pecking on a stump. "It is time we journeyed off to my sangha. It will be dark soon."

"What is a sangha?"

"It is a compound in the wilderness where people who are in search of interbeing gather to live in community."

"How many people live there?" asked the boy. "Do you have a wife? Do you have any children?"

"I have never taken a spouse, as I am unable to sire offspring. Even if I could, I am grossly unqualified to be a father. It requires more stability than one such as I could provide."

"Does that mean you live all alone?" said Uther.

"If one discounts the bugs, birds, and varmints who frequent my premises, your deduction is correct." Merthen took a step towards the western hills. "Indeed boy, it is just me."

Chapter IV: The Hunter Moon, AD 480

Potest ex casa magnus vir exire.

A great man comes from a hut.

* * *

Everything in Mister Merthen's hut smelled like smoke and wet hay. At least that was how it smelled to little Uther. Merthen's hut was round. Uther had never lived in a round house before, only square ones.

Mister Merthen had many round things. The broom he gave Uther to sweep out the rabbit hutch was round. The baskets stacked against the low mud wall of his hut were round. Even the big bronze stewpot in the middle of the clearing was round. Merthen stirred that pot all the time.

Merthen was always doing something. Sometimes he was carving a tool. Other times he was gathering water from the spring or twisting a leaf off a tree and looking at it. He seemed to like looking at things, mostly things he found lying around or growing in the forest.

Merthen was the busiest person Uther had ever met. All day long he puttered around. He even talked to himself, but not in the morning. As soon as he got up, Merthen would sit with his legs crossed and his eyes shut and just do nothing. Then he would go back to doing things.

Late one afternoon, Merthen twisted strips of bark and made a round thing. It was like a plate, but it had holes in it. He took some twigs and propped up the plate thing just above a pit filled with hot coals. Come to think of it, the plate thing had more holes than plate. Maybe it was not a plate at all? Was it a table?

Uther asked, "Is that a little table? Is that for me?"

Merthen laid a handful of shiny green leaves onto the woven frame. "No, boy. It is a rack for desiccating herbs. I am preparing mint for storage."

"Will we eat it? What does *desiccating* mean?"

"It means to dry something so thoroughly that no water remains."

Uther scratched his closely cropped hair. Sometimes his head still itched from where the lice used to bite him.

Above the smoldering fire, the air seemed to ripple. Uther followed it up past the top of the trees. A raven cawed somewhere up in the hills. Uther knew what a raven sounded like. He had heard them before.

Uther said, "I am hungry."

"As you should be. You worked rigorously this afternoon. You will make a fine monastic one day." Merthen curled his arm like a strong man. "*Sine labore non erit panis in ore.* There are tripe and crushed turnips in the skillet. Be mindful to thank the cow who gave us her organ meat."

Just for fun, the boy hopped toward the dinner pail on one foot. He scooped a mound of supper into his bowl.

Merthen shook the drying rack, and dumped its contents into a carved bowl. He flattened out a square of linen. Onto it, he poured out the dried herbs. A woodpecker went rat-a-tat, startling the old man. A dozen mint leaves flew off his rack, some landing on the hot coals.

Uther asked, "Some people call you *Merthen*, but some people call you *Ambrosius*."

With his finger tips, the old man picked up the four corners of the cloth. He created a fist-sized ball of herbs and crushed it. "I must confess to being rather inordinately well-endowed when it comes to pseudonyms. As I recall, my mother referred to me *Lailoken*, but no one else ever did. *Ambrosius* was the name I was given when I was baptized. I still use it professionally. Any more, most people call me *Merthen*, just like the town."

"*Merthen* is a town? Where is it?"

"Down the trail aways. That was what the wild Britons called *Carmarthen* before it became an imperial port. Unfortunately, the name *Merthen* was similar to the Frankish word for *turd*. Whereas Hadrian did not fancy landing his navy in excrement, he changed its name to the *Castellum Maridunum*, a stentorian moniker too convoluted for the Celts to pronounce, so they just called it *Carmarthen*."

Uther thought that was funny. Merthen said funny things, but not with a silly voice like in a puppet show. Merthen was not like most old men. Most old men were mean and smelled bad. Merthen did not smell bad, but he did smell sometimes. His breath smelled like garlic, and his farts smelled really bad. His armpits smelled like a shoe.

One of the fallen mint leaves in the hearth turned red and floated up on the rippling air. Uther waited to see if it would disappear or fall back down.

"My friends," said Merthen, "call me *Mister Merthen* in jest, for they say I am older than the Roman cobblestones."

"What does *Merthen* mean?" Uther took bite of stew and chewed it up. It was such a big bite, he had to chew it hard.

Merthen neatly tied up his crushed mint like a small bundle of wool. "I do not know, nor do I care to, just as long as it has nothing to do with dung."

Uther smelled hay, not wet hay, but burning hay. A single flame flickered in the thatch at the top of the hut. "Is that a fire?"

"*Caco santi!*" cried Merthen. "Fetch me a whisk broom straight away, the one with the long handle. Go boy!"

Merthen grabbed the ladder over by the wood pile and pushed it against the outer wall of his home. Uther scampered over with a broom in one hand. His dinner bowl was still in the other.

"That will do," said Merthen. He dunked the business end of the broom into Uther's half-eaten meal, then climbed the three rungs of the ladder. "Uther," he said while whacking the flickering flames with the stew-laden broom, "go draw a bucket of water."

The boy bounded off to the springhead dug into the side of the hill. It looked like a cave. If the roof burned down, maybe they would have to sleep in a cave? Merthen said there were caves nearby. Maybe they had bears? Maybe Uther and Merthen could go hunt them?

Uther filled a leather bucket and ran back. He found Merthen resting at the bottom of the ladder, rubbing the back of his neck.

Uther asked, "Did the fire go out?"

"For the most part." Merthen took the water. "I need you to perch yourself at the top of this ladder. You need not be afraid. Up you go."

Uther hopped up the rungs. "Afraid of what?"

Merthen, with bucket in hand, climbed as well. He nudged the boy forward onto the roof.

Merthen handed over the pail. "We need to douse the ashes. I want you to pour this onto the scorched area, but do it very slowly. Can you do that?"

"I think so."

Uther shimmied up to the peak. Merthen held onto the boy's legs.

Uther dribbled out the water just as he had been told. He heard a sizzle. A puff of grey smoke hit him in the face and he coughed. The sizzling stopped.

"Good job, boy," said Merthen. "The precipitation on this cursed island is nearly incessant, and yet it is *my* roof which chooses to ignite. *Hinc illae lacrimae.*"

There was a lone deer drinking from the stream at the bottom of the hill. Uther stood on his toes to get a better look.

Merthen touched his forefinger to a patch of unusually pale skin on the boy's knee. "What is that white spot on your leg?"

"It is white spot. I have one on my arm too." Uther lifted up his right elbow with his left hand and twisted around to show it off. In the process, he lost his footing, and flopped down onto the blackened thatch. He tumbled toward the eaves.

"Halt!" said Merthen. He tossed away the bucket and clasped onto the back of Uther's blouse. It ripped clean off, but the old man's effort did slow the boy's fall. Uther got his bearings and dove off the four foot wall into a stack of woven baskets, which tipped over and dumped him safely onto the ground.

Merthen's ladder teetered to the side. He launched off it just before it tipped, then stumbled backwards, tangling himself in a pine tree. The ladder hit the rabbit hutch. They thumped around, scared. Uther's favorite rabbit was a white doe with pink eyes. He called her *Lady Ygerna*. That was a pretty name.

Merthen, still hanging on to the torn-off blouse, asked, "Are you all right?"

Uther slapped his palms together. They were sooty. His bare torso was covered with shards of wet thatch. "I am dirty."

Merthen freed himself from the pine and massaged his lower back. "I know a geezer who is going to be sore come morning. I am too old for this."

"How old are you?"

Merthen, using the ripped up shirt like a rag, wiped the boy's face. "I am quite the antique, which is why you must learn self-sufficiency. At my age, the king of death stalks my every turn." He cleaned Uther's hands.

"What does that mean?"

"It means I may expire at any moment. Death comes for us all, but I am especially susceptible."

"With celery?"

"With *what*?" Merthen shook out the cloth.

"Mister Death's celery."

"Why would Death carry celery?"

The boy wiped his nose. "You said he had a stalk."

"No, Uther, I said he was stalking me, like a fox hunting a gosling." He spun the boy around and brushed the thatch from his back and shoulders.

Uther flicked off some of the hay stuck to his belly. "So," he said, "Mister Death does not like celery?"

"As far as I know, the grim reaper has no preference pro or con in regards to salad greens." Merthen looked at the roof. It was messy. "That will require a patch."

Uther asked. "Which name do you like better, *Ambrosius* or *Merthen*?"

"I prefer *Merthen*. It is more unique. *Ambrosius* is quite common. Our king is also named *Ambrosius*."

Uther shivered. "Why did your mother call you *Ambrosius*?"

"She did not. My master assigned it to me. I had another slave name as an adult: *Pig Eyes*."

"That sounds funny."

"And yet it brought me no merriment." He carried Uther into the hut. There was a wet spot in the floor. The old man lowered the boy onto his cot. Uther's teeth chattered. Merthen wrapped a towel around him. It was soft. It smelled like pine cones. Why did it smell like that?

"It is past your bed time," said Merthen. "When you stay up late you get grouchy. I interviewed a number of the matrons down at the market. They informed me that young boys require a great deal of sleep."

"Not me. I wake up all the time. I think I hear rats, but it is just you peeing."

Merthen unfolded Uther's nightshirt. "I fear my voiding is unavoidable." He examined the collar. "What is this?" He stuck his pinky through two holes in the fabric. "Must you chew on everything? I shall have to darn this, yet again!"

"You could teach me to sew."

"Oh, I shall." Merthen prepared the boy's bedroll. "You have to stop gnawing on things. It will not do, boy."

"I know," said Uther. He pulled on his night cap. "Could you tell me a story?"

"If you feel it would calm you, I will. Will it calm you?"

"Aye, it will. Tell me about Odysseus and the Cyclops!" Uther liked that story. It had monsters. The Cyclops was a monster, a giant with only one eye. He lived in a cave. Did the caves around here have any giants? They would need a big cave. Too small a cave, and they would get stuck.

"I cannot tell that story tonight," said Merthen. "It is far too athletic. What about Mount Olympus?"

"Is that the island where the man had a bull's head?"

"No. Olympus was the home of the gods, specifically King Zeus." Merthen tucked the boy in. "One day old Zeus decided to build a palace. Soon enough, he found himself on Mount Olympus, the highest promontory in all of Agamemnon's realm."

"Were there any giant monsters there?"

"There may have been a passing centaur, but they were of modest stature. Mostly, it was populated with humans called Greeks, but that was good. Zeus liked them because they could read, and they manufactured such nice pottery. I will teach you Greek someday."

The boy brought his collar up to his mouth. He quickly pulled it out. "What did the Greek humans eat?"

"Dried figs and black olives. And they loved to go to the theater. Thus, Zeus erected his estate on their territory. You know, the Greeks named their capitol after Athena, the goddess of wisdom. What do you think of that?"

Uther reached down and removed a piece of thatch from his trousers. It was poking into his skin. "Did Athena live there?"

"As I recall, she resides on the moon."

"Is your mother in Athens?"

"Oh, no. She passed long ago."

The boy stammered. "What happened? Where did she go?"

"It was not she who left." Merthen picked his teeth. "I was taken as a slave when I was… well, your age actually. The Visigoth who caught me told me that my mother was dead. For all I know he was right. I have almost no recollection of her. Needless to say, by the time I returned to Britannia, she was gone."

The boy yawned. "That is not fair. He should not have taken you."

"What can I say? Suffering exists. The First Noble Truth is annoyingly accurate."

Uther was not cold anymore. His cot was nice and warm. He closed his eyes. Then he quickly reopened them. "Where is your mother now? Is she on the moon? Is she with Athena? Maybe my mother is with her."

Merthen noticed a ladybug crawling up his beard. He shook it off. "Throughout the world, there is a diversity of cosmologies that speculate as to the status of the soul postmortem, none of which, to my knowledge, involve lunar habitation."

"What does that mean?"

"It means," said Merthen, "that here are many things we cannot see. *Ergo*, it is possible, albeit unlikely, that our mothers are on the moon." Merthen yawned. "Get some rest, boy. Tomorrow we shall go to market. We can visit Widow Blodwen. That will be nice, yes?"

The boy felt his eyelids drop. The hut smelled like ash and mint leaves. Merthen smelled like Merthen. That was a good smell. Uther fell asleep.

Chapter V: The Wolf Moon, AD 481

Contra vim mortis non est medicamen in hortis.

There is no herb against the power of death.

* * *

The Carmarthen Road rolled down from the slopes of the Cambrian Mountains, and westward to the bay. It was called *the Carmarthen Road* because it was the one *and only* road to Carmarthen. Given that the eastern side of the Cambrian Mountains was infested with Saxons, all the Britons who lived on the other side were relieved that there was but a single road.

All the mature trees along the Carmarthen Road had been cut down by the king's sawyers so as to keep marauding Germans from hiding behind them. At least that was the official story. In reality, the king was hoping to thwart the local bandits who robbed anyone returning from the market with a silver coin or an ivory button. They even stole nails.

Thus, the vegetation along the road to Carmarthen consisted of stumps in various states of decay. Upon these punky edifices grew clusters of toadstools, behind which stood damp grey sheep and equally un-colorful cottages, similar in form to the toadstools, albeit roomier. Just such a cottage was the destination toward which Merthen and the boy were traveling.

In front of this structure, a buck-toothed man with a bald forehead and a protruding Adam's apple paced about. He wore a priest's cloak with multiple patches, sewed with neat tight stitching. As clergymen went, this one appeared to fall into the category of *runt*. But still, he had a dagger in his belt. Upon seeing Merthen, the priest reached for it.

"I am not a Saxon!" said Merthen, raising both hands in surrender. "I am Ambrosius Merthen the apple seller. *Dominus illuminatio mea.* Widow Blodwen suggested I stop by, something about an injured girl?"

The priest sheathed his knife. "Beg your pardon, Sir. Your braids confused me. I am Father Thomasius. Are you the physician?"

"I am an herbalist. Where is the child?"

"She is inside. Let me get Mister Brynmor." Thomasius stepped into the cottage.

"What happened to her?" said Uther. "Is she all right?"

"She is ill," said Merthen. "She was bucked off a horse."

Out came the priest along with Mister Brynmor, dressed in thick leather boots and a peasant's smock.

Brynmor bowed. "Good day, Mister Merthen. Thank you for coming by. You heard about our Delyth?"

"Widow Blodwen informed me of her predicament. How did it happen?"

"You know Lord Carasius? His wife brought some of her ponies to market. My daughter managed to climb onto one of them. My son tried to push her off. It spooked the horse and it tossed her. She landed on her head."

"On the cobblestones?" said Merthen. "Was there any bruising? Did she pass out?"

"She had a blue mark on her head. She seemed fine. Then she said the back of her neck hurt. This morning, she got sleepy and fell down. Now we cannot wake her. She has a fever. Come inside."

Merthen said to Uther, "Stay out here, boy."

Brynmor and Father Thomasius had to duck to pass through the low hung doorway. Merthen followed. Inside lay Delyth, a girl no older than Uther. She rested on a clean straw mat, but she did not look restful. She was stiff and pale. Delyth's mother, Missus Gwenda stroked her un-reactive hand.

"Good day, Mister Merthen," said Gwenda. "Thank you so much for helping us."

"My pleasure, Madam. I need a lamp." Merthen crouched down. He pressed his fingers against the girl's shoulders, neck and scalp. She was not feverish. He asked, "Did she have any fluid coming from her nose?"

"Aye," said Missus Gwenda. She handed him a candle. "It came out her ears as well."

Merthen manually opened one of the girl's eyes. He brought the flame close to it and her iris expanded. Clearly, her faculties were still active. Back when Merthen was a drummer boy, he saw quite a few legionnaires carried off the field with a blow to the skull. The eyes were the first thing the physicians checked. Once the eyes died, the rest of the body followed.

Merthen said, "I have seen this sort of injury before. She has bruised her cranium. It is possible that she is bleeding on the inside. I know this may seem strange, but it can happen."

"Will she get better?" said Gwenda.

"Some can recover from this, others cannot. You need to boil a pot of water and gather some clean rags. I must speak with your husband."

Merthen went outside. Mister Brynmor and Father Thomasius joined him. Uther was down the road with a group of children. It was just where Merthen anticipated he would be. Whenever Uther got the opportunity, he would be off trying to out jump the other boys, or making a doll dance for a toddler.

Merthen addressed Mister Brynmor, "I am compelled to impress upon you how serious this is. Your daughter's brain is attracting aqueous humors. It is swollen with liquid. I fear that that in all likelihood, she will not make through the night. However, if we can drain her skull, she may survive."

Brynmor showed no outward emotion, but the pink drained out of his face. He asked, "How do we do that?"

"You need to get a wood auger. Whereas your daughter is so young, the bone on the top of her head is still thin. We can poke through it."

"Come again?" said Father Thomasius. "Are you suggesting we drill a hole through her head? No offense, Sir, but this procedure sounds more like, well... what some people might construe as witchcraft. I am not saying it is, mind you."

"We must release the pressure," said Merthen. "She may not live, but if she dies, she will go quickly. I observed this operation many times when I was with the legions. It was always conducted by Christians."

"Are you sure she will not get over it?" said Mister Brynmor. "Can you give her some herbs?"

"I could prepare an infusion of cherry stems, but she would need to swallow it. In her state, she might choke. I cannot make this decision for you. And I must reiterate in the starkest terms that whatever we do, we will most likely fail."

Mister Brynmor hung his shoulders. "We lost our first son when he was her age. His cut his leg. It was just a small damn cut. It took him months to die. If this happens again, my wife will go mad." He asked the priest, "What do you think?"

Thomasius considered his response. "Well," he finally said, "if it worked for the legionnaires."

"We should do it then," said Brynmor. "My brother-in-law has an auger." He ran down the road.

Merthen called out, "We need a curved quilting needle and some thread. And a long wooden spoon."

"My wife has that. I will be back in a moment."

Merthen sneezed and unfolded his hanky. Father Thomasius pivoted on the soles of his feet. Neither man spoke.

For Merthen, engaging in small talk was painful chore, especially with clergymen. This was not because he took issues with the teachings of Jesus. Rather, it was because so many priests attempted to quote the Bible despite having never actually read it. In Merthen's opinion, Saint Jerome's prose was undiluted genius. Hearing it mangled by a semi-literate cleric was a crime against eloquence.

"I have heard about you," said Thomasius. "Not by name, mind you. The locals say there is a hermit who grows apples in the woods."

"A peculiar hermit, no doubt. Do they say I am a druid?"

"I suppose some do. All I know is, I have never seen you at Mass. What are you doing here in Cambria?"

"Eking out a living. What are you doing here? Your accent suggests you come from Aquitaine?"

"I wanted to be a missionary up in Hibernia, but I have gall stones. I am hoping to establish a parsonage in Carmarthen. It seems like you folks need one." Thomasius continued. "You know, Bishop Zephyrinus is celebrating the festival of Saint Polycarp this Sunday. You should stop by. You have been baptized, yes?"

"If you have gall stones, you should drink plenty of water."

"Oh, I do. My wife is constantly nagging me about it. Is it true you once worked for King Vortiger?"

"I copied building plans for his architect."

Mister Brynmor ran up with an auger in his hand. "I will get the needle," he said. "My wife has rags." He dashed into the hut.

"Missus Gwenda," said Thomasius, under his breath, "her father and sister died last year. Her brother two years before."

The sound of children at play distracted Merthen. Uther swung from a tree upside down with his knees bent over a branch, giggling like a clown. Merthen was about to tell the boy to stop, when Uther set his palms flat on the earth, did a somersault, and landed butt-first in the grass, unharmed.

Thomasius withdrew out his dagger. "Take this. I just sharpened it."

Merthen accepted it, and the two men made their way into the cottage. The sun was low in the sky. Inside the windowless structure, it was already evening.

Next to the girl, Missus Gwenda had laid out a neat stack of folded rags. There was also a kettle of hot water and two threaded needles. Merthen tore one of the rags into long strips, and bound the girl's hands to her side. "I will need for you to hold her head," he said to Thomasius. "You must sit on her torso, but gently. Do not constrict her breathing."

Father Thomasius complied. He said to the parents, "Perhaps you should wait outside."

"What are you going to do?" said Missus Gwenda. "Why do you need that water?" She reached towards her child. Mister Brynmor held her back.

"I am sorry," said Merthen, "but you must go. You need to trust me."

Like a dutiful wife, she said nothing. Her husband led her out.

Merthen mindfully dipped the needles in the kettle, letting the threads drape over the side. "One more thing," he said to the dejected parents, "It is proper procedure for a mother to kiss her child before this treatment. Quickly now."

Missus Gwenda knelt down and caressed her child on the cheek.

"That will do," said Merthen. "Please wait outside. I would recommend you gather some woman - they all must be mothers - and pray to Saint Luke. Any prayer will be sufficient. The more the better."

"Aye," said Gwenda, "I will." She and her husband set off for their task.

Merthen submerged the tip of the knife into the simmering water. As the old legionnaires used to say, *hot metal heals, cold metal kills*. Why this was, not even Hippocrates knew.

Merthen lifted out the steaming needles. "Father Thomasius, I may ask you to dunk these in the water repeatedly. We must keep them heated, almost too hot to touch."

"Very well," said Thomasius. "I am ready."

Merthen wedged the handle of the wooden spoon in the girl's mouth. "Make sure that stays there. I am going to begin now."

Merthen positioned his dagger securely in his fist and recalled the first time he sliced through human skin. This time would be easier. After all, her eyes were shut, and she was not screaming for mercy. His wrist began to shake.

Thomasius asked, "Is something wrong?"

Merthen brought into his mind a statement he had meditated on countless times. It was a sentence of few words; *the past is an illusion, only the present exists.*

Merthen pressed the blade into her scalp. He carved out a flap of skin about the size of birch leaf, and folded it back. The girl struggled, then went limp. Too much pain and a person will lose all consciousness. That was something Merthen knew about as well.

With a quick twist of the dagger's tip, Merthen carved a hay-seed sized divot into the outer surface of Delyth's skull. He dipped the drill tip in the steaming water. Blood seeped out over the exposed bone. He centered the auger, and drilled down five cycles. There was a popping noise. A reddish liquid oozed out the hole.

Thomasius was breathing hard. "Is that a good sign?" he said.

Merthen was hoping the fluid would be clear. If it was, he would drain her braincase, sew her scalp back on, and sleep well tonight. Instead, a slow stream of blood, some of it dark and clotted, dribbled from her wound. Merthen checked her eyes. They had rolled up into her head. There was no noise. The flickering flame in the candle stood still.

* * *

A cricket with beady black eyes and bolt-like legs joints jumped onto Merthen's shoulder.

"Fear not," said the cricket, "I am Gopi."

Merthen did not let go of the girl.

"You wretch," he said, "leave me be."

He wanted to say more, but said nothing. Here he was, trying to save an innocent victim of fate, and all Lady Gopi wanted to do was interrupt him. How could she be so irresponsible? And the worst part was, Merthen had no one to blame but himself. It was *his* mind that created Gopi. It was *his* madness that would cost this girl her life.

Gopi hopped onto his red-stained hands. "I am sorry," she said. "The girl is dead. It was over the moment she fell off the pony. There is nothing you could have done."

BOOK II: THE MENTOR

CHAPTER VI: THE CORN MOON, AD 483

Perfer et obdura; dolor hic tibi proderit olim.

Be patient and tough; one day this pain will be useful to you.

* * *

When Merthen was a red-headed tike, the hedgerows of Carmarthen were awash in Frankish rabbits. Back then, Roman plantation owners shipped them over from Gaul and released them on their estates. But as the decades passed, the population dwindled, and the only long-eared nibblers left in Britannia were its native hares, a scrawny mule-faced race, with a strong musky aftertaste.

It was therefore an unexpected pleasure for Merthen to observe a genuine rabbit hiding itself behind the wall-like woodpile next to his hut. He whistled to Uther like a bullfinch. This was their agreed upon signal to indicate the appearance of game that might flee upon hearing human conversation.

Uther raised his bow in his hands. These were no longer the pudgy hands of a little boy. They were muscular hands; wood-chopping hands; and on some rainy days, bring-a-toad-inside-and-set-him-on-a-throne-made-of-sticks hands. Any woodland savage would be proud to have these hands, except for the splotches of pale skin that left Uther's fingers whiter than a shark's belly.

Merthen returned to stirring the pot in the center of his compound. Without moving his jaw, he muttered, "Wait till Mister Bunny looks away."

The rabbit took half a hop. Uther released his grip. The arrow spiraled through the air. It struck its target dead through the ribs.

Uther scampered toward the kill. "He looks scrawny."

Merthen dipped his bronze ladle into the stew. "They say that Attila the Hun was afraid of only two things: his mother and rabbits. He was under the impression that rabbits were spies sent down by the gods. At night they would hop up to the moon and report humanity's misdeeds to the Sky Bitch on the North Star."

The boy dislodged the arrow. "I can use this again."

"That would be very economical of you. We shall eat the giblets tonight. And, what does a good monastic do after spilling blood?"

Uther bowed toward the dead animal.

Using only a few cuts, Uther gutted the game. He delivered the innards to Merthen, who dumped them into the pot along with two pickled beets, a slab of lard, and a chunk of stale bread.

The boy dropped down and sat cross-legged. "Is it boiling?"

Using the side of his foot, Merthen slid over a basket holding a bunch of grapes. "Care for an appetizer?"

The boy popped one in his mouth. He grimaced.

"Problem, Sir? Shall I call the head cook?"

Uther gasped. "Sour! Are they all this bad?"

Merthen nearly laughed. "Not all of them."

The boy tried to wipe the juice off his tongue.

Merthen whispered, "Sour," and made his way, as if in a trance, into the hut. He shuffled through the bags and bundles stacked against the back wall.

"Should I stir the pot?" said Uther.

"Slowly," came the muffled response. Merthen reappeared with a cedar box. From out of it he produced a granular black bottle stopper. "This material is very hard to come by. The Greeks call it ασπηαλτοσ." Then, from the container he removed a small vase and a spool of copper thread.

"Are you going to sew something?"

"No, *we* are going to build something." He pointed to the sour grapes. "Get the grinder and mash those."

The boy darted off to fetch the mortar and pestle.

"When I was employed at the University of Nalanda," said Merthen, "I had an associate named Aturpat of Ctesiphon, a devotee of the prophet Zoroaster. Aturpat's father was a renowned magus, famous for pouring molten metal on his chest and then commanding it roll off like water."

Uther returned with the tools. "Did you see him do it?"

"No, that would never be permitted. Zoroastrians are quite insular. Aturpat was shunned for life simply for impregnating a Yazidi." Merthen reached onto the vase. From it, he took an iron bar and a tube-like copper cup that fit snugly into the neck of the vessel. "It was he who taught me how to make this."

Uther started crushing the grapes.

* * *

Merthen waited for Uther's next question, but the boy said nothing. Uther was frozen stiff. Up in the trees, no birds chirped. The squirrels stopped rustling in the leaves.

"Where are you!" said Merthen. He paced around to the forest's edge. An adder, hanging from the low branch of a sapling, flicked her tongue in his face.

"Great Caesar's ghost!" He spread hand over his chest. "You gave me such a start." He repositioned his grip on his ladle, then swung it at her.

Scaly Gopi slithered out of reach, unaffected by his attack. "Lord Satan has a question. He wishes to know more about Aturpat."

"Lord Satan? I thought your jury was packed with deities, not fallen angels."

"But it is my understanding," said Gopi, "that the Yazidis of Persia venerate the Serpent of Eden, so that he will not bring evil upon us mortals."

"That is not true," he said. "The Yazidis pray to the Peacock Angel of…"

Merthen stopped himself in mid-sentence. How the devil did Gopi know about the Yazidis? She was from India, not Persia.

She blinked her glassy black eyes with their slitted irises. It was only then that Merthen remembered she was neither Indian nor Persian. She was an illusion, hatched from the egg of his own deteriorating mind.

"This is lunacy," he said. "Why am I arguing with a reptile?"

"Lord Satan has just one question. Was Aturpat a close friend?"

Merthen had not thought about Aturpat for ages.

"He was more of a comrade," said Merthen. "Aturpat and I were both translators at Nalanda. His bench was next to mine. He was supposed to be translating the *Epic of Gilgamesh* into Sanskrit, but mostly he lounged around writing poetry. He taught me some herbal remedies and tried to interest me in astrology. It struck me as rather tepid. Why waste time predicting the future when one can help the needy today?"

Lady Gopi slid closer. "Not all people are as empirical as you."

"Why did Aturpat have to be so gullible? The last time I saw him, he had joined with a league of alchemists. They claimed to possess Chinese rocks that could transform copper into gold." Merthen shook his fist. "And this from a literate man."

"The philosopher's stones have captivated many a sound mind."

"Do you know what Aturpat's rubble turned out to be? An elixir of processed poppy sap! He and his colleagues smoked them in huka."

Gopi lowered herself to the base of the tree. "Habit energy can be fierce."

"Aturpat's craving drove him to madness. One evening, a knight caught him stealing a bracelet from a Brahmin's daughter. The soldier struck him dead." Merthen paused. "I fear the creative mind is like a city without walls, open to all muses, and thereby defenseless to the onslaught of less benevolent spirits."

The snake stretched up the tip on her snout. "At least you were able to learn from his suffering."

"In the *Epic of Gilgamesh*," said Merthen, "the hero kills the Bull of Heaven. In revenge, the gods strike down his best friend. The hero demands they restore his comrade to life, but the gods refuse, telling him, *when we gods created man, we let* death be his lot. May your days be full of joy. Cherish the child that holds your hand. Delight in your wife's embrace. For these alone are the concerns of humanity."

"It is never easy to lose a friend," said Gopi.

* * *

Uther tugged on Merthen's arm, "How does the lighting pot work?"

It took Merthen a moment to regain his bearings. "When filled with a sour extract," he explained, "this jug will generate a diminutive bolt of lightning."

"Like in the sky?"

"But much smaller. First, one must insert both the metal cylinder and the rod. The copper thread is then tied onto to this contraption, with the other end connected to an object composed of iron. After the juice is poured into the vase, the iron produces a stinging essence."

The boy gave the grape mash one final push. "What is that?"

"It means that any individual who touches the iron will receive a painful sting. Sometimes it is accompanied by a spark."

"Really?"

Merthen tucked the end of his beard into his belt. "Years ago, when I was performing on the streets of Paris, I connected my lightning pot to an iron chalice with the base broken off. My musician friend, James, suggested I call it the *Cauldron of Ceridwen*. He said the Romans would eat that up."

"Do you still have it?"

"Not any more. I had to leave the continent on rather short notice. That grail stayed behind. What do I have that is iron?"

"You have your sword?"

Merthen snapped his finger. "That will do." He unsheathed his weapon. "There are eels in Persia that can also generate a sting."

"Are they magic?"

"Of course not."

"I heard a sailor talking about a magic fish. It had the head of a dog."

"That was a sea lion." Merthen picked up a grape. With a twist of his hand, it disappeared. He lowered his arm. The grape rolled out from his sleeve. "Magic is all bunk, boy."

Uther smiled, then pouted. "There is no magic?"

"As Brother Tinh Tu use to say, interbeing is the only magic that actually pays off."

"So," said Uther, "is magic real or not?"

Merthen slid the grape mash into a cheese cloth. "Perhaps I should explain it this way." He squeezed the juice into the lightning pot. "When Saul of Tarsus was thrown from his pony and heard the voice of the Nazarene saying, *Saul, Saul, why do you persecute me*, he came to realize that he was connected to something greater than himself. Saint Paul experienced interbeing with the martyred bodhisattva. That was real magic."

"Saint Paul was a wizard?"

"No. In fact, genuine magic usually occurs in men who make no claim to sorcery. Let us say a German savage wounds a knight, but chooses not to kill him. That would be real magic: interbeing."

The boy rubbed his chin. "Would it be inter-be-ing if King Ambrosius stabbed a Saxon and let him go?"

"Indeed it would." Merthen patted the boy on the back. "An excellent example. Bully for you."

With the copper twine completed, Merthen assembled the lightning pot. He stuck the tip of his sword into the dirt and attached the twine to it. "You may touch it, but only very gently."

The boy cautiously extended his finger. When he finally made contact, nothing happened.

Merthen scratched his temple. "Something must have fallen loose." He grasped the sword to re-string it. He was immediately stung by a bolt of undulating blue light. The boy erupted in laughter.

Merthen shook his hand a few times. "How can this be?" He stomped forward and re-connected the device. Then he motioned for the boy to touch it. Uther grasped the handle. Again, nothing.

The muted half-smile of understanding crossed Merthen's face. "Uther," he said, "you only touched the leather swaddling around the handle. You must make contact with the metal. Your hand is so small you missed it altogether. Give it another go."

The boy eagerly grabbed the lower end of the great knife. A brilliant aquamarine flash exploded between his fingers, and his hair stood on end. He bolted backward, falling gracelessly on the hard packed earth. His eyes filled with tears. He stuck his throbbing finger in his mouth.

Merthen picked up the boy.

Uther's cries transformed into a wave of giggles. "Let me do it again!" He hopped up and down.

"No, it would not be safe. The only thunderbolt you need to touch is the one that emanates from the Buddha's mind."

"Can we do this some other time?"

"Perhaps when you are older." Merthen disconnected the wire with a stick.

The boy focused on the blacksmith's mark on the side of the blade. "What does that say?"

"Read it for yourself. It shall be today's grammar lesson."

The boy guided his index finger to the text. "It says, *Ex Calabr*. Is that spelled right? Where is that?"

"Calabria is a province in southern Italy. That is where the sword was cast. The swordsmith omitted the last two letters. The proper abbreviation should have been written as *Ex Calab*, but you were correct that the preposition *ex* means *from*. I award you a merit for the day."

"This came all the way from Italy?"

"Yes. But that need not impress you. I would never have purchased it, were it not for the substantial discount." He put the weapon back in its sheath. "It is a piece of cheap Italian junk, suitable only for slaying apples."

Chapter VII: The Hunter Moon, AD 483

Homo homini lupus.

Man is a wolf to man.

* * *

When he was out in the woods with Merthen, Uther often found himself in a valley he had never seen before. But Merthen always knew where they were. Sometimes, if was a nice day, Merthen would walk through the brambles where there was no path. Merlin called it bushwhacking, which made sense because when he did it, he had to whack through quite a few bushes.

There were thorns on some of the plants in the forest. When you rubbed up against them, they poked tiny holes in your shins. After Merthen and Uther got done bushwhacking, they would count the bloody spots on their skin to see who had the most cuts. Merthen usually won, but he had bigger legs, so he had an advantage. Those little cuts did not hurt much.

When it was rainy, or cold, Merthen would stay on the trail. No point to risk getting hurt when the weather is bad. That was why Uther and Merthen were sticking to the old elk path that led along the ridgeline. It was chilly and there was even some ice in shady spots.

Up above were leaves of red and yellow leaves. The wind whistled through the tall pines. Uther kept his cloak hanging open even though the air was chilly. Off on the other side of the mountain, a hawk screeched.

Merthen tapped the boy on the shoulder. "What do you observe?" He pointed to the top of the trees.

"Branches?"

Merthen curled an eyebrow. "Would I lead you on a two day trek simply to look at branches?"

"You might."

Uther pushed back the round straw hat Merthen had weaved to protect him from the sun. It was almost the size of a large frying pan. Its top was pointed, like the roof of circular stone well. Merthen said that Brother Tinh Tu taught him how to make it. In Tinh Tu's homeland, everyone wore them.

Uther scanned the trees. "Oh, I see, apples." He strolled off. "Are we going to pick them?"

"With alacrity!" Merthen untied his rucksack, revealing four woven bags. He positioned himself against the biggest of the trees. "Up you go."

Uther climbed up Merthen's back and into the branches like a mariner scaling a mast.

Merthen drew his sword. He popped a few apples off at the stem. "Fall my succulent prey. You shall not escape the sting of Lailoken."

"When did you plant these trees?" said the boy. He extended out his whole arm to reach some of the apples.

Merthen thought about it a bit, then said, "It was eighteen seasons ago, just after I arrived from the continent."

"How old are you, now?"

"I suspect I was four or five when Alaric sacked the City of Rome. That was sixty years ago. I can still remember that endless plume of smoke. Ashes rained down like black snow."

"You were there?"

"Just off shore. The Visigoth slaver who captured me planned to sell me in Rome. Needless to say, when we got there, we had to turn around. I saw the Eternal City for the first time on its very last day. So much for eternity."

Uther dropped down a few apples. "How did you get away from the slave ship?"

"I was sold to a Sicilian pirate who transported me to Cyprus. He traded me to a Phoenician for a half-bushel of pepper. At least I know what I am worth. From there I was carted off to Constantinople. Now *that* was a grand city, but it reeked of fish paste. You could smell it a mile away."

From around the other side of the hill, Uther heard a low moan like that of a deer or an elk. He tilted his head. "I hear something."

"I hear nothing."

"Shhh. You cannot hear baby birds, remember?" Uther peered out into the forest. All he saw was leaves. Again, he heard the call, but this time there was a reply. "Someone is talking."

Merthen stood still.

The boy scanned their surroundings. His mouth swung open. "I see savages coming this way. Up the hill from the other side."

"How many? How are they armed?"

"Four or five." Uther could only see them from the neck up. They were white blonds, Germans. One of them had some kind of stick across his shoulder. It was too thick to be a bow. "I think they have axes."

Merthen jiggled the eighteen beads around his wrist. "Climb down." He strapped on the rucksack that carried his belongings. "We cannot outrun them. Stay calm and keep your hands where they can see them. If they point at your white spots, just let them."

The cracking of twigs reverberated over the top of the ridge. Four young men approached, with pale skin and sagging pierced ears. Despite the autumn air, they were shirtless, with loose pants, woven capes, and fur boots.

Uther knew each German tribe tied their hair differently. Saxons had four long braids like Merthen, but these wildmen had five: two over each ear and three down the back. At the top of their foreheads were two woven strands as thin as yarn, knotted to form the shape of horns. Whoever these savages were, they were not Saxons.

"Our new neighbors," said Merthen. "The older one with the tattoos is a subchief." He pushed out his chest out to its fullest extent and greeted them. "*Gutten Tag. Ich kan Saxonische und Frankisch sprechen.*"

The subchief stepped forward. He was balding, with a scar on his belly and partially completed tattoos on his shoulders. Around his neck hung a bronze chain link necklace. From it dangled an oval silver plate about the size of a scallop shell. It was the lid from a fancy metal box that a Roman lady might own. Did that wild man have any idea what it was?

Merthen asked, "*Sind Sie von Herr Aelle oder Herr Hengst?*"

The subchief pointed to himself and his party. "*Jyde,*" he said. He motioned toward Merthen and Uther. "*Welschmann?*"

Uther had heard about Jutes, but he had never seen them. The Jutes spoke a funny kind of German even the Saxons could not understand. Widow Blodwen once said the Jutes were as white as ghosts and dumber than oxen. Merthen told her never to assume that any man is stupid, especially one who carries an ax.

"The boy and I are Romans," said Merthen. "Understand? *Wir sind Romanishe. Nos sunt Romanos. Verstehen Sie? Intellegeratis?*"

No reply.

Merthen picked up two apples and said one word, "*Apfel?*" He bit into one of them. "*Malus?*" He licked his lips and swallowed with an audible gulp. "*Afal?*"

One of the Jutes, a fellow whose right nostril had been largely cut off, moved forward. A sharp glance from his commander stopped him in his tracks.

"*Hixar,*" said the subchief.

That was a new word to Uther, but it sounded like the word the Visigoth sailors used to describe Merthen.

Merthen shook his head. "No, I am no witch, despite what you may have heard. I am however, somewhat skilled in manual prestidigitation."

One of the young warriors reached for his battle-ax. The subchief did not.

Merthen said to the boy, "I am about to do something that may be precipitously daft. Open your mouth."

Uther dutifully complied.

Merthen spread his fingers wide, demonstrating that both hands were empty. The subchief set his hands on his hips.

Merthen inserted his right thumb and forefinger into Uther's open mouth. When he pulled it out, he held a disc of clear glass. Merthen tapped it twice so as to prove it was solid. Holding the object up to his eye, he peeked through it. As Merthen moved the device towards the Jutes, his eye grew larger. This was a trick Uther had never seen before.

The subchief showed no outward sign of fear, but Uther could tell he was annoyed.

"Master Uther," said Merthen, "pick up the largest, driest leaf you can find, and hold it by the sides, as if you were serving pastries to a party of leprechauns."

The boy did as ordered, albeit with shaky hands.

Merthen directed his eyes toward the sun. He positioned the disc a thumb's length above the leaf. A thin column of smoke formed from directly below the center of the glass.

And then, a small flame licked up. Uther, somewhat startled, released his grip. The burning ash fell down and landed on his shin. He wanted to scream, but he was too scared. He shook it off.

Merthen said, *"Ich bin eine Hexe von Etzel der Huna. Wissen Sie Etzel?"*

The Jute with the wounded nose gasped. He elbowed the warriors next to him. They walked away. The subchief did not.

"Etzel," said Merthen yet again.

The subchief drew his battle ax up to his lips and gave it a kiss.

Merthen displayed the fire-inducing gem once more. With a flick of his hand, he caused it to disappear.

The Jute casually swung his weapon in the direction of Merthen's crotch and chuckled. Then he joined the rest of his band, not once looking back.

Uther did not understand the subchief's actions, but he was not surprised. Wild men did all kinds of strange things. Merthen said that when a German committed a murder, he would apologize to his victim's family and pay a fine. But if a savage killed a man in battle, the dead man's clan would seek out the killer and execute him. How could they get everything so backwards?

Merthen said, "Inform me when you become unable to see that warrior."

The boy stood on his toes. Merthen quickly stuffed a few apples into his purse.

"Now," said the boy.

Merthen lifted the bottom of his cloak, exposing his boney knees. "Very well. Let us flee." Into the opposite direction of the retreating Jutes, Merthen ran.

"But what about the apples we picked?"

"Leave them."

"But I am hungry."

From across the glade, Merthen called out, "You may eat, or be eaten. The choice is yours."

Uther gulped. Off toward his mentor he flew. On the way he scooped up two apples.

Merthen wheezed. "I recall seeing a brook when we came this way. We need to go there. Do you remember where it is?"

The boy banked to the left and sped down a hill. "This way."

Merthen followed as fast as he could. When he arrived at the side of the shallow creek, he waded in and slapped water onto his armpits, saying, "Dive in! We must lose our scent. They may have dogs."

Uther bit into his apple. "Big dogs?"

"Everything the Germans do is big. The hounds of Alsatia are no exception."

Uther let go of his apple. He rolled into the water.

Using his staff as a crook, Merthen shepherded the abandoned produce back into his possession. "We need to traverse along the stream bank. If we cross through the woods, the Jutes will find us. They are unparalleled trackers."

The boy stopped his cavorting. "Why did you talk to them in Latin?"

"I did not want them to know we were Britons. I tried to convince them we were Roman, but it appears they never even heard of Rome. Now *that* is what I call a bumpkin."

"Are they dangerous?"

Merthen heaved his saturated self out of the waterway. "If the snow barbarians capture a man who fought against them with outstanding valor, they will pull out his heart and eat it while it is still beating." He squeezed some water from his braids.

The boy hopped onto a mud flat. "But we did not fight them at all. We ran like baby girls."

"Selective acts of cowardice can be of great utility." Merthen bit into his apple.

Uther started to chew on his nails. "We should get going."

"I concur." Merthen smacked the boy's hand. "Stop mauling your claws."

They kept a steady trot. Uther slowed when it was obvious Merthen could run no more.

"Henceforth," said Merthen, "I forswear never to question your sensory abilities. If you ever hear anything out of the ordinary, inform me straight away. And should I fail to heed your warning, I shall present you with my posterior, and permit you to engage it with a swift kick of the boot."

"What is *Etzel*? Why did you say that word to them?"

"*Etzel* is the German name for Attila the Hun." Merthen sat down on a fallen log and removed his sopping wet boots. "Attila's cavalry laid waste the Rhineland some decades ago. To this day he is feared like a demigod. I wagered I might frighten those Jutes by pretending to be a druid under his patronage."

The boy plucked off one shoe. "I wish those wildmen would go away." He pounded it against the ground. "If we had more knights, we could make them go."

Merthen shot Uther a disapproving glare. "Watering the seeds of mindlessness begets only mindlessness. That is not how a monastic should behave. Besides, the Germans are so populous, attacking them would be like bailing the sea with a thimble." Merthen poured a stream of water from his boot.

"The king should make them go away."

"That oaf? I know barnacles with a stronger talent for strategy. Do you know what *strategy* is?"

"It is a catapult?"

"No, boy, it is a way of planning. For example, there was once a clever architect named Daedelus, who was imprisoned on an island with his son Icarus."

"Was it Hibernia?"

"I believe it was Crete. To escape this captivity, Daedalus fashioned wings out of wax and feathers."

The boy tied his shoes back up. "Is that true?"

"So say the Greeks." Merthen put on his boots as well. "Mister Daedalus gave his son a pair of wings and one day when the guards were otherwise engaged, they took flight. Young Icarus, caught in the sport, spiraled high into the firmament."

"Did they get away?"

"There is the rub. For when the boy flew towards the sun, the wax melted. Icarus fell, crashing into the foamy brine, whereupon he drowned."

Merthen began the hike home. The boy scampered up to his side, and said, "Do you think we should make wings?"

"No. My point is that Daedalus employed a flawed strategy. He had the right tools, but he failed to understand the human element. Our king makes the same mistake. He gathers taxes to purchase new weapons instead of sending envoys to froth up blood feuds among the Germans. That was how Augustus ruled the brutes."

The boy stopped walking. "He should have flown at night."

"What? Are you even listening to me?"

"Mister Daedalus was wrong. If he had flown when the sun was down, the wax would not have melted."

"But that would require abundant moon glow."

"Daedalus could wait for a full moon, right?"

Uther waited for Merthen to reply. Instead the old man tugged at his beard. That meant he was thinking. Uther could tell how much Merthen was thinking based on how long he held onto his beard. Merthen tugged on it three times. He placed his open hand on Uther's head. He shook the boy's scalp.

"Master Uther," said Merthen, "a gifted moralist, you are not. But I must opine, you are a brilliant tactician. Next time we go to market, I am going to buy you a pen. I think it is high time you started writing."

Once more, Uther checked the path behind them. No Jutes in sight. Then he asked, "What is a tactician?"

Chapter VIII: The Growing Moon, AD 484

Nomen est omen.

The name is an omen.

* * *

The saddle on display at the tanner's booth was in fine condition given its age. The seat had been recently replaced with Italian leather. Nothing wrong with that. It was the stirrups that were unsettling to Merthen. They were braided in the Ostragoth style, using a saddlery technique the Germans of the Danube had learned from the Huns. It was a technique Methen had mastered as well.

Although he tried not to stare at the Hunnish stirrups, Merthen found it hard to look away. In terms of general outline, a stirrup is shaped somewhat like a noose. Of course, a stirrup is not a noose. A noose kills one man at a time; a stirrup can exterminate an entire village. But these were dark thoughts. Merthen waited for them to pass.

Uther pretended to swing a sword. "You should buy me a knife. That would be more useful than a little quill."

"You should be mindful of how fortunate you are," said Merthen. "I wish I had a pen set when I was your age."

"But if I get a quill, we will have to buy parchment. It is very expensive, and we have hardly any money."

"Education is not just a diversion of the wealthy. You can practice your declinations on sheets of bark. Come to think of it, I could carve some phrases into the trees. Gathering wood will become be your grammar review."

Before the boy could respond, a Frank with a flowing handlebar mustache and a crucifix around his neck introduced himself. "*Salve* Sir," he said in Latin, "I am Oderic of Anjou."

Merthen checked to see if the back of Oderic's head was shaved. It was not.

Oderic produced a small scroll. "I need two copies of this contract. I was told you are a clerk."

Merthen bowed. "Ambrosius of Carmarthen, at your service. I will duplicate those for one denarius. Take it or leave it."

"Fair enough." Oderic pointed to a barrel. "Can you write on that?"

Merthen slid out two blank scrolls from the tube that hung from his belt. He said to the boy, "You can go play. Be sure to stay where I can see you."

Uther was large enough, and swift enough, to run away from any evil-intentioned adult. Nonetheless, Merthen was uncomfortable leaving him by the docks. Although the old man had no clear memory of his own mother's face, he could easily recall the sailor who locked him in a monkey cage.

"Aye," said Uther. "I will stay close." He scampered off.

Using a wool bundle as his chair, Merthen reviewed Oderic's document, saying, "This verbiage indicates that you sell apples. I grow a few orchards myself." He began to copy the text.

"Here? With all the rain? How do you control the mildew?"

"I plant all my groves on ridge lines. As soon as the water falls, it blows away." Off toward Saint David's dock, Uther was throwing pine cones into the bay with three older boys.

Oderic asked, "How large an operation do you have?"

"I work alone. Sometimes the boy helps." Merthen finished the first document.

"Interesting. Did your boy call you *Merlin* just now?"

"No, Mer-*then*. That is my Celtic name. Why do you ask?"

"There is a mystic in the court of Governor Syagrius. She claims her brother is hermit who grows magic apples Cambria. She calls him the Wizard Mer-*lin*."

Merthen's eyebrows perked up. Back when he was stranded in Paris, he performed sleight-of-hand in the market squares. He even formed a team with James, a street musician, who used to introduce Merthen as the *Wizard of Britannia*. That might explain part of Oderic's statement, but not all of it. When Merthen was stuck in Gaul, he never grew apples.

"And what," said Merthen, "would his woman's name be?"

"Morgan. Her father is supposed to be from around here. She says her brother is a druid."

"Does she? What kind of sorcery does she practice?"

"She reads the stars. Last time I saw her, she predicted the legions would march back into Gaul. The Romans eat it up. Puts on a good show, though. Red hair, green eyes. Nice hind end for a woman of her age."

Merthen began inscribing the second copy. "Is she old enough to be my sister?"

"Not even close." Oderic gently waved around the first copy to dry the ink. "She could be your daughter. Did you ever bang any Frankish girls?"

"Not me. My flagship stopped hoisting its mainsail back before my hair turned gray."

* * *

Merthen noticed a long-billed stork suspended in mid-air. And then a wasp flew past his nose.

"Your flagship?" said the wasp. She circled around his head. "When did you become impotent?"

"When did you become such a thorn in my arse?" He brushed her away. "Could you stop buzzing around? I am trying to work."

She landed on his chest.

"Not there. Get off."

"The Goddess Aestor wishes to know how you become educated," said Gopi. "She feels it will help her in evaluating your case."

"Evaluating my case? Tell me, Lady Gopi, why exactly am I am being tried? What charges have been levied against me?"

"There is a series of them. Related incidents. The gods wish to determine if you are genuine."

Merthen snorted. "Those lascivious, swan-seducing egoists are questioning *my* character? No, this will not do. Please inform the bailiff that I am requesting a change of venue. I want a jury of my peers: Cretins and Philistines preferably." He tried to write again, but the ink would not flow from his quill.

"Droll," said the wasp. "So, how did you learn to read? You were just a slave boy. The sooner you answer, the sooner I will be on my way."

Merthen pondered why he was experiencing repeated hallucinations. If his store consciousness was in conflict with his waking mind, it might explain why Gopi was so bent on agitating him. Perhaps this was a side effect of his decades of meditation. Or perhaps, his brain had sustained long-term mental damage when he was tortured by the Persians, or drugged by Huns.

Whatever the reason, he was not going to figure it out today. Instead, he just said, "My master in Constantinople was a solicitor of some means. I served as a domesticus to his son, Priscus. After his tutor gave a lesson, I would clear the parchment and deliver it to Judith the head cook. She used it to start the ovens at dawn."

"Another lady in your life?" said Gopi.

"No, she was a freed slave." Merthen flicked his pen. "One day I saw the tutor give Priscus an apple after the boy wrote the word μαλυσ. I reckoned it was a pretty good trick, so I painted it onto a pottery shard. A few days later I saw a clerk in the market. I showed it to him."

"Did he give you an apple?"

"No, but he read it. From then on I kept some of the exercises I was supposed to give to Judith. When I ventured into the streets, I would scan the public monuments, searching for phrases I found written on Priscus's scrolls."

Gopi swiveled her tail as if writing on his chest. "Just like the phrases you are going to write on the trees in your compound."

"I never thought of that." He straightened his finger and let the wasp clasp onto it. "Of course, Greek was an easy go. It was all we servants ever spoke. Learning Latin was more of a task. Needless to say, I became a regular at Mass."

"Hence your love of liturgy."

"The bishop was so impressed by the Celtic slave boy's piety that he wrote my master requesting I be baptized. Oddly enough, the first book I read in Latin was written by a Hebrew: *The Jewish Antiquities* by Josephus. I found it under Judith's bed after she died."

"She could read?"

"No," he said, "but she was a Jew. Somehow, she knew it was special."

"Fancy that," said Gopi. She wiggled her antennae and flew off. Her swift departure was no surprise to Merthen. His delusions tended to disappear on their own volition. Like pangs of hunger, once they were satisfied, they vanished.

* * *

From down at the docks, there was yelling. Merthen saw Uther run toward him. One of the boy's dockside playmates was with curled up, holding his crotch. The other was in tears with a broken stick in his hand. The third boy had a bloody nose.

"Boy!" said Merthen. "What have you done?"

"They were making fun of me." Uther's knees were scraped. "They called me spotty face and said I was an animal that lived in the woods. They called me *Uther-Arthur, Uther-Arthur*."

"What is he saying?" asked Oderic in Latin.

Merthen translated. "He says he got in a fight after some children were mocking him on account of the burns on his face. His name is Uther and the Celtic Briton word for bear is *art*, so they called him *Uther-Arthur*. They were teasing him."

In Celtic, Merthen continued to interrogate the boy. "And how did you respond to them?"

"At first I told them to stop. One of them threw a dirt ball at me, so I cracked him in the nuts. They tried to beat me up, but I got away."

Merthen rapped his knuckles on the boy's head. "I am glad you are well. But you should never fight when you are outnumbered. Be mindful, boy."

"But they started it."

Oderic nodded toward Uther. "Your grandson?"

Merthen replied in Latin. "Just a hired hand. How he wriggles out of trouble is beyond me. The word *caution* does not seem to be part of his lexicon."

"With spunk like that, he might make himself a great knight someday. Why, I can see him slaying a whole pack of them salt pricks."

"Salt pricks? Who in heavens are they?"

"The wild Franks from out in the marshes. You know, Chief Clovis's tribe: the frog-eaters."

Uther interrupted them. He spoke in Latin. "What did he say? Did he say I was going to do something? Did he say I was a *frog*?"

Oderic's face lit up. "You have taught him to speak Latin. By Juno, if this knight can fight and use the imperial tongue, he might just make himself a king. I can say I knew him when."

"What is he saying about me now?"

Merthen inhaled a long breath. "He is impressed with your ability to converse in his language. It is just as I told you, Latin a valuable skill."

"Did he say I would be a knight?"

Merthen batted his eyes. "He said that if you kept to your studies, you might have the potential to be a thoughtful soldier who fought justly in defense of the weak and downtrodden."

"He did not! I heard him say *frog*."

"Perhaps I embellished. But if you find my translation insufficient, you will simply have to improve your fluency."

The boy stuck out his chin. "Well then, maybe I will learn Latin. If you could do it, so can I."

Chapter IX: The Hay Moon, AD 484

Dux bellorum. Asinus asinorum in saecula saeculorum.

A duke of war. The greatest jackass in all eternity.

* * *

When Merthen was a student at university, the senior monastics were fond of saying, "*Before interbeing, chop wood and carry water. After interbeing, chop wood and carry water.*" In other words, the activities of daily life will never change, but one's perception of them can.

For the young men in Merthen's dormitory, this profound aphorism acquired a new meaning, namely, "*One of the professors just told me to paint a room, grind ink, or do some other menial chore, and I have no choice but to do it even though I was supposed to get the afternoon off.*"

Merthen recalled this metaphor every time he dipped his bucket into the cold spring by his hut. It was a memory he cherished, unlike so many that he would just as soon jettison. Of course, that would be inappropriate. Nothing in one's life should be tossed away; it all had value. What truly mattered was one's perception of it.

Merthen waited for his bucket to fill and read the words he had neatly carved into the trunk of a beech: *carpe diem, quam minimum credula postero*. Balanced upon the tree's largest root was a smooth round cobble. It had the potential to make an excellent grind stone. Merthen picked it up.

Lady Gopi asked, "Where are you taking me?"

"You have become granite, eh? I was not aware you were capable of petrological transmogrification."

The turtle stuck out her snout. "Your eyes are worse than I thought."

Merthen tipped the reptile over and laid her flat on her back. "Good day, Lady." He picked up his bucket and sauntered off.

"You cannot just leave me here!"

He stopped in his tracks. Who was she to give him orders? Lady Gopi was but a figment of his imagination. And *she* had the gall to tell *him* what to do.

"Am I unjust?" he said. "Is it unfair that I should treat you thusly? You descend on me as a snake and a stinging bee. I am to accept this?"

Gopi flailed her limbs. "I did not appear as a bee. I was a wasp."

He shouted, "This is insanity! Why are you asking me these bizarre questions? What is this trial? What have I done? What makes me a criminal?"

Gopi did not reply.

* * *

Uther bounded through the forest floor toward his mentor.

Merthen put down his bucket. "Boy, where is your hat? Every time you get sun burned your spots get bigger."

"I forgot to wear it." Uther was holding a sack, the lower end of which was soaking wet. "Look what I got. I shot them down by the stream."

"All this meat will be the end of me. Are they trout?"

The boy opened the bag. One by one, he lifted out a half dozen muskrats. The smallest one had sunk to the bottom of the pile. It was drenched in blood.

Perspiration dripped into Merthen's eyes. "The fire," he said, "is too strong. I am burning."

The boy stepped over to the hearth. It coals were bearly glowing. "How can you be hot?"

* * *

A blast of hot desert wind smacked Merthen in the face. The Persian sun baked down upon his naked back. A small stream of blood flowed down from his crotch, soaking into his sandals. His head was throbbing, his mouth parched. One of the Persians pounded on

Merthen's drum, while the centurion screamed. His cries for mercy sounded more like the howls of an animal.

Merthen fell to his knees. The Persian commander grabbed Merthen's red hair and forced him to his feet. The handle of a dagger was slapped into Merthen's palm. The Persian shouted his orders. Then Merthen felt the knife in his hand piercing the skin of the centurion's dark African neck. When he hit the centurion's jugular, blood gushed out. It oozed onto the desert floor, and quickly dried into a thin crusty layer, more brown that red.

The rat, slathered in a mixture of dung and human blood, squealed in pain. Although the Persian Commander had impaled it on the end of his sword, the rat was not yet dead. Its tail flapped from side to side, splattering gore into Merthen's face. The Persians laughed at him.

* * *

Merthen was about to cry out, when he observed the green leaves of the forest above. Somehow, he was thirty paces away from his compound. A searing pain radiated out from behind his testicles. He called out, "Boy? Am I lost?"

"Merthen?" said Uther.

"Over here, boy. Help me up. I have fallen."

Uther dashed over. "Are you all right?"

Merthen wiped away some tears. "I may have cut myself between the legs." He examined his crotch. It was fine. His only wounds were minor abrasions. He sat up. "How did I get here?"

"You disappeared, like a flash."

Merthen sighed. "I must apologize. I am stricken by a mania at times. It was that dead rat you showed me. They have a deleterious effect on me."

The boy pounded his fist on his own forehead. "I forgot what they did to you on the slave ship. I am so sorry. Really."

"And I forgive you. But for future reference, you should always keep a wide berth between me and any rodentia you may find."

"Never again," said the boy. "I will never do that."

Merthen caught his breath. Here he was, a grown man, running like a child. What kind of example was that for the boy? All these years meditating and pursuing the way of the Buddha, and still he was a lunatic, unable to control his passions. It was more than just distressing. It was humiliating.

Uther plucked a few leaves off Merthen's braids. "Did you have a vision?"

Merthen hoisted up the back of his blouse, exposing his spine. It was crisscrossed with long straight scars.

"When I was a slave in Constantinople," he said, "my master caught me reading, which bonded servants were forbidden to do. The fact that I had mastered this skill indicated that my master had been negligent in controlling his household. After giving me twenty lashes, he sold me off to one of his clients, a *Dux Bellorum* named Pertinax."

"What is a *Dux Bellorum*?"

"It is a Duke of War. Dux Pertinax commanded of a battalion of Armenian mercenaries. Because I could read, I was assigned to be a drummer boy. Dux Pertinax would copy his orders onto slips of paper. Runners would deliver them to us drummer boys. We would read them and bang out a signal directing the troops. When a battle is raging, drums are the only sound one can clearly hear."

"You were important."

"Life-threateningly so. The Persian archers were rewarded a full cup of salt for every drummer they struck." Merthen, still shaken, rose to his feet. He checked one last time to make sure there were no Persians in the woods.

Uther asked, "Did you ever go to battle?"

"I fought against Bahran Gur, the Emperor of Persia. The Persians had raided some Roman outposts in eastern Anatolia. Dux Pertinax was thrilled. His father was a senator who invaded Persia many years before. It ended in a costly stalemate and the senator lost his office. It brought great shame on his family."

"So, Pertinax was not a real soldier."

"Not even half. He was a politician's son with a penchant for issuing inept oratory. My commanding officer, the Centurion Aethiops, was constantly giving him advice, all of which he spurned."

"What is a centurion?"

"That is a field marshal." Merthen limped toward the hut. "Aethiops was a professional soldier, the son of Negro slaves. He knew our battalion was unfit to defeat the Persians on their own territory. Pertinax ignored him. He was blinded by vendetta."

"How long did the war last?"

"Three pathetic weeks. Dux Pertinax wanted to go to battle in the worst sort of way, and oh, how he succeeded. That moron led us into a desolate valley searching for a cache of weapons. We found nothing. His spies had lied to him."

Merthen faltered as he walked. Uther helped the old man keep his balance.

"We were ambushed," said Merthen. His shoulders slouched. "From up on the ridge, a double row of Syrian archers let loose a rain of arrows. Our Armenian troops turned and ran, back to Armenia I suppose. When the Persians captured Pertinax, they stuck nails through his penis, tied him to a tent post, and let him die of thirst."

"How did you get away?"

"I did not. The centurion and I were stripped naked and forced to ride on a square fence rail like a hobby horse." Merthen jiggled the bracelet on his wrist. "They tied weights to our ankles and hoisted the timbers on their shoulders. My crotch was pretty well ripped up. Then they whipped us and ordered us to talk. They said they would kill us if we did not comply."

"Did you? Did you talk?"

Merthen pushed back his hair. He knew that if the boy was to become a monastic, he would have face life's un-pleasantries. Suffering exists. Accepting this precept was the first step toward overcoming ill-being. This was how Brother Tinh Tu trained Merthen. This was how Merthen would train the boy.

Merthen resumed his normal upright posture. "The Centurion Aethiops was a good man. He never ordered us to do anything that he would not do himself. Needless to say, he felt honor bound. He would not betray our forces. They tied ropes around his wrists and ankles, staked him spread eagle onto the ground, and abused him most wickedly."

The boy swallowed hard. "What did they do to you?"

Merthen replied with some hesitation. "They handed me a dagger. They told me to slit his throat, and before I was even aware that I did it, I did it. If I had been a man of character I would have thrown the knife away."

"Did they let you go?"

"They released me, but I was not free. If I had returned to Constantinople, they would have hanged me. I suspect there is still a price on my head. Instead, the Persians sent me to an outpost in Kabul near the Indian border. For two years I clerked with an architect building a fort. He was a cold-hearted man. There was a grove of apple trees nearby. I used to go there for shade."

"The centurion," said Uther, "he was not going to talk. They would have killed him anyway. Right?"

Merthen closed his eyes. "I will not shirk my responsibility. It was I who made orphans of his children. A monastic should be mindful of his shortcomings no matter how shameful they may be. Do not forget that, Uther."

"But you were just a boy. You were afraid."

"The Buddha never took a man's life, not even in war."

"I will not bring home any more rats. I promise."

"I know that I should not dwell on the past. And yet, I am struck by habit energies and pointless rumination. Such foolishness."

"No," said Uther. "The centurion was your friend. They made you do it." The boy scooted off toward their simmering meal. "We should get something to eat."

* * *

Uther hopped over a log, but did not land on the other side. He hovered in mid air, not moving up or down.

A turtle crawled up to Merthen's feet. She asked, "What were you trying to run away from just now? What did you see that so frightened you?"

Merthen rested his heel on her back. There was nothing more he wanted to do than crush her. Her shell was her spine. He pressed the sole of his foot down onto it. "Do you," he said, "have any idea what all I could do to you?"

She did not retreat into her shell. "You did not tell Uther the whole truth, did you?"

"You wretched little monster. Do you wish to know each lurid detail?" His wrist began to shake. "When I was but a boy, I witnessed the Centurion Aethiops tied face down. The Persian commander cried, *Let him have it*, and then I sat there and watched as two of his officers positioned a bronze pot with an iron cover upside down on top of the centurion's naked buttocks. Then they pulled the lid away."

"What was in the pail?"

"At first the centurion pleaded. After that, he just screamed. Those bastards held my chin. They forced me to look. It was a rat, covered in excrement and shards of the centurion's bowels. The Persians had starved it for days. It was trapped."

"Was it the rat you were running from?"

"That metal bucket," said Merthen. "They placed that filthy animal in it and tipped it on top of Aethiops. The rat burrowed up into the centurion's anus. It had nowhere else to go, so… the damned thing ate its way out his torso."

Gopi stopped asking questions.

"They told me to give them information. I was a stupid drummer boy, for Christ's sake! As if I knew anything? I told them whatever they wanted to hear: truth, lies, utter nonsense. What did it matter? They asked me if I would kill newborn Romans rocking in their cradles. And I said, *Yes*."

Gopi said, "A promise sworn in a moment of desperation has no meaning. The court will not hold that against you."

"Your court be damned," said Merthen. "I am not one to swear falsely. When I said I would kill babies, I meant ever word." He lifted his foot off the turtle. "If you think that I was running from that rat, think again. In point of fact, I was fleeing from an even more despicable beast."

"What was that?"

"*Ecce homo*," he replied. "I was running from myself."

BOOK III: THE TEACHER

CHAPTER X: THE GROWING MOON, AD 485

Nascentes morimur.

From the moment we are born, we die.

* * *

Merthen may have been more fit than men half his age, but he was still twice as old as them. Come noontime, he had the habit of lying on his back in the sunniest spot he could find. He called it *recumbent meditation*. Uther called it *dog sleep*.

Uther rather liked it when the old man spontaneously nodded off. These naps left the boy free to eyeball all the young maids who swayed across the marketplace. Some of these tall, round-hipped women were the same skinny girls he played with last summer. That bothered Uther a bit. He still had the body of a boy. Why was he so small? Was it because of the white spots on his skin?

Merthen farted, and not delicately, so much so that it woke him up. "Boy?" he said, rubbing his eyes. "Oh, there you are. What were we doing?"

"You were testing me on my vocabulary. I told you it was boring."

Merthen dusted a few shards of grass off his cloak. "Nonsense, how far had we gotten?"

"You asked me the cardinal directions."

"So I did. And what are they?"

In a monotone, Uther replied, "*Oriens, occidens, septentriones, et meridies.*"

"And the three primary colors are?"

"*Ruber, caeruleus, et flavius.*" Uther pushed back the conical straw hat that shaded his face and shoulders. "How do you say *brown*?"

"*Spadix*," said Merthen. "Although technically speaking, *spadix* only refers to a chestnut-like hue. Latin has no direct translation for *brown*."

"How can they not have a word for something?"

"Easily. We call man *deaf* if he can not hear, and *mute* if he cannot speak, but we have no way to describe someone who lacks the sense of smell."

"I think we do. I heard it once."

"Oh, really? What is it then?"

Uther rested his chin on the heel of his hand. "*Smoof?*"

Merthen erupted with laughter.

Uther never understood the old man's sense of humor. When someone told a joke, Merthen reacted by nodding, as if recognizing that the punch line met the criteria for that which was known as *funny*. And yet, when Merthen spent all day carving a pitchfork, only to have it snap as soon as he tried to use, he would howl with delight.

A little girl came running toward them, waving her arms. The cross on her necklace flapped up and down against her chin. It was Paulina, Father Thomasius's oldest daughter. One of her braids had unwound and was flailing around.

"My father needs you at the vicarage," she said, out of breath. "Missus Myfany has fallen. You must come straight away."

Taking hold of his staff, Merthen launched himself to his feet. "Is she hurt?"

"My father thinks she broke a bone."

"Old women have been known to do that," he said to Paulina. He took hold of her hand. "Take us to your home."

Paulina led them to the informal dirt path that snaked around the back of the market.

"Who is Missus Myfany?" said Uther.

"Her husband was a blacksmith," said Merthen. "A few years back, she bought some rabbits from me intent on breeding them. Within a year they were all dead. She has been hounding me for a refund ever since."

"Were they sick?"

"They were as healthy as Adonis. She packed them on a dingy cloistered hutch. I told her they needed more room."

The dirt trail came to an end at the steps of the Roman-brick chapel. The thatched roofed vicarage stood next door.

Paulina pointed toward a toddler standing out in front. "That is my sister Columbia."

Tied around little Columbia's waist was a rope securing her to the hitching post like a dog leash. Columbia was throwing a splint of wood in the air and giggling. Paulina trotted up and took it away.

From inside the cottage, came the creaky voice of an old woman saying, "Oh, bugger!"

Merthen and Uther entered the two-room homestead. It had a wood floor, but no windows. The only light came from the embers in the fireplace. Missus Myfany, a toothless white-hired crone with a prominent mole on her cheek, was sprawled out on the floor. Her blouse was saturated with some sort of fluid.

Merthen knelt down by Myfany's side. "Are you bleeding? Have you been cut?"

"This is water." She winced, gritting her teeth. "I was carrying a bucket when I slipped. You still owe me four denarii."

"I cannot help but admire your tenacity. Your practicality is another matter. What is wrong with you?"

"I was birthing Father Thomasius's wife. I think my shoulder is broken. You have to go in there."

"Does it hurt?"

She clamped her eyes shut. "Like bloody hell! Now get in there and deliver that baby."

Merthen addressed Paulina. "The baby is not yet born?"

"Aye," said Paulina. "Mum is in the other room with father."

Missus Myfany yelled out, "Get your boney arse in there you cheap old bastard."

"Madam," said Merthen, "I am not a midwife. My training is all military."

"Go, damn it!"

Paulina tugged at the end of his sleeve. "Come this way."

Merthen patted Uther's arm, and tilted his head toward a basket of rags. "Boy, clean up this mess."

Uther got to work, but his eyes stayed fixed on Merthen in the bed chamber.

Through the door, Uther could see Father Thomasius, with bags under his eyes, gracelessly petting the cheek of his wife, Eira. She was on her back, exhausted but awake. Her skirt was pulled up to her hips and her legs were splayed open.

"Thank goodness you have come," said Thomasius. "Missus Myfany has been telling me what to do, but I am rather at a loss. We have been waiting all night."

"Are you well?" said Merthen.

"Just tired. There was a fire in the sanctuary Tuesday night. Neither of us slept much."

Merthen peered into the woman's crotch as discretely as a former Buddhist monastic could. "One moment," he said. He dashed into the adjoining room.

Missus Myfany still lay on the floor holding her visibly swelling arm.

Merthen whispered, "What am I supposed to do? She looks ill. Should I give her something?"

"No. The baby should have come out already. I suspect it is dead. You must not tell Missus Eria."

"Dead? How can you tell?"

"Something is wrong. She has given birth four times. This one should be easy. I think the baby is too big for her." Myfany motioned for him to come closer. "Last night there were three crows above the doorway. Did you hear about the fire in the chapel?"

Merthen's pursed his lips as if he had swallowed a sour grape. This was a facial expression Uther knew all too well. It was the one Merthen exhibited whenever he saw someone misquoting the Bible, or throwing away a bent nail rather than straightening it for future use.

Merthen propped his fists onto his hips. "Are you certain you observed three crows on the roof? Perhaps one was a grackle with a sore throat?"

Missus Myfany's eyes bugged out. "Listen you old witch, if that baby is stuck inside her, you will have reach in and pull it out… piece by piece if need be. You must not let the father know."

Merthen grasped her arm and ever so slightly twisted it. Using a circular motion, he pushed his thumb into the ball of her shoulder. "Your arm is dislocated," he said, "not broken." Then he seized her by the elbow, and yanked it with a sharp strong twist. There was a pop. She screamed with all her might.

Uther started shaking. Myfany gasped for air, then fainted.

Father Thomasius came running out. "Is everything all right?"

Merthen flung off his cloak and rolled up his sleeves. "Yes, I set her arm back in place. She will be fine. Widow Myfany gave me instructions on how to care for your wife. Go outside and gather twelve smooth pebbles all the same size, no smaller than your thumb. Wash them clean and bring them to me."

"I understand," said Thomasius. Off he went.

Merthen snapped his fingers. Uther jumped up. They both approached the bedchamber.

In hushed tones Merthen said, "This is a dire situation, boy. Father Thomasius's wife will likely die. Be mindful and strong. Just do as I say."

Uther asked, "What do the crows mean?"

"Crows are just crows, boy. You can tile the roof with them. It will change nothing."

"Why did you tell Father Thomasius to get stones?"

"It is best for him to be out of the house for a while."

Uther gazed down at Missus Eria's exposed torso. "Her hole got bigger!"

Eria released a belch, then screeched. Merthen spread her legs open manually. The baby's head began to appear. Eria exhaled a long low moan.

Uther had seen generations of rabbits give birth. He knew it was messy. When it got too messy, Merthen would pull out his dagger and end the mother's misery. Would the old man do that to a Missus Eria?

Merthen asked, "Is she still breathing?"

Uther put his ear to her mouth. "Aye."

"Stay here boy." Merthen rushed back into the main room and slapped Widow Myfany on the cheek.

"Wake up you lousy hag! Can you hear me?"

She cracked open her eyes. "Aye. How is the baby?"

Merthen said, "Partially extruded. I can see the top of its head. Should I conduct a Cesarean?"

Myfany made a fist with her good hand. Tears streamed down her face. "What is that?"

"It is a surgical procedure. I can make an incision in her belly and pull the baby out. That is how Julius Caesar was born. I am unable to properly deliver this baby, Madam. But I know how to stitch and dress a wound. How long till the mother expires?"

"She should have been dead at sunrise. If she goes, we will tell the father that we cut the baby out after it happened. Agreed?"

"I concur." He hopped up and scooted back to Eria's bedside.

"What are we going to do?" said Uther.

Merthen rolled up the mother's skirt revealing her entire belly." He removed his sword from its scabbard. "Stand behind me, Uther. Close your eyes and do not open them, no matter what you hear."

Uther complied, and again Missus Eria cried out. "Thomasius!"

Uther re-opened his eyes.

Merthen wiped the surface of his sword on the bed cover. He positioned himself beneath the mother's legs. With his left hand, he gripped onto her distended belly. He pressed the blade to her skin. Merthen's right hand was shaking, almost violently. "*Gah-tay, gah-tay, para gah-tay,*" he said to himself.

Uther had seen the old man pull off some amazing feats, but never when two lives were at stake. Could he actually slice deep enough to cut Missus Eria's belly, but not so deep as to endanger her child?

Uther detected something move. Where did it come from? From out of Missus Eria's vagina, there emerged an infant's face.

"I see the baby!" cried Uther. "Yuk."

Merthen dropped his weapon. There was a spurt of fluid and the baby was forced out. Merthen grasped it by the shoulders. He untangled the chord. Missus Eria passed out.

The slippery wet newborn lie limp Merthen's hand. He brought the baby's face up to his. It was not breathing. He thumped its breastbone with his finger tip. No signs of life. He examined the placenta scattered out at his feet, and said, "Poor child. At least the mother is not bleeding."

And then Merthen lost his grip. The infant slipped from his palms and fell head-first toward wooden floor planks. Merthen tried to it catch it, but lost his balance. He nearly tumbled over.

The newborn's skull was ready to crash against the floor, when Uther sprang forward. He pounced, landing on his knees, and snatched onto the baby by the ankles, one in each hand. The infant's head jerked back. Uther, wide-eyed and panting, held up the dangling baby.

Merthen wiped the perspiration from his forehead. "Good catch, boy."

Father Thomasius bolted into the room. "Is she alright?" His wife wheezed, unconscious, but still alive.

From the other room Myfany called out, "What is going on in there?"

Merthen placed his hand on Thomasius's shoulder. "I have some rather unpleasant news for you, father."

Thomasius hung his head and let loose the twelve stones in his hands.

There was a high pitched cough, almost like that of a small animal, followed by a baby's cry. It came from the newly minted mortal who Arthur was holding in his grips. The boy looked down at its crotch. "He has no penis!"

The infant began to clench and unclench her hands. She wiggled her toes. Merthen laid her on her mother's breast. "Father Thomasius," he said, "it appears that I need to revise my previous statement. It is my pleasure to inform you that your wife has given birth to yet another daughter. Congratulations, Sir."

Chapter XI: The Mead Moon, AD 485

Baptizavi autem et Stephanae domum ceterum

nescio si quem alium baptizaverim.

I baptized Stephanis and his family, but I cannot remember if I baptized anyone else.

* * *

Into the soil of the field behind the chapel, a gang of sweaty Cornish sailors pounded down the iron stakes securing the tie ropes for a large canvas tent. Underneath this temporary structure, acolytes in ecclesiastical tunics scurried about. They arranged the communion chalice, paten, and ciborium on a makeshift altar composed of three pine coffins stacked one atop the other.

Uther and Merthen listened to the workmen singing tight multi-layered harmonies to the rhythm of their hammers.

A priest with wavy black hair called out. "*Entschuldigen Sie, bitte. Sind Sie Deutch?*"

It took a while for Merthen to realize the cleric was hailing him. "No father," Merthen replied, "I am a Briton. Ambrosius of Carmarthen, at your service."

The priest bowed, "I am Father Mercurius of Tuscany. I meant no offense, Sir."

"None taken."

"I wonder, why do you keep your hair like a German?"

Merthen lifted up one of his braids. "I live by the Saxon frontier. I find the brutes less inclined to toss an ax at my spine if they see a quartet of ponytails dangling from my scalp."

"You are well spoken for a frontiersman. Are you educated?"

"Somewhat. I was drummer boy with the legions."

"Really? Did you fight in Gaul?"

"No, Persia. I spent my youth in Constantinople. I was slaved off when I was just a tike."

"That is an awfully long trip for a little boy."

Merthen scratched his bald spot. "I was light and easy to pack."

"Were you baptized in the Eastern Diocese? You are Nicean, yes?"

Merthen puffed out his chest. "By all means."

Father Mercurius said, "You need to speak with Monsignor Camillus. This way please."

He led Merthen and the boy to an empty sheep shed. It had a tarp spread over its roof, like the field headquarters of a Roman legion. Outside this ad hoc office stood two burly Swabians from the Alps. They wore Roman breast plates, so well polished, they shined. Uther was dazzled. Merthen dragged him indoors.

Father Mercurius bowed to the monsignor, a middle-aged cleric with the tan skin of a Moor and woolly black hair of a Negro. Perhaps he was a half-breed bastard, left as an infant on a church door step. Many churchmen were.

Father Mercurius spoke first. "Monsignor Camillus," he said, "this man is a Briton named Ambrosius of Carmarthen. He is quite well traveled. He informed me that he was baptized in Constantinople."

Monsignor Camillus folded up the note he had been reading. He tucked it into the drawer of his portable secretary's desk. "So," said the monsignor, with no sense of urgency, "what brings you into town today?"

"Why the Eucharist, Your Grace," said Merthen. "I was hoping to expose the boy to a properly-executed mass. I have been training him in Latin, and there are so few in these parts who can pronounce it correctly. I thought the archbishop would be a good example."

"That he would," said Camillus. He fingered his rosary. "You are, of course, aware that the Patriarch of Constantinople has been excommunicated."

Merthen stammered. "What? How did this happen? Is there a new Patriarch?"

"No." Monsignor Camillus slid back his bench. "The Patriarch refused the Pope's order to resign. The Holy Father had no choice but to excommunicate the post. All the Eastern Dioceses are now heretical."

This was bad news for Merthen. If the Patriarch of Constantinople was a heretic, then so was Merthen, and that was worse than not being baptized at all. The last few Popes had systematically wiped out the Gnostic, Donatist, and Pelagian Christians. The only Arians left were the Visigoths. Having eliminated all the black sheep, the Vatican was now targeting those whose hind legs were still strong enough to kick the sheepdog.

"*Deus Misereatur*," Merthen finally said, "this is sad."

"Tragic I would say. So tell me, when were you last in Byzantium?"

"Thirty years ago. After the Hunnish war I settled in Gaul, but the Franks got to fighting. So, I sailed here to make my fortune… or lack thereof."

"Was that when Vortiger was still king?"

"Yes. I arrived just before the Saxons killed him."

Camillus rose from his seat. "Well, at least you are not a pagan, despite your hairdo."

"No all who own a harps are harpists. Will that be all, monsignor?"

"Not quite. I need to seek guidance from the archbishop's secretary. Stay here. If you need anything, the guards can help you. They speak Latin."

Monsignor Camillus left the building with Father Mercurius close behind.

Uther bit his thumbnail. "Are we in trouble?"

"I suspect not. They just want to verify I am a Nicene Christian. I tell you boy, this modern church is nothing but politics."

* * *

A pink-lipped lamb wandered into the room. The pitter-pat of its delicate hooves was the only sound Merthen heard. The ever-fidgeting Uther was immobile, as were the Swabian sentries outside.

"Good day," said the lamb, on wobbly knees. "I have a question from Lord Khnemu."

"Khnemu? What is he? Some sort of goblin? Or perhaps he is an elf? Or maybe he is one of those three-eye flaming demons who haunt the outcrops of the Katmandu Valley?"

"Lord Khnemu is the oldest of all of Egypt's gods."

"Let me guess, does he have the body of a man and the head of a jackass?"

"No, a ram. You would like him though. He is quite the creative sort. He sculpted the very first human from a lump of red clay."

"Sounds eerily familiar. Then again, once a miracle becomes fashionable, I suppose all immortal beings feel pressured to pull it off."

"Lord Khnemu is interested in your view of Christianity. The court is aware of your familiarity with the Bible. What would you say is its most important verse?"

"I find it rather telling," said Merthen, "that when we last met, I was writing a receipt, and you asked how I learned to read. Now, when I speak with a priest, you ask about Christianity. There seems to be a trend forming, yes?"

"People can see patterns in anything. Now then, what is your favorite Bible verse?"

Merthen could not help but recall a line of text he stumbled upon it when translating Paul's Letters during his stay at Nalanda University.

"I would opine," said Merthen, "that the most important verse in the Bible is Corinthians, chapter one, verse sixteen. In this woefully unappreciated paragraph, Paul notes that he cannot remember the names of some fellows he had previously baptized. I find it most diagnostic. If Paul was prone to forget things, the other gospel writers may have forgotten things as well. Thus, it is possible that some of the words of Jesus were inaccurately transcribed."

"Which implies that the Bible is not the whole truth?"

Merthen displayed his open hands. "Human fingers," he said, "are incapable of writing the whole truth."

"And what of ecclesiastical dogma?" said Gopi. "Your interpretation of scripture suggests that the church should not believe its own holy text. Was this what Christ wanted?"

"You can ask him that yourself next time you flitter off to heaven. All I know is this: Jesus roamed the streets, sat with lepers, and initiated a brawl with some bankers. Tell me Lady, do these strike you as the actions of a man who intended for jewel-encrusted temples to be erected in his name?"

* * *

The Swabians by the door saluted. An athletic, grey-haired priest entered the makeshift office. Gopi was nowhere to be seen.

The muscular cleric introduced himself. "I am Father Michael of Candida Casa, Executive Secretary to His Grace, Bishop Patricolus." He settled down behind the desk. "Your name is Ambrosius? Is this your grandson? What is wrong with his skin?"

"He is a hired hand. His mother claims he was scalded as a child. Myself, I have no issue."

"You were in Britannia when Vortiger was king," said Michael. "Did you ever take communion from a cleric named Father Agricolus? He was the assistant to the king's chaplain."

"Certainly. He was a Burgundian. I knew his daughter as well. She died last winter."

With pen in hand, Michael jotted down some notes. "Were you aware that Agricolus was a student of Pelagius the Briton? Have you heard of him?"

"I know of him. He was a Scot, not a Briton, a rather portly one from all accounts. He ended up somewhere in Africa. I always assumed he was a Stoic."

Michael put down his quill. "So tell me, how do you view original sin? Do you believe it to be true?"

Original sin, along with all the unoriginal ones, featured prominently in Merthen's world view. As a boy, he wondered how it could be that the bad men who stole him away from his mother ended up earning a half barrel of pepper. It was only after met Brother Tinh Tu that he finally got an answer. *Suffering exists,* said Tinh Tu. *And if you should happen to find out who started it all, suffering will still exist, so why bother?*

Merthen's response to Father Michael's question was, "When I was with the legions I was taken captive by the Huns. They once punished a traitor by crushing his hands and feet with a stone, sewing his mouth shut, and throwing him into a pit to starve, along with the bodies of his children whom they had just decapitated. For me, original sin is not a question of belief. It is *de facto.*"

Michael unfolded his hanky.

Merthen asked, "Good father, why do you ask me about this?"

Father Michael sneezed. "Professor Pelagius," he said, "was dangerously misguided. He taught that there was no original sin."

Merthen breathed in, and then he breathed out. There was no point in arguing with Father Michael. The cage of dogma he had constructed around himself had protected him from some unspoken fear, and protected him well. But by the same token, its cold bars constrained him from any further growth.

Merthen said, "It would appear that you too are a Scot. There is still some red in your hair."

"You have a keen eye. I was born a Pict."

"Fancy that? I was not aware that the Picts had been re-converted."

"They have not, but they will be. *Deo adiuvante.*"

"Myself," said Merthen. "I was shipped oversees in container designed to hold monkeys. It was decades before I was able to get back home. I gather your path to redemption has been an arduous journey as well. It is commendable you wish to ease the voyage of others."

"I am a soldier of the Lord, nothing more."

Merthen folded his hands.

Father Michael scanned his notes. "You are free to go. I recommend you return to the frontier, and do so quickly."

"I shall depart following the Eucharist."

"No. I can not permit that. You were not properly baptized, and I do not have time to resolve this. You are a complicated man, Mister whoever-you-really-are. When Father Patricolus holds mass this afternoon, there will be no complications."

Merthen put his hand on Uther's shoulder. "If possible, might the boy attend? I swore to his mother that I would arrange it."

"Very well," said Michael, "but you cannot accompany him."

A barn swallow flew out the doorway.

Merthen bowed. "Good day then. *Pax vobiscum*." He kneed Uther in the hip, and the boy did likewise.

Father Michael did not rise, nor did he offer his signet to be kissed.

From up in the meadow, there was a round of applause. The Cornishmen had finished erecting their tent.

Merthen and Uther skulked out of the stable in silence. They quickly assimilated into the mulling crowd, then strolled down to Widow Blodwen's fish stand.

The boy asked, "Do all priests have blue legs?"

"Blue legs? Why would they have that?"

"Father Michael's ankles were covered with drawings of animals. They were blue. He had a face on his kneecaps."

Merthen released an uncharacteristic blast of laughter. "An eye on the ground to watch his steps. Oh, how special."

The boy tilted his head. "What?"

"Father Michael is a Pict. They are infamous for their extensive personal adornments. They rub white lye in their hair and form it into spikes. Their entire skin is covered with tattoos. Their very name is derived from the Latin word *picit* which means what, boy?"

"Picture?"

"It means *painted*. It is a false cognate. When the Picts are young, they are embossed through an arduously slow process. Pigment is deposited on the tip of a metal prong that punctures the upper layers of the skin." With his finger, Merthen pretended to poke himself around the wrist.

"Does it hurt?"

"Like a bee sting. The Picts regard this self-mutilation as a form of moral training. It would appear that Father Michael participated in the Pictish rite of manhood."

"Is he a savage?"

"No, just a Scotsman. You see, Uther, savagery is not indelible. One can overcome it though education." A double mast was anchored close to shore. In front of it Widow Blodwen was packing salt cod.

"So," said the boy, "if the Saxons were taught things, would they stop being wild?"

"Precisely." Merthen patted his ward on the back. "All souls have the potential to be gentlemen. Keep this in mind as you pursue your monastic training."

"Even the Jutes?"

Merthen shook the beads on his wrist. "Brother Tinh Tu used to explain it this way. When one is happy, one exudes joy and civility. *Ergo*, if you observe a man who is snarling and treating everyone with cruelty, you know he is a man who is fundamentally unhappy. A German waving an ax is really just a crying baby."

Down by water's edge, Widow Blodwen hailed the detoured pilgrims. "Ahoy, Mister Merthen! Did you hear the news? The swamp Franks burned the port at Boulonge. All the Romans had to ship out."

Uther ran up and gave her a hug.

She pointed her knife toward the tents. "I thought you were going to mass?"

Merthen replied, "Our itinerary has been modified."

"Fancy that. I thought it was only snakes that ran away from Father Patricolus?"

"You know, Missus B, there are times when I consider challenging you to a duel of wits, but I loathe the idea of assailing an un-armed opponent."

She wiped some scales off her hands. "My third husband was killed in a duel. I told him to stay home."

"Sage advice." He gave her an apple. "Might I trouble you to take the boy to today's event? In the interest of my health, I think it would be best if I were to spend the afternoon resting in your stall."

She did not ask Merthen for any further explanation. Instead she said, "He can join my brood if he wants. I have to make a delivery to the archbishop's cook. Can your boy carry a bushel basket?"

"Handily." Merthen addressed his charge. "You will behave for Widow Blodwen, right boy?"

"I will," said Uther.

"Off you go, then." Merthen laid his palm flat on the boy's head. "And make sure to sit where you can hear the archbishop. His Latin is excellent. I want you to pay close attention to his pronunciation."

"I will try to remember everything he says."

"No," said Merthen, "just listen to his diction."

Chapter XII: The Storm Moon, AD 486

Caelum non animum mutant qui trans mare currunt.

They change the sky, not their soul, those who run across the sea.

* * *

The scent of baking sourdough inserted itself into Merthen nostrils, and dragged him over to Mister Pryderi's redbrick oven. It was an odor no man, saint or sinner, could resist. If the Lord Almighty's face shone with radiant light, and his voice was heralded by the blare of trumpets, then surely the smell of God had to be that of hot fresh bread.

Uther cleaned out his ear with his pinky. "Is it lunch time yet?"

A line of dark-eyed women and children queued up in front of Mister Pryderi's bakery stall. Instead of shoes, they wore sandals, more fitting the tiled floor of an Italian villa than the cold hard cobblestones. Their eyes were red, as if they had a rough crossing of the channel. Like all proper Roman women, their hair was unbraided.

A straight-postured matron with a fine, but patched overcoat said, "I know you." She did not say it loud, and yet Merthen heard it. She opened her palm, as if to offer him something, but it was empty.

"You used to perform," she said, "on the corner with James the cithara player. I am Lucretia of Paris." She curtsied, as proper a curtsy as Merthen had ever seen. Her Latin was exquisite.

He bowed his best bow. "I am Ambrosius Merthen of Carmarthen. I do not recall your acquaintance."

The wind off the bay blew one of her salt and pepper tendrils over her sunburned cheek. "Lord Marcian," she said, "I am his wife."

"Lord Marcian's wife! I say, I hope he is well. Do you still run Inn of the Fountain? What brings you here?"

"They stole it. Filthy salt pricks. Clovis gave our inn to his bloody whores."

"Clovis?" said Merthen. "Clovis the Salian? Why would he be in Paris? Where is Lord Marcian?"

Lady Lucretia clasped onto the sleeve of Merthen's cloak. Her hands were gaunt. She had lost that lovely layer of fat, all the Roman gentlemen adored. The feminine physique should display dimples, not bones.

"We need your magic," she said. "Put a curse on him. Kick him to hell."

"I am not a sorcerer, good lady. I sell apples."

"No. You have the hidden knowledge." Lucretia waved two of her companions over to her side. "This is Morgan's brother. He can help us."

Merthen remembered Lucretia as she once was; stylish and dignified. She let her husband make the decisions. He kept her in silk, and she furnished his house with wall rugs and bone-inlay furniture. She never asked if Lord Marcian was keeping a mistress. When he did, he did so discretely.

"The Wizard Merlin!" cried one of the women. She clapped her hands in celebration. Gwallter the weaver stepped out from his stall. So did his son.

"I am not a wizard," said Merthen. "And my name is Mer-*then*." He addressed Lady Lucretia. "Madam, some years ago you showed me good will. It would be a disservice for me to pretend that I can assists you, if I cannot. Why have you come to Britannia? Why are you asking for my aid?"

Three more women appeared, one with a boy and a girl in toe. The baker and his wife glanced up from their oven.

"We cannot find our Morgan," said one of the women. "We need your spells."

"I have none to offer, dear girl."

A small child asked its mother. "Is he a witch? Is that boy a leper?"

The weaver's son called out from the back, "Is who is a witch?"

Merthen searched to see of there were any priests in the crowd. There were none. There were, however, enough church ladies around to spread the news. Merthen announced. "I am in no way a druid and this boy burned his skin as a baby."

Into the fray swaggered Sir Plotinus, the knight constable. "What is all this then?"

"I am Merthen the apple seller. I came to town to buy a rabbit. These women claim to know my sister, but I have none."

Merthen knew Sir Plotinus. More to the point, he knew his father, a man of Roman extraction who claimed, perhaps accurately, to have been of senatorial stock. As a result, Plotinus got to marry the king's niece, and landed a plum job patrolling the market.

A woman in the crowd shouted, "Someone said he was a witch."

Plotinus grabbed onto Merthen's arm. "Come with me. Everyone else, clear out."

From up above, Merthen heard the snort of a horse, and the clink of chain mail. Mounted upon a one-ton Percheron was a barrel-chested man, six foot ten inches tall. His strawberry-blond beard stuck out at all angles from his harelip. One eye was covered with a patch. His nose was crushed flat like a ram's. This was a face everyone recognized. It belonged to Ector, Duke of the Cavalry.

"L-let him go," said Ector in his deep stuttering voice. The weaver dashed back to his stall. Mister Pryderi, the baker, quietly shepherded Lady Lucretia and the Roman women away.

Plotinus saluted. "I have taken care of this, Sir."

With a twist, Duke Ector tightened the reigns around his leather gloved fist, generating a barely audible screech. "Did you h-hear me?"

"Aye, Sir, but this is a civil affair."

Ector repositioned himself on his mount. His expression did not change. He simply sat there. When Merthen first met Ector, he was merely a soldier -

albeit the biggest one - in King Vortiger's cavalry. Ector said little back then. Now, he said less.

Plotinus let go. "Very well, Sir. But I am notifying the harbor master. I am just doing my duty, Sir."

"As you should," said Ector. He kicked his mount and trotted away.

Merthen dug a denarius from his purse and slapped it into Plotinus's hand. "No harm done."

Plotinus squeezed the coin. "Stay out of my way."

Merthen bowed. He snapped his finger and Uther appeared by his side. They scurried off to Widow Blodwen's fish stand. A drip of sweat rolled into Merthen's eyes. He wiped his forehead, half expecting to see a hallucination, but none materialized. No, this was not madness; he was scared.

"Who was that horseman?" said Uther. "Is he a Cyclops?"

"No. Duke Ector is a simply an inordinately large human who once stopped an arrow with his face."

"Did it hurt?"

"I cannot imagine it tickled. The Jutes regard Ector as the only Briton whose heart is worth eating."

"Is that good?"

"I think we can say it is a unique distinction."

Uther lifted his thumb up to his face. It was pure white, as was most of his mottled face and hands. "Did I really get burned when I was a baby?"

"No, boy," said Merthen. "But you must say you were, lest you end up quarantined at a leper colony. That is something you do *not* want to do."

Widow Blodwen twirled her fillet knife in the air. "Ahoy, old salt. I hear those Roman girls are pretty hard to impress but you seemed to be drawing them like flies to a turd."

Merthen asked, "What are they all doing here?"

"You have not heard? Governor Syagrius is dead. The Salian Franks took Paris. Clovis is now the King of Gaul, all the way out to the Rhineland."

Merthen's mind bubbled over questions. Governor Syagrus's enclave was the last holdout of Caesar's Empire. All the Romans north of the Alps had flocked to his castle. If he was gone, what would become of them? And what about the Christian Franks? They had been cleaning Romans' stables for so long, they had forgotten how to live in the wild.

Widow Blodwen stabbed her knife into her butcher block. "Clovis killed off Syagrius and his officers," she said, "but listen to this: he let the middling Romans keep their plantations. Clovis is calling them his *citizens*. They even started wearing pants. Imagine that, some wooden-shoed frog-eater from the Belgian swamps calling his people *citizens*."

A Manx mariner strolled up and fingered a flounder by the gill.

"Those are from yesterday," she said.

"A chieftain is now a king, eh?" said Merthen. "*Mens sana in corpore sano, volente Deo*. Let us pray he does a better job than Vortiger did. What is the Pope saying about this?"

"Whatever Clovis tells him to say. That crazy Frank has an army of wildmen swinging Roman swords. He shipped all his wives off to the Frisians, and got engaged to some cardinal's granddaughter."

"That should keep him occupied till he negotiates for a suitably lucrative princess."

Lady Lucretia's refugees huddled by the road, watching everyone go by. There were no grown men with them. Lord Marcian's sense of propriety would never have permitted him to leave his wife in this condition. He must have been one of the Roman holdouts Clovis killed.

"So," said Merthen to Missus B, "this is how an empire ends. The Visigoths overran Lisbon, the Vandals sacked Rome, and now the Franks rule in Paris. Not one single city in *Europa Major* remains under Roman governance."

The Manxman would wait no more. "So are you open or not?"

"Aye, Sir," said Blodwen. "What can I do for you?"

Uther tugged on Merthen's cloak. "Why did those ladies say you were wizard?"

"There is a misguided spiritualist in Gaul who told them that I was a sorcerer. It is a lie, yet they conceive it to be true."

"Why?"

"They lost everything. When people become desperate they revert to a childlike state." He patted Blodwen on the back. "It is time I was off. Thank you for the news."

Accepting the impermanence of all things was one of core principles of Merthen's monastic training. And yet, the demise of the last Roman colony was almost unconceivable. Before Rome, Europe was a vast nowhere, visited only by crafty Greeks who sought to extract her treasures. But now, without Caesar to care for her, what would she become?

Merthen and the boy wandered off to the docks. Uther sat down and dangled his legs over the wooden planks. Merthen lowered himself into a cross-legged position. He removed four apples from his rucksack.

"That Roman lady," said Uther, "she said you had the power of God."

"I noticed that as well," said Merthen. He handed over two red apples. "Unfortunately, no man has that power… or perhaps I should say *fortunately*."

Uther bit into his lunch, and stared at two seagulls gliding overhead. He rested his snack in his lap, and asked, "Is God real?"

Merthen unwrapped a package of smoked rabbit legs. "I suppose it is a possibility," he said. "Then again, is anything real?"

"Aye. All kinds of stuff."

"Like what, boy?"

"You know, trees, fish. Everything."

Merthen tapped on the head of his walking stick. "What do you see when you look at my staff?"

"A duck? No wait, I remember. It is a swan."

"You are mistaken Uther, it is a walking stick." He rapped it against a mooring post. "It may appear to be a waterfowl, but that is only because a woodwright carved it so as to appear that way. Do you see the difference?"

"Aye. But what does that have to do with God?"

"Almost everything. You see Uther, most people perceive what they expect to see rather than things as they genuinely exist." He bit off a chunk of rabbit jerky and chewed on it. "The church fathers," he continued, "find God in heaven, because that is where they look for him. Some day I shall teach you about the discoveries of Plato. He had a great deal to say on this subject, as of course did the Buddha."

"How come no one else ever talks about Mister Buddha except you?"

"His teachings have not yet arrived in the Occident, but one day they will."

"When?"

"Eventually. It took centuries for the Buddha's Practice to cross the Himalayas. It may well be eons before it enters Britannia."

"Are you the only one around here who does the Practice?"

"I know of none other."

The boy finished his apple. "It would be nice if you had some Practice friends to talk to." He set his core down on the dock.

Merthen yawned. "Fear not, brave comrade, for I am, at this very juncture, implementing a strategy to ameliorate that woeful paucity. There may yet be a monastery in Britannia."

"What does that mean?"

"It means you will just have to wait and see."

Merthen displayed his apple core between his thumb and forefinger. With a flick of his wrist, it disappeared. Then he lowered his arm at the elbow. The core rolled down from up his sleeve, and into his palm. He tossed it at a gull resting nearby. It missed by so much, the bird did not even flinch.

Uther hopped to his feet. "You should let me go hunting," he said. "I am a very good shot." The boy threw his whittled down apple core at the very same seabird Merthen attempted to hit. Uther, however, struck his target square in the chest.

Chapter XIII: The Hare Moon AD 486

Certum est quia impossibile.

It is certain because it is impossible.

* * *

The morning sun rose through the gaps in the forest. All Uther wanted to do was lie on his back, but the rope binding his wrists to the trunk of a maple made that impossible. His stomach still churned from the smoked venison the savages fed him. The soil around him reeked of the diarrhea that struck him during the night.

Uther forced open his heavy eyelids. He heard voices, but only two. One was that of a Saxon girl, a bit older than him. She had been tied to the same tree he, was, but now she was over by the fire. She was saying something to one of the savages who had captured Uther. The rest of the wild men were gone, out hunting perhaps.

The Saxon girl's wrists and ankles were still bound together. Nonetheless, she managed to pull up her skirt revealing her buttocks. She leaned over on her elbows. Uther tried to stand up so he could see what was going on.

The blue-eyed savage next to the girl loosened his trousers. His rounded blond beard was trimmed short, except for a pair of thin, four inch-long braids that jutted out from just below the tip of his chin. Both ends of his foot-long mustache were twisted back around his head, and tied in a knot. This was no Saxon.

It appeared to Uther that the girl was doing something with her hands. Indeed, she was undoing the twine around her wrist. The young man positioned himself behind her. He gripped onto her hips and she let out an artificial moan.

Then, with one swift move, she snatched a log from the fire, spun around, and cracked her lover across the nose. Sparks flew. He screamed and clawed at his eyes. She punched him in the testicles. He collapsed.

With both hands on the log, she hammered at his skull. After two blows he went limp. She gave him a few more more, then stole his dagger, cut her legs free, and ran off into the forest.

Uther found a rock, and awkwardly pounded it against the rope that secured him to the tree. He could hear a pair of feet approaching, rustling though the underbrush. The fatigue that had plagued him for the last three days evaporated. He did not look up. If he could get loose, he knew he could escape. He was fast enough to outrun anyone, even a German.

A whispering voice called out, "Follow me."

Merthen, holding his sword in one hand, touched his finger to his lips. "Stay quiet." He cut the boy free. They fled, but not before Uther observed the trembling body of the fallen savage. He was not yet dead.

Uther's burst of energy faded. He stumbled.

"Up boy," said Merthen, "I cannot carry you." The old man's sky blue eyes, which usually had a youthful shine, appeared old and haggard. One of his long white braids was missing, as if trimmed off by a barber.

Uther forced himself up, and put one foot in front of the other. He was not so much running as falling, without quite hitting the ground. Branches smacked him in the face. He began to think of elephants.

Merthen once said that in India, a baby elephant would hold onto the tail of its mother, following behind her even though it could see nothing but the back of her massive body. Like most of Merthen's stories, this one had some sort of moral, but whatever it was Uther forgot it. A thorny bramble scraped a gash into his shin.

The rocky woodlands gave way to the muddy floodplain of a broad flowing river. Merthen bent down and picked up a bundle of fags, four feet long, tied together with what had previously been a length of his own hair. Merthen's ash wood staff was stuck in the middle. A neatly cut chestnut branch sporting an umbrella of leaves was wedged into the contraption, creating a sort of canopy.

Merthen knotted his purse and his sword together. Then he strapped them around his back like a rucksack. "What say we go rafting?" He waded into the river, pulling the makeshift watercraft behind him. "This water is chilly. Mind you, do not splash."

Uther joined him.

"Keep your body below the surface," said Merthen.

Together, with the bundle securely in their hands, they floated into the center of the stream. The leafy green branch obscured their heads.

They glided silently around a bend, and Uther scanned the valley. All he could hear was the tap of a woodpecker; no Germans. That did not guarantee there were none there, but it was a good sign.

Merthen glanced over into the boy's sunburned face. "I found you two days ago, but had no opportunity to free you. I have been worried to no end."

Uther wept. "I got lost. The wild men took me away. My skin hurts. Am I going to turn into a white freak?"

"Not at all. Most people prefer a pale complexion. Aside from that, are you well?"

Uther rubbed his hand against his cheeks. "I was gathering walnuts. I saw a deer with fourteen points so I followed him. Then I saw the Saxons. They were following him too."

"Those men were Angles, not Saxons. You can tell by the well-trimmed beards. I saw them out hunting this morning."

Uther stopped crying. "I ran away, but one of them called out to me in Latin. He had a big nose and curly hair. Why would a Roman live with savages?"

"He was adopted. What did he do to you?"

"He showed me his hands. They were empty. Then he grabbed me. His friend wrapped a rope around my wrists." The boy started to weep once again. "They tied me to a tree next to that girl. Did she kill that man?"

"A crafty lass. She is a Saxon. I fear her paramour is paralyzed. He will die soon."

"I was so scared. Were they going to eat me?"

"No, they were going to take you as a captive. When the Germans lose a relative in battle they steal a child from their enemy and raise him as a replacement. I suspect they kidnapped the Saxon girl so she would make babies for them." Merthen reached into the water and retrieved a bag of wet raisins. "Eat this."

"They wanted me to be a wild man?"

"Precisely. And now you know, one must never trust a savage, even if he speaks Latin. Germans live in a constant state of war, loyal only to their own clan. Respect their abilities, but do not expect mercy."

Uther said, "I never want to get lost again."

Up above, a trio of crows was harrying a hawk.

"When I was a bit older than you," said Merthen, "I worked for an architect building a fortress near Kabul. One night I ran off with a bag of figs and a butcher knife. I swam down a river, and floated all day until the waterway became a gully-wash. I hiked along its shoreline till the rivulet disappeared."

"Were did it go?"

"It evaporated. I found myself in a desert. My water ran out in three days. The heat of the sun drove me mad. Judith of Philadelphia guided me by the hand."

"But she died when you were little?"

"She was a hallucination. I was wandering aimlessly in a dry floodway. Judith's sang a song to me. *Eits chayi hi lamchazikim ba, vetomecheha meushar.*"

"What is that?"

"It is a lullaby. It means *there is a tree of life to those who hold it fast, and all who cling to it find happiness.* After Judith serenaded me, I saw a dark cloud. I presumed it was death. Then I felt a drop of rain. Soon a great deluge released from the heavens."

"Was Judith's ghost still there?"

"She began to dance, and I joined her. Puddles formed down at my feet. I attempted to move to higher ground. Unfortunately, the gully banks were lined with slick clay. I could not climb them. It was then that I heard a roaring sound."

"What was it?"

"Although I did not know it at the time, I was witnessing the annual inundation that drenches the otherwise dry plains that separate Persia from India. A churning torrent of mud barreled towards me. It hit me like an elephant gone rogue."

Merthen and Uther stood up. The river was now shallow enough that they could walk along its bottom.

"How did you get out?" said Uther.

"I became entangled in a tree that had been ripped from its roots. Then, like Jonah, I was cast up to the surface. I found myself riding the trunk."

"You held onto the tree of life. It was just like in Judith's song."

"Eerily so. I held on through the night, but when the sun rose, I passed out. When I came to, I was lying on a cot. I had landed in Talaxia, a frontier community in northwest India. The people there fed me naranga fruits. They called me *Puskar Aska*."

"What does that mean?"

"It is Sanskrit for *blue eyes*, but it refers to an aquatic flower called a lotus." Merthen started kicking his legs. "Upon arriving in India, I was sent to the governor's palace and interviewed by a young prince named Skandagupta. He was touring the borderlands on behalf of his father. We spoke in Persian. He asked me if I drank dog milk."

"Dog milk? Did they drink that in India?"

"No, they would never do that. There are, however, pony barbarians north of India who drink it with glee. I informed the prince that I was a Roman and that I could read. That caught his interest. He knew a number of stories about Alexander the Great, but he called him *Iskandar the Invader*."

"The invader?" said Uther. He paused to think. "Oh, I get it."

Merthen repositioned his hands on the float. "The prince told me that his father, Emperor Kumaragupta owned a book of Latin text written by Jerome the Cave Dweller. This document dealt with Κριστοσ, a martyred bodhisattva who was hung by nails. It was presented as a gift by a party of seafaring Arabs who had no need of it, as they only followed the laws of the Venerable Moses. The prince asked if I could translate it."

"You mean the Bible? Did you really translate it?"

"Every page. Within a month, I was delivered to a monastic who transported me to the University at Nalanda. Of course, I had to learn Sanskrit first. All together, the project lasted fifteen years. Those were the happiest days of my life."

"You got lucky," said Uther. "You should have drowned, but instead you got to go to school."

"I would not regard it as fortuitous. For if you follow the events that led me to India, you will find they begin with my slitting the throat of Aethiops the Centurion."

"But," said Uther, "you would have lived your whole life as a slave if you had not become a drummer boy. It was lucky you got free."

"I only became a drummer boy because I was a slave. Being locked in a cage is not good luck."

"I know. But if none of that had happened, you would have stayed in Carmarthen, and become a farmer like everybody else. And when my mother died, you never would have taken me in. So in a way, your bad luck was my good luck. That is kind of like being lucky, right?"

"I suppose," said Merthen. "You know boy, I do not fancy you getting captured again. I believe it is time we procured you some protection."

Chapter XIV: The Hay Moon AD 486

Gratia Domini nostri Iesu Christi cum omnibus.

May the grace of the Lord Jesus be with everyone.

* * *

When he was in India, Merthen never carried a dagger. As Brother Tinh Tu said, "*Everyone carries thoughts of violence, thus it is the presence of the weapon which leads to death.*" Merthen also had a less philosophical reason for not bearing arms. When he strolled the streets of Nalanda with his pale face and red eyebrows, he had to constantly reassure the locals that he was not a demon. Even a paring knife might be perceived as a threat.

But now, Merthen's hair was no longer red, and his home was not an ancient city, flush with scholars and the fragrance of temple incense. Instead, he was an exile, scraping by on a blustery island infested by savages and corruption. In this sorry land, a war knife was essential, which was what led Merthen and the boy to the daggers on display at Mister Eusebius's cutlery stall.

Having examined a solid yet reasonable priced model, Merthen said, "We will take that one." He deposited ten denarii onto the table. "And we can haggle till midnight, or you can just take this, since it is all I am prepared to spend."

Mister Eusebius said, "It is worth twelve… but ten will do." He scooped up the money and handed over the dagger. "What is wrong with your boy?"

"He was burned in a fire." Merthen replied. He gave Eusebius a bow and addressed Uther. "Now remember, boy, this is a tool not a toy, and a very expensive one at that." He placed the weapon into Uther's mostly white hand.

Merthen flicked his wrist and a coin appeared in his fingers. "We have one denarius left in today's budget. I recall seeing a honeycomb for sale next to the cooper's stall. What say we go there?"

Miss Rhonwen, the carter's old maid sister, flittered on by releasing a loud sneeze.

"It needs a name," said Uther. "I think I will call it *Lord Thunderbolt*. What is your sword called?"

"It has no name."

"Yes, it does. It is written on the side."

"My sword is not named *Ex Calabr*." Merthen withdrew the weapon from its sheath, just enough to expose the blacksmith's stamp. "That just indicates it was cast in Calabria."

"You could call it *King Thunderbolt*. Then they would match."

With overly-dramatic enthusiasm, Merthen shook his beaded bracelet. "Better yet, I could call it *Buddha's Thunderbolt*. Are you familiar with that term?"

"No. But it sounds boring."

Missus Angharad, the butcher's wife, sneezed. Merthen hailed her. "I say Madam, you are the third person I have seen huffing wind this afternoon. Is there something in the air?"

"Snuff," she said. "There is a Frank selling mummy dust down by Saint David's dock. He said it clears the sinuses, and by Juno, is he right." She showed off a small bag.

Merthen bent over and smelled it. It was pepper and ginger, nothing more.

Uther asked, "Can I show my knife to Widow Blodwen?"

"Certainly, but do not run. I am going to take a stroll to Saint David's dock. I will meet up with you at the fish stand."

Uther ran off. Did that boy ever listen?

Missus Angharad sneezed again. She said, "The fellow selling it has a bit of a hunchback." She wrapped up her snuff and bowed. "Good day."

Merthen headed down to a collection of docks that looked much like those at the port of Constantinople, or along the shores of Lake Sambhar. While most men never traveled more than a day's walk from their farmstead, Merthen had survived four score years of almost constant walking. And yet here he was, back at Carmarthen Bay. The net gain of his life's journey: just a few yards.

Close to shore, a small flock of women were clustered around a stoop-shouldered man wearing an apothecary's hood.

"My grandson has the croup," said Missus Haf. "Will this help with that?"

"It may be too powerful for a child," said the hunchback. "I would recommend adding half a tablespoon to a pot of hot chicken soup every day for a week. It will not cure the illness instantly, but it should degrade the symptoms, provided he gets enough rest."

"Thumbs!" said Merthen, "Why are you selling these people pepper and ginger?"

Thumbs grinned and bowed. "Well look who it is! I was hoping to run into you. There is someone you need to see." To his customer he said, "Pepper and ginger are two of the key ingredients. They permit the potent components to be fully digestible."

"Mummy powder?" said Merthen. "Really, Thumbs."

Thumbs wedged his lock box under the armpit of his gimpy arm. "Ladies, if you will give me a moment, I must speak with your wizard." He drew Merthen in close. "Old boy, you need to come with me. There is a bookseller on my vessel. He wants to meet you."

"I am not a wizard."

Thumbs hobbled toward his ship. "This friend of mine came all the way from Corinth. He is collecting books for a bunch of rich Greeks."

Merthen stood firm. "Why am I going to him? If he wants to meet me he, can come out here."

Thumbs checked to see if anyone was near. "He is a Jew, and quite afraid to land. Can you blame him? He is right up there." Thumbs hobbled onto the deck.

Merthen recalled the old legend, probably a modified Hindu tale, in which the Buddha appeared as a sticky man. Once you touched him you could never get him off. That was Thumbs all right, a rolling ball of glue.

Merthen grudgingly made his way up the gangplank of the ship. There he saw a grey-bearded Jew perched on a wool bundle reading a book. He did not turn the page or look up.

*   *   *

The crowd waiting on shore for Thumbs did not make a sound. Merthen awaited Gopi's call. She said nothing.

He called out, "Stop being coy! What are you this time, a deaf mute narwhal?"

Merthen paced around a bit. Then he peeked over the shoulder of the immobilized Jew and viewed the page of the open book. It read, *Chapter Forty-six of Book Eighteenth: Of the birth of our Savior, whereby the Word was made flesh; and of the dispersion of the Jews among all nations, as had been prophesied.*

There was a second iota above the letter *i* in the word *prophesied*. Inside it was a pair of black mandibles attached to an off-white larva.

"Welcome to *The City of God*," said the bookworm. "Please allow me to show you the sights. As the sole inhabitant of this metropolis, I am uniquely qualified to direct you to its many dining opportunities."

"You scoundrel, do you have any idea how valuable this manuscript is?"

"I have always had an appetite for fine literature," said Gopi. "I hate to spoil the ending, but let me tell you, the last few chapters are delicious. That Augustine is a genius. Have you ever read his *Confessions*?"

"Why must you eat this? *The Book of Numbers* would be just as filling and nobody would miss it. I should squash you. That would be the ethical thing to do."

"Which leads to my next question. The Goddess Guan Yin wants to know if you regard yourself as a Christian."

"Why would a Chinese goddess ask about that?"

"There are Nestorian Christians in western China. How did you know Guan Yin was Chinese?"

"How did I know? How did you know? You are supposed to be a noblewoman from India. Why would you know anything about the gods of China... or Germany for that matter?" He smacked his own forehead. "Fifteen years at university, and here I am arguing with a grub."

"Just answer the question," said Gopi. "Are you really a Christian?"

"Certainly. Do I behave in an unchristian manner?"

"No, but you have been known to venerate the Buddha. Is that what a Christian would do?"

"Well, it certainly should be," said Merthen. "In *The Book of Matthew*, Jesus proclaimed, *blessed are the poor*. In so doing, he proposed that people who with no material attachments are fortunate, because they will enter the kingdom of heaven, and thus be free of ill-being."

"So?"

"Well, as it happens, the Buddha espoused that in order to achieve interbeing, an individual must lose all attachments, even attachments to the very notion of *the self*. Thus, one can only be free of ill-being if one is poor. Clearly, Jesus and the Buddha were brothers."

"But the Buddha was just a wise man. Jesus was the Word made flesh. He rose from the dead."

"Did he?" said Merthen. "Or was he in such harmony with the universe that he was reincarnated as himself?"

* * *

Merthen heard the uneven stomp of a hunchback's twisted legs. The Jew looked up.

"Mister Sira," said Thumbs, "this is my friend Ambrosius Merthen. He is the one I told you about. He spent many years in Byzantium."

Sira closed his book and bowed. "My name is Sira of Corinth," he said in Greek, "I am a Jew. May I speak with you?"

Merthen bowed in return. "Certainly, Sir," He said in Greek. "I have spoken with Jews on many occasions. In fact I was raised by one." He closed his eyes. "She used to sing me a nursery rhyme. *Vezot hatorah asher sam Mosheh lifenei benei Yisraeil, al Adonai beyad Mosheh.*"

Sira stepped back. "Why, Sir, that is the Torah. What was her name? Perhaps I know her family."

"I do not know her lineage. She called herself Judith. Her father was a learned rabbi from Philadelphia-on-the-Nile. Her mother was Ethiopian, one of her father's servants. And yet, he publicly accepted Judith as his own."

"Like Abraham and Hagar," said Sira. "What was the rabbi's name?"

"Judith never told me," said Merthen. What he did not say was that Judith's father gave a fiery sermon after Emperor Theodosius outlawed all the Jewish patriarchs. At least that was the rumor. The good rabbi ended up with his head in a basket and his family on a slave ship. Whatever really happened, Judith would not say.

Thumbs jiggled his lock box. "I have customers waiting. I will catch up with you later." He scurried off.

Merthen asked, "What can I do for you, Mister Sira?"

"My kinsman, Mister Thumbs has informed me that you are literate in both Latin and Greek. I am wondering if you are a scholar, Sir?"

"No, just a clerk. By the way, Thumbs's claim to be Jewish should be taken with a grain of salt, large enough to choke an ox. He has a marked tendency to embellish."

Sira batted his eyes. "When it comes to issues of religious affiliation, I find it best not to probe. But, on to business. I have a contract to acquire books for the Academy. Mister Thumbs thought you might have some to sell."

Merthen straightened his posture. "*The* Academy. *Plato's* Academy? I thought the church shut it down?"

"Not entirely, Sir. The professors are forbidden to teach the Dialectic, but the library still functions."

"I am impressed."

"Thank you, Sir." Sira folded his hands. "Specifically, I am looking for a set of publications once owned by Governor Constans. I have been told they are now the possession of a young maiden. My informants suggest that they include a number of Plutarch's *Lives*, some volumes pertaining to Pericles, and perhaps the *Tuscan Disputations*. Apparently, she inherited them from her late father, the grandson of Governor Constans. There would be a dozen books in all."

Merthen found this rather difficult to believe. Most men of letters, even in India, would count themselves lucky to have a library that large. The entire time Merthen was in Paris he saw no more than ten books, aside from the Bible, and very few Frenchmen wanted to read that. How could so many books be here?

"Quite the mother lode," said Merthen. "Did you know that the king of Britannia is also the grandson of Governor Constans?"

"Indeed Sir, I had heard reports."

"This girl that you mentioned. What is her name?"

"I do not know. Her father was called Riothamus Minor or Riothamus Aurelianus. As I understand it, he was the son of the general who fought so bravely in Gaul." Sira brushed some lint off his cloak. "Until he disappeared. I thought perhaps Riothamus Minor might have relocated to Britannia, as it was his father's homeland."

"I wish I could help you Sir," said Merthen, "but I have heard no news of this girl. Have you considered speaking with our king? Based on your research, he would be a cousin to Riothamus Minor."

"I would not want for your liege to come under the impression that I was looting his family heirlooms. I understand that His Majesty is not a man a Jew would want to disturb. As the Venerable Bion said, *though boys throw stones at frogs in sport, the frogs die not in sport but in earnest.*"

Merthen was thrilled to hear someone quoting the Philosophers, in their natural Greek no less. He had always wanted to visit Athens, yet never did. Nalanda may have been a cultured metropolis, but in the final analysis it was just like every other city: a walled in fortress surrounded by peasants. Athens, however, was more than that. It was built *by* the citizens and *for* the citizens.

Through his peripheral vision, Merthen saw Father Thomasius approaching up the gangplank, waving his standard clumsy wave.

"Excuse me Mister Merthen," said Thomasius. "Sorry to interrupt. Might I ask you a question?"

"By all means. What is it you want?"

"Bishop Zephyrinus requested that I pop round and conduct an investigation. Apparently a Jew has landed in Carmarthen. The bishop wishes to interview him."

"Really, about what?"

"He did not say. It struck me as a bit odd, but I am sure he has his reasons."

Merthen addressed Sira in Greek, "Sir, you must get out of here. Set sail as soon as possible. Our bishop is looking for you. I will divert this priest. Just nod and look happy."

Merthen said to Father Thomasius, "This is Mister Shariputra of Phoenicia. He only speaks Greek, the Kione dialect. He and I were discussing the new cathedral being built in Constantinople."

Thomasius bowed. "How nice. Too bad my Greek is so rusty. Actually, it was never that good to begin with. Perhaps you could invite him to mass tomorrow? We will be blessing the animals."

Merthen snapped his finger. "I think I know who the Jew is. We need to go back on shore." Merthen spoke to Sira in Greek. "Good luck with your travels, Sir. And may I say, what an honor it has been to speak with a man so highly regarded by the Platonic Order, that they would employ him as their consultant. Had I a house, I would gladly offer you my bed. I bid you *Shalom*."

The Jew bowed. "*Pax vibosum* to you as well, Sir."

Merthen bowed yet again, even lower, then aimed his walking stick over the bow at Thumbs. "There is your Jew!"

"Oh good," said Thomasius. "I know they have them in Paris. I never actually met one."

Merthen bounded down the gangplank. Thomasius trotted behind.

111

"Perhaps you could come to mass too?" said Thomasius. "You could bring some of your rabbits. The children would love that."

"Thumbs!" yelled Merthen. "I need to speak with you."

Thumbs accepted a payment from a young mother and limped over. "Were you able to help Mister Sira?"

"No, but I had a nice conversation with Mister Shariputra *up on that ship*. This is Father Thomasius. Bishop Zephyrinus sent him to gather up a Jew who has come to our town. As I recall, you once performed under the name *Julius of Judea, the Juggling Jew*."

"I did?"

"Yes, back in Paris." Merthen elbowed Father Thomasius. "In addition to being a talented apothecary, Mister Thumbs is a wonderful acrobat. Tell me, Thumbs, are you really Jewish, or was that just a stage persona?"

"It was... a form of persona." Thumbs began to pack up his belongings.

"So you are *not* actually a Jew, then? That must be what happened. Someone who saw your act told the bishop you were Jewish. Just a misunderstanding."

"I could not agree with you more," said Thumbs. He tossed his jars of mummy dust into a sac. "Why I am a full blood Roman. To prove it, I will drop my trousers." He unbuckled his belt.

Father Thomasius put up his hands. "No! You need not do that."

Merthen patted Thumbs on his hump. "I am glad this was cleared up. I hope we did not delay your departure. Give my best to your wife and children. And I will pray for our friend Mister Sira. I know that without the assistance of your medications, his life may be in *imminent danger*."

Thumbs slammed shut his lock box. "Aye. Thank you for your kind thoughts. Well, I must be going. Nice meeting you, father."

"One more thing," said Thomasius. "Do you really juggle? Could we see some?"

"I am," said Thumbs, "rather out of practice."

Merthen picked up three stones. "Use these."

Thumbs threw them in the air with his one good hand. He dropped them. "The palsy," he said, "hit me rather hard a last winter." He bowed and ran off.

* * *

Attached to the sleeve of Merthen cloak was the bookworm. Everything else was still and silent.

Gopi said, "Do you blame the Jews for killing Jesus?"

"Why are you asking all these religious questions?" said Merthen. "Why do your gods care about what I do - or do not - believe? A man should be tried for his actions, not his beliefs."

"That may be true for mortals, but the gods have a broader jurisdiction. So tell me, who killed the Messiah? What is your perspective on that?"

Merthen replied, "The first full manuscript I ever read was Josephus's history of the Jews. In it, he presents a rather unimpressive paragraph describing a faith healer who ran afoul of the gentry. Josephus noted that Jesus's followers continued to gather, even after he was executed. It was a humble passage, yet quite insightful."

"Old Josephus was not one to mince words," she said. "Matthew, Mark, and Luke each needed an entire book."

"You miss my point. You are a student of history. How many men have had their philosophy carried on after their deaths?"

"Well, there were Greeks, the Hebrew prophets. Kung Fu and Lao Tsu. Who else? Oh, yes, Zoroaster. And of course, the Buddha."

Merthen rested her in his hand. "There are but a handful of sages whose epistles have survived the crucible of time. I have heard men say that Christ's divinity was demonstrated by his resurrection, but in my opinion, the proof of his transcendence is the sheer persistence of his teachings. How he died is immaterial. You ask who killed him? I say, everybody."

"I believe they have a word for that sort of an evaluation. They call it *heresy*."

"When I was at University," said Merthen, "I related the narrative of the Gospels to Brother Tinh Tu. His comment to me was only this: *It is not a miracle that the Bodhisatva of Nazareth walked on water. It is a miracle that he walked at all.*"

BOOK IV: THE HEALER

CHAPTER XV: THE WOLF MOON, AD 487

Rara avis in terris nigroque simillima cycno.

A rare bird upon the earth and very much like a black swan.

* * *

If only Merthen had some bay leaf, he could boil it in a mash of ginger, mint, and garlic. Such a poultice was not a cure-all, but it would serve as an effective decongestant. Unfortunately, bay leaf bushes only grew in the sunny Mediterranean, and Merthen was far from there. Instead he was huddled in a thatched-roof hut, tending to a boy who lay on a cot.

Uther lay unconscious and drenched in perspiration, his breathing weak. The boy coughed. He mustered up enough thoracic strength to hack up some phlegm. Merthen checked it. Still green. When a sailor's clothes were saturated for too long, he would attract feverish humors. If his phlegm was yellow, he would break the fever. If it was green, the fever would break him.

Every jack-tar knew the dangers of getting wet, but not every growing boy. Just a few days earlier, Uther went hunting and struck a buck. It started to rain, but Uther chased the animal down anyway. It was a poor decision, but one Merthen understood. A few brown whiskers had recently sprouted on Uther's otherwise white face. He was a boy, who wanted to be a man.

And so, Merthen stayed up till dawn brewing an infusion of cherry stems to wipe away Uther's sweat. This posed a calculated risk. During his enslavement with the Huns, Merthen had developed a debilitating insomnia. It was only through meditation that he kept it at bay. He had no desire to return to those nights he spent pacing around a pony corral repeating the words *gah-tay gah-tay*, over and over again.

Merthen swabbed the boy's neck. The sun was setting. Merthen rested his head in his hands. He sang the healing chant, *namo valo ki-teshvaria*. He supposed to chant it three times. Or was it four times? Brother Tinh Tu told him the right number once, but what was it? Of course, Brother Tinh Tu would have said there is no right number.

Unable to stand, Merthen lay on his own cot, hoping to catch a few winks. Drips of perspiration trickled down the sides of his face.

* * *

Drawn to the sound of flapping of wings, Merthen gazed out the window at Sambhar Lake. A flock of pink flamingos arose from the water's shallow surface.

Something soft and warm brushed against his shoulder. A black-eyed woman snuggled her head against his chest. He felt her smooth black hair. The moonlight reflecting off the lake illuminated her almond colored skin. She kissed him. Her tongue licked against his. He got an erection. It hurt a bit near the scars that led back to his testicles.

"The boy," she whispered, "tell me about the boy."

Merthen, still as naked as she was, got out of bed. From the back of his spine, he felt a large rope-like appendage wrap tight around his neck. It dragged him out the door, down the palace hallway, and into the royal hunting grounds.

A voice called out to him, "Merthen, Merthen, Why do you persecute me?"

Two eyes blinked, small with long dark lashes. Two gray ears flapped in the wind above a pair of oblong ivory objects.

"Your move," said the elephant.

The sweet figgy fragrance of blossoming bo trees wafted through the gentle wind. The violet blue of the early evening sky was spotted with pink clouds, and stars that burned not white, but orange.

The elephant moved his right foreleg toward the Chaturga set, a square game board divided into ten rows of ten squares, alternating black and white.

"How can I play?" said Merthen. "You have six arms. I have but two?"

With his trunk, the elephant blew life into the nostrils of the red clay game pieces. They transformed into cherubim and flew away.

Merthen clenched the pointed claws that sprouted from the tips of his fingers. His arms and legs were covered with short black fur. He touched his face, a long snout with two jutting teeth. He had become a rat.

Merthen asked, "Who are you?"

"I am who I am." The elephant hovered his massive foot over Merthen's head, almost brushing the fur of his pointy rodent ears.

Merthen crawled onto all fours. "Please Lord Ganesha, do not crush me."

Lord Ganesha drank a sip of Brahma milk from his translucent jade bowl. Then he declared, "All things are a manifestation of our thoughts. If one's thoughts are confused, then one becomes lost in the manifestations of those thoughts, the same way that a cart follows a horse."

Merthen had heard this before, but where? Was it something Tinh Tu taught him? No, it was a quote from the Buddha. Merthen read it when he was first learning Sanskrit. He remembered how nonsensical it seemed to him at the time. How could external objects arise from intangible ideas? Now, it seemed obvious.

Merthen asked Ganesha, "Have you been trained as a monastic?"

Ganesha leaned forward from his mountainous cyan sofa and scowled. "Why do you deny my brethren? Has not King Woden the potential for interbeing? Has not Yahweh an inner Buddha? My kindred, Ahura Mazda and the Sky Bitch, they also toil in samsara. Suffering is not yours alone."

Ganesha touched his third eye. Merthen lifted his snout toward the moon. It was in fact Ganesha's missing tusk, the very tooth he threw into the heavens after the sky mocked him for being so portly. Ganesha had suffered as well.

Merthen grasped his forepaws together. "Punish me Lord," he cried. "It is I who have sinned. Do not take it out on the boy. He had nothing to do with the centurion. I beg of you."

Ganesha sneered, "Why do you refuse to honor to me? Am I not suitably intellectual? If I were to grant your wish, would you worship me then? I think not."

Merthen wept. "I am trapped."

Ganesha was not yet finished. "You never give us credit. The God of Abraham keeps his dwelling down the road, and yet you pass him by. You arrogant brat! Who would fault me if I were to strike you down?" *Ganesha unsheathed his scimitar and brandished it high in the air.* "But then again, why tarnish an evening so lovely as this?" *His weapon turned into peacock feather.*

Ganesha scratched the wisps of hair beneath his chin. With a sly grin, he said, "I believe I shall heal the boy. This obstacle shall be removed."

Merthen sang a blessing in praise of Ganesha's protection. "Ganesha sharanam, sharanam Ganesha. Jay Ganesha, Jay Ganesha!" *This was a chant the Hindu yogis cherished. The rational Buddhists at Nalanda spurned it as superstitious nonsense, a mindless plea for dependency. Prayers would not lead a man to find his inner Buddha. And yet, despite all this, Merthen had committed it to memory.*

"Furthermore," said Ganesha, "it is my intention for you to remain alive. I shall continue to mold you, to transform you, not simply until death, but beyond. This could go on for millennia. What sport!"

Merthen cowered before him. "As you wish, My Lord."

"Indeed, Pig Eyes, I will grant you substantial continuance, but it shall take place in my realm. You will become like me, imprisoned in the universe of metaphor. Let us see how you enjoy it when mortals question your existence. How will you like it when they say the Wizard Merlin was just a myth, his life's labor a fairy tale, his heartache a literary construct?"

Ganesha reared up on his hind legs. He trumpeted an all-encompassing "Om." It reverberated through Merthen's knees, past his pelvis, radiating upward along his spinal chord. Ganesha's monumental exhale divided into four pairs of siroccos. They swirled against the rat and threw him to the ground.

* * *

Then Merthen heard Uther's voice.

"I am thirsty," said the boy.

Merthen opened his eyes. "What time is it?" He pushed the hair from his face. His head was throbbing. The front door was wide open. Sunlight blasted in. "It is morning? I must have slept all night."

Uther coughed. "I think I am better." He hacked up a clump of phlegm. Merthen eagerly examined it. It was yellow.

Into a drinking bowl, Merthen poured a serving of ginger water. "Drink this."

Uther took a sip. Merthen felt the boy's forehead. It was almost completely devoid of pigment, but it was not feverish.

Merthen handed him an apple. "You know, Uther, as long as you keep your belly covered, I doubt anyone will notice your condition. Your hands and face are almost entirely white."

"What is that?" said the boy. He pointed at a box covered with a checkered tablecloth. Upon it sat forty wooden disks, twenty carved from a red cedar branch, the rest from white pine. Each had a mark on top.

"I whittled these while you were ill," said Merthen. "Whereas you will be disabled for some days, it is my intention to teach you Chaturga."

"Is it a game?" Uther bit into his apple.

"Yes, but not some trivial hopscotch affair. They say it was invented by Ashoka, the Elephant King."

"Was he an elephant?"

"No, but he did have an army of them. Upon their backs, King Ashoka's architects constructed armored platforms, like the rook of a castle. From this lofty perch, his archers would shoot."

"Moving rooks? Is that true?"

"That was how he conquered India. But then, wise Ashoka underwent a transformation. He ordered his knights to lay down their swords and travel afar teaching the way of interbeing. They began waging peace. It was a most dangerous campaign."

"What was so dangerous about that?"

"Consider this, boy: a well armed warrior must have courage to face his opponents. It takes an even bolder heart to engage one's enemies empty handed."

Merthen arranged ten of the game pieces in a row. He centered each of them in a square. His head still throbbed. He needed to stoke the fire outside. But that could wait. The boy was willing to learn Chaturga. That was how they would spend the morning.

Uther asked, "Who did you play this game with? Did you have a family in India?"

"The monastics were my family. I never wed. Since I cannot sire children, I am worthless to a woman."

"Did you ever have a lady? A lady who is not your wife."

Merthen rubbed his neck. "You have been spending too much time at the docks."

Uther finished his bowl of water. "Was she pretty?"

Merthen shrugged his shoulders. "She had good teeth."

"Where did you meet her?"

"She was a chaperone to one of King Kumaragupta's daughters. We met in a palace next to a shallow salt lake. It was an impressive structure with extensive floral latticework. Those Indian masons were no shirkers."

Uther lay back down on his cot. "Did the lady of the lake want to be your wife?"

Merthen unfolded a fresh blanket for the boy. "All I can say is, sometimes when one is immature, one is overcome with the flowery arrows of craving."

Merthen recalled the few times he tried to have sex. It proved tremendously painful. Up until his hair turned white, he would regularly wake up with an erection that felt like someone was inserting needles into his penis. Those Persians that hoisted him on that square rail had no idea how long their torture would last. But then again, maybe they did.

Merthen realized that he was ruminating so hard, he failed to notice that Uther had fallen asleep. Fortunately, this was just what the boy needed.

* * *

The fire in the center of the hut stopped flickering. It had not gone out, it was just no longer moving. There was honking noise outside. Merthen peeked through the doorway. Over by the hearth, a black swan was flapping her wings.

Gopi asked, "Who was the lady in your vision?"

Merthen sat next to her on a log, and replied very matter-of-factly, "I had a hallucination about a woman I knew in India. It was before I followed the path of the Buddha. Past memories periodically arise. Such things happen."

The swan waddled up to him. "You may have no memory of who your mother was, but clearly she raised you well."

Gopi's statement caught him off guard. It was so out of place. What did that have to do with the trial? Gopi had never asked him about his mother before, not that it would do any good. He drew a blank every time he tried to remember her.

Merthen looked into the swan's jet black eyes. "So," he said, "the gods are giving me a grilling, eh? From what you have told me, I gather that Athena is serving as my defender. This leads me to inquire, who is pursuing the case against me? Who is my prosecutor?"

"That would be the Elephant God, Ganesha." Gopi rested her head against his chest. "But I suspect you knew that."

"I fear," he said, "that good old Athena may have her work cut out for her." Merthen stared silently into the fire, but he did not push Gopi away.

Chapter XVI: The Storm Moon, AD 487

Disjecta membra.

The scattered remains.

* * *

Almost everything within Merthen's field of vision was muted shades of grey-green and tan. The wet sandbar into which he dug his harvesting rake was only a trace lighter than the sea that washed against it. This overcast coastline reminded him of the monochrome ink paintings that the Chinese students at Nalanda used to hang in their dormitories.

Merthen teetered beneath the bushel of wet cockles perched upon his shoulder. He huffed over to a dingy beached on the mudflat. The nearby beach was deserted, with no noise save the gulls. Merthen deposited his basket into the small boat and checked on Uther, who was furiously digging with a short handled rake.

"Time to go," yelled Merthen. "The tide comes in quickly around here."

Uther responded by waving his conical straw hat. He scraped his rake across the sand and uncovered another large cluster of bivalves. He called back, "This is a good spot. How much money do you think we are going to make?"

"None if the ocean sweeps us away." Merthen crawled into the dingy and positioned himself on the seat.

A small wave spread out into the wet sand, its foamy upper layer lapping against the bow of the boat.

Merthen picked up his oar. "Get a move on, boy. *Vita brevis.*"

Uther gave his rake one last drag across the sand. He uncovered an even larger cluster than before. "I hit a goldmine!"

Merthen smacked his oar in the water to get Uther's attention. "Leave them for next time. If you delay any longer you will not be able to get on board."

A wave washed over the crest of the mud flat. It covered the cockles Uther had just unearthed. The boy was ankle deep in water.

"That was quick," said Uther. He sloshed over to the boat with his partially filled basket. A sizable wave hit him in the knees. The bottom of his basket was soaked, making it suddenly much heavier.

Merthen reached out his open arms. "Hand it over."

Uther gave it to him, but by now the little boat was floating a few inches higher. A small, flat section of polished wood floated by. Uther waded over to it.

"What is that?" he said. "Is that a barrel stave?"

Merthen snapped as him. "*Caco santi!* If this water gets any deeper you will not be able to get on board."

Another wave rolled in. Uther became submerged up to his hips. He waded over to the boat and grasped the side. Merthen leaned in the opposite direction.

Uther attempted to climb on board, and the boat lurched. The boy fell into the waves.

"I cannot get in," he said. "The water here is too deep."

Merthen shook his fist. "Which is just what I have been telling you. Try again."

Uther sloshed his way to the front of the craft. "I saw a sailor do this once. Just stay where you are."

"Boy! Get down from there."

Uther latched his fingers onto the tip of the stern and, in one smooth move, hoisted himself up. For one brief movement, he was perfectly balanced with his arms straightened directly beneath his torso.

The front of the dingy sunk down. The back of the boat, where Merthen sat, jerked up about a foot. Uther's arms buckled. He tipped face first into the cockle baskets by Merthen's feet. In the process, the boy succeeded in jamming his wrists against his testicles. He let out a moan, but he was in the boat.

Merthen gave him an oar. "Row, young Socrates. The currents are shifting. We need to get this hulk on shore."

Merthen began paddling. Uther, still hunched over, assisted as best he could. Another piece of wood floated by.

"Jetsam," said Merthen. "A ship dumped her load in the storm last night."

Uther said, "I see someone coming this way."

Merthen responded with a simple, "Keep rowing."

"No really," said Uther. "There is someone walking on the beach. I think he is waving."

The dingy was now in the surf. The crashing waves pushed it toward the sand. Merthen yelled, "Row, row, row," to keep the two of them in tandem. As soon as they hit the shore, Uther hopped out. Merthen threw him the rope, and the boy dragged the boat in farther. There were bits of wood everywhere, broken planks mostly. Quite a few had nails in them.

"We should collect all this lumber and burn it tonight," said Merthen, "Come tomorrow we can gather the nails from the ashes and sell them."

There were two figures approaching. One was running toward them, shoeless and clothed only in a tunic, not the dress of a German.

Merthen retrieved his sword from the stand of marsh grass where he had stashed it. "Keep your dagger handy, Uther. Those strangers may not be saints."

The barefoot man ran yelled, "*Hei, Brueder! Ob Sie uns hilfen kann? Unsere Schiff ist im gestern Abend wegen Sturm hinuntergegangen.*"

Merthen cupped his hand to his mouth and shouted, "*Bin Ich nicht Sachsonisch. Hier is Cambria. Sprechen Sie Lateinisch?*"

The runner replied, "My Latin stinks, but I speak *Welschmann* pretty good. My name is Christophe of Frisia." His loosely braided hair was covered in sand. He bowed. "My ship sunk last night. Have you seen any of my crew? All I have been able to find is an old man we were ferrying to Britannia. How far are we from Swansea?"

"Quite," said Merthen. "I am Ambrosius, a Briton of Carmarthen." He bowed with all due respect, even though he suspected this orphan of the sea was one of those wandering fishermen who dabbled in smuggling and, when the opportunity arose, piracy. Who else would risk crossing the Celtic Sea through the storms of mid-Lent?

Christophe stuck his fingers in his mouth whistled. Off in the distance, the second figure approached.

"Who is that?" said Uther.

"His name is Leithleach. How he survived is beyond me. He is older than Adam's knob. How far are we from Carmarthen?"

"It is a day and a half south by boat," said Merthen. "Three, if you hoof it. Did you see any bodies? We saw only flotsam." He offered him an apple.

Christophe dug into it. "That was one wicked storm. It came out of nowhere. Me and a few mates hung onto what was left of the mast, but the currents kept pushing us out. Come dawn, we had to swim for the coast. I thought I was the only one who made it, till the old geezer showed up."

The other survivor, Mister Leithleach, was now clearly visible.

Uther shaded his eyes. "He has tattoos on his face? Is he a Pict?"

"Beats me," said Christophe. "We picked him up in Hibernia."

Leithleach stepped up and bowed, but not very much. He was a tall, broad shouldered man, about Merthen's age and height, wearing a long white robe. The front half of his head was shaved. He had long white hair, all unbraided. His beard was longer than Merthen's, but aside from that they looked quite similar. They even shared the same sky blue eyes.

The tattoos on Leithleach's face were a combination of birds, painted eggs, and twisted knot designs. High on his forehead was a crescent moon with both points facing up.

Merthen turned to Christophe saying, "This man is a druid. Where were you taking him?"

"Hell if I know. The skipper booked the passengers."

Liethleach extended his hand, as if to tell them to stop. Then he said, "This mariner knows nothing. And I have nothing to fear. I am ready for rebirth."

"In that case," said Merthen, "you may not have long to wait. This is Christian territory, Sir. If an officer of the church finds you, you will be roasted on a spit. Britannia is not safe for you. What possessed you to come here?"

Liethleach gazed out at the sea. "Hibernia has gone mad. The Irish are chopping down the holy oaks to make meeting halls for the Pope's book. My brother judges elected that I should travel to Wessex and request assistance from the Saxons. What kind of fool builds a house for a stack of paper?"

A strange slapping sound echoed out from the surf. A wave crashed, carrying something with it. A seagull dove down to peck at it. Uther ran over. "I see a hand!"

Christophe followed close behind. A limp body rolled along with the churning water. Uther dived in.

Merthen cried, "No boy! There may be sharks."

Uther reached his elbow around the neck of the body and started to swim. Before he got very far, a wave came up and tossed him toward the beach.

Christophe waded in and dragged them both to shore. "Ambert!" he said, "are you all right?" He and Uther laid the young man on his back.

Ambert had a few whips of adolescent whiskers on the side of his face. His body was pale, but not stiff or bloated.

"He is gone," said Liethleach. "His soul has been transferred to the gull."

Merthen knelt down and put his ear to Ambert's chest. He propped Ambert's head back and opened his mouth. Ambert's tongue was blue. Merthen folded Ambert over and pounded on his back five times. Ambert coughed. A small gush of water shot from his mouth.

"Is he alive?" said Christophe. "He is the captain's son. I though I heard him yelling after the ship went down."

Merthen squeezed Ambert's nostrils shut, then blew a breath into his mouth. Again something came out. It was vomit, but not much. Merthen wiped

Ambert's face with his blouse and repeated the process. Ambert coughed a few more times. He started breathing on his own.

Christophe stammered, "How did you do that? Are you a druid too?"

"No," said Merthen. "I enjoy reading too much."

Liethleach pulled a twig of mistletoe from the purse around his waste. He pointed it at Ambert and began to shake.

Merthen sat up straight. "Is that really necessary?"

Christophe leaned close to Ambert and said, "Wake up, son. Can you hear me?" He slapped him a few times. No reaction. Merthen held the young man's hand. It was not entirely limp, but when he let go of it, it fell. Merthen manually opened Ambert's eyelids. His eyeballs were locked in place, unblinking.

Christophe hung his head. He swore an oath in Frankish and said, "The mermaids got him. His mind is frozen. We were too bloody late."

"Damn it," said Merthen. He curled his hand into a fist.

Uther asked, "Is he going to die?"

Christophe put his hand on Ambert's shoulder.

"What should we do?" said Uther.

Christophe replied, "Take him back to the sea. That will be quick."

Merthen sighed. "Yes. I concur."

"It is just as I prophesied," said Liethleach. "His soul has been reborn in the seagull. Clearly his drowning fulfills a desire he requested during a previous life."

Christophe scanned the old druid from head to toe, then punched him square in the jaw. Liethleach fell backwards onto a stand of sea grass. His mistletoe spiraled high into the air. Merthen lurched up his hands to keep Christophe from taking another swing, but it was not needed.

Without further ado, Christophe clasped onto Ambert's wrists. In a workmanlike manner, he dragged the doomed lad into the surf. They all watched Christophe rest his heel on the chest of his captain's son and press down. A few bubbles bobbed to the surface. Then they stopped.

Merthen helped Liethleach back onto his feet.

Christophe pulled Ambert's body from the churning surf. He kissed him on the cheek, then pushed the corpse back into the ocean. Christophe slapped the sand off his hands, and marched away.

"I say," Merthen called out to him, "where are you going?"

"Carmarthen," said Christophe. "I need to get a job."

"What about your passenger?"

"Burn him. If they need some kindling to start the fire under his arse, be sure to call on me. I would be more than happy to light him up."

Uther asked, "What are we going to do?"

Merthen tugged on his beard a few times. "I fear," he said to Liethleach, "that you are in a predicament. Even if we cut your hair, your tattoos will give you away. I can give you some food, Sir, but I cannot risk having you travel with us. I recommend you go north. Find a stream and follow it east till you reach the hills. The Saxons go hunting there. Make enough noise, and they will find you."

Liethleach shook the sand off his pure white robes. "Do you think I am so weak that I cannot survive in the wild? I am in communication with all that lives. The birds will guide me. Magic crystals will invigorate me. I see all my past incarnations and those that are yet to come. This life is of minor consequence."

Merthen paused. Then, in a very scholarly fashion, he inquired, "Is it true that it takes a druid twenty years to memorize the unwritten mystic code?"

"Aye," said Liethleach, "if you are among the truly skilled."

"And if I may ask, what do the wiccan teachings say regarding the concepts of charity and mercy?"

Liethleach laughed. "Clearly you have no idea of the power of the transcendent masters. The in-born knowledge I possess is like a sharpened blade cutting though the veil of this realm. It connects me to the cosmos and gives me an understanding of the ancient ones. When one has the power to see the future, the triflings of this life mean very little."

Merthen took an apple from his purse, and smacked it in Liethleach's hand.

"Head for the hills," he said. "Good luck."

Chapter XVII: The Harvest Moon, AD 487

Aut insanat homo, aut versus facit.

The fellow is either mad, or he is composing verses.

* * *

The chore of raising rabbits is an exercise in maintenance. A peltier must keep his animals free from parasites. Fleas and ticks can cause skin lesions, resulting in gaps in the fur that reduce the value of the pelt. For Merthen, the problem was lice, a trio of which were attached to the ears of his best breeding doe. He cradled her in his arms and pinched the offending insects.

The rabbit released a cascade of oval droppings.

"Sorry about that," she said. "Not really something I can control."

Merthen shook his boot clean.

Gopi extended her forepaw toward a lock of loose hair hanging by the bend of his elbow. "You seem rather unkempt today," she said. "Why have you undone your braids?"

"It seemed the prudent thing to do. Might we discuss this at a later date? I am rather occupied at the moment."

"Lord Quetzalcoatl, the Winged Serpent, has a question."

Merthen lowered her back into the hutch. "Let us just hope he shows mercy on all those poor mortals who attempt to pronounce his name. Where does he come from, the Grand Duchy of Shibboleth?"

"He oversees a western empire," said Gopi, "or an eastern one, depending on your perspective. The gods thought it wise to consider his observations as he is wholly unfamiliar with your background. Every jury should have an impartial member."

"So be it. What does Quetza-whozits wish to know?"

"Why is it that you became a hermit? Was it a quest for spiritual purity?"

"No, it was more a quest for corporeal continuation. King Vortiger asked me to become one of his courtiers, which would have been a fine career except for the painful death that inevitably befell all his employees. Whereas I am an inveterate coward, I ran for the hills and set up shop beside the savages, who may score low in terms of personal hygiene, but have never posed any meaningful threat to me."

Merthen nestled Gopi back in the hutch. She crept into the corner and nibbled a sprig of sedge grass.

"Actually," said Gopi, "the only reason the Saxons did not kill you was because they feared the wrath of your rabbits."

Merthen kicked away the cluster of turds by his feet. "Oh really? Since when do fuzzy bunnies possess the capacity for wrath?"

"Among the Germans," said Gopi, "white rabbits are regarded as bad luck. When they find a dead one, they keep its feet to frighten the live ones away. That is why the Saxons never attacked your compound. Were it not for my cotton-tailed cousins, you would have been diced up ages ago."

Merthen frowned, much like a child who just dropped his sugar plum in the dirt. "But, I always thought they were afraid of me?"

"Oh no," said Gopi, "who would be frightened by you?"

* * *

Once again the birds began to sing. Merthen's attention was diverted to a party of six knights approaching along the deer path.

"Ahoy," said the knight-in-command. "My name is Duke Gaius Felix. I come on order of His Majesty King Ambrosius Aurelianus. I am looking for Merlin. Is that you?"

"I am Ambrosius the Furrier at your service." Merthen bowed. "How nice to see you. Please sit down."

"No thank you, we cannot stay. We are looking for Merlin. Do you know where he is?" Gaius rapped his knuckles on one of the trees covered with Latin script. "Who wrote this?"

"I did. They are prayers. They keep the Germans away."

"Germans?" said Gaius. "Are there Saxons in these woods?"

"It is infested with them. When the savages read the word of God, it makes them run."

Gaius surveyed the forest around them. "The merchants say there is a fellow up here with long braids who grows apples. Is that you?"

"No, Sir." Merthen laid a log on the hearth. "That is my brother Merthen. He is not here."

"Old man, I need to find him. Tell me were he is." Gaius unsheathed his dagger.

"Merthen is not here. He is dead Sir. It was last winter. The Germans took him."

"They killed him? Where is his grave?"

"Grave Sir?" said Merthen. He tilted his head, confused. "Why, no Sir, he fell. I tried to get him back to our hut, but they dragged him away. I supposed I should take down his bed."

Merthen attempted a half step forward, but Gaius raised his weapon, stopping him. Sir Iorwerth, the Sergeant-at-arms, peeked into Merthen's round hut and said, "There are two cots in there."

Gaius put away his knife. He blew a nostril full of snot onto the ground. "What kind of Germans were they? Saxons, Angles?"

"They were in disguise, dressed as wolves. They ripped him to shreds. I told mother I would look out for him."

"And these Germans dressed as wolves," said Gaius, "did they have four legs and a tail?"

"They curse me. I hear them at night." Merthen threw a stick out into the woods. "Do you know were my brother is?"

Sergeant Iorwerth spoke up. "He is balmy, Sir. There are no Germans here."

"I am not." Merthen patted himself on the chest. "I live in this forest all by myself. People who say I am crazy are slanderous. If I was wrong headed, could I keep this estate on my own?"

"You mean this shack?" said Gaius.

Merthen shook his finger at them. "My brother was very educated too. He knew Greek, every word. Those people in the market are just jealous because he can read."

"I thought you said your brother was dead?" said Iorwerth.

"He fell on the ice." Merthen grew teary eyed. "My baby brother was named Lailoken. He disappeared down by the docks." The rabbits thumped in their hutch. He tossed a fist full of greens at them. "Why are you looking for him?"

"Merlin," said Gaius, "I am looking for Merlin."

"I never heard of Merlin."

"So I gather. Did your dead brother wear an orange kerchief like the one around your neck?"

"Orange?" Merthen untied the scarf and examined it in the sunlight. "This scarf was red when I bought it. No one uses quality dyes anymore."

"Did your brother wear a scarf like that?"

"Oh, yes. Back in my day everyone wore one. After the Romans withdrew from Britannia, all of Governor Constans's subjects wore a red kerchief to show we were still with him. I became a citizen of the Empire when I was only sixteen."

"Sir," said Sergeant Iorwerth, "we should take him in. At least the king will know we tried."

Merthen grinned at Iorwerth and blathered on. "I remember when the legionnaire's came marching through Londinium. All us lads nabbed red hankies from Uncle Ignatius and tied them round our necks like capes. I never knew why Uncle Iggy had so many red hankies."

Duke Gaius took a swig from his water sack. He wiped his mouth. "Was your brother ever called a wizard?"

"No. That was just a nickname. They called him that because he told so many stories. He fought in Europe under Riothamus. Lailoken knew slight of hand."

"I was referring to Merlin."

"Who?" Merthen scratched his crotch. "The Germans killed my rabbits once. You tell King Vortiger to watch his back. Those Saxons are crafty. They read Latin, you know." He peered suspiciously into the trees and sniffed the air.

"He does not even know who the king is," said Iorwerth. "His mind is stuck in the past." He asked Merthen, "Old man, who is the Pope?"

Merthen squinted. "Why, he is the head of the church! I should think you would know that, soldier."

Duke Gaius put his hand against one of the inscribed trees. "I am not inclined to deliver a lunatic to His Majesty. It is not professional." He stared Merthen straight in the eyes. "It is getting late grandpa, and I have other duties. I will return before All Saint's Day, and you must be here when I do. On order of your *current* king, Ambrosius Aurelianus, I am forbidding you to go anywhere until then."

"I have nowhere to go but Zion. Which is to say, yes, I will do as you say. I am a loyal subject. Ask anyone in town, they will vouch for me."

Gaius motioned for his soldiers to leave. "I intend to do that."

"And if anyone tells you I am touched, it is a lie. I was a highly regarded scribner in my day." He stepped sideways, putting his foot in a bowl of porridge near the hearth.

"I am sure you were. Good day."

The soldiers marched down the trail to Carmarthen. Merthen waved goodbye. When they were well out of sight, he called out, "Boy!"

From beneath the rabbit hutch crawled Uther. A clump of white fur was clinging to the sparse hair of his sideburns. Merthen had been meaning to teach the boy to shave. Buddhist monastics shaved their entire scalp, a task that requires two monastics. Back in India, Merthen and Tinh Tu shaved each others heads.

Uther asked, "What did those knights want?"

Merthen cleaned the food off his boot. "That company of men belong to the Dragons, King Ambrosius's henchmen. Tomorrow, they will return." He put on his cloak. "You must listen closely and do exactly as I tell you. Understand?"

"Aye."

"Very good. When those soldiers come back here, make sure that you stay well out of sight. Do not utter a sound. Once they are done disturbing the place, wait for them to leave. Then and only then, you must build a new camp, three hundred paces to the north. There is a cave there near a stand of apple trees. How many paces?"

"Three hundred. I got that."

"Correct. I must inform you that I may be away for a while. If I do not return within ten days, you must go to court and find Sir Ector. He is a monstrously big man with a disfigured face and one eye. He stutters, but do not be afraid of him. He is a former colleague of mine and an individual of genuine honor. Tell me his name again."

"Ugly Ector."

"It is proper to call him Duke Ector. You must speak to him in private." Merthen threw six apples and half a loaf of bread into his rucksack. "Tell him that I wish to give him *another pastry*. That should perk up his ears. Then tell him everything that happened today. Tell him the truth. Do not lie to him, ever."

Uther fidgeted. "I am," he said, "scared. Can I come with you?"

"No. I need you to be here on the outside." Merthen jiggled the string of wooden beads on his wrist. "I wish that I could say something to ease your mind, but I cannot." He untied the bracelet. "String this around your ankle. If you are afraid, shake it and the Buddha will calm you." He handed it over. "These got me through Catalonian Fields; they should do the trick for you."

Uther bent down to secure the beads to his mottled leg. "I thought you said magic was all bunk."

"Perhaps I overstated the case. Nothing is completely anything."

Merthen drew his sword with his right hand. He gathered his loose facial hair in his left hand at chest height. With one smooth stroke, he cut off the lower half of his beard, making him look more like a tradesman than a hermit.

Uther finished tying the anklet. "Are you sure you want to give me these beads. What if you need them?"

A muted half-smile crossed Merthen's face. "Or could it be they are just pieces of rosewood?" He gathered together the long white locks that flowed down his back, and held them near his shoulder. He sheared them off as well. His hair was now so short, he could pass for a Christian. He patted the boy on back. "Promise me that you will follow my instructions."

"Aye, I will."

"One more thing. As you know, I have known many great men from Rome to India. Of all of them, there is no one whose comradeship I have valued more than yours, not even Brother Tinh Tu."

Merthen joined his palms together as if in prayer, but instead, he brought them to his forehead. He positioned them over his heart and bowed toward the boy, a deep bow. Then he walked away.

Chapter XVIII: The Harvest Moon, AD 487

O praeclarum custodem ovium lupum.

An excellent protector of sheep, the wolf.

* * *

The throne room of King Ambrosius Aurelianus was a barn-sized building. Merthen had always been impressed with the quality of its massive stone walls. Jutting out from up near the square oak rafters were black iron hooks. From these, there once hung wool carpets, used by the Romans to insulate their buildings. Merthen could only imagine how nice it must have looked back then.

He tapped his finger on the shoulder of Lord Chamberlain, Sir Goronwy, and said, "I suspect this structure was designed to hold more weight. Have you ever considered replacing the thatched roof with a clay tiles?"

Sir Goronwy scowled and adjusted his ceremonial bronze breastplate. "Oh Yay, Oh Yay," he cried, "*Domino optimo maximo*. The Court of His Majesty, Ambrosius Aurelianus, King of Britannia is now in session. All rise!"

The king, a swarthy broad-shouldered Roman of modest height, entered with a minimum of pomp. His retinue of officers wore light armor. The hall was hushed save the jingle of their spiky Frankish stirrups echoing off the floor.

The assembly bowed and His Majesty took his proper place upon a high-backed chair that passed for a throne. He twisted his signet ring around his finger and, getting on to business, said, "Old man, you live in on the frontier, yes?"

Merthen bowed, "Indeed, Your Highness, I am Ambrosius Merthen, the apple seller, at you service."

"You share a Christian name with Us, eh? Have you met Our court astrologer?"

Merthen grinned broadly enough to hold back the reservoir of suspicions he reserved for both kings and soothsayers. He replied, "Why no, I have not had the pleasure?"

"Well, We ought to fix that then."

The king set his eyes on a statuesque woman dressed in a gown of patterned blue silk. She was decked in pink and yellow ribbons that were secured above her breast with two silver pins, one depicting a stag, the other a flower. Her ever so slightly graying red hair was elegantly organized by a mother of pearl comb.

Although her emerald eyes were in no way common, they struck Merthen as somehow familiar. For some reason, he thought of James, the cithara player who used to perform with him on the streets of Paris.

"Good Lady," said the king, "may We present the Wizard Merlin." It was an unsettling introduction. The king and his men seemed bent on referring to Merthen as *the Wizard Merlin*. But why a wizard? Was it simply honorific? And why were they calling him *Mer-lin*?

The lady curtsied, and smiled a dazzling, yet unsure smile. She looked to the king for an explanation, and upon hearing none, said, "Good day venerable Sir, I am Morgan of Paris, at your service."

It was her voice that finally jogged Merthen's memory.

Back when he and James were giving shows at Inn of the Fountain, there was a young beer wench who was always in the crowd, usually attached to the arm of a visiting merchant. They called her *Little Morgan*, but her name was really *Faye*.

"Faye," he said to her, "it is I, Ambrosius of Britannia. I was friends with James the harpist."

Her eyes opened up, exposing much of the white surrounding her piercing green irises.

"You are," she said, "still alive?" Her initial shock was short lived. Regaining her composure she added, "They told us you were dead… *my dear brother.* My sweet, sweet Merlin, I thought I would never see you again." A tear rolled down her cheek. "Oh please, come embrace *your sister.*"

She thrust herself into Merthen's arms. He fell limp. She caught him. Merthen climbed to his feet, grabbing onto her wrist, with its many silver bracelets. Were these gifts from Governor Syagrius, or payments for services rendered? Or, did she take the opportunity to rummage through the Governor's coffers after King Clovis stuck his head on a pole.

"Could this be my sister Morgan?" said Merthen, a man who knew full well when to play along. "*Gloria in excelsis Deo*, we are together again."

"My brother," she whimpered, "my dearest Merlin."

"Half brother," he said. "After all, I am a full blood Briton, and here in Britannia they call me Mer-*then*, the fine Celtic name my crimson-haired pappy gave me."

"But of course you wish to honor you father… *King Meurig*. It has been so long since I last saw you. I had forgotten how proud you are."

"Yes, it has been a while." He slipped his hand into his into his pocket. "*Tempus fugit*. I will always think of you as the young prankster I knew down at Lord Marican's wine bar. Ah, the tricks you turned, little Morgan."

She released him from her hug, but not before deftly poking her long thumbnail into the back of his neck.

Merthen said, "I have heard so much about you, dear sister. You once provided a forecast to Governor Syagrius, did you not? Something about the Roman Legions?"

She sighed. "Poor Syagrius, I fear he was too kind hearted. He never should have trusted his Frankish guards."

Merthen could not help but recall his conversation with Oderic the Frankish pear vendor. "I have also heard," he said, "that you frequently speak of me with pride. If His Majesty permits, could the lady relate one of the tales that she is so fond of telling about me?"

"An excellent idea," said King Ambrosius. He clasped his hands. "We have been very impressed with Lady Morgan's stories."

"Well," she said batting her luscious lashes, "if it pleases Your Majesty, how can I refuse?"

The king signaled for the Royal Steward, Sir Illtyd, who appeared with an additional pillow. The king slid it behind his lower back.

Morgan raised her hands, positioning them like a statue of Saint Cecelia preparing to pluck her harp.

"As you know," she said, "King Vortiger foolishly invited the German savages to live on his eastern shore, and soon after was betrayed by them. Fleeing west to Snowdonia, his troops constructed a mountain fortress at Dinas Emrys. He built it using his own design, and so it was no surprise when the edifice came tumbling down. Straight away, he commanded that it be reconstructed, but again it fell. No one could find the cause."

"Oh, he tried," said Merthen.

Morgan continued unfazed. "Vortiger's wicked chaplain, the heretical druid Pelagius, declared that the castle's foundation was infested with fairies. Pelagius called for a sacrifice, a tithe of human blood. He ordered his witches to erect a giant wicker man and set it ablaze. My own brother was to be chained inside of it."

Merthen clownishly winked at one of the young maids-in-waiting. "I was to be fricasseed alive, protected only by my diaphanous flaxen undergarments." The girl stifled a giggle.

"And so," said Morgan raising the volume of her voice, "the wicked Professor Pelagius arrested brave Merlin, intent on slaying him. But when this proud Celt was brought before King Vortiger, he declared that beneath the fortress lived two dragons, one red and one white. The red dragon, spoke in sweetest Latin, while the white spoke with the grunts and growls of the Saxons brutes. The dragons fought endlessly with neither one victorious."

Merthen waved his hand like an eager schoolboy. "Actually, the white one was more of an ivory color."

Illtyd, the royal steward rolled his eyes.

"Aye," said Morgan. "My venerable brother then decreed that the fortress must be moved to another hill. Furthermore, Merlin prophesied that no king who embraced the sinful ways of Pelagius would ever defeat the Saxon savages."

"That Pelagius was one corpulent Scotsman," said Merthen. "Too much haggis I suppose."

The king stood and massaged his thigh. "Do go on. We bruised Our hip on maneuvers yesterday. Unfortunately this throne is rather hard on the arse. We much prefer Our saddle." Everyone laughed at the appropriate level.

Morgan bowed. "King Vortiger was so overwhelmed by the visionary power of the Wizard Merlin that he spared his life, and ordered his knights to rebuild the fortress on another peak. It stood strong, and saved many a knight from the Saxon ax. But was Vortiger grateful?" Morgan waited for Merthen to reply.

He scratched his ear. "Not as I recall."

"No!" she exclaimed. "Vortiger's Pelagian warlocks convinced him to exile Merlin to the eastern woods, in the hopes that some Jute would boil his bones in a stew pot."

King Ambrosius cleared his throat. "The Lady Morgan's testimony," he said, "is of great interest to Us. But We are also interested in some other news that We have recently heard."

Morgan fluffed out her dress. "Do tell, Your Highness?"

"Just last month," said the king, "Our lord chamberlain spoke with a hunchback who was delivering a shipment of food stores from Our associate King Clovis. He informed Us that a sorcerer by the name of Ambrosius the Briton was living in the Cambrian hills. Apparently this wizard had lived among the Romans of Paris for some time after having served for Attila, King of the Huns. We were told his chap wears an orange kerchief."

Merthen untied his neckwear. "Perhaps I should clarify," he said. It is true that some decades ago, I did live amongst the Huns, but in no way was I an accomplice to Attila. Like so many others, I was captured in battle and sold into slavery."

"You were a knight?"

"No. I served as a drummer boy in the legions when your grandfather was Governor. Having learned to read some, I eventually clerked for a company of sappers, all of whom wore these." He shook his orange neckwear, then tied it back on.

"You are an architect then?"

"More of a draftsman. Nonetheless, my unit was assigned to build a fort in Balkans. We had only just begun it when we were overrun by Attila's hoard. I was taken captive and forced to sew saddles."

"So you *did* work on behalf of the Huns?"

"At first I refused, and my master whipped me." Merthen rolled up his blouse to expose the scars that disfigured his back. Some of the more easily-pained courtiers had to avert their eyes.

"When he threatened to kill me," said Merthen, "I told him to draw his knife. That he did, and with it, he decapitated a Roman maiden right before my eyes. From then on, I complied with his wishes." He tucked his clothing back into place.

The king said, "Do you swear to this testimony?"

"Unfortunately, I do. There may be those who allege I was a collaborator, but if Saint Peter pronounces judgment upon me, at least I will not be tried before a jury of headless cherubim."

Lady Morgan inched forward and asked with genuine curiosity, "Just how did you escape the Huns?"

"After the Romans defeated Attila at Catalonian Fields, I was granted my liberty. I lived for a time in Paris, performing slight-of-hand in the marketplace." Merthen flicked his wrist while saying, "*Quae vide*," and made a denarius appear. "Through the charity of our cousins in Brittany, I was able to board a ship and return to my native land."

"When you served under King Vortiger," said the king, "you built the fortress at Dinas Emrys, correct?"

"On that project," said Merthen, "I was initially the copyist. After Vortiger ordered the architect torn apart by horses, I was assigned to finish the job. The outer wall was nearly complete when the king's Saxon guards revolted. I fled here to Cambria with everybody else."

The king tilted his head toward Chancellor Goronwy.

"This tale I have related," said Merthen, "is true in every detail. It contains no dragons, but let me tell you, the breadth of the horrors I witnessed during my captivity with the Huns could put any winged sphinx to shame."

Chancellor Goronwy slipped out of the room.

"This greatly clarifies the rumors We have heard," said the king. "And yet, We are confused. If you served my grandfather and then King Vortiger, why do you withhold your talents from your current sovereign? A trained architect could be valuable to Our court."

Merthen replied, "My patriotism is as robust as always. I did my best to serve King Vortiger, but after the peace conference, I had reason to fear the Germans might seek my head as a trophy. They believe that literate men carry magic in their skulls. Thus, I fled to the highlands and planted apples."

The king asked, "Did you witness the Kent Council Massacre?"

Merthen chose to reply with a simple, "No," instead of detailing the stupidity of the whole affair.

King Vortiger's only talent was extorting cash from the Romans stranded in Britannia after the Empire collapsed. If he had any political skills, he would not have gone to Kent for a council with the Saxons. It was a short meeting. After the Germans skewered him, they took his peace treaty and wrapped his liver in it. It was sent to Sir Ector, the only knight of rank they did not kill that day.

"My father," said the king, "was among the knights slain in Kent."

"That he was," said Merthen. "I knew him, Your Highness, but not well. He deserved better that what he got. They all did."

The king sat down and sipped his wine.

"Your Majesty," said Merthen, "you asked why I have not presented myself to your offices. My explanation is simple. I am old. Although I once was of utility, I can no longer ride nor swing a sword."

The king placed his goblet on the side table. "Do you have a son?"

"That would be impossible. When I was in the legions, I suffered a battle wound to my pudenda. It rendered me as inactive as Saint Origen, that early father of the church who sliced off his own testicles lest he be distracted in his search for salvation. If only all of Christendom's clergy would show such enthusiasm."

"And yet," said the king, "some of the lads down at the docks claim that you have a grandson named *Uther-Arthur*. They say he has spots."

"Well, of course *Arthur* has spots," said Merthen. "Perhaps, I should explain. As a woodsman, I am occasionally visited by a spotted bear, who has become accustomed to my presence. The market folk tease me by saying I have a son named *Arthur*. As a purebred Roman, you may not be aware that *art* is the vernacular Celtic word for *bear*. I am certain Sir Goronwy is familiar with the term."

The king snapped his fingers. Into the room marched Sir Goronwy. Behind him was Uther, flanked on either side by Duke Gaius Felix and Sergeant Iorwerth. They bowed. Uther hung his head, red faced.

Merthen fought the urge whip out his sword and separate the royal head from its shoulders. But as the Buddha so wisely noted, morality springs from what a man does, not what he considers. Merthen permitted this anger to dissipate. After all, killing one tyrant would only make room for another.

The soldiers shepherded the boy up to the throne. King Ambrosius put his arm on Uther's shoulder.

"Might this be the *Arthur* you spoke of?" said the king. "Or perhaps not? Either way, We believe that it would be best if this foundling were to live here in Our court. One cannot help but think how unfortunate it would be if something bad were to happen to him. That would be *sad indeed*. Would you not agree, Mister Merlin?"

Merthen had learned a few things performing with James the cithara player. Old James held that all performances - from a troubadour's song to the epics of Ovid - were just artfully crafted lies. Lying to an individual was deceptive. But lying to a crowd was entertainment, and people would gladly pay for it. From this observation, James developed his guiding rule of stagecraft: *Do not lie, lie big.*

Merthen straightened his posture and strode to the center of the court. He breathed in, and then he breathed out. With a sudden windmill-swirl of his arm, he pointed his walking stick at Uther like a warlock brandishing his wand. A few people even gasped.

Merthen released a long low moan. "I have seen this boy before," he said, "but not in an earthly realm. Last night I dreamt of a bear cub standing before the gates of this very castle. In the cub's right paw he carried a wounded lamb; in his left, a legionnaire's sword, its green blade dripping with Saxon blood. Before him lay a quartet of angels fast asleep: one Celtic, one German, one Persian, one African."

The king began to speak.

Merthen cut him off. "Forgive my boldness, but I now understand the meaning of this riddle. The Roman sword is you, Your Highness. The blade of green is your Celtic knights. The lamb is Britannia, a nation blessed by the Great Shepherd. It has been wounded by pagan savages and Pelagian lies."

"The bear?" said Morgan. "Why was he a cub?"

"Young Arthur is a boy," said Merthen. "Ergo, the bear is a cub. In my vision, he carried both the lamb and the sword, for it is Arthur's generation who shall defend the True Faith and Your Majesty's kingdom."

"And what of the four angels?"

"They are the peoples of the earth; the freckled Briton, the blond Saxon, the swarthy Sassanian, and the black-skinned Moor. For one day, all of humankind, north, south, east, and west will hear the tales of Britannia and her bold defenders."

"But why do they sleep?"

"They can only dream, dear sister. The knights of Britannia have yet to begin their glorious exploits, but mark my word, that day is nigh." He re-aimed his stick at the king. "Your Majesty, you have pronounced that there would be misfortune if ill treatment were to befall this child. Indeed, you are correct, for if Arthur were to be hurt, the sun would be blotted from the sky, and night would follow night from Sabbath to Sabbath."

The king remained quiet.

Merthen curled his hand into a fist until it trembled. "If Arthur, the bear, were to be wounded, a frost would cover the green fields of summer, and famine would haunt this island for a generation."

Morgan lifted a finger. Merthen's maniacal glare stilled her eager tongue.

"If this Arthur were to be killed," he said, "a plague like none that befell Pharaoh's Egypt would spill across Caesar's once mighty realm, and curdle the blood of saints and sinners for winters numbering a thousand."

Sweat poured down Merthen's face. He eyeballed each person in the hall with utter contempt. He was not actually angry; he just needed to appear insane. All true prophets were. How ironic that he had to pretend to be crazy simply to get their attention. Years before, when he actually had lost his mind, everyone pretty much ignored him.

The king spoke up. "Very well then," was all he said.

"My brave Liege," said Merthen, "there is immediacy in this vision. It compels me to serve in your court, starting today. Although I am frail, I the Wizard Merlin, will dedicate my remaining days to ensuring that that your fortress is built to the highest standards of Roman military engineering. Indeed, I have been too long in exile."

The king removed the pillow from behind his back and returned it to Sir Illtyd.

Merthen took it as an endorsement. "Furthermore, young Arthur shall forever be under my patronage. He shall be sent to receive his training from Field Marshal Ector, a capable duke and Christian gentlemen." Merthen extended his walking stick far above his head, and brought it down to the ground with a crash. That was another one of James's rules: *Finish every gig with a bang.*

The king addressed Sir Goronwy. "In two days," he said, "We and Our dukes will hold a private audience with Wizard Merlin to better understand the full measure of his abilities. Arrange a council for the afternoon."

"A most skillful plan," said Merthen. "If it pleases Your Highness, I would now beg permission to take my leave. Having arrived at dawn after traversing all evening, I am quite weary."

"Aye, that will do. My steward shall assign you to your quarters." The king nudged Uther with his foot.

The boy skulked across the courtroom to his mentor. Merthen was taken aback by the immense sense of relief he felt just having the boy by his side. It was a form of attachment he knew he should avoid. And yet, there it was.

Merthen bowed and called out, "*Vivat rex!*" He elbowed Uther. The boy bowed as well.

With no more theatrics to perform, there was nothing left for Merthen to do but retreat to the wings. He bowed to Lady Morgan. She curtsied as gracefully as any well-bred Roman of Paris.

Sir Illtyd stoically led Merthen and the boy into the foyer, and down the musty passageway that led to the guests' dormitory.

Merthen retrieved two silver bracelets from out of his pocket. "Take this, *Squire Arthur*. Now that you are to be trained by Sir Ector, you will need to acquire some armor. Feel free to use these trifles to finance the acquisition of your military vestments. It appears your monastic robes may have to wait."

"Is this jewelry?" said Uther. "Where did you get these?"

"They were transferred to me via my sister, Lady Morgan." Merthen examined the chestnut planks in the ceiling. "Best if you keep mum about it. She does not wish to receive undo notoriety."

The boy tightened his grip around the gift. "Thank you very much, *Wizard Merlin*." He hid the booty in the side of his boot. "So," he asked, "are you really going to build a castle?"

BOOK V: THE WIZARD

Chapter XIX: The Storm Moon, AD 488

Quod licet Iovi, non licet bovi.

What is permitted to Jupiter is not permitted to a cow.

* * *

Merlin was a light sleeper. His boyhood weeks spent caged in the hull of a ship scarred him with an animal-like sensitivity. The mere suggestion of dawn was enough to rouse him. On good nights, he would fall back asleep, or at least remain under the covers, one eye propped open like a bitch nursing her puppies. On bad nights, he had to meditate until his galloping mind slowed to a trot.

As youth in Constantinople, Merlin woke up at sunrise. As always, Judith would already be in the kitchen, lighting the bake oven. He would lie in the waning darkness, and listen to the shuffle of her sandals against the tiled floor.

In later years, Merlin would attempt to revive this bygone sense of stillness in the meditation halls of Nalanda University. And yet, he was never able to match the sense of peace and comfort he felt hearing the sounds of a solitary old lady, sifting flour and kneading dough.

But now, it was Merlin's turn to start a fire at dawn. He lit his three-flame lamp, and rested it on the oak table in the exchequer's hall. A fiduciary spread sheet was sprawled out before him. Undeniably, it would be easier to read it by the noonday sun, but by then, Merlin would be too distracted with interruptions.

Sir Ector stooped his head below the doorway and, using his free hand, adjusted his eye patch. The strap that secured it to his head created an odd part in his explosive mound of hair.

The Germans referred to Sir Ector as *Der Strewel-strubel*, which could be roughly translated as *the tangle-headed destroyer*. It was not an insult. The savages appreciated a spectacle. For them, the angular red tufts that sprouted from Ector's hare-lipped moustache were not some freakish anomaly. Rather, they were a warning sign delivered to this realm from the god of war himself.

Using just one of his truck-like arms, Ector dragged across the room a squat, bald-headed man in his bedclothes. The prisoner was gagged and bound at the wrists and ankles.

"Could this be the infamous Antonius Puglius?" said Merlin from the comfort of his cushioned high-backed chair. "I was wondering when he would drop by. If memory serves, I formally requested a meeting with him *three weeks ago*. Perhaps he misplaced my invitation?"

Ector kicked close the lid of a large lock box, and sat Antonius onto it.

"Shall we see what he has to say?" said Merlin.

Ector untied the gag.

"*Non capisco,*" said Antonius. He sat up. "*Che ore sono?*"

"Come now, Mister Puglius," said Merlin, "everyone knows you can speak Celtic. Or if you prefer, we could converse in Latin? I am also fluent in German, just like the king of Italy. Tell me, how is Naples faring now that the Ostragoths are running things? I suppose the place rather smells of sauerkraut."

Antonius folded his calloused hands. In Celtic, he said, "What am I doing here? You pull me out of bed like a common criminal. Is this how you treat all your guests?"

This was not Merlin's first run-in with freemasons. He had initially encountered them in Persia, and more recently when he was building King Vortiger's castle at Dinas Emrys.

Freemasons were skilled craftsmen who knew exactly how valuable they were. If one war lord would not pay them, they would haul their hammers down the road till they found another one who would. Although they would always bow their head to the king, they would never bow completely.

"For some few decades," said Merlin, "I had a career copying financial documents. My recent appointment has given me the opportunity to review a multitude of invoices previously issued by this office. Based in my research, it appears that you have been skimming to the tune of fifteen percent."

"Skimming? I do not know that word."

"And yet you have fully mastered the concept. You have been squirreling away cash budgeted for the construction of His Highness's fortress."

Antonius laughed, only a few short bursts. "Oh, I see. So, you blame the Italian, eh? You know Mister Exchequer, I always try to be respectful, but now you are disparaging me. I have important things to do today, much more important than listening to some Roman wanna-be insult my lineage."

"I am not saying that you are a crook because you are an Italian, I am saying you are a crook because you are a free mason."

Antonius poked his thumb against his breastbone. "If I was a Roman, you would not tie me up this way."

Antonius's argument had some merit. No one trusted Italians. Rome may have been located in Italy, but it was a world away from the illiterate stock that populated the rest of the peninsula.

While the Romans argued in the Senate; the Italians plowed the fields. And once the well-bred families of Rome concluded the Ostragoths were going to crush them, they sailed off to Constantinople. The Italians, they just got crushed.

"*Pisano*," said Merlin, "In my youth, I was trained as a mason's apprentice. I know how the *Manus Magnus* operates."

"Your king is lucky I work for him at all. Do I ever get paid on time?"

"You are operating a criminal organization."

"As a member of royal court, you should know all about that."

"Indeed I do."

"Listen, you old witch" said Antonius, "if it is your intention to kill me, then do it. If not, stop wasting my time."

Merlin wiped off the tip of his quill and said, "Myself, I abhor waste. The only thing I despise more than frittering away time is squandering money."

Antonius picked a fleck of food from his teeth. "Then why did you take a job in government?"

"My good man, if I were to tell the king that your nimble digits have found their way into his purse, I suspect he would insert an iron spike betwixt your ample Neapolitan buttocks. I beg of you, does this need to happen?"

Antonius yawned. "And once I am gone, who will build your wall? There is not a chisel man between here and the Danube who is not related to my guild."

"Of course, there is another option. I could simply cast you in the dungeon. People get lost down their all the time. By summer's end, some other mug will have taken over the racket you established down at the market. From what I can tell, you are garnering protection money from everyone but the minnows."

Antonius planted down his heels like a bull in a pen, and said, "When the vendors at the market need something, they come to me. If I can do them a favor, I do it. What do they get from that pretty Roman you work for... aside from bastard grandchildren?"

Duke Ector removed his gloves. Antonius straightened his posture.

"Myself," said Merlin, "I care not if you steal from the king. Pry the rings from his fingers if you must, but heaven help you if you bollix up his fortress."

Antonius stretched out a crick in his neck. "I am a businessman, not a lord. I have debts, and people expect me to pay them. If my pockets are empty at the end of the day, I have nothing to eat."

"And yet you appear so well-nourished. Nonetheless, here is my proposal. You and I shall establish a merchant's guild. You shall serve as governor; I will be the secretary. For the next three years, you may skim no more than ten percent of the royal funds allotted to you."

"Twelve is as low as anyone goes."

Merlin rolled up his ledger. "Three-quarters of this ill-gotten currency will be yours. One eighth shall finance a charitable endowment to feed the beggars who would otherwise pilfer from the vendors. The remaining balance will be set aside for a commercial loan program. If the bay market makes a greater profit, your take of it will similarly increase. *Capisce?*"

"The church will stop you. They have spies everywhere. It never works."

"Perhaps not in Europe. But I can assure you the clerics on this island are no threat. Father Thomasius could be browbeaten by a door mouse, and Bishop Zephyrinus only ventures outside his gate to purchase pastries for his larder."

Antonius directed his eyes up toward the ceiling. When Brother Tinh Tu was thinking, he used to do that as well. Could it be that a greedy mason and a charitable monastic could have such similar habits? Why not?

Antonius scratched his chin. "This is a rather complicated scheme. I suppose it could generate some spare cash. But at the end of the day, what do I get that I do not already have?"

"Me," said Merlin, "I clerked for a mason in Persia. I know formulas that your carpenters never heard of. My recipe for concrete is a long shot better than that Frankish mud you use. Of course, if you spurn my assistance, I can always take it up with His Highness."

"Blackmail?"

"I prefer to think of it as effective governance."

Ector took his dagger, and buffed it on his sleeve. "Sounds g-good to me."

Antonius yawned again. "I will have to clear this with my brothers. It may take a month or so. I need to get approval from my associates on the continent."

"I will grant you three weeks," said Merlin, "not a day less. Your crew may have sway Europe, but in here Britannia my king is still the biggest brigand."

Antonius Puglius tapped his fingers on his knee. "So be it," he said. "I can deal with this. But keep in mind, your boss has a knack for going through wizards. By the time you get this organized, you may be out of a job."

Merlin extended his right hand. "Do we have a deal?"

Antonius staggered to his feet, then the squeezed Merlin's spindly digits with the meaty grip of a man who spent his life in a quarry. Merlin pretended not to feel the pain.

Antonius lifted his wrists, still bound, and directed them toward Ector's dagger. The duke cut the ties, as well as the ones round his ankles.

"*Gratia*," said Antonius. He strolled off toward the exit. "If we were in Europe right now, your throat would be slit by noon. *Memento mori*."

"And by the way," said Merlin, rolling up his broad sheets, "there are going to be some changes to the design of the castle. I have already drawn up the plans. Send one of your men over to pick them up this afternoon. Good day."

Antonius silently waved his hand as if to say, "Just get away from me."

Oblong beams of orange sunlight flooded through the window slits.

Merlin tied up his ledger, despite his throbbing hand. "Well I certainly handled that, did I not?"

Sir Ector slipped on his gloves. "Be c-careful."

"When am I not?" Merlin tossed his scroll into a nearby open crate. "General, on your way out you will find two esquires waiting by the entrance. One is your son, so I presume you will recognize him. Could you send them in?"

Ector responded by raising a finger, like someone making a point. Then he leaned into the hallway and yelled, "Lads!"

The sound of clumsy adolescent stumbling echoed off the walls. Arthur and young Sir Kay dashed to the threshold and stood at attention. Both wore esquire's cassocks and page boy haircuts. Their necks and spotty whiskers had been shaved last week, leaving their faces with a crop of stubble.

Arthur's clamshell-pale arms were looking almost normal, spotless all the way to the elbows. Merlin was relived that the boy's hair showed no signs of turning white. If Arthur transformed into an albino, people might think he was somehow cursed, or worse yet, blessed.

Merlin asked, "What were you doing out there?"

"Sleeping," said Arthur, and yet he had a half-chewed toothpick in his mouth. "Who was that that man in his nightshirt? What were you doing?"

Merlin slid back from the table. "You should always be up before sunrise. How are you doing these days, boy? I never see you anymore. It is high time I started teaching you Sanskrit. Every monastic should suffer through that."

"You saw me two days ago," said Arthur. "Every time I come by you are at court."

Merlin hobbled up to a standing position. "Alas, I must cede the point. But this morning, it will be different. I need you to assist me in a tour of the timbers we are harvesting for the drawbridge. I have arranged for it to be a cloudy day, so you need not worry about getting sunburned."

"Should you be walking?" said Uther. "I though you twisted your ankle?"

"Actually, I bruised my Achilles tendon stomping Satan into a molehill. Thus, I will require you and Sir Kay to transport me to the woodruff." Merlin extended his arm around Arthur's shoulder for support. Together they limped out into the courtyard.

Kay asked, "Are we going to carry him all day?"

"Bear in mind," said Merlin, "I am a much lighter burden than the armor you would be wearing this afternoon. A barrow is parked by the stable out front. That will be my stagecoach and you shall be my steeds: Argo and Bucephalus."

"I thought Argo was a dog?" said Arthur.

"And what a dog! You should have seen him pull a chariot."

* * *

A passing hay cart came to a sudden halt. Its wheels stopped moving, as did the flies buzzing around the snout of sweat-drenched cow, securely bolted in its yoke. She, however, licked her mouth with her pink leathery tongue.

Merlin hailed her. "Good day, Lady Gopi. If in fact that is who you are."

"Yes, this is me," said the cow. "Were you expecting someone else?"

"No," said Merlin. He patted her on the haunch. "I was expecting you to be you. The question is, are you in fact *you*."

"I am hoping that is a rhetorical question."

"Or," Merlin continued, "are you in actuality, a manifestation of my mental processes? Could it be that my store consciousness - which would be you - is engaged in a battle with my waking mind - which is me? Your weaponry is illusion, irrationality, and hallucination. My defenses are logic, fact, and mindfulness. Which side will prove victorious?"

"I am not sure I like this use of military metaphor. I have done you no violence. All I do is ask questions."

"Fair enough," said Merlin, "but even you must admit our relations have been adversarial. Clearly, my store consciousness and my waking mind are in conflict. Why is this? How can I solve this puzzle?"

The cow said, "You are confusing me."

"Ergo... I am confusing *me*."

"I cannot argue with that," said Gopi. She swished her tail. "Now then, the Goddess Ashera needs some clarification. It is clear from your testimony that the teachings of Brother Tinh Tu have had a profound influence on your world view. How did this come about?"

"When I first arrived at Nalanda University, I was assigned to the Persian dormitory. If I was sleeping and someone outside my room spoke Persian, I would bolt up and scream *rats*. Rather than install me in a madhouse, they let me room with the Chinese students. It was there that I learned to eat with sticks. The Chinese felt it was unsanitary to touch food and rude to cut it while dining."

"So, Brother Tinh Tu was Chinese?"

"No, but he came from a province east of India that was ruled by the Chinese. He told me it was coastal land of mountainous jungles. His people built houses from tubes of a tall woody grass. They raised bison that swam in the swamplands. His native tongue was Vietnamese."

Sweaty Gopi said, "I could stand a nice swim right now."

"Brother Tinh Tu's talent for languages led him to become well known as a child prodigy. Thus, he was sent to a monastery for further education. After his ordination, a clique of Vietnamese noblemen who hoped to establish their own monarchy, burned down the Chinese governor's harem, killing three of his infant sons. The governor responded by boiling three baby boys from every village. Tinh Tu called on all both sides to end the slaughter."

"Shall I assume," said Gopi, "Tinh Tu did not leave his home by choice."

"Not quite. One day he received an invitation to attend the University at Louyang in Northern China. It was delivered by a company of Chinese cavalry. Not being stupid, Tinh Tu let them escort him to Louyang. But when he arrived he pretended to be a half-literate Vietnamese bumpkin. Not knowing what to do with him, the university sent him off for schooling in India. I suspect they were hoping he would never come back."

"You were both world travelers," said Gopi.

"We were both rejects. But we did have some grand times together. Our instructor for Sanskrit grammar was the renowned Professor Kumarajiva. We use to call him *Ball Breaker*. His specialty was delivering skewering verbal jabs. We were not so much his students as his pin cushions."

"Well, you have been known to tease Arthur and Kay a bit too," said Gopi.

"After class, Old Ball Breaker served a stimulating drink brewed from the leaves of the *t'e* bush. He mocked me for being so fond of it. He said I should be forbidden to take *t'e* back to my homeland, for if I did, the population would become addicted and invade the Gupta Empire just to get a sip. The thought of tiny Britannia conquering mighty India gave us all a good laugh."

"That would be amusing."

"After I finished translating the Bible, Brother Tinh Tu was offered a post at Chien Kang University in central China, this time without the armed guards. He asked me to come with him. I told him I would be a poor model for any student. After all, I had come to the Buddha's Practice as an adult, having squandered my youth on mindless diversion. Tinh Tu reminded me that these were all traits I held in common with the Buddha. Within a month, we were climbing the Silk Road through the Himalayas."

Gopi asked, "Did you make it all the way to China?"

Merlin thought about the last time he saw Brother Tinh Tu. It was a spotty memory, as is common after catching multiple blows to the head. "Indeed," said Merlin, "we made it to China."

Chapter XX: The Hay Moon, AD 490

Timendi causa est nescire.

Ignorance is the cause of fear.

* * *

Arthur may have grown up among the trees of Merlin's forest compound, but he was equally at home at the bay market. Lacking aunts and uncles, he took instruction from a motley collection of coopers, cobblers, carters, and crockers. These merchants negotiated mercilessly, told predictable dirty jokes, and chipped in for a pine box and a widow's basket when one of their members could haggle no more.

Arthur had been what the locals called a *dock runt*. But now that he wore the cape of the king's soldiers, the name no longer fit. The vendors who saw him would smile and remark how tall he had grown, but they left it at that. After all, Arthur served the crown, the same crown who levied taxes, and beat you blue if you failed to pay them.

Still, Arthur enjoyed visiting his old haunt, if for no other reason than to drop in on Widow Blodwen.

"Just look at you!" she said to Arthur and Sir Kay. "All dolled up in your fancy uniforms." She wiped some loose scales off her hands with a tattered rag. "Back when I still had my looks," she said, "all the squires were queuing up to get a crack at me. I was all set to marry one of them, but the Saxons got him. He had thighs like wild ponies."

"These are just our regular clothes," said Kay. "Sir Illtyd sent us for the herring."

From behind her stall, Widow Blodwen rolled out a large clay pot. Its lid was tied shut with twine, as if something might pop out. "You lads can carry this, right?"

"Where is the other one?" said Arthur. "The steward told us there were two?"

"Aye," she said. "One of them went bad. You tell Sir Illtyd that I will make it up to him next month." She nudged Sir Kay. "You keep an eye on Arthur, here. That bounder stole a fish from me once: a four foot tuna!"

The clang of cowbells split the briny air. Two knights were ringing them. Behind these soldiers limped a bedraggled parade of people, young and old, draped in sackcloth. Arthur assumed they were beggars, till he noticed the dignity with which some of them walked. One was even a Roman with curly black hair, except for the blistered patches where his scalp had peeled off. Everyone cleared out of their way.

"Who are they?" said Arthur. "Where did they come from?"

Blodwen did not look up. "Lepers."

Kay asked, "What are they doing?"

"The king," said Blodwen, "he is shipping them off to a hostel. It happens from time to time."

Kay asked, "Where is it? Is it on an island?"

Arthur knew what a hostel was. Merlin told him all about them. They were large houses where knights rested after a journey, or recovered from a battle. Hostels were staffed by wounded veterans, whose injuries left them too lame to fight, but uniquely fit when it came to waging war on disease. As far as Arthur knew, there were no hostels in Britannia, and certainly none accessible by boat.

"Do they really need a bodyguard?" said Arthur. "Are they even well enough to go to sea?"

Widow Blodwen said nothing, nothing at all.

A barefoot girl, covered with red sores struggled to keep her balance.

Arthur asked, "Are they really going to a hostel?"

"Hush," said Blodwen. "The Dragons will hear you."

"Dragons are make-believe."

"She means those knights," said Kay. "They are with king's special unit."

"What makes them so special?"

Widow Blodwen smacked him with her rag. "Just let them pass."

Arthur crossed his arms. "The king should send those lepers up in the hills. No one lives there. The Saxons would be afraid of them. They could be like border guards. All they need is a place to live, right?"

The infected girl fell down. Her exhausted companions barely noticed. Arthur waited for someone to pick her up. No one did. He grabbed his rucksack.

"No!" cried Blodwen. She tried to stop him from marching off, but Sir Kay kept her back. Arthur helped the girl up to a sitting position. The baker's wife screamed, "Leper!"

"Are you all right?" said Arthur to the girl. "Are you thirsty?"

"Hungry," she said

Arthur retrieved an apple from his bag. For a brief moment, not only did his fears evaporate, but so did all of his thoughts. It was just him, the girl, and the apple. It almost seemed like this was the same apple Merlin had given to him so many years ago. Who did Merlin get it from? Where did the apple start? Was it Eve's? After she gave it to Adam, maybe he gave it to Cain?

Sir Cadwigan of the Dragons charged up. "Are you insane? Get away from her."

"She needs food," said Arthur. He gave her the apple. "Why did you let her lie here?"

Cadwigan shook his sword. "Step away esquire. That is an order."

Arthur uncorked his canteen. "After I give her a drink."

"I said now! You will kill us all."

Arthur rolled up the front of his blouse to reveal his belly, blotched with large white splotches. "Go ahead. Do you really want the blood from this gamey skin on your hands?"

Cadwigan half-stepped back, nearly tripping.

Arthur passed his canteen to the girl. "Here, drink this."

Widow Blodwen called out, "Uther, stop that!"

Cadwigan addressed her. "What is wrong with him?"

"Oh, he is just headstrong. Arthur, you let that girl be."

"Come on, Arthur," said Kay, "you will get sick."

"I think he already is," said Cadwigan. "What the devil happened to his stomach?"

Blodwen replied, "He was scalded when he was a baby. He is perfectly healthy, just a jackass. Get over here, boy!"

Arthur remained focused on the girl drinking his water. Although he heard the shouts being aimed in his direction, they seemed distant, like Germans on a far off hill, practicing their yodels at sundown. Merlin once said that when a monastic was deep in meditation, he could be slapped on the back with a strap and not even be aware of it. Was this what he meant?

Arthur corked his canteen. "As a knight," he said to Cadwigan, "I am honor bound to help her."

"Spare us the sermon, Father," said Cadwigan. He positioned himself behind the little girl, a good two paces behind, and shepherded her back to the rest of the group. "Ector is going to hear about this, squire. Now get out of my way."

Widow Blodwen latched onto Sir Kay's ear and gave it a good sharp twist. "Go back to your quarters and come back here with clean clothes for Arthur."

"Clothes?" said Kay. "What for?"

"I am going to dunk Arthur in a pot of lye, and burn everything he is wearing."

"What will I tell my sergeant?"

"You might start with the truth." She handed him the herring. "Make sure this gets delivered. And if it happens that you crack it, I will crack you even worse. Now, off you go."

Kay started to salute, then stopped himself. He hoisted the clay pot on his shoulder and took off.

Arthur untied the sides of his cassock. The rush of heroism was sinking away. All that was left was the inevitable month of latrine duty and a scowl from Ector, which would be more searing than all the insults he would get from his drill sergeant.

"I suppose I should thank you," he said to Blodwen. "Will Merlin find out about this?"

"Will he?" Her face flushed red, just a few shades shy of purple. Her neck puffed up like a bullfrog swallowing a cinder. "That was the most dangerous, half-witted stunt I have ever seen!" She pounded her heels on the cobblestones. "Who do you think you are, you bloody lunatic?"

Arthur knew that whatever answer he gave, even if it was just one word, would be monumentally wrong. He steeled himself, awaiting her next barrage. She would show him no mercy, which was what he deserved.

Widow Blodwen wiped away the sweat running down her face. "You are reckless hard-headed fool," she said, shaking her fist with every word. She sat down on her keg of salt with a thump. "And if was still a maiden," she said, her voice rising to near falsetto, "so help me God, I would marry you here on the spot."

Chapter XXI: The Hare Moon, AD 491

From quod non mortalia pectora coges, auri sacra fames.

What can you not bring men to do, miserable hunger for gold!

* * *

The royal dock was a fantastic waste of money. Merlin could testify to its exorbitant cost, because it was he who managed its construction. Since the days of Governor Constans, the Port of Carmarthen had functioned perfectly well with just three landings. But, the king wanted one of his own, located away from the others. And it had to be longer than the rest, which it was by four feet.

This new dock was to be used exclusively by the king's navy - which did not yet exist - and also for visiting ambassadors, none of whom ever arrived. Nonetheless, vessels did land there, albeit rarely, staying only long enough to pick up supplies. Everyone assumed they had something to do with the Dragons, but no one dared inquire.

Merlin's wagon stopped in front of a ship moored to the royal dock. Upon its planks paced a burly light-eyed knight. Like most of the population of Carmarthen, this soldier was an infant when Merlin first returned to Britannia.

Merlin climbed down off the passenger's side of his cart. He thanked the driver, then hailed the knight. "*Vale*. I was sent by Sir Gaius. I am supposed to conduct an inventory for the king's guards. Could you direct me to them?"

"That would be me," said the knight. "I am Sir Cadwigan."

"Cadwigan?" Merlin bowed. "I thought all the Dragons were Roman?"

Cadwigan did not return the gesture. "You thought wrong. Come this way."

Cadwigan plodded up the gangplank of the ship. Merlin followed. Up on deck was a young squire. The lad dutifully bowed, then slid a ladder down the hatch into the cargo hold.

Cadwigan climbed down. Merlin followed.

The moment Merlin touched his foot onto the uppermost rung, he became engulfed by the reek of sweat and stale urine. He ducked his head under the low ceiling that capped the dark musty room.

Before him sat a collection of Saxon females, all of them young. They were shackled together, except for the little girls, who were simply roped by the waist. In one corner rested a water bucket and waste pail, which was stained red, as were the loose skirts of those women who were old enough to menstruate. They had been in there for at least a month.

The clanking of an iron mast chain in the rigging above sounded all too much like the rattling door of a monkey cage. Merlin's heart fluttered.

He inhaled and tried to slow his mind. "Where did these wenches come from?" he asked with bureaucratic impassion. "How many are there?"

"I never counted them," said Cadwigan. He strolled down the aisle that separated the wide-eyed captives. "The king has been conducting raids on the coast. We are taking out one village at a time. Nobody knows about it, and that is how it is going to stay. We kill off the warriors and sell the breeders to the King Clovis."

"Why do you require my services?"

"We had a problem with the last shipment. We need you to write up a description of each one. That way we can be sure who all gets delivered."

"What does Clovis do with them?"

"Who cares? As far as I am concerned, he can grind them up for bait." With the tip of his boot, he kicked away a pile of brown pellets on the floor: rat dung.

While at Nalanda University, Merlin had learned that a core element of mindfulness was to see yourself in others. Their suffering is no different than yours. This was a precept one should to apply to all souls, even one's enemies.

Such a noble perspective usually required a great deal of effort. On this ship's hold, it was easy. Merlin had no need to intellectually appreciate these Germans' suffering. He knew what cold shackles felt like.

Merlin uncapped the leather tube that held his scrolls and pens. "I will need a plank to write on. And two more lamps."

"What for?"

"I am old. I cannot see in the dark. This cabin lacks sufficient illumination. If you prefer, we could haul them all on the deck?"

"Two lamps then," said Cadwigan.

"And be quick about it. This stench will ruin my cloak."

Cadwigan silently surveyed his captives, then crawled up out of the hold. The stomp of his boots reverberated across the boards above, then down the gangplank.

Merlin peeked out through a small high porthole like a wary field mouse scanning the clouds for falcons. He whispered, "*Wissen Sie Celtische?* Can any of you speak Celtic?"

A young girl tied to the bench raised her hand. "I can, Lord. I speak *Welschmann.*"

He asked her, "How did you get here?"

"The blue skins came and took us. It was night. They killed my brothers and took me and my cousin. She is over there." She pointed her sunburned hand at a young woman chained to the others. "She only speaks *Saxonische.*"

Merlin asked, "Blue men? Do you mean the Picts? Tell me girl, were those the ones who attacked you? Were they tattooed? Did they have spiky white hair? *War ihr Haar weiss?*"

"*Ja,*" said the girl's cousin, "*Schottischen mit weiss Haar.*"

"They took us to an island, Lord. Then the *Welshmann* outside put us on this boat."

Merlin rubbed his temples. "So, now I traffic in slaves, eh? There was no battle, was there?"

"The blue men took us."

Merlin slapped his hand on his thigh. "I am about to do something that is traitorously daft." He placed his hand on her shoulder and spun her around. "I cannot save your sisters here. Tell them that." He began to untie her knot.

"*Er sagt, dass er nicht Sie speichern kann,*" she said.

"But I can save you, girl. Can you swim?"

"Aye, Lord."

Merlin withdrew his sword, intending to quickly cut off the little girl's long ponytails so she would look like a boy. But as soon as his blade inched near to her neck, her cousin gasped. Old Merlin observed the sharp metal, so close to her youthful skin. His wrist began to shake.

"*Namo Tassa Bhagavato,*" he muttered to himself. He closed his eyes. Then he slit off her hair and said, "Girl, tell your cousin that I am going to help you escape, but I need her help. When I go up on deck, I will knock three times with my staff. When she hears that, she must start a fight. Then I will throw you overboard."

She translated the message.

He rustled her newly cut hair. "You must tell people you are a boy." He stuffed the shorn locks down his shirt. "Pretend your name is *Lailoken*. Find a river and walk up it until you are high in the hills. You will find your people there."

"Why me, Lord?" she said. "My cousin swims better."

Merlin recalled a day long ago when he was in the scribe's hall at Nalanda, translating the *Book of Exodus* into Sanskrit. He read the story in which God told Moses to lead the Israelites to freedom. Moses said, *No, Lord, please send someone else*. It seemed like a reasonable question. After all, why did God pick him? The Bible never explained it. Merlin decided to give the girl a straight answer.

"You are small," he said. "Your cousin is too big for me to smuggle out of here."

Merlin untied his purse from his belt. He dumped out it contents: two small apples and fifteen denarii. He tied the empty cloth sack around her shoulders, and said "Use this as your ruck sack." Into it he dropped the apples and four of the coins. "You can trade these bits of silver for food and shoes. One piece for each shoe, one piece for six loaves of bread, and once piece for a cloak." He slipped rest of his money into the ankle of his boot. "Never give anyone more than one at a time."

Merlin heard the jangle of spurred footsteps on the gangplank. He lifted up the back of his cloak. "Hide under here, girl. Hold onto my hips. Do not cry or make a sound."

Her cousin, who was able to hold back all but one tear, whispered, "*Drei Klopfen.*"

Merlin stuck his walking stick under his armpit. He gripped the handrails of the ladder, and hoisted himself up onto the first rung. The little girl let go and awkwardly slapped her bare feet on the flooring below. Perhaps this was *not* going to work.

But then the German girl extended her arms forward. She gripped the rung above Merlin's ankles and began to climb so that the top of her head hit him in the bum. This nudge was all he needed. Moving like a half-drunken spider, their eight limbs successfully negotiated up the ladder. Merlin's head emerged through the hatch. The esquire was no longer on the deck, but Sir Cadwigan was.

Merlin yelled, "What took you so long? It stinks down there." He tossed up his walking stick. It flew in Cadwigan's direction. The knight jumped back to avoid it. This diversion permitted the girl to scamper onto the deck. Merlin repositioned his cloak. The girl tucked herself beneath it.

Sir Cadwigan presented two lamps, one in each in each fist. "Here you go."

"Where is the other one?" Merlin bent over, stiffly, so as not to expose the girl. He picked up his stick and farted, but the little girl stayed still.

Cadwigan said, "You told me you needed two."

"No. I said three."

"That was not what you told me."

Merlin curled his knobby fingers around his staff. "I said three!" With each syllable he pounded it against the floor. From down below there was a screech followed by the crash of chains. The ship rocked.

"Blood hell!" Cadwigan put down the lamps. His assistant esquire on shore dashed up the gangplank. "In the hull," said Cadwigan. "Those bitches are at it again."

The two soldiers went below decks. Merlin heard punches and the slap of a belt, followed by shrieks of pain. It was a beating worthy of Pontius Pilate.

Merlin and his hidden charge shuffled backwards to the seaward side of the vessel. He unfurled his coat and propped the girl up onto the ship's railing. Her big blue eyes stared out at the sea.

He kissed her on the cheek, then tossed her into the bay. She landed with a splash, no bigger than a diving pelican.

Merlin checked to see if anyone on shore noticed. No one did. Crates and baskets fell into the water all the time. He checked once more. No one seemed to care. He said, "*Gah-tay, gah-tay, para gah-tay, parasam gah-tey, bodhi svaha.*"

He watched her swim off. Germans had a reputation for being lead-footed landlubbers who swam like three-legged dogs. But this little girl, she glided like a swan.

* * *

The screaming from below came to a sudden stop. The German girl floated motionless. Why was she stopping? Was she panicking? What was going on? Merlin's heart started pounding.

A dragonfly landed on the tip of his walking stick. "You certainly are having a full day," she said.

Merlin asked, "Is that you Gopi?"

"None other," she replied. "So, Lord Wizard, how does it feel to be a liberator?"

"Exhausting!" He sat down on the lid of a barrel. "I am reminded of a story," he said. "Brother Tinh Tu once told me about a student of the Buddha who requested permission to go into the hills and teach interbeing to the savages."

"Did the Buddha permit it?"

"Of course not, it was a crazy idea. The brutes would rip him to pieces. But the young man kept insisting. Eventually the Buddha caved in."

Merlin tugged a few times on his beard. "There was a very impressive moral to this tale, but for the life of me I cannot remember what it was. I hate forgetting things. *Mendacem oportet esse memorem.*"

"What happened to the Buddha's student?" said Gopi. "Did the wild men kill him?"

"No one knows. The story ends with him hiking up the Himalayas."

Merlin thought back to when he first climbed the Himalayas, a journey that ultimately ended in woeful Britannia, an island cut off from the civilized world. He wondered if the Buddha's student ended up like him, dressed like a barbarian, employed by a callous war lord, and unable to transmit the Way of Interbeing to anyone but a street urchin.

"You did the right thing," said Gopi. "Despite all the crimes the Germans have committed, that little German was innocent."

Merlin did not dispute the point. Freeing the Saxon girl was something of which he could be proud. Brother Tinh Tu would have approved.

"And yet," said Merlin to the dragonfly, "I cannot help but contemplate, how many of my friends her ax-wielding offspring may one day massacre."

Chapter XXII: The Winter Moon, AD 491

Libenter homines id quod volunt credunt.

Men gladly believe that which they wish for.

* * *

Merlin never much understood the draw of gems. What were they, other than glittering rocks? For him, they paled in comparison to the elegant beauty of a well rounded river stone, sculpted by the deft hand of *natura mater*.

When he was a lowly slave boy in Constantinople, Merlin heard the tale of Demosthenes, the venerated orator who would practice his recitations with a hand full of pebbles stuck in his cheeks. Merlin tried it once. He nearly chipped a tooth. His jaw was sore for a week.

Having survived this experience, Merlin determined it was best to deposit skipping stones into his purse, rather than into his person. During his years as the royal exchequer, he had compiled quite a collection of such rounded rubble. He used these as paperweights to hold down the stacks of invoices and dog-eared receipts piled high in his office chambers.

Upon each of these flat stones, Merlin penned a word in Sanskrit. Funding requests sent to him from the staff at the royal kitchen were kept under a stone marked with शांति signifying *contentment*. Invoices relating to the king's personal belongings were filed under भ्रांति, which would be translated as *delusion*.

Most people who visited Merlin's office assumed these Sanskrit words were astrological symbols, which was just fine. If Merlin was cast to play the part of the wizard, he would deliver his lines loud enough to be heard in the back of the amphitheater. It reminded Merlin of something James the street musician used to say: *The plebeians always ask for bread and circuses, but if you give them a good enough circus, they will go home and swear they just ate bread.*

Merlin, who sat cross-legged on the floor sifting through his papers, was interrupted by Sir Percival, a fit young officer with curls of dark blond hair.

"Your Excellency," said Percival, "are you ill?"

Merlin did not look up. "I am fine… albeit tangled in a Gordian knot of accountancy. I keep coming across documents written by one *Spadix of Exeter*. I have no idea who this chap is, but I am rather impressed with his talent for misrepresenting the facts."

Percival presented a scroll. "Here is a voucher for supplies requested by the Lady Morgan. Duke Ector thought you should approve it."

Merlin cracked the seal. "Baby sister needs provisions, eh?" He perused the document. "Ten bolts of silk? That is a rather exorbitant amount."

"I would not know, Sir."

"Wild Ethiopian fennel?" Merlin dipped his quill and crossed the request off the list. "By chewing on these seeds, a woman can fornicate with abandon and produce nary a bastard." He marked out another item, then a third. "I am only authorizing those purchases that are not excised. Make sure you get receipts in Latin with nice straight printing, none of that wobbly Frankish scribble."

Merlin handed back the parchment and returned to his spreadsheets. Sir Percival remained standing at attention.

Merlin said, "Is something on your mind soldier?"

Percival stammered, as if gathering his thoughts. "Is it wise to eliminate so many items? It might disturb the Lady. There are those who say she has unique abilities, if you get my drift."

"Are you saying my sister is a witch?"

"Not at all, Sir. She is an upstanding Christian." Percival checked that the hallway was empty. "They say she has in her possession a magic grail. None but Morgan can touch it without being stung."

Merlin opened his mouth, ready to launch an armada of rants, but chose a more diplomatic tack, simply saying, "That little snot, she stole my act! And where exactly did she procure this mystic soup tureen?"

"They say it is the vessel that Joseph of Aramathea used to collect the sweat of Christ. Anyone who drinks from it can restore a corpse to life."

"And Lady Morgan bought it at auction?"

"Why no, she inherited it from her mother. As I understand it, her family comes from a village that was founded by Mary Magdalene."

This was a story Merlin had heard before, far too many times. He could never understand how anyone could believe that a peasant prostitute from Judea sailed all the way around the boot of Italy with a rather spectacular cup, which, for some inexplicable reason, none of the thirteen disciples felt was noteworthy enough to use, hold on to, or document in their writings.

Merlin put his pen down with a slap. "That," he said, "is hogwash."

"But they say she was heavy with child. According to the Parisians, it was the Savior's child. That is why she had to flee."

"Well if she was pregnant, then of course she would want to climb on a boat and shack up with a bunch of Frenchmen." Merlin hoisted himself to his feet. "Charlatans have been spreading variations of this fiction for decades. It is simply untrue. Every nation claims to be descended from one of the apostles."

"But Sir, I have met learned men who will testify to it."

Merlin slid over his copy of the Bible. "I have read the Old and New Testament extensively, and I assure you there is no mention of any punch bowl, chafing dish, or other erstwhile piece of dinner ware being passed around by the folks at Golgotha."

"But they say…"

Merlin shook his quill. "If I hear you say *they say* one more time, I shall crack you on the head with my own flagon, which is quite secular, but will nonetheless cause welts to arise upon your scalp as if by supernatural design."

Percival bowed his head. "I meant no offense, Sir."

"Good Sir Percival," said Merlin, "you are a brave young man with a kind heart, and I would gladly stand shoulder to shoulder with you in battle. However, when it comes to matters of critical evaluation, you are a gullible bumpkin of the highest magnitude. The civilized mind accepts only those facts that can be directly observed. It is called *empiricism*."

"I am not familiar with that term."

"Well, you should make a study of it. This grail upon which you are fixated is a flight of fancy. You should not waste your time with it." Merlin sorted a pile of notes into a stack. "Now, be off with you."

Percival bowed, albeit awkwardly, and left the room.

Merlin retrieved an errant receipt that had slipped out of its assigned pile. The text was rather small. He searched for his glass disc. It was still on the floor. Once again he got down on all fours. A small white owl with clipped wings hooted in the doorway.

"A harbinger of wisdom," he said to the owl. "Come to come to enlighten a poor fool, have you?"

Instead of responding, the bird scampered back down the hall. Merlin went back to work, until he heard a woman sneeze.

"I overheard your conversation with Sir Percival," said Lady Morgan. Her silky red braids were intertwined with golden ribbon. "I am pleased to hear that I am not a witch." She sauntered into the room. "Have you seen my pet owl? She seems to have wandered off."

Merlin replied, "Was she an Indian noblewoman working as a court reporter on behalf the Goddess Athena?"

Instead of answering, Morgan unleashed her dazzling smile. "You know, Ambrosius, you and I are not that different. You stumbled into notoriety your way. I took another route."

Merlin detected a whiff of perfume, lilac. "I stumbled." He returned to his accounting. "You dove."

"Fool yourself if you wish. You could have found some unassuming work in the countryside. Instead you set your sights on Paris. I saw you old man, you loved performing. James may have been a master harpist, but you were the one playing the crowd."

When Merlin was in India, he read a legend about Mara, a yellow-haired red-skinned demoness, prone to sensuality, and fits of joy and sadness. Ananda, the Buddha's attendant, once saw her on the road, and tried to frighten her away. But the Buddha, who was willing to face all facets of the universe, invited her to have a seat. It was as if he was saying, *Show her in, Ananda, she has an appointment.*

Merlin slapped his hands on his knees. "Is there anything of substance you wish to discuss?"

Morgan picked up a pen and flicked its feather. "I do not wish to be your enemy. Never did."

"Then you should not have told lies about me. By the way, my name is Mer-*then*."

"To be honest - Mister *Poop* - I thought you were dead. We all did. When you shipped out with a keel of Germans, we figured they would boil you for *Fasnacht*."

"They tried. Turned out I was all gristle."

She almost laughed. "Where did you get that pale boy? That was kind of you to let him pawn my bracelets."

"Carmarthen," said Merlin. "When his mother died, I hired him to pick apples. It seemed the economical thing to do."

"You had mercy on him. You saved him from a life of misery."

"And your point is?"

Her green eyes locked onto his. "Nobody saved me. Perhaps I had to slander you, but if you were in my place, you would have done the same."

Back in Paris, it pained Merlin to watch Little Morgan whoring herself off to the drunks at the Inn of the Fountain. He assumed his strong empathy for prostitutes was due to his own close call.

As a boy, Merlin nearly got buggered by a trade minister, who was staying the night at the house of Merlin's master. The visiting gentleman discretely crept into his Merlin's bed chamber and told him to stand and lift up his bed shirt.

Being clumsy, Merlin knocked over a table. The noise woke up Judith. When she shuffled down the hall, the would-be assailant fled.

Merlin scratched his chin. "If I am a showman, so be it. But when I lie, I lie to protect the weak."

"So you are an ethical liar?" She opened a scroll on the table and gave it a quick scan. "Which one of us is pretending now?"

"Correct me if I am mistaken," said Merlin, "but I have noticed you have a tendency to gravitate towards only the fair few whom Jupiter loves. Of course, poverty has never been fashionable, has it?"

"You have worked for as many kings as I have." She stepped towards the exit. "Assuming Vortiger actually was a king. And as far as worldly goods are concerned, it is not I who sits in the royal counting house. The word *opportunist* comes to mind."

"Guilty as charged. But let me ask you this, when you die, what works will you leave behind? What will people say of you?"

"They will say I forged my own destiny."

"While the rest of the world starved."

"And you Lord Exchequer, how many souls have you fed?"

He clasped his hands together. "Just me and the boy. Although lately, he seems to be the one feeding me. Either way, an orphan gets a meal."

"How droll. And what a fine way to divert the conversation."

He picked up the stone marked परिग्रह for *acceptance*. "I am guilty of many things," he said, "but you can never accuse me attempting to deaden myself from suffering, either that which I have caused, or that which has shaped me. Through my many missteps and blunders, I have come to witness my pain. When I cradle it like a foundling baby, only then can I calm its raging."

She chuckled. "I am beginning think they were right about you. You have gone balmy." She disappeared down the corridor, much like the owl. Her silk ribbons trailed behind her.

Chapter XXIII: The Growing Moon, AD 492

Video barbam et pallium; philosophum nondum video.

I see a beard and a cloak, but I do not see a philosopher.

* * *

Sir Ector set forth that no soldier under his command was ever to be seen sitting down while uniform, at least not in public. At first, Arthur did not understand the rationale behind this policy, but that all changed as he rose through the ranks. Just as a red-frocked bishop must always be godly, so a breast-plated fighting man must always be ready, and thus forever on his feet.

Field Marshall Ector explained it this way: *There are two kinds of knights. Those that are standing, and those that are dead.*

As a result, Sir Kay had little choice but to stand, perhaps with an occasional lean, at his post outside the harbor master's house. It was light duty, suitable for an esquire. But if said esquire performed it well, he might get to accompany the harbor master on his rounds. That was a plum assignment. The vendors were prone to offer gifts, and the ship captains always kept a rich supply of bribes.

Sir Kay's glazed-over eyes were aimed at the docks, but focused on nothing.

Arthur snapped his fingers to get his attention. "Ahoy, young laggard, I am here to relieve you."

Kay yawned. "Tell me, Arthur, why are there so many ugly girls around here? All we got is bags of bones. How come we never get any with meat on them?"

"Maybe they just run away when they see you. Anything to report?"

"They got cider for sale down by the white smith's."

"Nothing happened then?"

"A fat man tried to beg some onions off me. How does a beggar get fat? And why did he think I had onions? It makes no sense."

Old Missus Heulwen, shaking with palsy, struggled by with a cane in one hand. In the other, she held a sheet of inscribed parchment.

"Is that a bulletin?" said Arthur.

Kay replied, "I saw the rag-and-bone man with one just like it. Why would old Hopcyn have that? He can barely talk let alone read."

A bayside gust blew the paper from the old woman's unsure fingers. It floated up then snagged in a plug of cattails sprouting from a mud patch. Once the wind had calmed, the scroll slipped down the plant's long leaves, destined for the gooey muck by its roots. Arthur bounded over and caught it in mid-fall.

Arthur scanned the document. It was written in formal Latin script.

> *"To Protarchus from Ptolemaeus. Protarchus and Ptolemaeus agree that they have come together to share equally in the ownership of a vineyard covering twent- acres located in Campania, south of the River Sarno, and that Ptolemaeus agrees to transplant not less that one hundred and fifty grape vines, grown from seed..."*

"Bless you," said Missus Heulwen. "You saved my prayer. I say, are you the boy with the spots? What is it they call you?"

"My name is Arthur."

"Oh forgive me, I though you were Master Uther. You look so much like him."

Sir Kay snickered.

Arthur rolled up the scroll and inserted it snugly into the sleeve of her blouse. He asked, "Did you get this from a book?"

"No, a monk. He is hocking them down at Saint Clear's dock, three for a denarius." She winked her eye. "I bought me a prayer to Saint Jude. With my grandson's breathing troubles, it will be a good to have one. I know my saints!"

Arthur asked, "A monk was selling prayers? Who is he?"

"A Frank. Charming fellow. Bit lame. Calls himself Pollox. The archbishop of Paris sent him over to raise funds for crippled children. Rather kind of the archbishop to be thinking of us."

"Do you need help getting home?" said Arthur. "We could escort you."

"Not today, lads." She waved goodbye. "I got Jude watching my back."

As soon as she was out of ear shot, Kay whispered, "Her grandson died few months ago. I knew him. He was sick for a long time."

Arthur fingered the handle of his sword. "I think you and I should go see this monk."

"You have to stand post. I can go talk to him if you want."

Arthur pivoted on his heels and marched away.

Kay called out, "Where are you going?"

"That was no prayer. It was a contract. This is a sham. Missus Heulwen told us the monk was named Pollox. *Pollox* is Latin for *thumbs*. What kind of monastic would call himself Brother *Thumbs*?"

Kay ran up behind. "Maybe we should report him to the harbor master?"

A modest crowd was chattering down at Saint Clear's. Some had sheets in their hands. The rest were busy cutting deals to raise the cash needed to make a purchase.

"Do you have a prayer to Saint Nicholas?" said old Missus Tiwlip. "My son is a sailor. I worry with all those Germans in the channel."

"A grave concern," said Thumbs. The right sleeve of his monk's robe was rolled up to the elbow. He shuffled through his box of papers. His stunted left arm hung in a sling. "I could have sworn we had a few prayers to Saint Nick, but they seem to be all out. Quite popular with the mariners, of course."

Tiwlip slouched her shoulders. "I suppose Saint Christopher would do."

Thumbs dug down to the bottom of the pile. "Let me look one more place." He pulled out a sheet. "Here we go, the last one."

She pressed it against her breast. "God bless you, brother."

He winked at her. "You are having a lucky day, Madam."

Arthur cupped his hands over his mouth and called out. "Do you have a prayer to Saint Siddhartha?"

Thumbs rubbed his chin. "Who is he the patron of?"

"Drummer boys and runaways. He carries a walking stick with a swan carved at the end."

"Oh him!" said Thumbs. "I think I *may* have one."

Arthur grinned at Kay. The two of them stood behind Thumbs.

"Here it is," said Thumbs. "Rather an unusual item, this."

Arthur whispered, "I have a dagger at your back and I can read. What say we take a walk over to the baker's stall?"

Thumbs stood up as straight as his crooked spine would let him. He announced, "I am going to have a chat with these fine fellows. Checking my license. Nobody go anywhere, this will just take a moment." He limped off flanked by the emboldened esquires.

"Those are not prayers," said Arthur.

"Lads," said Thumbs, "I cleared this with the harbor master. You should speak with him."

"We work for Sir Ector," said Kay.

Thumbs reached into his purse. "I did not realize that was the arrangement." He dug out two coins. "How about a nice silver denarius for the two of you?"

"You think we can be bought?" said Arthur. "We are in training to be knights. You have to give them back their money."

Arthur's face beamed. He had the hunchback just where he wanted him. This was going to work out perfectly. Come tomorrow, Arthur would gather his friends in the esquire's hall, and describe in great detail how he unmasked the scoundrel and forced him to return his booty.

Thumbs popped the coins back into his purse. "So," he said, "you are a moralist then? Tell me Father Augustine, what am I doing that is wrong?"

"You are impersonating a monk," said Kay.

"Not really. A monk passes around a collection plate and gives nothing in return. Me, I am selling hope. Who else would let these villagers buy a little chunk of heaven? Look at them. You will never see them this happy in church."

Arthur had to admit, it was like a festival.

"You are lying to them," said Kay.

"There is a long queue for that, and I am far at the back if it. Tell me good squire, where did you get that cape? Who bought your shiny dagger? It was those peasants and their taxes. Can you honestly say your armaments make them feel any happier?"

If Merlin were here, he would know what to say, but Arthur did not.

"Some young mother has a dying child," said Thumbs. "I cannot save it, and neither can you. But at least I can make her feel like she tried. She scrubbed a floor all week just so she could earn enough to buy this piece of paper. What is a prayer, anyway? Just a bunch of Roman words nobody understands."

Arthur's first thought was to haul the grifter away. But then again, how could he tell all those people that their prayers were nothing but a con?

Kay kicked a stone on the ground. "There is no point is taking him to the harbor master."

Arthur stuck his dagger back in its sheath. He let it drop with a clink. "True," he said. He tugged a few times on the sparse whiskers of his beard. Behind him, Baker Pryderi was pounding on a powdery mass of dough.

"Mister Pryderi" said Arthur, "how much bread can you bake today? What would it cost for me to buy all of it?"

The baker wiped his hands on his apron. "I got two bushels of flour. If I can find some more eggs I could probably get you twenty dozen loaves. That would set you back fifteen denarii, assuming you got that kind of change."

Arthur snatched Thumbs's purse and threw it over to Pryderi.

"Give that back!"

Arthur jumped up onto a wool bundle and released a long sharp whistle.

"Excuse me," he said to the crowd. "Brother Pollox has just informed me that because today is the Feast of Saint Gautama, he will be distributing fifteen dozen loaves of bread as a gift to all of his customers. What say we give the good brother a round of applause?"

A cheer rang out.

"You little *Welsch* bastard," muttered Thumbs. "That will eat up half of my profits!"

Arthur hopped down from his perch. "Brother Pollox, I fear it would be irresponsible if we let this rabble to get out of hand. I am going to have to insist that Sir Kay and I stand guard, so as to assist you with your charitable work. Would you not agree, Sir Kay?"

"Aye," said Kay, "that sounds like an excellent idea."

BOOK VI: THE PRAGMATIST

CHAPTER XXIV: THE CORN MOON, AD 492

Tantum religio potuit suadere malorum.

So potent was religion in persuading to evil deeds.

* * *

Aside from the king, the largest landowner in the Carmarthen's shire was the church. Soon after Bishop Zephyrinus arrived from Gaul, he consecrated extensive tracts of land for new burial grounds, despite the fact that the existing cemeteries were not even half full. Most of this sanctified pasture was so hilly, even the Romans never bothered to plow it.

Having amassed this estate, Father Zephyrinus acquired an impressive flock of sheep, and even accepted the services of a stud ram as donations. The wool his acolytes harvested was some of the finest in Britannia, and its sale financed the bishops' pilgrimages to Paris, which he took every other year departing on the last full moon of summer, and returning for Good Friday.

Under Zephyrinus's management, the flock grew. After additional fields were donated by the king, the bishop offered penitents the option of maintaining the roads throughout these properties. As a result, Merlin's wagon wheels hit scant few potholes as it rolled past ewes, munching on the autumn grass.

Steering the wizard's horse-drawn cart was Tristan, a pale-skinned esquire sporting the red-blond hair of his grandfather, Sir Ector. The king had ordered Tristan to guard Merlin's person, at all times, even at night. This arrangement was part of the king's overall effort to keep an eye on the wily old man.

Behind the ridgeline, a spire of smoke coiled up into the afternoon sky. "Towards that conflagration," said Merlin to his driver.

"Aye, Sir," said Tristan. He cracked the whip, and they creaked up the crest of the hill.

A crowd was milling about next to a large stack of logs. It was not yet ablaze, but a nearby stoking fire was. A sturdy fence rail had been erected in the center of the wood pile. Tied onto this makeshift post was a young woman, naked from the waste up. She was one of the prostitutes that worked the bay market. Merlin recognized her. She grew up an orphan.

He called out, "Who is in charge? Was this woman tried?" Tristan brought their vehicle to a stop.

Sir Gawain, a wiry freckled knight with an offset broken nose, saluted. "I am the officer on duty. His Grace Bishop Zephyrinus passed judgment on her."

"Did the bishop interview her? Where is he?"

Gawain lifted up a scroll. "He left it to his secretary. It is all written up in here. Feel free to check it."

"What was her crime? Where are the witnesses?"

"She drowned her infants in a bucket: two of them, one newborn. Three people saw her pull the toddler from the pail." Gawain pulled off his gloves. "Go ahead, ask her."

Merlin climbed up onto the pyre as close as he could get to the accused. In a low voice he said, "Miss, I am about to do something that may appear daft." Then he said, "Tell me the truth, did you dispatch your children?"

The prostitute's eyes darted around with no focus. "I am a bride of Satan."

"Be that as it may. Did you slay those babies?"

She thrashed back and forth. "Aye!" she screeched, "it was me!"

Once, while Merlin was first studying the Buddha's Precepts, he accidentally stepped on a caterpillar. The heel of his sandal crushed its hind quarters leaving the rest of it wriggling in the hot Indian sun. Did the Precepts direct him to smash it and end its pain, or leave it there, so that it might be eaten by a song bird in need of nourishment? Which would cause less suffering?

Merlin addressed the villagers from his pulpit of tinder. "This woman has committed murder, and the laws of His Majesty the King are quite specific as to the penalty for a capitol offence. This woman shall be hanged."

No one dared dispute his proclamation, but there was some whispering.

Still standing by the pyre, Sir Gawain said, "Bishop Zephyrinus sentenced her to burn."

"And she shall be, after she is executed. That fact that she is a witch does not relieve her of civil punishment."

"What?"

"The king is the sovereign, Sir, not the bishop. If you take issue with my reading of the legal code, I would be more than happy to let the king decide which of us is correct."

The prostitute whimpered, "I must burn."

"All in good time," said Merlin. He nudged Gawain with his staff. "Go loop a rope in that tree."

Gawain tucked his gloves in his belt. "I have no idea why you are doing this. But I know when I am outranked." He untied the knots that held the prostitute in place.

"Young Lady," said Merlin, "your victims are now in heaven. Is that correct?"

"I had to protect them. I am bound for hell."

"A common malady. Nonetheless, would you like to join your children? If you admit to your transgressions, you can join them in the hereafter."

Gawain snapped his finger, and his esquire led his horse over to the condemned. The two of them hoisted her onto its saddle, a clumsy affair given that her arms were still bound at the wrists.

"I need a Bible." Merlin scanned the crowd. "Come now, this is a witch burning, one of you must have one." A young lady produced a dog-eared copy. Most of the Old Testament was missing.

Sir Gawain hopped off the wood pile. He mounted his horse and rode up next to the prostitute.

A toothless old woman offered up her apron. "Drape this over her eyes," she said.

That Gawain did, using the strings to secure it like a sack placed on her head. His esquire tossed him a rope. At one end, Gawain tied a noose. He threw the other end over a tree branch.

Merlin pushed the Bible toward the prostitute's trembling hands. "Do you confess?"

She began to weep. "Do not let me touch it. It will burst into flame."

"Do you actually think," said Merlin, "that the Lord of Abraham, who breathed life into Adam, could be intimidated by lowly sinners like us?" He slapped the book into her palm and cried out, "*Apage Satanas!*"

Her entire torso trembled.

"Do you," he said, loud enough for everyone to hear, "believe in God the Father Almighty, who crafted the heaven and the earth? Aye or nay?"

"Aye."

"And in Jesus Christ his only Son our Lord, who was conceived by the Holy Ghost; was born to the Virgin Mary; suffered abuse from Pontius Pilate; was crucified till he died; and was subsequently entombed?"

Some of the village folk fidgeted. "Is he praying?" asked one of them under his breath. Another answered, "No, it is not Latin."

"Whereupon," said Merlin, "he descended into hell. Then on the third day, he rose from the dead and rose into heaven, where he now sits at the right side of God the Father Almighty, and judges both the living and dead. Do you have faith in the Holy Ghost, the holy universal church, the communion of the saints, the forgiveness of sins, and the resurrection of the flesh to a life without end?"

The witch did not reply.

"Well woman, do you or do you not?"

She hunched forward. The rope drew taught around her neck. The front of the cloth covering her head was saturated with tears. With her bound hands, the prostitute made the sign of the cross. "I do."

"In that case," said Merlin, "*in nomine Patris et Filii et Spiritus Santi*, you are forgiven."

With his right hand, he raised the pointed end of his staff a foot above the horse's rump, and prepared to jab. His wrist began to shake, harder than ever before. He struggled to keep control of his arm. Why was it so hard to execute the prostitute? After all, she was guilty. He was giving her what she wanted.

He chanted, "*Gah-tay, gah-tay, para gah-tay, para sam gah-tay, bodhi svaha.*" With his left hand, the hand around which his rosewood beads were strung, he clutched the horse's tail. He yanked at it with all his might.

The horse bolted. The prostitute jolted backward off the saddle. There was a clearly audible snap from the cracking of the vertebras in her neck. She shivered a bit, swung from front to back, then went limp.

* * *

Merlin had to close his eyes, but instead of seeing nothing, he saw the dark brown face of Aethiops the Centurion, a broad shouldered man, who always grinned but never showed his teeth. Aethiops used to tell his troops that they had the best damned job in the world. Who else gets paid to ride horses all day? And yet somehow, that proud warrior ended up with his neck slit by a skinny red-haired drummer boy. A brave man extinguished by a coward.

* * *

Merlin wiped the perspiration from his forehead. His shaking arm was calm, but it was flushed and tingled. Almost inaudibly, Merlin said, "Light her up."

With one swift stroke of his sword, Gawain cut the rope from which the lifeless corpse now dangled.

Merlin simply wandered off. He rested himself beneath an oak tree. Above him, the branches stretched out like the loving arms of a mother. Throughout his life Merlin found comfort in trees. He had no idea why. When he read in the *Pali Cannon* that the Buddha had achieved interbeing under the shade of a bo tree, it seemed perfectly reasonable.

Back at Nalanda University, Brother Tinh Tu once presented a linguistic study in which he documented that the bo tree was known as *the wisdom tree* long before the Buddha was born. Tinh Tu proposed that the story of bo tree might be little more that an old pagan legend some historians mistook for the truth.

Merlin became furious with Tinh Tu for questioning the veracity of the *Pali Cannon*. Tinh Tu countered that as long as humankind benefited from the Buddha's Practice in the here and now, who cared where he sat?

Merlin smelled the scent of smoke. He had been so occupied mulling over his argument with Tinh Tu, that he did not notice Gawain and his squire laying the prostitute onto the pyre. They curled her up like a sleeping child, then touched their torches to her skirt.

An inchworm spiraled down from a strand of silk and landed on his shoulder. Instead of brushing it off, he said, "Gopi?" The worm said nothing because worms cannot talk.

No one cheered. The flames licked higher, transforming flesh and bone to ash with god-like efficiency. The air was scented with the odor of cooked meat. Layers of skin and sinew blistered and popped. Fat dripped into the embers. One by one, the villagers shuffled on home.

When Merlin was in China, he and Brother Tinh Tu cremated the dean of the University at Chien Kang. They could not find dry wood, so they stripped the thatch off houses left deserted by the famine. After the pyre got to burning, scores of Chinese peasants add their dead relatives to it. It turned into a day-long bonfire. The dry bones on the bottom fueled the corpses on the top.

Merlin rose from his resting spot. He returned to the site of the holocaust. Gawain and his squire were warming themselves by its embers.

"At harvest time," said Merlin, "the citizens of Rome ate a meal at the graves of their parents."

"Did they?" said Gawain.

Merlin leaned on his staff. "That is why the Romans punished traitors by burning them. Petty thieves got nailed to a beam so that the rats and wild dogs would run off with the remains. If there was nothing left to bury, the crook's family would have no tomb to visit. For decades after a man was crucified, his children would be punished."

The fire snapped. A log tumbled down. With it came a small piece of off-white kindling. It was a rib.

Merlin tossed it back in. "The Jews," he said, "regarded crucifixion as unsanitary. Their purity laws forbid them to have contact with human blood, let alone some sad lot decaying on a stick. That is why the Hebrews stoned their criminals. It is a clean execution."

The fire finally subsided. The sun was going down.

"In much of the Orient," said Merlin, "cremation is accepted as a high honor. Internment is also eschewed by Zoroastrians. They expose their dead to the vultures, so as to permit the body to rejoin with the cycle of nature."

Gawain's squire got onto his saddle. Sir Tristan took a leak, then readied the bridles of his horse.

"Will that be all, Sir?" said Gawain.

Merlin shook the dust from his cloak. "Yes, thank you." He climbed onto his wagon. "I will commend you and your squire to the king for your professional demeanor this afternoon."

Gawain stuck one foot into his stirrup. A puzzled, almost childlike look came across this face. Merlin rarely saw that in a military man.

"Wizard," said Gawain, "how could it be that Jesus was crucified? If the Jews killed him, he should have been stoned?"

* * *

Gawain and his horse stood perfectly still.

The inchworm, still on Merlin's shoulder, said, "Amaterasu the Sun Goddess, would like to know what happened when you arrived in China?"

Merlin replied. "As soon as Brother Tinh Tu and I crossed the Himalayas, we found a throng of refugees fleeing for the mountains. Our Sherpas warned them they would freeze, but they said it was better than starving. When we crossed the border into Southern China, we found utter chaos. The Yangtze River had overflowed. Crops failed. Generals and governors fought endless wars.

The peasant said the emperor had lost the Mandate of Heaven. They were terrified."

"What did you do?"

"We trekked to the City of Chien Kang, but the University was deserted. When we finally located the dean, he was emaciated. He had previously served as a tutor to a prince in Northern China, so he suggested we go there. The next day the dean dropped dead. We carried his passport with us, hoping it would give us safe travel, which it did for a few weeks. Then we got arrested."

"What for?"

"The emperor had a wizard named Kou Chien Chi. He was a Taoist xenophobe, who claimed that all of Northern China's misfortunes were caused by Southern Chinese spies and non-Taoist infidels." Merlin tugged on the orange kerchief around his neck. "Tinh Tu got wind of this, so he made us to tear up our saffron monastic robes, and wear only a kerchief beneath our clothes. He wanted us to blend in. I rubbed soot into my hair to make it look black."

"How did you escape?"

"We did not. They bolted us in shackles and paraded us around the palace grounds. As soon as we entered the royal chamber, one of the emperor's eunuchs aimed his long painted fingernail at me and cried, *Xiongnu!*"

"What is a Xiongnu?"

Simply hearing Gopi say the word *Xiongnu*, was all Merlin needed to set him ruminating on the past.

He recalled the eunuch's first punch, an unexpected blow to his lower back. He fell to the floor. A kick to his groin doubled him over. One of the eunuchs withdrew a saber. Tinh Tu lunged forward to protect his fallen brother. In the process, Tinh Tu was struck in the neck. The last thing Merlin saw before passing out, was a pool of blood expanding across the ornate tiled floor.

"You were fortunate to have met Tinh Tu," said Gopi. "Most people have never had such a friend."

Merlin cleared his throat. "Interesting. That is the very sort of thing Tinh Tu would have said."

Chapter XXV: The Storm Moon, AD 493

Habent sua fata libelli.

Books have their fate.

* * *

Most of the old cabinets stored in the harbor master's office were moldy, broken, or both. There was one box however, that had always kept its contents dry. It was sealed with tar, lined with a layer of tin, and polished with mercury to keep the bugs out. Within this container, the habitually drunken former harbor master kept a unique collection of texts. It was his stash of pornography.

This library of erotica sat unopened until Merlin stumbled upon it. Like any other archival papers, Merlin saw fit to evaluate them. What he found was a survey of sketches depicting grinning idiots from throughout the civilized world, engaged in unrealistic acts of acrobatic copulation. Was he surprised? No. The streets of Carmarthen teemed with sailors eager to bribe a lowly bureaucrat.

What these fine calfskin parchments lacked in moral guidance, they more than made up for in durability. Never being one to stomach waste, Merlin bleached the ink off of them. He bound them onto a book, with a thick black cover scavenged from an ox hide saddle bag. Upon each even page, he penned in a grid of rows and columns. The odd pages were reserved for commentary.

Merlin, sitting at the desk of the newly appionted harbor master, ran his finger along a row of numbers. "You have listed the contents of the ship," he said, "but no assessment? Why are all these spaces blank?"

"There was no value," said Harbor Master Galfrid, a balding former novitiate with a close cropped beard. He had a tattoo of a turtle on his arm, a throwback his former life as a pilot on Carmarthen Bay.

Merlin tapped the page. "How can a ship full of wine be of no value? Did they pour it into the bay? They had to have sold something."

"No sir, they bartered. No money was involved. There was no figure to enter."

Outside, a pair of seagulls cawed.

"But I told you," said Merlin, "this book needs to inventory every vessel that lands in Carmarthen. If no currency is exchanged, you must record an estimate."

"Beg your pardon, Sir, but there is no way I can keep track of that. Most of the deals at the bay market are contracted between *Welshmen*. They just trade."

Merlin chomped his teeth. "Firstly, the hard working folk at this market are *Britons*! If I ever hear you using that that Germanic slur again, I shall thrash you to the bone. Secondly, the point of this exercise is to estimate the value of goods. I need to know the total volume shipped each month. Not just some of it."

Arthur rapped his knuckles against the front door, which had been propped open to let in the midday sun. His head nearly touched the top of the doorway.

"Ah, there you are boy," said Merlin.

"Do you need me for anything?" said Arthur. "Can I wait outside?"

"I suppose. There is shade in here. You will burn in that sun."

"I will be outside then." Arthur propped himself against the hitching post out front, then slid down to a sitting position and wedged a piece of sedge grass between his teeth.

"That boy is always moping," said Merlin. "What has gotten into him?"

"A lad of his age gets a little touched in the head," said Galfrid. "As soon as my sons got whiskers, I had to throw a slop bucket on them just to get them out of bed."

"Fascinating. But I digress. You must keep better records, Galfrid. I chose you for this position specifically so that the young boys passing by the head house could see a Briton just like them, reading and writing. You are an example. I expect more of you."

"I know, Sir. But you have to understand, my inspectors never enforced the shipping code before. They barely know which end of a quill goes down."

Merlin could not dispute this sad assessment. Aside from himself and Galfrid, whose rampant spelling errors made his blood boil, everyone working at the port was illiterate. Merlin wanted to establish a competent bureaucracy, but where was he supposed to find good bureaucrats? This was not India, nor China. And it certainly was not Rome. After all, Rome was no longer Rome.

"We need consistency," said Merlin. "Shippers do not mind paying a tariff as long as it hits them all the same." He closed the ledger. "If you need more men, tell me. And if it happens that your deputies cannot perform their duties, feel free to sack them. I know you are trying, Galfrid, but you must try harder. This is not glorious work, but it can save our nation like no battle can."

"Aye, Sir." Galfrid rolled out a docking schedule. "There is one more matter. We have a ship sailing under a Frankish flag that is acting rather queer. The captain is a Roman Spaniard."

"What has he done?"

"Nothing. He has neither loaded nor unloaded. He landed here in February on his way to Hibernia. Then he returned just after the *Kalendae* of March, claiming he got stuck in a storm, yet his ship showed no damage. Now he is back, destined for Gaul. He just lands and sails."

"He does not wish for the stevedores to see what he is carrying. He better not be trafficking in boys. Is he still here?"

"Aye. He is moored to Saint Catherine's Dock. If he is shipping weapons to the Scots, I will have to call for backup. Can I get your approval to gather a posse?"

"No need for that. I have a knight at the ready." Merlin slipped on his cloak and shouted. "Domesticus! I have a job for you."

Arthur, not bothering to stand up called back. "A job? What kind of job? Will it take long?"

"Excuse me Sir," said Galfrid, "I meant a real soldier."

"He will do." Merlin retied his belt. "*Vale*, and good day, Galfrid. Remember, the Black Book of Carmarthen must hold everything you see or hear. It is your Bible. Cherish it."

"As you wish, Sir. But as soon as you leave, I am going to send for a proper knight."

"Then he will have to catch us." Merlin puffed up his chest and marched out toward the docks. Using the bird-beak end of his walking staff like a grappling hook, he dragged Arthur along by the collar of his blouse.

Arthur shook himself free. "Where are we going? I thought we were supposed to buy ink."

"A smuggler is afoot. You know boy, the Venerable Kung Fu proposed that a well functioning civil service could serve as the spiritual foundation for an ethical society. I should instruct you on his teachings. I fear your monastic training is faltering as of late."

"Why do you need me?"

Merlin raised a finger. "You are essential to me as there are very few people with whom I can discuss Confucianism."

The two men walked along the newly rebuilt planks of Saint Catherine's Dock.

"That was not what I meant," said Arthur.

Merlin shined up an apple and bit into it. "I know what you meant, boy. We are going to have a bit of an adventure. Just stand by me and look menacing."

"And should I be prepared to run?"

Merlin stomped his boot heel on the ship's gangplank with a loud thump. "Always." He strolled up onto the ship's deck, still chewing.

The vessel's captain sat on a low stool. He wore high-strung sandals and a Roman work toga. In front of him was a modest sized sow. He dumped out the contents of the bucket - fish heads - and the pig gobbled them up.

The captain swiveled around, "Ahoy. Get off my ship!"

Merlin saluted with a fingery wave. "Believe it or not, I am the Lord Exchequer to his Majesty King Ambrosius Aurelianus. I am inspecting your barge, so you better clean the chamber pot."

The captain blocked their path.

"What is your name Sir?" said Merlin. He tossed the rest of his apple at the pig. "Where is your crew?"

"On shore. My name is Appollinaris of Brittany. What do you want?"

"A tour of your craft, skipper. If you prefer, I can bring along some of the king's special knights, but they do have a tendency to break things. Is it true you are Spanish?"

Appollinaris put down his pail. "My father was. What are you looking for?"

"This and that; knickknacks; do-hickeys; thingamabobs." Merlin descended into the hull. It was loaded to capacity with wooden crates, held together with nails, not dowels and glue. Arthur followed.

Merlin asked, "What is in these boxes?"

"Cheese. The Romans of Paris pay good money for it."

"Rich fools, eh? *Deliriant isti Romani.*" Merlin patted his hand against a case. "I must request that you open it, Sir."

"This smells rotten," said Arthur. "What is cheese?"

Merlin replied, "Month-old curds left to molder in a cow's digestive organs. The Irish regard it as pure ambrosia. Myself, I never touch it. Like we used to say in the legions, if you cannot peel it or skin it, eat it not."

Appollinaris drew his dagger. He pried the lid off of a crate. A blast of funky air filled the cabin. The seaman sunk his arms into an enormous mound of hay. Out came six wheels of cheese as big around as a legionnaire's shield. He rolled them onto the floor.

Each of them was encased in a skin of bee's wax. The smudged fingerprints of the tradesman who packaged them were still visible on the outside.

"Will that be all then?" said Appollinaris.

Merlin tugged on his beard. "Tell me Sir, why is it you have chosen such a roundabout itinerary? You travel from Gaul to Hibernia and back again without loading or unloading. You are not some slack-jawed jack-tar. Surely you know how suspicious that looks?"

Before the Roman could reply, Arthur brought a wheel up to his still youthful eyes. There was a hand print embossed in the wax covering. "It has six fingers," he said, "two thumbs."

Merlin's mouth twisted into a crooked half-smile. He tapped the lower end of his staff against each crate, first on the lid, then on the side, and lastly near the base. The three strikes generated a thud, a thud, and another thud. When he hit the second container, three distinct tones were produced: a thud, a thunk, and a subtle yet resonant *bong*.

Merlin licked the last vestige of apple juice off his lips. "How many of these have false bottoms?"

Appollinaris rubbed the back of his neck.

"The disfigured freak who hired you to run this goose-chase," said Merlin, "what name did he use? And keep in mind, if you lie to me, I have the authority to set this ship ablaze, with - if I so deem it - both your testicles tied to the mizzenmast."

Appollinaris jiggled his purse, and grudgingly said, "His name is Claudius Pollox. Most people call him *Thumbs*."

"My old friend. What is that shyster up to?"

"You will not believe it."

"I am nothing if not ecumenical. Do tell."

Appollinaris straightened his toga. "Thumbs hired me to sail his cheese to Hibernia and back. He wishes to make it appear as if it is Irish. The Romans of Paris shell out three times what they would pay for local product."

"But this is not what Thumbs is hiding from me."

"You are correct, Sir. Some of the crates have false bottoms. Thumbs is hiding books under there, a baker's dozen."

"Thirteen?" said Arthur. "That must be the biggest library in Gaul!"

"I loaded the ship at night," said Appollinaris. "Thumbs came to the docks with a young woman and a girl. I believe the child was a deaf-mute. Her older sister was talking with hand signals."

Merlin asked, "Who was the maiden?"

"I have no idea. However, she was Roman of some rank. Her chauffeur unloaded the parcels off her wagon. They all seemed to be rather easy to carry. They were too light to be weapons."

"How could you tell what they were?" said Arthur. "Did you see the pages?"

"She opened one of them and asked for a torch. She was reading it."

"Splendidly false," said Merlin. "But why sail them half way round Britannia? And where did Thumbs get the cash to finance this? He is a back alley grifter, not a lord."

Appollinaris gathered up the wheels of cheese and tossed them back in their container. "You would have to ask Thumbs that. *Sua cuique voluptas.*"

"For a sailor, you are awfully well spoken."

"My grandfathers served as senators from Iberia."

"You are a true pillar of the Empire then?"

Appollinaris sealed the lid back on the crate, and pounded them down with his fist. "What empire?" he said. He adjusted his toga.

Any more, Merlin rarely laid eyes on a toga-clad man. In China, the Buddha was always depicted wearing a toga, a *Roman* toga. Chinese artists knew Gautama was a prince from the south, so they painted him like an effete Persian dressed in the Roman style. Brother Tinh Tu thought it was hilarious. It reminded Merlin of the German Christians who drew Jesus with a beard. The Greeks never did.

Merlin paced between the stacks of boxes. "Could it be that we see before us the *Lives* of Plutarch, imprisoned beneath a mountain of soured cream?"

Arthur's eyes grew wide. "Are we going to look at them? Would it hurt if we peeked at it?"

"Alas boy, I am going to show remarkable restraint. We came here looking for weapons and slaves. Having discovered none, it is time we disembarked and allowed this voyager to continue his trip."

"But the books? What if the ship sinks?"

"If we seize them, we must deliver them to the king, and he will simply squander them. If these manuscripts are to survive, we must invest our faith in the young lady who appears to be protecting them."

Appollinaris asked, "Am I free to leave?"

Merlin loosened his purse string and counted out thirty denarii. He stacked them on a crate in three piles of ten. "Tomorrow, I will instruct Master Galfrid to fine you twenty denarii - yes, *twenty* - for failing to properly register your vessel. He will order you to remove your craft from this port by sundown, weather permitting. When you arrive in Gaul, you shall report to Thumbs that I conducted a thorough search and found nothing."

"I can do that." Appollinaris scooped up the coins.

"Indeed you will. Or else you will never do business in Carmarthen again. King Clovis may rule half of Europe, but this corner of *terra firma* is still mine."

* * *

Something tugged the end of Merlin's cloak. It was the captain's pig.

"Thank you for the apple," she said. "It was a nice change of fare from chomping on day-old fish skulls."

"I was not aware sows had such discerning pallets."

The pig snorted, "My race is actually quite intelligent. You can be rather cunning yourself. Is that how you escaped from China?"

"In Manchuria," said Merlin, "they caution that a man should fear fame, like a pig fears getting fat."

Gopi sat on her hind legs. She had jet black eyes. That was odd for a pig.

"How long were you imprisoned?" she asked.

"A few months. After I was beaten senseless by the eunuchs, I awoke to the sound of trickling water. I opened my swollen lids to see a short stocky fellow with Asiatic features, urinating. He had branding scars on both cheeks, two eight pointed stars, one beneath each eye. The front of his head had been shaved from the ear to ear, with one tight braid down his spine."

"Was he a Xiongnu?"

"Using Mandarin Chinese, I notified him that I was a monastic from Nalanda. He seemed not to understand me, so I repeated it in Persian, which he spoke fluently. I told him I was an ambassador from India. He said his name was Scottas, son of Bleda. Then he asked me if I was a Buddhist.

"I said I was, and he informed me that he sacrificed to the Sky Bitch. He then notified me that the Buddha could stick his head up her arse, and there would still be room for Kung Fu and Lao Tsu. He asked why I was arrested.

"I explained that one of the royal eunuchs accused me of being a Xiongnu because I had blue pig eyes. Scottas began to laugh because he himself was a Xiongnu. Turns out his sons had captured a Chinese general, and the Chinese needed some Xiongnu prisoners to trade. Since they could not catch a real Xiongnu, they settled for me.

"He told me that I looked like the fair-haired Xiongnu from out west. When the Xiongnu defeated a nation, they would ask their captives to join them or die. Those declared that they would rather be killed than submit to the will of their enemies, were spared and adopted by the Xiongnu. The rest were decapitated as mercy-begging cowards, their skulls stacked up like a pyramid.

"Over the years, Scottas's family had assimilated thousands of warriors, some with blue pig eyes like mine. The Persians called them Epthalites. Scottas said his uncle Attila had an entire army of them.

"I asked if some people called his uncle, *Attila the Hun*? Scottas wanted to know where I heard that. He asked me if I was Roman. I asked him if he drank dog milk. He smiled wide revealing his teeth, chiseled sharp like a Hunnish wolfhound. *Why*, he said, *I chug bitch wine by the barrel!*"

Chapter XXVI: The Harvest Moon, AD 493

Pax melior est quam iustissimum bellum.

Peace is better than the most just war.

* * *

The forest should have been silent, but a dull clomping noise echoed out from the underbrush, as if some wooden-shoed trekker had stumbled over a log. Arthur considered making a run for it, but if they had arrows - and the savages always did - a solitary rider galloping on uneven ground would be an easy target.

Arthur quieted his horse. Whoever these graceless brutes were, they were not saying a word. Perhaps they were drunk? Arthur delicately unsheathed his sword. The sound of feet shuffling through the leaf litter drew nearer. He raised his shield to breast-height.

An odd kind of high pitched whine pierced the autumn air. Arthur tightened his reigns, preparing to bolt. Then, from behind a vine covered maple there appeared a muscular bull elk. Three does, each with a fawn in toe, trotted close behind. These were not Germans.

Arthur's horse snorted. The stag lowered its head, displaying a formidable rack. This was one of the famously large elk that roamed the Severn Valley: the no-mans-land that separated the Britons from the Saxons. With no men present to hunt them, the wildlife grew to a ripe old age, chewing on the wild grasses that sprouted from the ruins of once productive Roman plantations.

The father elk stomped his hooves and rippled his shoulders. This display was not difficult to decipher. Arthur had been delayed enough already, and this battle was not part of his mission. He steered his mount around to the left, and with a whinny, it galloped up the mountainside.

When Arthur reached the crest of the hill, he surveyed the landscape below. A stand of pines obscured a column of soldiers, mostly infantry, marching behind two rows of equestrians. A low gravelly call bellowed out from within this company. It was Sir Ector atop his Percheron, a massive workhorse he chose to ride because no other breed could hold him.

Sir Ector cried out to his field commander, "Have the scouts reported yet?"

"No, Sir," said Captain Galahad, a short but stocky, Romano-Briton half-breed, "They should have come back by now."

"Keep going. The infantry is spread out too thin in the rear. I am going to head back there and stick a burr up their arse. If you get to the clearing before the rest of the battalion gets here, wait."

Arthur navigated down slope to join them.

Ector continued, "Once they arrive, start your flanking. If I am not there, go on without me." He addressed Arthur, "Ahoy Squire! Did they get my message?"

"Aye, Sir. I delivered it to Gawain."

Ector winked his un-patched eye. "Looks like you earned your keep today." With that, he kicked his spurs and sped into the woods.

Sir Galahad motioned for Arthur to come closer. "Once we hit the clearing, you fall behind and wait for Ector."

"Aye, Sir," said Arthur. "Has Sir Ector stopped stuttering?"

"He loses it in battle." Galahad rode toward a section of woodland felled by a windstorm. Arthur trotted alongside him. Up slope a ways, a party of some dozen gray-haired men walked out into the far end of the log-strewn hillside. A few carried shovels, others hoes. None of them had proper boots.

In Celtic they yelled, "Do not shoot! We need to speak with Ector. Where is he?"

"Whose army is this?" said Galahad.

Arthur heard the pounding of hooves, large hooves, charging forward from behind him.

Sir Ector, his sword extended, raced past with thunderous speed. "Attack! Those are Ten-acres! Attack, damn it!"

Galahad, whose head had been exposed to the elements, slipped on his chain mail hood. "Go to the infantry," he said to Arthur. "Tell them to attack… attack now. Tell them the enemy is Ten-acre Britons. Go!"

Arthur snuck a quick peek at the group of old men. Behind them, crouching low, were young men.

Galahad withdrew his sword and said, "You have your orders, Squire. Go!" Then he yelled "Charge!" at the top of his lungs. Upon hearing this, his cavalry launched into the clearing. The troops marching behind them let out a roar.

A volley of arrows whizzed by. Arthur's horse bucked, then galloped into the forest. As Arthur rode, low growing branches smacked him in the face. He dared not slow down. He had to close his eyes.

Merlin once told Arthur that practicing the Buddha's Precepts was like riding a horse. Most of the time you were in control. But when you came to a log in your path, you simply had to let go and trust the horse to jump.

When Arthur re-opened his eyes, his horse was dashing toward a supply cart, piloted by Sir Gawain, Duke of the Infantry.

Arthur waved his arm. "Sir Galahad sent me!" he said. "There is an army of Ten-acre Britons up ahead. They attacked at the clearing."

Gawain whistled to his troops. He stood up in the driver's seat, and threw off the wool cloak draped over his shoulders. "Ten-acres attacked Galahad's cavalry." He hopped off the cart, and tied the reigns to a tree. "Follow me men, double time. This is it."

Gawain's foot soldiers marched through the forest, dodging stumps and boulders only to close ranks again, much like any other herd of animals.

Gawain shouted back to Arthur, "You must go to the king. Tell him that the Germans met our northern flank." He picked up a stick and threw it off to his left. "Ride that way till you find a gully. Follow it until it becomes a stream. The king will be there in the lowlands."

Arthur snapped his reigns. "Aye, Sir." Once again he was galloping through the woods, not so much riding his horse as holding on to a saddled beast. At the edge of the forest, Arthur noticed a hawthorn tree. Before he could steer away from its thorny branches, his horse had veered around it. Arthur was always a bit puzzled when Merlin said, *Trust in the universe.* Was this what he meant?

The clang of metal reverberated from up ahead, along with the muffled cries of men, angry or in pain. Arthur rode on. It began to rain.

When he got within sight of the battlefield, he dismounted and ran over to Palamedes, the captain of the archers, a black-haired mercenary everyone called *the Syrian.* He had a thick Frankish accent.

"I have a message from Sir Galahad," said Arthur. "Sir Ector's northern flank was attacked. I have to speak with the king. Where is he?"

The Syrian asked, "Who attacked them? Infantry or cavalry?"

"They were on foot. Ten-acre Britons."

The Syrian wiped the sweat from his face. "*Ces putains*," he said. Then he called over to his men. "This esquire needs to report to the king. We have to form a turtle, boys, *tout de suite*."

There was a screeching sound on the battlefield as two horses careened into each other and crashed to the earth.

Arthur said, "But, I am not a knight."

"Neither am I," said the Syrian.

Arthur always admired the archers. They were never worried. Every archer had a nickname like *Skinny* or *Punch*. They slept until noon, practiced till sunset, and tossed darts all night. If you could shoot straight and hold your ale, the archers would seek you out, regardless of how high or low you were born. They were always kind to old ladies, and even kinder to the young ones.

The Syrian opened his mouth and pressed his upper canine tooth against the top of his bow. Then he plucked the string while squealing, and in so doing generated a high pitched twang that cut through all the other noise. Ten of his archers rush to his side. The Syrian asked, "How many shields do we have?"

"I lost mine," said one of them. His head was gashed.

"You better stay in the rear. If they try to run up our arse, shoot everything you got, hear? Everybody, give him all your arrows. Go to it, *mes frères*."

The archer's huddled together. They arranged two square shields in front, two on each side, and three above. Their efforts resulted in a jury-rigged tortoise shell with human legs.

"Squire," said the Syrian, "stick your head against my bum. Lucky for you, my arsehole smells like rose petals." He dragged Arthur behind him into the center of the scrum.

The Syrian's men marched their armor-plated box into the center of the fray. They slipped on mud, a mixture of water, churned up sod, and the occasional dead man slit open at the neck or stomach. Germans and Celts had one thing in common, they always aimed for the soft spots.

The Syrian yelled, "Open up!" and four sets of hands gripped Arthur by his thighs. They haul him high into the air and balanced him on the Syrian's shoulders. Arthur teetered there, face to face with the king.

The king, astride his saddle, yelled, "Report!"

An animal-like instinct directed Arthur's attention to a cluster of white-blond Jutes no older than him. There were being marshaled by a tattooed subchief, who pointed the back of is battle ax at Arthur's unarmored chest. The tallest of the Jutes set an arrow into his Frankish-made longbow, and aimed. He let loose his shot. A horse ran into it.

"Damn you!" screamed the king, "I said report!"

The Jute sniper reloaded.

"Sir Ector's flank has been attacked," said Arthur. "Infantry, on foot."

The straining turtle, which was now attracting a tide of savage missiles, lurched a bit to the side. Arthur felt the brush of a feather swoosh by his ear.

The rain stopped.

Arthur tried his best to stay focused on the king, but could not help but notice the Jute sniper pulling back on his third arrow. The Syrian lost his footing, regained it, then lost it completely. Arthur tipped over, like a falling tree. The Jute's arrow passed through the air. It hit a stone dead elm. Decaying bark scattered everywhere.

Arthur landed face first in the mud. He rolled to a stop, and found himself staring across the field at the face of the very Jute who was trying to kill him.

The Jute subchief gazed up. A rainbow had formed. A fearful expression spread over the faces of all the Jutes. They all kissed their respective palms, then threw their kisses toward the sky. The Jute sniper lowered his weapon; perhaps in deference to a message received from some heavenly overlord.

Behind the Jutes, a massing of Angle axmen was retreating. Arthur could identify them by their round beards. Upon their shoulders they carried the lifeless corpse of their subchief, a balding fellow whose partially-severed hand swung from his wrist bone, attached by only tendons.

Long-braided Saxons chased after them and screamed insults. Arthur could make out a few of their words. "*Sheistkopfe! Feiglinge!*"

King Ambrosius cried out, "Attack the breech!" Twelve of his horsemen joined together. They slammed into the German line.

Arthur got up on all fours. Someone grabbed him by the hair. The pain was temporarily paralyzing. He tried to pull out his dagger, but stopped when he saw the face of the Syrian, who was dragging him back into the turtle.

"Syrian!" screamed one of his men. "Stop! Reverse!"

Arthur peered through the unprotected hole in the back of their mobile fortress. A company of dog-eared peasants with sharpened pikes were running, stumbling, and falling toward them. It was the Ten-acres.

The Saxons roared. They broke out in howls, yodeling their victory songs.

The Syrian squatted down. "*Merde.*" He propped his shield in front of him and curled up in a ball. His men did likewise.

Arthur wrestled a loose shield from a dead German. He clamped his eyes shut. The rumbling of hooves was all he could hear. Horses' bellies were barreling over him. The boots lodged into the stirrups jingled with Frankish spurs. None of the German tribes had tack that good. They barely knew what a saddle was for. This battalion had to be Sir Ector's cavalry.

Then there came a searing pain. Something, as large and solid as the handle of a shovel, crashed against Arthur's scalp. The living air was pushed out of his lungs. Everything went dark.

* * *

Arthur continued to hear the clop of galloping hooves, but it was muffled and soon faded off into the distance. Arthur rubbed his eyes. He did not see the battlefield, but rather the ships on Carmarthen Bay. He ran barefoot on the cobblestones with a slippery eel in his hand. Was the fat lady with the knife still chasing him? Then he hit his head on something.

A skinny old man with long white braids and blue piglet eyes toppled over. Arthur's forehead hurt, but not enough to cry. The old man's walking stick had a bird carved onto its head. It looked rather like a duck and Arthur asked if that was what it was. "No," said Merlin, "It is a piece of wood."

* * *

Arthur awoke from his dream, shivering. There was a layer of dew on his skin. The sun was down, and it was too cloudy for star light.

The Syrian lay still. A splinter of bone jutted out through his cheek. Above his eyebrow, there glistened a round wet surface. Upon closer inspection, Arthur could tell it was a fold of exposed brain. The Syrian's skull has been crushed in by the u-shaped stomp of a horseshoe. Vomit welled up into Arthur's throat. He hobbled to his feet.

The valley below glowed with scattered firelights, generating enough illumination to silhouette the outlines of dead and dying men strewn across the field. Blasts of warm breath periodically shot up from those who still had it.

Four figures with torches roamed through the mist. They carried arrows to shoot at wounded horses, and razor sharp daggers to put down paralyzed men.

"*Vivat rex!*" said Arthur. He felt dizzy. "Do not shoot. I am Arthur, Ward of Merlin."

"Squire?" said Galahad. He waved his torch. "Come here. Are you wounded?"

"No, I just got hit in the head." A large welt throbbed just above Arthur's ear. "The Syrian is dead. How is Sir Ector?"

"Stuttering again. You need to go to camp and lie down. Did you pass out?"

Arthur's hands were encrusted in dried muck. "Did we win?" He wiped them on his trousers. They were filthy too.

"Stalemate," said Galahad. "Bloody Ten-acres. We shot at them until we ran out of arrows. They had no shields. They were nothing but boys."

Arthur's ear started ringing. "Why are they called Ten-acres?"

"When the Saxons killed King Vortiger, every Briton who could ran off. But some got stuck behind. High Chief Hengst offered ten acres of land to every householder that had a plow. Most of them took it."

"The Ten-acres are Britons?"

"Not really. Most of them are half-breeds. Only the old timers can still speak Celtic."

From in front of the field marshal's tent, a figure called out, "Ahoy, Galahad, is that Squire Arthur? Ector needs a clerk." It was Sir Gawain.

"Aye Sir," said Arthur. He ran over, even though he was feeling a little nauseated. Gawain led him through the entrance. A low fire simmered in the center. To the right, Ector was conferring with his deputies.

To the left, reclining on a blanket of white ermine was High Chief Aella. His graying beard was short and round like an Angle's, but down his back were the four long braids of a Saxon. He wore no shirt, which showed off his hairy chest and the tattoos etched on his upper arms. A twisted gold bolt, hung around his neck. His client war chiefs, and a few elderly peace chiefs, sat behind him.

A Jute chief scowled at Arthur and asked, *"Ist er sien Sohn?"*

"Who is he?" said the German's interpreter, a toothless white-haired Ten-acre. He wore a threadbare smock. "Is he your son?"

Sir Ector tilted his head towards Arthur. "He is my c-clerk. He belongs to our w-wizard."

"*Er ist der Sohn des Hexe mit weisse Kaninchen,*" said the Jute. "*Ist der Knabe ein Hexe?*"

Chief Aella interrupted. "*Nein, nein. Er is nur sein Kind.*"

Ector said, "What is g-going on?"

Before the Ten-acre could translate, the Chief Aella positioned his throwing ax under his bottom. He invited the Jute to do likewise and motioned for Ector to join them. Duke Ector laid down his dagger, and sat on it.

Chief Aella and the Jute spoke to each other in Saxon and Jutish. Their conversation deteriorated into a shouting match.

The Jute asked Ector, "The *Vater* of the boy. Is he from Apfal-on? Has he *ein Stein*? Makes *der Stein* a fire?"

Sir Ector said, "Where the blazes is Apfalon?"

Chief Aella had a brief back and forth with the Jute in German. Then he said, "This *Jyde* says there an island in the forest where you *Welschmann* grow big red grape trees. He says there is druid with rabbits and a stone that makes fire. Who is this?"

Arthur recognized the Jute. He had a chunk of skin cut from his nostril. "Aye," said Arthur, "we met you in an apple grove when I was a boy. Your war chief had a Roman medal around his neck."

The Ten-acre translated.

Upon hearing this, the Jute froze. "*Er ist der Hexe von Etzel! Er fahrt mit Hengst.*"

Chief Aella tried to calm him down. "*Sei ruhe. Er is kein Hexe.*"

The Jute whistled to his warriors. Curses flew. Chief Aella and the Jute stood chest to chest. They shouted at each other.

An Angle peace chief had to physically separate them.

Ector said, "Settle d-down, Herman."

The Ten-acre spoke up, saying, "The Jute says your king has Etzel's witch. They think your wizard is a Hun. They say he crossed the channel with Hengst the Saxon."

"Well," said Arthur, "Merlin was taken captive by Attila."

One of the younger Jutes jumped to his feet. "Attila! He is with Attila!" He addressed the Saxons, saying, *"Der Knabe sagt das der hexe fur Eztel arbietet! Etzel!"*

The Jute chief stuck out his tongue, licked his thumb, then rubbed his saliva across his eyebrows with one swift insulting move. The rest of the Jute warriors all did the same. The Saxons barely contained their rage. The Angle peace chief tried to speak with them, but they all stomped out without saying a word.

"Where are they g-going?" said Ector.

Chief Aella stabbed his finger toward Arthur. "This boy. Those dumb Jutes, they think he is magic."

"They fear him," said Ector. "They fear Etzel's s-sorcerer."

"They are fools," said the Ten-acre. "Your king is wounded. Your men are hurt."

Sir Ector grinned, exposing his twisted teeth. "Your snow dogs will n-not bite, Aella. We still have h-horses."

Aella stuck out two fingers. "Shove your nose up my arse, Tommy. I have enough men in Wessex. That boy is no druid. Magic is crap. Where is your *Keonig, Welschmann?*"

Ector reached into his blouse. He pulled out a blank parchment. "Sign a t-treaty."

"Paper? Wipe your hole on it, *Fraulein*."

"Make no war with us for as long as you l-live." Ector folded it to a crease and ripped it in half. He handed both pieces to Arthur. "Sign this and we can go our ways."

Gawain gave Arthur a quill and whispered, "Write down what Sir Ector just said. Keep it simple. Make two copies."

Arthur had difficulty hearing due to the constant high-pitched tone that was now buzzing from inside his head. It modulated with every heartbeat. He almost felt like he was going to upchuck right then and there. He started writing.

The Ten-acre translator extended his hand. "We will sign it, *Herr* Ector."

Chief Aella snarled, "*Schmutzig Welschmann!*"

"*Kein mehr Krieg!*" shot back the Ten-acre. "We shoe your horses, *Deutchsman*. You stop this war, or we will join *Herr Strewel-struble*. *Kein mehr, kein mehr.*"

Arthur blew dry the two documents. Ector signed them with an *E*.

The muscles in High Chief Aella's jaw tightened up. "Only, I will sign," he said, pushing the Ten-acres behind him. "I have a Frankish boy in my village, Mister Ector. He can read like the Pope. If your paper has a trick, I will wrap your liver in it. *Verstehen Sie?*"

Chief Aella snapped his finger and the Angle peace chief presented him with a formal painted chieftain's ax. Aella raised it waist high, then let the head-end of it fall straight down. It stuck into the soil.

The Angle peace chief said to Ector, "You drop your long knife, now. Yes?" Ector unsheathed his sword and lodged it in the earth.

"Pen boy," said Chief Aella to Arthur, "you tell Ector *Strewel-struble* this."

The high chief covered his heart with his hand and began to speak, not in German or in Celtic, but in Latin, good clear Roman Latin. It was easy for Arthur to translate.

"I shall sign this paper of yours," said the chief, "but keep in mind, we Saxons know all about paper. Back in the Rhineland, my grandfathers signed a paper with Valentinian, *Kaiser* of the Romans. He promised to feed us and love us if we became his *feoderati*. We fought the savage Huns. We drove *Etzel* from the Alps. But did Valentinian keep his word? No, he betrayed our nation. We fled to the swamps, lost in *volkerwanderung*. We watched our children starve.

"My fathers signed another paper with Vortiger the Celt, *Keonig* of the *Welschmann*. He promised he would feed us, and love us. We rowed our keels to Britannia and became his warriors. We spilled our blood to drive the blue-skinned savages back to *Irlandt*. We killed the *Schottisch* raiders. But did your

Vortiger keep his word? No, he slandered us. He called us invaders, when it was he who begged us to live in his land.

"Now we sign a paper with your new *Koenig*, Ambrosius Aurelianus, grandson of the Roman Governor. We will abide by it, because ours is an honorable nation. Take this paper back to your *Koenig*. Tell him this will be the last. No more paper.

"I was born in the Rhineland, where my father and grandfathers are buried. My sons and grandsons were born here in Britannia. It is all they have ever known. Essex, Wessex, Sussex, and Kent; these lands are now our *Vaterland*. My grandsons will never be removed from them. We have burnt all our keels. We will row no more.

"The Angles, the Frisians, and the Swabians, they are my brothers, and I will die for them. Even those stupid yellow Jutes are dear to me. I will love them forever, as I will love the Ten-acres, for they have never lied to us and have given us many wives. I swear this as an oath by my ancestors. I swear it by *Herr* Woden, Lord of Thunder. I swear it by Jesus Brown Beard, God of the Squared Timbers. May I die a coward's death, banished from Valhalla if I should fail to uphold it."

Chief Aella snatched the quill from Arthur. Upon each copy of the treaty, he drew his pictogram, a two-headed eagle grasping a thunderbolt in each claw.

Arthur's entire head was overcome by a wave of heat. The pounding in his ears was deafening. The tent began to spin. He fainted.

BOOK VII: THE MYSTIC

Chapter XXVII: The Harvest Moon, AD 496

Vox populi, vox dei.

The voice of the people is the voice of God.

* * *

The feast of Saint Michael marked the autumn equinox, the day when hogs were slaughtered, and the end of battle season. From now till spring, Saint Michael - the Satan-stomping drill sergeant archangel - permitted all mortal warriors six months leave. Sprains and lacerations would have time to repair until after the spring thaw, when troops would once again take to the field.

To mark Michaelmass Eve, the Knights of King Ambrosius Aurelianus assembled in their hall. These young men celebrated their victories, and recalled their fallen brothers the way all soldiers do: they drank. With slurring voices, they sang off-key, and bumped into the serving girls who spirited away down smoky corridors perfumed with plum cake and pork fat.

Sir Arthur wiped a fluff of beer foam off his mustache. Like all the other officers, his beard was neatly trimmed no longer and no shorter than the king's. It was a kind of uniform all the king's men wore, even when naked.

At the front entrance to the hall, Arthur observed another beard trimmed like his, but it was jet white and attached to the face of a cantankerous old man with a small beer cask under each arm.

Merlin barged his way through the mulling revelers. He nodded a half bow to Sir Kay, stern-faced and sober, who stood sentry in the center of the festivities. Kay's mission was to break up any fights, and make those who fought them regret it.

Two young esquires, both reeking of alcohol and talking far too loud, blocked Merlin's path. One of them said, "So, the Scotsman puts the duck back in his pants and leaves. Just then the matron turns to the innkeeper and says, *Well, I have seen one that big before…* "

Merlin interrupted. "*But, I have never seen one eat a walnut.* That joke was an antique when Methuselah was wetting the bed." He elbowed them aside with a sharp jab, and charged on.

Arthur nudged Sir Ector and asked, "Is that our learned wizard carrying the king's personal stock? How can this be? I thought the Buddhist philosophy forbids its adherents from committing theft?"

Merlin thumped the barrel down onto the table top. "The Precepts of the Buddha," he said, "are mental guideposts, not commandments. And whereas, His Royal Majesty has passed out, I felt compelled to free these innocent bitters from his evil grips."

Arthur responded with his best imitation of Merlin. He sat up straight and tugged at his beard a few times. "That seems rather inconsistent with the Practice. Would it not be more mindful to submit to the will the universe? In time, it will manifest a resolution for all of mortality's gross inequities."

Merlin cleared his throat. "Sometimes the universe requires a kick in the arse." He knocked the stopper off the keg. "Now, do you want a swig or not?"

Ector filled his bowl. Into Arthur's he poured equal parts beer and water. He slid it over and said, "You have b-bear's heart, but a dove's bladder."

Merlin raised his vessel. "*Nunc est bibendum.*" They all slurped in unison.

Merlin twisted a grape from a bunch on the table. He popped it in his mouth.

"I thought you w-were a teetotaler?" said Ector.

"That would be correct, I should not be drinking." Merlin rested his elbows on the table. "I should also refrain from telling falsehoods, fomenting ill will, or groveling for money. And yet, I seem to have made a profession of them all. Would you like seconds?"

Ector nodded *yes*. He bit into a slab of pork rind floating in his soup. A few slurring knights began to sing a barely-comprehensible sea shanty about a sailor named *Bilibra*, whose two-pound cast-iron testicles led him into various misadventures.

Arthur asked, "Should so many knights should be drinking? What if the Germans attack? Will we be ready?"

"Herman is having a p-poke," said Ector.

Merlin set down his drink. "What our taciturn colleague is so obliquely communicating is that the Saxon savages are currently occupied in amorous pursuit. In the month of *Winterfylleth*, the Germans honor the goddess of the corn by imbibing the bock till the spigot runs dry. Suffice it to say, fornication ensues."

Ector called out, "Bread!" From across the room, a loaf was hurled. Arthur caught the hearth-baked missile in mid-flight.

"He is quick," said Ector. "He will make a g-good knight."

Merlin jutted out his chin. "And just what is a good knight? Why, I would opine he is a servant whose sole occupation is to implement the policies of a king. And what is a king then? Why, he is a pimp! He beats the Johns to protect his girls, then beats his girls to ensure his income."

"I serve a king," said Ector. He sipped his soup.

"As do I. Does that make us good? No, it makes us highly polished revenue collectors. Contrast this to the German chieftains who distribute all of their booty, even to the least of their brethren. If only our supposedly advanced monarchs could practice such equanimity."

Two knights on the bench next to Merlin climbed up on their table and began to sing, "There once was a Roman hag, who never got a shag…"

With a gentle touch of his hand, Merlin pushed them off. They fell into their comrades, spilling brew everywhere. In the confusion, a young esquire ran up and stole Merlin's half-empty barrel. Sir Kay stepped forward.

"Let him go," said Ector.

Kay returned to his corner. "That lad digs latrines till Saint Crispin's Day."

Ector winked his eye in approval.

Arthur said, "You say that kings are unfit to govern. If so, who is? Would the senatorial system would be better?"

"Those pandering elitists? *Ubi solitudinem faciunt pacem appellant!* We Britons seem to forget that Rome, whose practices we take such great pains to emulate, invaded our island and subjugated our forefathers for centuries."

Ector poured himself another ale.

"But the Romans brought us literacy?" said Arthur. "They gave us medicine. What about the codes of justice?"

"They taught us to be sheep, then abandoned us to the Hibernian wolves. They were tyrants and dictators, like every other king."

It was pronouncements like this that made Arthur wonder how Merlin had lived for so long. The way Merlin slandered figures of power should have sent him to the gallows. And yet, the nobles he mocked never took offense. Perhaps, no one took him seriously because he was so odd. His strangeness was an armor protecting him from humanity, but also separating him from its warmth.

Ector drained his bowl. "People like k-kings."

Arthur concurred. "Ector has a point. If kings are such a disservice, why do nations replace them when they die?"

From across the room, one of the knights attempted to ride a goose, as was the traditional sport of this day. The bird flapped itself loose, and the knight, having failed the task, was pelted by all manner of small objects.

"The problem with Britannia," said Merlin, "is that we are not fully maturated. If we were, we would realize that we do not require a monarch."

"Who leads then?" said Arthur. "Who will govern?"

"A στρατεγοσ. That is the title the Athenians gave the venerable Pericles after he refused to rule as a king."

"I barely s-speak Celtic," said Ector, "now you give me Greek?"

Merlin bowed in apology. "Forgive my insensitivity. A στρατεγοσ is a leader chosen by a nation's freemen to preside over their daily activities. He has no higher standing, but he is accepted by his community as its executive."

Ector asked, "Did this Greek chap hold c-court?" He loosened his belt to accommodate his beer-filled gut.

"He did indeed," said Merlin. "But in the dominion of Pericles there were no royal commands. Instead, Pericles gathered his citizens at an amphitheater. There he would pose a question to his countrymen regarding the governance of the nation." Merlin's voice began to slur. "Each man would drop a stone into a pot, white for yes and black for no. These pebbles would then be counted; the majority opinion would become law. This, the Athenians called δεμοκρατια."

"Again with the G-Greek."

Merlin said, "Δεμοκρατια is the west's greatest gift to humanity. I have seen it nowhere else in all my travels. I can say without reservation that the δεμοκρατια of Pericles is as important to human progress as any of the Buddha's teachings. I say Arthur, you may wish to make a study of Pericles for your monastic training."

Ector rested his back against the wall. His mouth hung open. Merlin extended his forefinger and poked the old duke in his belly. Ector let out an enormous belch.

"Quite often," said Merlin, "when I listen to the king blather on - with all the stilted eloquence of Puncionellus berating his hand puppet wife - I imagine how grand it must have been to hear the dulcet oratory of Pericles, addressing his circle of citizens."

"He must have had a big table," said Ector.

Arthur added, "It would have to be round. How would you build that?"

"Rather h-hard to move. I suppose you c-could roll it."

Merlin glared. "Dear Ector, must you view everything from a purely mechanistic perspective?"

Sir Ector grinned exposing the crooked teeth he usually kept hidden behind his goat-like lips. He tipped himself sideways, and just before passing out, released a voluminous thundering fart.

Merlin waved the stench away. "I have often pondered," he said, "why the Lord of Abraham chose to endow humanity with the capacity for flatulence?"

Arthur gathered up the bowls from the two old friends. Merlin's was still half-full, but enough was missing to get him drunk.

Arthur said, "You should stop now. You have affairs to attend to in the morning."

Merlin folded his hands. "I have developed a hypothesis that in days of yore, before the inception of musical arts and lyric poetry, breaking wind served as the only available means of entertainment." He closed his eyes and rested his head on the pillow of his arms. "Indeed, that is what farts are for."

Chapter XXVIII: The Growing Moon, AD 497

Hunc tu caveat.

Beware of this man.

* * *

The Festival of Saint Alphius's Day was a sneeze inducing event. The calves awaiting auction chewed on loose piles of hay that scattered in the ocean breeze. Vendors unloaded crates of kiln-baked Iberian pottery, tossing the packing straw everywhere. By mid-morning, the cart wheels and horses' hooves had crushed these sun-dried shards to grist, well suited for airborne dispersal.

A caravan of red-caped Frankish knights rode by, kicking up clouds of dust. A fowler's wagon, stacked high with hens in crates, rolled into a rut, and lurched to the side. Feathers flew everywhere. Through this swirl of irritants, Merlin observed a flash of iridescent orange. Next to drawbridge, a Sardinian clothier with slick black hair and a huge nose was shaking out a sheet of orange silk.

Merlin pushed his way through the traffic, and said, "I have been trying to locate fabric like this for ages. This is a toga-quality weave."

"The gentleman knows his cloth," said the Sardinian. "You are the court wizard, yes?"

"Alas, I fear my position is much more mundane. I am the lord exchequer. What is your offer for ten yards?"

"For you, Your Excellency, thirty five."

Merlin thumped his staff. "I do not accept gratuities nor do I solicit them. You should be asking fifty denarii for material like this. I am giving you forty-five." He dug into his purse. "Have your boy deliver this to the counting house. *Factum est.*"

The Sardinian twisted his moustache. "Or... I could do forty?"

"You will take forty-five!" Merlin thrust his over his payment. "I cannot believe that I am actually haggling for a higher price."

The Sardinian bowed and deposited the coins in his lock box. "And how charitable of you, Your Excellency."

From behind him, Merlin heard a voice. "Ambrosius! How pleasant to see you."

Merlin pivoted around to see a red-haired knight, one of the visiting Franks. This soldier was fit, with a strong chin and a fine Roman sword. There was something vaguely familiar about him.

"Good day, Sir," said Merlin, "I am the Lord Exchequer, Ambrosius Merlin. Have we met?"

"I am King Vortiger's son," said the knight. "My name is Pashent. You used to call me *Patty.*"

"By Jove! The last time I saw you, you were in nappies. You seem to have done quite well for yourself, Your Highness."

Sir Pashent grinned at the three knights with him. "You need not call me that. I am an officer of King Clovis, nothing more. Besides, my father was more of a chieftain than a king. You know, I still remember listening to you tell Ector's wife about your travels. Living with the Huns and sewing saddles."

"Those were not my stories. I fought against Huns and learned saddlery from the Ostragoths."

"My mistake then. I understand you are building a fortress with Antonius Puglius of Naples. Do you know his elder brother, Nicholas Parvus? He is married to my late wife's sister."

Merlin rubbed his nose. "I have never met him. But then again, I tend not to socialize."

"We ought to share a meal sometime." Pashent shook some hay off his red cape. "Tomorrow, perhaps? I have an audience with your sister this afternoon. After that, I should be free."

"I was not aware that you were on Morgan's calendar."

"Aye. We are old friends. When she offered me a passport to visit Britannia, I felt I could not refuse."

"It is the king who issues passports, not the Lady Morgan."

"But of course." Pashent glanced over to his comrades. "I must get back to my men. I do look do forward to meeting with you."

Sir Pashent bowed and rejoined his company. He slapped them on the backs.

Merlin knew both of Pashent's brothers. The Saxons had no trouble killing those plonkers. Pashent, however, was sharp, like his mother. If Pashent was back in Britannia, there had to be a reason, one which apparently involved Lady Morgan. The fact that she had been King Syagrius's mistress should have made her King Clovis's enemy. Then again, Clovis was known to cozy up to old foes.

Merlin called to his attendant, "To the armory, Tristan." He stomped back up the drawbridge and marched across the courtyard.

Tristan followed behind. "Who was that Frank?"

"He is no Frank." Merlin barged through the door of the arms house.

Sir Ector pried the lid off a crate of armor he and Gawain were unpacking.

Merlin found a blacksmith's stool and sat down. "Does the king know Sir Pashent is here?"

Ector reached his meaty fingers into the wooden container and from it pulled a shield. "Leave us f-for a bit," he said to Gawain. The knight left the room, taking Tristan with him.

Ector examined the handle straps on one of the shields. "His Majesty signed Morgan's p-passport. I saw him do it."

"Why did Morgan bring him here? What does the king want with him? Does he have any idea how dangerous he is?"

"I spoke with Pashent this m-morning," said Ector. "Clovis sent him to spy on us. He t-told me some cock-and-bull story and g-gave me a gift."

Ector pointed his thumb toward the far side of the stable. There, atop a bale of oats, was a saddle of mottled horsehide leather decorated with Scythian ornamentation.

Merlin focused on its dangling stirrups crafted with ornate bars of Damascus wootz steel. He began to perspire. A drip of sweat rolled off the tip of his nose. It fell down onto the dusty ground.

* * *

The vast horizon sprawled out before Merlin's eyes. There were no trees, only scrub shrub for miles on end. The Siberian wind whipped through the steppe grasses. A herd of shaggy brown ponies huddled together.

Merlin smelled the scent of roasted groundhog. In the distance, a throat-singer played a light air on a horse skull fiddle. The sun was nearly down. The encampment hummed with the muffled chortles of infants being tucked into bed, and young couples having sex in their yurts.

Merlin paced a never ending circle in the middle of the corral, trying to stay awake. Down in the valley, a family of Hunnish wolfhounds was devouring a carcass. The puppies whelped. The dominant males snarled to scare off their would-be successors. The blood that had soaked into Merlin's furry boots was now cold. His red-stained hands were both curled into fists. Inside each of them was a dismembered human ear.

* * *

Then he heard nothing.

"Merlin?" said Ector. "Can you h-hear me?"

Merlin opened his eyes. He lay on a cot in Ector's stable. It was empty except for four horses, and a goat fast asleep in the corner. A single lamp flickered by the door. Ector sat on a bench.

"What happened?" said Merlin. "What time is it?

"Late. You spoke in t-tongues. Did you have a vision?"

"I must apologize. I am prone to mental distempers. They afflict me sometimes." He rubbed his forehead. "I must tell you something. That saddle Pashent gave you, I have seen it before. More to the point, I made it."

"But that is s-savage tack."

Merlin sat up. "When I was a younger man, I was taken prisoner by a tribe of Asiatic horse barbarians known as the Xiongnu. That was the language you heard me speaking."

"Was that back east?"

"Actually, it was east of east."

Merlin never spoke about what drove him mad. Not even to the boy. It was a secret, and one he hated keeping. The Buddha left his wife, and squandered a decade in a selfish quest for spiritual purity. But instead of hiding his shortcomings, the Buddha used them to demonstrate how even a flawed man could overcome ill-being. Merlin had always been too ashamed to do that.

"When I first rode with the Xiongnu," said Merlin, "we used a primitive saddle with no leg support. It was very inefficient. After a few days, my thighs were so cramped that I feared I could go no further. I asked for a strap of leather, so that I might make a stirrup. One of the warriors gave me a rope."

"They did not have stirrups?"

"They had never even seen them. In India, we used thin rope stirrups that looped around the big toe, which is possible to do when one is wearing sandals. But, whereas I was dressed in the fur boots of the Xiongnu, this device was useless to me. I even fell from my pony."

The wind outside picked up. The lamp nearly blew out.

"The Xiongnu warriors," said Merlin, "mocked me for my graceless horsemanship. In my mindless rage, I dismounted and re-tied the stirrup. I wrapped it around my entire foot and charged forward a ways." Merlin's voice began to tremble. "I twisted at the hips so that I was facing them, leaning back over the horse's hind end. I pretended to fire an arrow."

"The Parthian shot?"

"I had seen knights do it when I was in Persia. They had to train for years to master it. I found that with the added stability of my full boot stirrup, even I could do it." Merlin shook the rosewood beads of his bracelet. "They asked me to build them a saddle with a stirrup, so I did. Within a few years, every savage from the Great Wall to the Rhineland had them. I let those killers become masters of the horse. It was me."

Ector said nothing.

"After I saw the horrors that sprang from my invention, I determined that I would sew no more saddle, regardless of how wickedly they might abuse me. Scottas, my master, was an excellent judge of character. He knew I cared little for my own life. He swore to kill one of his captives every time I refused to sew for him."

Merlin's wrist began to shake. "To show he was in earnest, he propped a terrified little Chinese girl in front of me, and slit her throat. He carved off her ears and ordered me to hold them all night long. If I let go of them before the sun came up, Scottas would kill her sister as well. He fed her body to his war dogs. The Huns never buried the souls they dispatched. Their wolfhounds always needed good meat."

Ector said, "Does Pashent know this? Can he b-blackmail you?"

"No one knows. I was destitute when I first arrived in Paris. To make ends meet, I stitched a few saddles in the savage style. I became friends with a fellow named James who played cithara on the street corner. One evening, he told me some Roman knights were looking for me. They had heard I was a Hunnish witch. Next morning, I hopped a ride to Sussex with some Saxons. I was on the same keel as Chief Hengst. The Germans probably still remember that. Wildmen have excellent memories."

Ector tossed a horse blanket onto a straw pile. "I will k-keep watch on Pashent. Go to sleep. You have a c-castle to build." He unbuckled his belt and laid down his sword.

"My life's history sickens me," said Merlin. "I was weak. I was foolish."

"Aye," said Ector. He blew out the lamp. "That makes you just like the r-rest of us."

Chapter XXIX: The Hay Moon, AD 498

Noli turbare circulos meos.

Do not disturb my circles.

* * *

In Merlin opinion, Britannia was sorely wanting in terms of aesthetics. Her architecture was uninspiring, her food was bland, and her weather ranged from *cool and damp* to *damp and foggy*. And yet, on some spring days when the sky forgot how cloudy it was supposed to be, the island erupted in a verdant blanket of budding heath and ivy. *New green* was what Brother Tinh Tu used to call it.

Taking advantage of such a sunlit day, Merlin spread out a scroll of construction plans on a table in the courtyard of the half-built castle. His task was to calculate the costs for building supplies. The most expensive items were the new drawbridge gears, which had to be imported from Paris.

This purchase required cash, which posed a challenge since King Vortiger stopped minting coins a few years into his reign. Since then, Britannia lacked its own currency, leaving Merlin no choice but to spend weeks at the market accumulating foreign denarii before he could buy anything of value. The process was beyond inefficient; it was ridiculous.

Merlin detected the astringent odor of cracked walnut husks. On the other side of the yard, Gwalter the weaver was dipping an oar-like wooden ladle into a simmering cauldron of dye. Taking a break from his task, Merlin strolled over and dipped his index finger into the brew. When he withdrew it, the skin around his fingernail was blue. "Excellent!" he said. "How much is there?"

"We should get three barrels. It will be much darker. Give it a few days."

"You do good work," said Merlin. "If we mix this with some ochre, we might just have ourselves a decent purple flag."

* * *

The blue dye stopped boiling. A black cat jumped onto the table. Merlin said, "I have been looking for you? Where have you been?"

Gopi replied, "One of your big fat rabbits got loose. I have been stalking it all day, but it keeps hopping out of range."

Merlin scratched the scruff of her neck, and said, "Did I ever tell you the story about the Brahmin Priest who came up to the Buddha and asked, *What can I do to achieve interbeing*? The Buddha replied, *You are a Brahmin priest, follow your training.* It was a somewhat controversial tale. After all, why would the Buddha say that a man who is not a Buddhist could achieve interbeing?"

"No, you never mentioned this."

"Of course, my good friend, Brother Tinh Tu had a different interpretation. He argued that this parable demonstrated that the Buddha was not rigidly attached to anyone's teachings, not even his own. What do you think of that?"

The cat hopped down to his ankles.

"It is an interesting interpretation. Why are you telling me this?"

"I believe that I have been too rigidly attached to my rational mind."

"You have?"

"Yes. That is why I have been unable to wrap my noggin around this trial you keep talking about. But now, I understand it."

"And what is the nature of this epiphany?"

"It appears, good Lady, that the trial is a symbol. The gods sent Arthur as a test. They wanted to see if I would stick to my principles. Could I influence him into becoming a true gentleman despite his low origins? Would I train him to be proper Buddhist, even though I was surrounded by Christians and pagans?"

"So, according to your analysis, the trial is *the very act* of raising Arthur?"

"Exactly. As you yourself have said, the gods wanted to find out if I was genuine; a genuine Buddhist who held fast to the Practice even when the whole world was against him. That is why they were asking all those theological questions. They wanted to see if I would trip up."

"But I thought you did not believe in the gods?"

"True. But I do believe in the interconnectedness of all things. If the gods are part of that unity, so be it. I have always accepted that there are forces greater than man. If some old witch wishes to name them and carve their faces into a tree, who am I to stop her?"

"This is quite a turn of events. Does it mean you accept my existence as well?"

"You are uncredulous, I will grant you that."

"*Uncredulous?*" Gopi meowed. "What does that mean?"

"If you were credulous, I would believe you *bona fide*. If you were incredulous, I would regard you as something that should not be believed. You, however, are a manifestation of my own mind, but still, I have learned things from you. And why not? Ultimately, the universe I perceive is the only universe there is. Therefore, since you have the possibility of being real, I am willing to suspend my critical thought, and engage with you as if you were undoubtedly real. Hence you are uncredulous."

The cat rubbed up against his leg. "You silly man. *Uncredulous* is not a word. You just made it up."

Merlin tugged lightly at her tail. "The human lexicon is a fluid institution. I see no reason not to give it an occasional stir."

* * *

The sound of splashing water over by the drawbridge caught Merlin's attention. Sir Galahad and Sir Percival where hauling a shirtless man out of the moat. They had just dunked his head in it. He gasped for air and wriggled to get free of the ropes around his wrists. They dunked him back in and kept him submerged.

Merlin jogged out to them, "I say! What is going on?"

Galahad had a grin on his face. "We caught a spy!"

"Red handed," said Percival. He waved a scroll of paper with his free hand.

Merlin thumped his staff against the torso of the partially submerged man. "How long do you intend to leave him down there?"

Galahad rested his elbow on the spy's back. "Just a bit more."

Merlin noticed a crucifix strung around the prisoner's neck. "What say we pull him up? I wish to interview him."

The knights hoisted the wet spy up to his feet.

Merlin said, "Gentlemen, I am about to do something which, upon initial review, may appear to be daft."

Merlin asked the spy. "What is your name lad? *Sprechen Sie Welsch?*"

The red-faced spy coughed up some water. "Horst. My name is Horst."

"That was not what he told me," said Galahad.

"So, Herr Horst," said Merlin, "are you any relation to old Chief Horst? You know, I sailed across the channel with his brother. Where did you learn to speak Celtic?"

"My grandmum."

"One of our wayward cousins, no doubt. I see you wear the Cross. You being a German, you must be one of those Arians?"

"Who?"

"The Arians. The followers of Arianus. Do you believe Jesus was a good teacher or God incarnate?"

Horst looked at Galahad, and then at Percival. They said nothing.

"He was," said Horst, "a teacher?"

"Just as I thought, you are an Arian." Merlin extended his arm around Horst's shoulders. "All things considered, I rather agree with Arianus, but you need not mention that to the Pope. Now then, let us look at these papers of yours."

Percival unrolled them and presented them to Merlin.

"We found these stuffed in his boots," said Galahad.

Merlin scanned the documents. They were charcoal sketches of the fortress. "These are quite good. Nice line weights. Were you trained as a clerk?"

"Who me?" said Horst.

"You really missed your calling. If you moved to Paris you could rake in some serious cash." Merlin tapped his finger against the diagram. "These six marks here, I presume they mean sixty paces? Actually, the outer abutment is slightly longer than that. Here, let me show you." Merlin led him across the meadow.

"We left a space of sixty-two yards between the wall and the first ring. I prefer to use the standard Byzantine yard myself. Much easier to measure than the old Roman yard. I know the Franks prefer it, but what does King Clovis know about architecture? He grew up in a mud hut."

"Mud hut?"

Merlin directed the tip of his staff toward the wall. "Now then, when you look out at that field, what do you see? Is it flat?"

"Aye. I suppose."

"No, you fool, it has rise-to-tread ratio of three divisions of ninety, which happens to be the sharpest incline one can grade a landscape and still have it appear to be level. Do you know what that gets us?"

"No."

"Well consider this, sixty yards is as far as an arrow can fly, even a Hun arrow. That ever so slight tilt gives us an opportunity to shoot from our tower, thus striking your comrades in the stomach. However, when your warriors send a return the volley, where will all their arrows land?"

"In the fort?"

"Certainly not! They will strike the wall, exactly one yard below the top. Geometry is so fascinating. I have been meaning to read Archimedes, but who has the time? Here, let me show you this." Merlin led him in through the main gate.

Galahad, following behind said, "Should we be taking him in there?"

"I just want to show him the walls." A white rabbit hopped over into a shady corner. "I raised that bunny," said Merlin. "Someone ought to put her back in the hutch."

Horst jumped back in horror.

"Problem, Sir?" said Merlin.

"It is just a rabbit," said Percival. He threw his cape over it and picked it up. Horst covered his face.

Merlin scratched his head. "You Saxons are a silly bunch. Here have a seat. I want to show you something."

Galahad dropped Horst on a stool by Merlin's table. Percival deposited the rabbit in an open barrel.

Merlin wandered off. He returned with a jug of wine and two large flagons. He sat down next to Horst and poured out a small sample for each of them. "These walls are pure granite. If you can find a castle with a foundation this solid, you should buy it."

Merlin took a sip, swished it around his mouth. "Please, try some. It was fermented using white grapes, just like in the Rhineland. Does it taste like German wine? Give me your honest opinion."

Horst gave his flagon a sniff. He drank some.

Merlin flicked his wrist and his Chinese glass appeared in his hand. He held it over Horst's knee. "Lovely afternoon is it not? Not too many days as sunny as this here in Cambria."

Within a few moments the wet cloth covering Horst's leg began to sizzle. He fidgeted in his seat, then screamed. He attempted to jump up, but Galahad and Percival forced him back into his chair. Merlin positioned the Chinese glass over the center of Horst's face. Soon, the skin on the tip of his nose began to burn.

"*Wissen Sie Etzel?*" said Merlin, "*Ich bin eine Hexe von Etzel.* That is where I learned to build this fort, by the way. It is so good to have a trade."

"*Bitte! Bitte!*" said Horst. "*Nein, bitte.* Stop!"

Horst struggled to get up. He blinked his eyes. Then he slumped over and fell to the ground.

Percival stammered. "Is he dead?"

"No. I drugged the wine. He may upchuck. You best tip him onto his side."

The two knights did as directed.

"Galahad," said Merlin, "this man will remain asleep until tomorrow. I want you to shave off every hair on his body, then dunk him in that vat of blue dye. Chop the heads off of three of my white rabbits and tie them around his neck like a necklace."

"Like a... *necklace?*" said Galahad.

"A bloody one. Just south of this fortress grows a stand of pines. Pick one of the red toadstools that grow at their base, but make sure to wear gloves. Then take Mister Horst up into the hills and set him under a tree. Pull the cap off the mushroom and rub it on his lips. Do not place it in his mouth, that will kill him."

"You want to let him go?"

"When he awakes, he will spend a day or so running about like a berserker. When he regains his wits and goes back to his people, they will not know whether to believe him or not."

"But he has seen our fort?"

"And over the next few days, he will see some even stranger sights. You see, Sir Galahad, when you sow the seeds of fear in your enemy, you have achieved very little. There is always a young man who will volunteer to face it. But when you fill their minds with uncertainty, you take one great step toward victory."

Percival said, "You drank the same wine he did. If it was drugged, how come it did not knock you out?"

"Actually," said Merlin, with a yawn, "it will." He poured the contents of his almost overflowing flagon. "I filled my cup to the brim with water, thus the toxins I ingested were substantially diluted. Our guest drank only the pure stuff." Merlin rested his elbows against the table. "Might I trouble you to carry me to my cot?" He closed his eyes and slumped forward, asleep.

* * *

The woman who appeared before Merlin was not simply beautiful, she was perfect, which was not to say she was unblemished or entirely symmetrical. After all, the moon is perfect, even with its flaws. She was, by any measure, the very ideal of the feminine form. In her strong yet delicate hand was a huntress's bow. She wore a brilliant bronze hoplite's helmet pitched back on her head like most ladies might wear a summer hat.

"It is time for your testimony," said Bright Eyed Athena, "You need not be afraid, just tell the truth. You always do."

"I would dispute that," said Ganesha, straddling a fine saddle secured to the back of a rat. "The only soul he never lied to was Judith the Jew, and he hid his literacy from her."

Quetzalcoatl the feathered serpent hissed, "We have already addressed this issue. Let us hear from the accused." He fanned himself with the green and yellow plumage of his tail, while a hummingbird sucked nectar from the orchid that bloomed on his crown.

Diwi the Rice Goddess nodded in agreement. She flexed her wings and returned to combing her hair. The sun setting over the red wine waters of the Aegean Sea reflected off the looking glass she held in her fingers. The scales of her mermaid tail glistened like disks of jade.

Lady Athena led Merlin to the center of the circle. Gathered around him were the gods, each reclining comfortably on the furniture of their choosing. This was no agitated mob. They simply wanted the facts. To the north, atop a high flat topped hill, the temple fires were glowing in the Acropolis.

"We are in Athens!" said Merlin to Athena. "I have always wanted to go there."

"Be still," she said. "Hear my voice."

In his right hand, Merlin was holding the Persian officer's dagger, still wet with the warm blood of the Centurion Aethiops.

"I was just a boy," said Merlin.

The Goddess Guan Yin washed the blade clean with her jar of pure water, then pointed her willow branch at the noose in his left hand. "What about the peasant girl?"

Merlin replied, "What would you have me do? You have wind and waves; all I have is… these two hands. How can you expect any more from me? We only have what you have given us. If you wanted us all to be saintly, you should have made all of us saints."

Bearded Wotan rested his hammer down by his muscular legs, "Should we take that to be a confession?"

"Take it however you wish," said Merlin. "I know I am guilty. Did I ever claim to be innocent?"

"Your plea is accepted," said Ganesha. "Whereas he has admitted his culpability, I propose to the court that this human be reincarnated as a maggot, that he might burrow through the corpses of individual like those whom he murdered."

Athena countered, "Surely that would be a waste. The evidence clearly indicates that the accused has a heartfelt dedication to serving humanity. Certainly there are mitigations to be considered. He was shown so little compassion in his formative years."

Reeking of brimstone, Satan asked, "What exactly are you proposing?"

"I would suggest," said Bright-Eyed Athena, "that he become an elephant, one who is domesticated and so remains under the watchful supervision of his trainer. That way he could continue his assistance to the inhabitants of the mortal realm."

The Goddess Pele, straight-backed and carrying her egg-shaped sister under her armpit, arose from a lava flow and said, "Let us bring it to a vote."

One by one, the gods and goddesses in the circle opened up his or her hand, wing, paw, or fin. They each held two voting stones: one black, one white.

Merlin closed his eyes. He jiggled the beads of his bracelet and said, "What about all my other crimes? I left Brother Tinh Tu to die. Is he of no consequence to you?"

*   *   *

A rooster crowed. Merlin rolled over in his cot and rubbed his throbbing head. On the floor next to him, Arthur was sleeping on a soldier's bedroll.

"I say, boy," said Merlin, "have I ever been dishonest with you?"

Arthur opened one eye. "You are all right then? We were a bit worried."

"I know I can be a prevaricator, but I have never hidden anything from you, have I?"

"Not that I know of." Arthur propped himself up on one elbow. "Is there something you want to tell me?"

Merlin lay back and positioned his arm over his eyes to shield them from the rising sun. "No," he said, "I just needed confirmation."

Chapter XXX: The Winter Moon, AD 499

A fronte praecipitium a tergo lupi.

A precipice in front, wolves behind.

* * *

In Constantinople, the olive was king. Every meal included a plate of them. And even though the pagan temples had been toppled centuries before, everyone still celebrated the end of winter with a gift of olive oil, enclosed inside a hollow statuette of Jupiter with ribbons tied to the stopper by his feet. It was as if the feast of Saturnalia had never been eclipsed by the Mass of the Nativity.

It was pepper, not olive oil, which wooed the palate in India. Every village had its own variety. Cities like Nalanda dedicated one square exclusively to vendors hawking a pantheon of peppers. Of course, neither olives nor peppers were eaten in Britannia. This mossy island was perhaps the only province in Caesar's empire that never capitulated to Roman cuisine.

These thoughts arose in Merlin's consciousness as he sipped a bowl of mutton broth. His did best to ignore the caterwauling of the knights all around him. It was the Feast of Saint Sylvester, and the king's dining chamber was packed with solders getting drunk on winter ale.

Down the hallway and off to the left, a less muscular contingent of court bureaucrats was holding its own grand meal with somewhat more sober men. Logic would have dictated that Merlin should have been with them, but logic did not rule this kingdom, the king did.

The king slid his silver setting off to the side. He called out, "Another flagon!" He bit into a joint of venison. A serving wench passed a tray of blood pudding to the king's dinner guest, Sir Pashent.

"Venerable Wizard," said Pashent, "I have some excellent wine you should sample. It comes from Burgundy. They say it is as old as you are."

Merlin buttered his bread. "Then surely it has turned to vinegar."

The king elbowed Pashent in the ribs. "If you challenge him to a battle of insults, you will lose. Besides, he does not take alcohol."

"Not even a drop?" said Pashent.

Merlin whistled to the court hounds. One of them trotted over. "I drink one bowl of beer in the month of Octavius. I am not an extremist."

"And he always gets the last word," said the king with a wink.

By way of response, Merlin bowed. He wiped his hands on the dog's coat.

"See what I mean?" said the king. The two noblemen roared with laughter.

Merlin gave his mustache a final lick. He did not relish being mocked by the king, but put into perspective, the ribbing was quite tame. King Vortiger was fond of pummeling his staff with a bronze-tipped riding crop, and Attila played polo with the heads of those who gave him bad advice.

Merlin excused himself. "I beg your leave, My Liege, but I must be off to bed. I am meeting with your stone mason at sun up."

"Excellent. You keep up the good work. We need that castle done by spring."

"I will be sure to pass your urgency on to Mister Antonius."

Sir Pashent carefully placed his knife onto the plate of one of his deputies.

Merlin bowed and scooted down the hallway, past the old crones washing pots and kettles. The door to his bedchamber was unlatched. He usually latched it, but not always. Next to his cot was a pitcher of water, his bowl, and an apple.

Merlin took off the cloak that covered his orange toga. He sat cross-legged on his straw mattress. He drank a sip of water and began his evening meditation.

"The Bhodisattva Avalokita," he chanted to himself, "while moving in the deep course of perfect understanding, shed light on the five skandas and found them equally empty." Merlin began to perspire. "After this penetration he overcame…"

* * *

The pungent scent of fish paste wafted through the window.

Merlin heard a woman's voice ask, "Did you drink it?" She spoke to him in Greek. Her accent was Egyptian.

Merlin opened one eye to see an old lady in the doorway.

She had brown skin and broad lips, and was wiping flour off her hands. She gently reprimanded him. "You should be more careful, boy."

"That water tasted funny," he said to her. "What are you doing here? You should be in the kitchen."

She cleaned out his bowl with her apron. "It is the dish that offends you."

Beads of sweat rolled down Merlin's face. He felt sleepy.

"You are ill, Ambrosius." She brushed aside his curly red hair and dabbed his forehead with a cool wet rag. Her clothes smelled like toasted flat bread. She sang a song: "Eits chayim hi lamachzikim ba, vetomechehe meushar."

"Do you have to leave?" said Merlin. "I miss you."

Judith's ghost kissed him on the cheek. "Be still, boy. Hear my voice."

Touched by the comforting caress of her lips, he fell into a deep sleep.

* * *

What Merlin noticed first was the odor of mildew. A layer of crusty pus had formed on the edged of his eyes. He was lying on a cot somewhere. A sharp pain shot up from his hip. He lifted up his blouse to find an enormous blue-gray bruise on his thigh. Outside, there was a light patter of rain.

"God in heaven," said Tristan, "you are alive!"

Merlin coughed. "What is going on? Where is Arthur?"

Tristan handed him a canteen. "We are in a cave, hiding. There has been a coup. My grandfather and Duke Arthur had you delivered here. They are organizing a counter rebellion."

"Rebellion?" Merlin's mouth was dry, he chugged down a swig of water.

"Young man, I want you to give me a formal report, focusing on the events that led me to be sequestered in this cavern."

"Aye, Sir," said Tristan, now standing at attention. "Three days ago the king became ill after supper. His Majesty was taken to his bed. A number of the Dragons fell sick, but none of the company under Sir Pashent's command. Sir Cadwagan accused Pashent of poisoning them. A fight broke out. Pashent killed the king."

"The king is dead! *Caco santi!* How many of our troops were killed?"

"Half of the officers are dead," Tristan stared straight ahead. "Including my father, six cousins and my Uncle Kay."

A crack of thunder broke the silence. It began to rain in earnest.

"I am sorry for your loss," said Merlin. "I knew Kay back when he was your age. You honor your lost relatives by maintaining such composure. At least you still have Ector. How is he faring?"

"Well enough. He lost some fingers."

Merlin sighed a loud guttural sigh. "I should have seen it coming. But please, continue."

"Duke Ector was called away to the western front," said Tristan. "The border guards reported that Chief Aella's warriors were on the march."

"But that cannot be! Chief Aella has been crippled for months. Two of his wives got in a fight and pushed him into a fire. What did Arthur do?"

"He rode out to join Ector, but he thought the Germans might be ambushing them. He sent a sortie back toward the castle. One of scouts saw the sentinel tower burning. When he came closer, Sir Pashent's men were stabbing the watchmen."

"Our ever suspicious Arthur," said Merlin. "Now I understand. Pashent planned to take the court, regroup, and attack Arthur and Ector when they returned. *Latet anguis in herba.* How was Pashent was dispatched?"

"He fled on horseback. Ector's cavalry shot an arrow in his back."

"Where is Ector now? Is Arthur with him?"

"Duke Ector rode to Carmarthen to close the port. Arthur is mustering an infantry. Everyone is afraid the Saxons will attack."

"Or the Scots or the Franks or the Visigoths. As it now stands, we could be conquered by a quartet of gnomes armed only with macramé hooks."

A drop of musky water splattered onto the floor.

"What are we going to do?" asked Tristan. "We have lost so many of our knights. The Dragons are all dead."

Merlin stroked his chin where he used to tug at his beard. "Hired swords are easy to find. Unfortunately, we have neither gold nor land with which to pay them. What we need is some sort of a device, something that would attract a good sum of mercenaries to this gloomy little island."

"Like what?"

Merlin examined his surroundings. "Where in blazes are we?"

"We are one hundred paces north of the compound where you used to live. Sir Arthur said the savages fear to come here because of the apple trees."

"Deep in the bosom of Apfalon, eh? The Jutes believe that my orchard is full of fairies, a misperception I have endeavored assiduously to cultivate. Speaking of evil spirits, where is the Lady Morgan?"

"She disappeared."

Merlin coughed again. He was highly phlegmatic and had slept for days. The symptoms would suggest a dose of nightshade. He ran through a possible scenario. The lethal juice was rubbed into the king's cup and those of the Dragons. Wine is one of the best agents for hiding toxins. It increases the potency while masking the objectionable flavor. That was why Pashent so graciously offered it.

Merlin snapped his finger. "Morgan LeFay tried to poison me."

"But why did it not kill you?"

"Temperance! I drank only water. She should have used foxglove infused with ginger. Little Morgan, what an amateur you are." Merlin peered out at the downpour. "This foul weather favors our cause. The rebels will not be able to sail."

The fire at the mouth of the cave flickered, sending shadows dancing across the walls. Plato proposed that reality was the fire. We mortals could only perceive the shadows. Conversely, the Buddha taught that perceptions were the only reality: only shadows, no fire. How strange that two such perceptive men could reach such opposite conclusions.

Merlin was overcome with a surge of nausea. He laid back down. "When I was taken captive by the Huns," he said, "I was given an opiate to make me sleep."

"Were you captured in battle?"

"Alas, mine is not a tale of bravery. I was a civilian clerk who fell into the clutches of a misguided wizard. He traded me to a Hun war chief in exchange for a pudgy effeminate toady."

Tristan added a log to the fire. "Were the Huns as wicked as everyone says?"

Merlin wrapped himself in his blanket. "No, just wickedly effective. Whereas they had no homeland, their life revolved around the family. Hun warriors collected wives so as to sire an army of children. Similarly, women of rank married a man *and* his brothers."

"That would be some wedding."

"They were sordid affairs, full of poetry and fermented dog milk. Throat singers sang epic songs accompanied by a long fiddle fashioned from a horse's skull."

"What did it sound like?"

"Remarkably hypnotic as far as I can recall. Of course, my judgment was rather spotty back then. I was *non compos mentis*." Merlin bent his leg and winced.

"What does that mean?"

"It means I went bonkers. I spent weeks reciting the Mantra of the Prajnaparamita. All night long I did nothing but chant, *Gah-tay, gah-tay, para gah-tay, parasam gah-tay, bodhi svaha.* In time, I deteriorated to the point where I was only able to say one word: *gah-tay.* I was afraid to sleep. I just paced around in circles."

"I have never known you to be a mad man," said Tristan.

Merlin almost laughed. There were those who claimed the Buddha was insane. Fortunately, he had trained himself to step back and observe the irrational components of his mind. When he meditated, they all just drifted away. Perhaps it was better to describe the Buddha as being half-crazy. After all, he was human.

Tristan asked, "What are we going to do?"

Instead of replying, Merlin directed his attention out toward the entrance. "You are a fine student of conversation, Tristan. Once this deluge rests, I suggest we trek out to my old hermitage."

"My orders are to keep you here."

"And you have fulfilled them. Can you shoot us some game? If you could lend me your sword, I would gladly dress the carcasses."

"Your sidearm is under your cot," said Tristan.

Merlin reached down for his sword. "Let us see what Buddha's Thunderbolt can do."

* * *

The raindrops stopped falling in mid flight. A bat crawled out of a crack in the ceiling. Merlin raised his walking stick. When he lowered it again, Lady Gopi hung upside-down on the handle. Using but one finger, he stroked her chin.

"You are not afraid I will bite you?" she said. "We bats have a nasty reputation."

"Not in the east. The Chinese regard your ilk as harbingers of good fortune. They smile upon seeing your elongated digits flitting about the pagoda. So you see, Madam, I am quite lucky to have you in my company."

"How sweet of you to say so. So tell me, when you were with the Huns, how did you regain your wits? The Goddess Ceridwen wishes to know."

"The Huns," said Merlin, "had military witch doctors who were especially adept at potions. The night before a battle, their cavalry chewed a root that dulled the body to pain. Upon waking they drank an infusion that enhanced the mind's ability to react. And just before the attack, they snuffed a powder that washed away all fear of death."

"Did they drug you?"

"Let us just say I was medicated. After I descended into babbling lunacy, most of the Huns shunned me. But my master Scottas did not want to lose his investment. He was angry that my madness kept me from reading for him. So, he directed his medicine man to spike my canteen with opium. After that, I slept. Eventually it returned me to sanity."

"It is not every man who receives mercy from Attila's Horde."

Merlin scratched Gopi's fuzzy chest. "Attila was actually a dwarf, albeit a large one. All his saddles were customized. He could barely walk, but on a pony, he was Mercury."

"What was he like?"

"He ate from a wooden bowl. The Huns viewed wood as a luxury, as there is none of it in the steppes. In their opinion, men who hid behind stone walls were cowards."

"He must have hated the Romans."

"And the Persians and the Chinese. Great Father Attila was none too fond his own people either. When one of his nephews hinted of competition, the lad woke up with a tent spike in his neck."

"Where did you meet Attila?"

"He called a war council on the north shore of the Danube. My master Scottas trotted me in for a show. When Attila's secretary found out I was Roman, he interrogated me."

"Attila the Hun had a secretary? I thought Huns were savages?"

"Savage, but not stupid. It always bothered Attila that that Huns had no written language. He realized its military value. To resolve this paucity, he kidnapped a clerk, a Macedonian named Alexander. In time, Alexander was adopted as an Epthalite. He even acquired some Hunnish wives."

"What did he ask you?"

"He was interested in the topography north of Italy. He asked if anyone had ever taken Rome. I told him Hannibal of Carthage had done it, but then had to retreat after the winter killed off his elephants."

"But that is not true," said Gopi. "Why did you say that?"

"I wanted Attila to invade Italy. More specifically, I wanted him to march through the Rhineland to get there. Five centuries ago, the Germans massacred Augustus Caesar's army in the forests of Tuteborg. There were no survivors. I reckoned Attila's horsemen might suffer the same if they entered Saxon territory."

"Did Attila's secretary believe you?"

"Not one word. Alexander threatened to have my tongue ripped out, so I up and lied some more. I told him that the Romans never spoke well of Hannibal, but that in Africa, the bards still sang of his victory.

Alexander clapped his hands and called out, *Speck!*

"I watched as a little Negro, only waist high, somersaulted into the yurt. Brass bells jingled on his ankles. His skin was pitch-black. On each stubby finger was a golden band. He grinned like a clown. Alexander asked Speck the Negro if he knew of a man called Hannibal. Speck said that Hannibal was a great general. He attacked Rome on an elephant but was defeated.

Alexander smiled at me, and said, *Looks like you lose your tongue, Pig Eyes*. I was so terrified, I spoke directly to Attila, which normally would have gotten me an appointment with a flay knife.

I told Attila that Speck would agree to anything Alexander said. After all, Speck was a jester. I then asked Attila if he actually believed the Romans could have defeated an army of elephants? Did that make sense? Why would an African commoner like Speck even know Hannibal's name if Hannibal had been a failure?

Attila showed some interest in my argument. Everyone fell silent. He asked little Speck if the elephant king did in fact take Rome?

Speck pouted like a baby. My heart pounded so hard I thought it was going to shatter my sternum. Then Speck said, *Aye, Great Father. Mister Pig Eyes has it right. I did not wish to offend Mister Alexander, as he is a like a son to you.*"

The bat splayed out her wings. With one quick flap, she landed on Merlin's shoulder. "Why did the Negro say that? It was not true."

Merlin answered, "Indeed, Speck may have acted foolish, but Speck, he was no fool. Like me, he yearned for freedom, and that would only come with Attila's demise. After the council, Attila assassinated all his nephews, including my master Scottas. And then Attila, the Great Father, Lord Consort of the Sky Bitch, coronated himself *King of the Huns.*"

"He was not a king before then?"

"No, and he was not much of one afterwards. It was a ploy. Attila needed to be a king so that he could sign a treaty with the king of the Ostragoths, who really was a king. Together, their armies marched west. They planned to take City of Rome from the north, and invade Constantinople by sea."

"I did not know the Huns could sail."

"They never got the chance. The Ostro-Hunish confederation so frightened the Romans they formed an alliance with the Visigoths and combined their forces. Caesar's army met the Huns in a field in Gaul. It was down the road from a decommissioned fort full of old Roman soldiers and their Frankish wives. Just a few huts and a wine bar."

"Orleans?" said Gopi. "Did you fight at Catalonian Fields?"

"I ran like a baby. Just before the Visigoths overran our camp, I stripped naked and tied my own hands. I told the solders who found me that I was a Latin grammarian, forced to read by the Huns. They set me free."

"Ironic," she said, "it was a Visigoth who first enslaved you."

"After my release, I met up with some Syrian archers working for the Romans. They delivered me to their centurion's headquarters. He asked me what

I knew about the Huns. I gave him all the intelligence I knew. We stayed up till dawn."

"You aided the victory. Perhaps you were a better soldier than you admit."

"There was no victory. It was a draw. Attila's Ostragoth mercenaries were worthless prats. They ran off as soon as the legionnaire's infantry leveled their pikes at them. King Attila was forced to pull back. Then the Visigoths fled into the woods, and the battle was over. The Romans were livid."

"Was that when Attila was killed?"

"He died twenty years later. He had added an Ostragoth maiden to his harem, and was in the throes of conjugal embrace when he was caught by a mortal seizure. I always thought the Germans were the only race capable of slaying him. Who would have wagered a woman's charms would be their weapon of choice?"

"What became of the Huns?"

"After Attila was gone, the Franks and Visigoths slaughtered them. The survivors fled down the Danube, hoping to find a haven with the Ostragoths. Instead, the Ostragoths hanged the women and drowned the children. What few remained were sold to the Romans and burned alive in the streets of Constantinople. As far as I know, the Huns have been cleansed from the earth."

"I wonder," said Gopi, "could it be you are the last one who still speaks Hunnish?"

"I suspect so," said Merlin. "*Sic erat in fatis.* And to think, Attila's dynasty could have ruled Europe for centuries, had it not been for that one little Speck."

Chapter XXXI: Winter Moon, AD 499

Aliqaundo et insanire iucundum est.

Sometimes it is pleasant to act even like a madman.

* * *

The ash produced from the immolation of a thatched roof is especially fine. Arthur walked through a layer of it, kicking up grey puffs that spiraled up into his face. He sneezed into his glove. His snot was streaked with that same ash. He had been breathing it for three days. His clothes he reeked of it as well, which could have been remedied by laundering them. But Arthur had no time for that.

The half-burnt timbers of the royal stable were still smoldering, and would periodically reignite, forcing Arthur to marshal what able-bodied men were left to haul water buckets from the mill pond behind the burned-out gatehouse. How that caught fire was anyone's guess, but one of the cooks swore she saw the king's horse galloping in circles with its tail on fire.

Arthur waved his conical straw hat to get the attention of the village folk crowded around in the courtyard. He let out a thundering whistle to quiet them, then called out, "We have no more bread today. All we have is grain. Father Thomasius will give a quarter bushel to each household who wants it. I think that is fair, aye?"

Everyone grumbled. "What are we supposed to eat? Where did our taxes go?"

The rhythmic pounding of hooves, enormous hooves, drew closer. It was Sir Ector approaching on his Percheron. Everyone jostled to get out of his way.

"Is the port secure?" said Arthur. "How did it go? Did you get any provisions?"

Ector dismounted. "A t-train of supplies will be here by sun up. Only two ships were l-left at the docks. We emptied them." He headed off toward the doorway that led to the royal courtroom. The door was broken off at the hinges.

Arthur joined him, and the two of them entered the building. A railing from the guard tower had fallen and poked a gaping hole in the roof. Loose thatch covered the floor. Dried blood was splattered on the back wall.

Ector flung off his glove, and said, "Someone l-lynched the mason." He carefully unwrapped the strips of linen covering his two scab-covered finger stumps. "They stuck a chisel in his eye and jammed t-two coins up his nose."

"It was probably his own men. Did you find Morgan? What do you hear from up north?"

"Morgan hopped a b-boat to Brittany. The Scots are raiding, but no more than usual. We found Bishop Zephyrinus clubbed to d-death. His lock box was next to him, b-busted open. Pashent must have p-paid him off."

"We cannot let this out," said Arthur. "We will have to say that the bishop was bucked off his horse. I will send Galahad to get the body. Father Thomasius must not know."

"How is the c-court?" said Ector. "Any news from Sussex?"

"The court is secure, but the farmers are too scared to go back to the fields. Gawain got word of a flotilla of Jutes sailing south from Kent. They are supposed to join Chief Cedric's village. Do you know him?"

"Cedric's father was Cynric, one of King Vortiger's b-bodyguards." Ector opened his canteen and drank. "I trained him to ride. His son needs to p-prove his salt. He will attack us by summer. You can b-bet on that."

"Can we raise an army by then? Half our knights are dead. Did you get find any horses?"

"Just two. I can g-get more. How is Merlin?"

"I sent Tristan to guard him, but he slipped away. He could be anywhere."

A shouting match was erupting out in the courtyard.

"Here we go again," said Arthur. He stomped out. An old crone with a long head smock was gripping onto a sack of grain. Father Thomasius was delicately trying to wrestle it away from her.

"Madam," said Thomasius, "I understand you are hungry, we all are. But Duke Arthur has been very fair about this. Only a quarter sack per household."

She reached her fist into the sack, stuck out her foot, and leaned against the Father's shoulder. Father Thomasius stumbled in one direction and the she fell in the other. She let loose her grip. A stream of golden grain sprayed into the air. Her cloak spiraled upward. Everyone tumbled over each other, as if on cue.

Arthur ducked for cover. Bodies and wheat scattered everywhere. The only one left standing was a stranger with his head shaved clean. He was beardless and wore only a loincloth. His half naked body was covered in soot. Arthur shaded his pale white eyelids to get a better look. He saw an orange neckerchief. It was Merlin.

"Woe Britannia!" Merlin moaned with his hands on high. "Will the Lord of Isaiah strip this land of her sons, just as Nebucadnezzar rid Jerusalem of the Israelites?"

"Where did he come from?" said Father Thomasius. "Did you say *Nebucadnezzar*?"

"Oh, lament!" said Merlin, almost howling. "I have been sealed in a cave for six days, with neither food nor drink. And on the seventh day, I saw above me, a dove of pure white with an olive branch. What did I do?"

Arthur wedged his way through the mob. "Damn it, *Merthen*! Where have you been?"

Merlin responded with a friendly wave and launched back into his patter. "I followed this bird of peace off toward the sanctuary. And there I espied a winged sphinx, its eyes like burning lanterns, its claws like mighty grappling hooks." He stared directly at Father Thomasius. "The angel spoke to me in Aramaic."

"You speak Aramaic?" said Thomasius.

Merlin poked the father in the belly. "No, and yet I understood every word. The beast said, *Give up thy arm*. And though its glorious radiance nearly blinded me, I presented my weapon."

"Your walking stick?" said Thomasius.

"No, Father, my sword, *Ex Cala*..." Merlin paused. "My sword of pure wootz steel, *Ex Calibur!* I handed it to the monster, and swoosh! It burst into flame. Bolts of lighting sprung forth from the weapon's shining surfaces. It was a thunderbolt incarnate."

Arthur stepped up to Merlin. "You look ridiculous. What are you doing? What happened to your hair?"

Merlin covered his face. "I hid my eyes from this fabulous being. When I cast up my eyes, I saw the creature aloft in the sky. He flew at me, striking me in the thigh like the seraph that wrestled Jacob." Merlin lifted up the side of his loincloth and revealed the large bruise on his hip. "It was then that I realized that this creature was no beast of mortal flesh, but rather an angel of the Lord."

There were many things Arthur never understood about Merlin. If Merlin was as dedicated to the monastic life as he claimed, why was he such a showman? Merlin idolized his friend, Brother Tinh Tu, for the simplicity of his insight. But whenever Merlin got the chance, he would go out of his way to tell the most convoluted tale he could muster.

Arthur crossed his arms. "And what did you do then, you mangy old goat?"

Merlin strolled through the refugees. "Good question, boy. I cried out, *Deo gratia. Have mercy on me.* Imagine my surprise when the angel replied, *Mercy shall you have. For soon Britannia shall have a king.*"

"A new king?" said Thomasius. "Well, this is news. Who might that be?"

Merlin replied, "Actually, Father, I asked the very same question. But instead of replying, the seraph exploded into a column of brimstone. It scorched me so gravely my hair was singed to a strand, and my clothing reduced to cinders."

Merlin shook his arms and his legs. A puff of ash came off of his body. There were a few laughs.

"The angel said, *Your king will be the one who has protected fair Britannia by dispatching those heathens who would oppose the true cross. You will know him, for he and he alone will hold Ex Calibur aloft upon the harvest season.*"

Ector stomped up. "Somebody got a h-haircut."

Merlin crawled on all fours. "I cowered low, afraid to stand lest I be burned to a crisp. When I dared to looked up, I saw that my sword of steel, Ex Calibur, had been wedged into an outcrop by yonder lakeside, inserted there by the awesome power of this heavenly denizen."

In a monotone, Ector said, "Have you g-gone crackers?"

Merlin rose to his feet, grasping bits of hay in each fist. "And then the angel was gone." He opened his hands and the straws fell downward. "Dispersed into the ether from which it emanated. Cautiously, I extended my hand to touch the sword Ex Calibur. When I did, a mighty bolt of lightning sprang forth from the metal, stinging me so profoundly that that I could hold no more."

Arthur noticed Merlin was not wearing his sword. Granted, Merlin was not wearing his pants either, but still, this was a dangerous time. By now, every German from Wessex to Kent had heard of the king's assassination. Chief Aella's warriors could expect a great reward for killing the king's wizard. Surely Merlin knew that. Why the devil was he unarmed?

Merlin displayed his trembling fingers. "I asked myself, *What portents does this fiery vision hold?* And then, touched ever so tenuously by the hand of providence, I understood the angel's message."

"And you saw all this?" said Thomasius. "Here in Carmarthen?"

"Yay verily, this weapon was not meant for me. It was meant for our new king. Ex Calibur had punished me, for I was not worthy of wielding her. No, that honor would only go to the man noble enough to dislodge the blessed blade from its petrological sheath."

Merlin aimed his staff at Sir Ector. "Honorable Duke, may I humbly request you post a guard at the rock containing Ex Calibur, and forbid anyone from disturbing it on pain of death. For it must be known throughout the land, and even abroad, that any knight who has slain the savages in defense of our fair Britannia, shall be offered the opportunity to remove this confined cutlery from is craggy holster."

"You want w-what?"

"Good Duke," said Merlin, "whosoever, by the grace of God, is successful in dislodging Ex Calibur, shall be coronated King of Britannia, forthwith." Merlin pranced off to the lake with one hand on his loincloth. "Come join me! Come and behold Ex Calibur."

No one followed the crazy old man, except of course, for Arthur, who had been doing just that since he was but a street urchin. Since that time, Arthur had learned never to fear Merlin's talent for swirling fact with fiction, philosophy with mind games. Even when Merlin was beset by hallucinations, he was always kindhearted and ethical. Few sane men could claim that.

Ector said, "This better be g-good."

Arthur could now see the outcrop. The handle of a weapon stuck out of it.

"Noble Field Marshal," said Merlin, "you have slain many a son of the Rhineland in defense of our blessed island have you not?"

Ector approached the exposed rock. "What of it?"

"Today is Sunday when the leaves are turning. Therefore, I entreat you, remove this weapon from its halter." Merlin pantomimed a pulling motion.

"This?"

"All I ask is that you give it a tug. What harm can there be in that?"

Ector, unimpressed, extended his unwounded hand. The moment his palm touched the handle, a bolt of blue lighting shot towards him. It slithered up the sleeve of his chain mail coat like a glowing serpent. The shock sent him reeling into the truf. The crowd became silent.

Father Thomasius said, "Oh my."

Arthur said nothing. As far as he could tell, Merlin had created a foxfire that would appear at his command. Arthur scanned his memory, trying to remember when he had seen this trick. Then again, it could be a new trick. Merlin still spent quite a bit of time grilling the sailors at the docks. Perhaps one of them taught him how to generate Saint Vitus's fire? Or maybe, he figured it out on his own.

Duke Ector gazed up at Merlin. "You old troll," he said, shaking his hand. "What kind of h-hobgoblin spawned you?"

Chapter XXXII: The Hare Moon. AD 501

Mendacem oportet esse memorem

A liar must have a good memory.

* * *

When Merlin accepted ordination as a Buddhist novice, he agreed to pursue a life of celibacy. Having come from a Christian nation, he viewed chastity as a practice that protected one from the corrupting draw of animal desire. He assumed that a monk could only function properly by freeing himself from such distraction.

But as Merlin aged, he realized that the value of a sexless life had nothing to with evading sensual traps, and everything to do with avoiding connections. A monastic could not marry nor sire children. With no in-laws to borrow from, and no sons to lend to, the monk rarely needed to ask favors or grant them. As a result, celibates possessed a kind of neutrality unknown to most men.

It was because of this impartiality that Ector and Arthur elected Merlin to resolve those occasional small claims which spring up in any community. Thus the old man found himself addressing two shepherds, who stood uncomfortably in the well of what was the formerly the king's throne room.

"So," said Merlin, "all parties agree that Mister Gruffyd ended up with eleven lambs sired by Mister Trahearn's ram." He jotted down a few notes.

Farmer Trahearn nodded in agreement.

"Mister Gruffyd," said Merlin, "you are to deliver five sheep to Mister Trahearn. And make sure three of them are ewes."

Gruffyd protested. "But Your Excellency, my son arranged the deal, not me. That is not just."

"Perhaps, but it is just enough. You ended up benefiting from your offspring's actions. If your boy returns with the money he owes Mister Trahearn, I would gladly reconsider my decision."

"Not likely," said Trahearn.

Merlin shot him an ugly glance. "Mister Trahearn, I am ruling in your favor. It is in your best interest *not* to annoy me." He stamped his staff the floor. "*Me iudece*. This case is closed. If you are unsatisfied, feel free to submit an appeal to the church's court. I am sure they can cook up a reason to remove the sheep from both of you."

* * *

A beetle flew in through the window slat. It landed on Merlin's quill. He was about to flick off when he noticed everyone had stopped talking, not to mention blinking or breathing.

"Sorry to call on you at work," said the beetle. "Satan has another question. He wants to know why you always mock the church?"

Merlin attempted to turn the page of his book, but it stayed where it was. "They have created a monopoly," he said. "In India, the Gupta dynasty employs Jain bankers and Buddhist diplomats. Chinese citizens may choose from Taoism, Buddhism, Confucianism or any combination thereof. When we occidentals show such tolerance, perhaps then I will pop in for a snack at Pope Anastasius's house of holy wafers."

The beetle flapped her wings. "You play the satirist well, but every cynic I ever met was just a scorned romantic hiding beneath a philosopher's coat."

Merlin refuted her assessment. "Me, a cynic? No, I have never been a student of Diogenes. He was a world negator. I take the middle way."

"And yet you remind me so much of him. Have you ever read Cicero's account of his run in with Alexander the Great? It was written up in the *Tuscan Disputations*."

"Why no. I was not aware they met."

"One day," said Gopi, "when Alexander was traveling through Corinth, he heard of a strange philosopher who claimed to want nothing. After searching the city, Alexander found Diogenes lying on the ground, basking in the morning light. Alexander hovered over him and said, *I am king of all the known world. Name anything you desire, and it shall be yours.* Diogenes simply replied, *Just now, stand a bit away from the sun.*"

Merlin reared back, and almost giggled. "I will have to use that line."

* * *

And then, Gopi was gone. Merlin scanned his agenda. "Who is next on the docket?"

Into the courtroom strode a small stooped-shouldered man wearing a purple silk cape and a finely tailored red hat. It flopped over the left side of his head. Behind him was a man nearly as tall as Arthur, with brown hair and hazelnut eyes. He cut a fine figure in his leather short coat.

The foppish visitor bowed with a flourish, saying, "Allow me to introduce myself. I am Lord Claudius Pollox at your service." He motioned to his assistant. "This is my deputy, Cassius of Brittany."

Cassius bowed. "Good day, Your Highness."

Merlin scribbled down their names. "I am a civil servant. You will refer to me as *Your Excellency*. Now then, are you the defendant or the accuser?"

"Neither. I am the Emissary of His Highness, King Clovis. I come with an urgent message for Your Excellency and Chancellor Ector."

"Lord Ector only holds court on Tuesdays. May I see your papers?"

"I was not aware that Ector was semi-retired?"

Merlin stroked his clean-shaved chin. "Have we met?"

"This is my first visit to your court. But I am often told I have a familiar face."

Merlin nearly dropped his quill. "Thumbs!"

Thumbs winked an eye, the gray one, not the black one. "Perhaps we have met. Did you ever perform on the streets of Paris? As I recall, you had a sister named Morgan. I say, how is she doing these days?"

"Why you conniving sideshow freak." Merlin hailed the bailiff by the door. "Get the field marshal straight away."

Thumbs presented Merlin with a scroll, sealed with the signet of King Clovis. "How fortunate that I will be able to meet the renowned Duke Arthur."

"Oh, stop it," said Merlin. He did not accept the scroll. "And by the way, I would appreciate if you would stop telling people I was a Hunish witch. Do I tell people that you are a Jew?"

"Half Jew," said Thumbs.

Arthur entered the hall. His boots were muddy.

Merlin settled into his chair. "Good afternoon, boy. I have a treat for you. For at this special moment, I have the dubious pleasure of introducing you to one of nature's most asymmetrical productions."

Thumbs bowed to Arthur.

"Take off the glove," said Merlin. "Unless you have something to hide."

Thumbs puffed up his chest. "There are many who may claim to have two left thumbs, but ever so few who can prove it." He removed his glove exposing his left hand, a disfigured appendage with three and-a-half fingers and two wiggling thumbs.

Everyone laughed. Some gasped.

"And yet," said the undaunted Thumbs, "through God's Grace, a twisted figure such as I has ascended to some pleasant estate, which I regard entirely as testament to the stable governance My Liege, His Highness, King Clovis."

Thumbs gave his papers to Arthur, who cracked open the seal.

He unrolled the document and read it. "This man is Ambassador Claudius Pollox. He was sent by King Clovis. He is a royal emissary."

"The famous Duke Arthur is literate as well," said Thumbs. "It is not every day one sees an educated soldier."

Arthur examined the scroll again. "Have I met this man?"

Thumbs grinned at Merlin. "My papers are genuine, old boy. If you wish to have me thrown in the jail, I cannot stop you. But then you will never get the news I carry."

"I am willing to risk that. Do we have a cage for this thing?"

"Wait!" Thumbs hobbled up to the table. "You need to speak with my sister-in-law. She is outside with my wife. This is what Clovis instructed me to do. If, after this interview, you still think I am scamming you, I will set sail immediately. I can do that, you know. I own my own ship."

Arthur said, "I saw two Roman girls outside. What say we bring them in?" He left the room.

Thumbs and Merlin waited.

"My compliments to your tailor," said Merlin. "Your vestments make you look almost human."

Thumbs replied, "You must give me the name of your coiffeur. With that oblong hairless head, I am amazed you have yet to garner a bride."

Merlin re-arranged his papers. "I say, whatever happened to James the cithara player? He was always a good bloke."

"He quit drinking and got married. Then he fell down a stairwell and died. His cithara was smashed open. On the inside, somebody had glued a Star of David, and three gold coins from Alexandria. Some Jew must have hid them there long ago. James's widow used the money to open a nice little ale house."

"And you expect me to believe that?"

"Well, I am willing to believe that a street magician who once sewed Hunnish saddles in Paris is now the Lord Exchequer of Britannia." Thumbs readjusted his hat. "This is an age of such wondrous possibilities."

Arthur entered the court with two dark-eyed daughters of Rome. The younger one, with jet black hair, was visibly pregnant. The elder was taller and less plump, with curls of chestnut brown. Her nose was long and Mediterranean.

"May I introduce my wife," said Thumbs presenting the shorter of the two, "the Lady Honoria Aurelianus."

Merlin bowed and smiled. "How pleasant it is to meet you. I presume you are from the house of Governor Constans?"

She curtsied but did not speak.

"You must forgive her," said Thumbs. "She is a deaf mute." He turned to her sister. "And this would be my sister-in-law, Lady Guinevere Aurelianus."

Merlin bowed again. "Happy to meet you. I take it you can hear?"

"I am honored to meet you, Venerable Sir." She spoke in Greek. "I would like to apologize for my brother-in-law's behavior, but if I did a proper job of it, we would be here till dawn."

Merlin sat up in his chair.

"I have a message for you and Duke Ector," she said. "It involves the request for military assistance you included in your last letter to King Clovis. Lord Pollox knows none of the details. He cannot speak Greek. That is why King Clovis sent me. I have been directed to speak to no one but you, and then only in the presence of Chancellor Ector."

Merlin reached for his water bowl. "How does a girl come to be such a fine grammarian?"

"My father was Riothamus Minor. He had no sons. When he was killed, I inherited his library. My mother took great pains to teach me to read, so that I would not squander his legacy."

"You still have Governor's Constans' library?" said Arthur in Greek.

"Yes," she said somewhat flustered. "You speak Greek? I was under the impression only the Lord Wizard spoke it. Are all your knights literate?"

"Well, this is just lovely," said Thumbs. "You three just keep on chatting. I will wait here."

"Shut up, Thumbs," said Merlin. Then he spoke to the lady. "Duke Arthur is an oddity among military men. He reads Greek fairly well, but he can barely understand it when spoken. I told him to stick to his studies, but did he listen?"

"Not much use for it," said Arthur. He pulled the hay from his mouth. "But I am Ector's eyes and ears. If you have something to say, you might as well say it now. I know half of it already."

"Very well," said Guinevere. "King Clovis intends to honor the request you included in your letter. In late April, a ship will arrive bearing a contingent of knights led by a duke named Lancelot du Lac. Lancelot will serve as the commander of all the mercenaries King Clovis will provide."

"That could be acceptable," said Merlin. "Go on."

"Throughout the spring and summer, Clovis will send troops. Most will be Frankish and French Romans. He will also send mercenaries from the Visigoths and other races, as they become available. They will come in small ships. Clovis does not wish to give the appearance that he is moving troops."

"I am having difficulty understanding all of this," said Arthur. "How will Clovis be sending his troops?"

"In drips and drams," said Merlin. "Continue Lady Guinevere."

"King Clovis does not wish for the Saxons of the Rhineland to know he is lending you support. If they see him sending troops to Britannia, they will assume he is being attacked from the west, which will embolden them to attack him from the east. You must ensure that none of the Saxons in Britannia uncover this ruse. They must think the soldiers are all yours."

"Easily done," said Merlin. "If anyone asks, I will tell them that Duke Lancelot has come to our shores in the hopes of pulling Ex Calibur from her stone. Clovis can send as many men as he wants."

"Who is Ex Calibur?"

"You will meet her later." Merlin sipped his water bowl. "No offense Miss, but I find it highly irregular that Clovis chose the weaker sex to serve as his courier. How can I be sure you have properly transmitted his message?"

"If a ship arrives bearing a duke named Lancelot, you will know. As for Clovis, keep in mind, he was born in a nest of reeds and now rules half of Europe. Nothing he does is regular."

Merlin leaned towards Thumbs. "Your brother-in-law is a bunko artist."

"He is many things. When Clovis ascended to the throne, he executed hundreds of Romans, including my father. Thumbs pretended to be a slave trader, specializing in young girls. His trickery saved scores of Romans ladies."

"Which would explain how he got so rich."

"He saved my library as well."

Arthur interrupted. "So it was you. You hid the books on that ship?"

"They still smell of it," she said. "And I must thank your venerable wizard for not impounding them. The captain told me of your noble actions."

Merlin said, "It appears I should have given him a bigger bribe."

Thumbs waved at them. "Have you heard what you need from the Lady?"

Merlin put down his bowl. "Yes, why do you ask?"

"As you may know,' said Thumbs, "cheese is all the rage among the Franks. There is a yellowish variety favored by the Celts of Hibernia. My agents have informed me that the Ten-acre Britons of Wessex are now manufacturing it. They live in a coastal town called *Cheddar*."

"And you believe I will be able to provide you access to it by sea? That way you can bypass the Saxons."

"Aye. I would like to form a trading colony right here in Cambria. It can serve as a distribution center for my dairy operations. I would also like to launch a trade mission to Hibernia, as there are now so many Christians there. I am certain the citizens of that sunny isle would happily trade their produce for British ale and Frankish wine."

"*Erin* is wet and cloudy," said Merlin, "and her inhabitants prefer highly distilled malt, which they drink while singing woefully long dirges in which everyone ends up dead."

Thumbs smiled. "A rich poetic society. I presume you will levy a reasonable tariff for the upkeep of your docks?"

Merlin ran his fingers along the crest of his head. "Why not? If a flock of gluttonous continentals with heavy purses wish to squander their wealth on a clump of old milk wrapped in a goat's colon, who am I to stop them."

Chapter XXXIII: The Mead Moon, AD 501

Hostis humani generis.

An enemy of the human race.

* * *

As a child, Merlin spent countless afternoon shelling peas while bathed in the aroma of Judith's ever-simmering soup kettle. While at Nalanda, his long arms snatched flatbreads out of the oven to sustain his brother monks. In Paris, he and James practiced their act by the hearth at the Inn of the Fountain, where the chef, an effeminate music aficionado, was delighted to boil them up an egg.

Merlin was less welcome at kitchen at Castle Camaloudensis, a yeasty kingdom ruled by beleaguered matrons, who tossed scraps to the lazy old court hounds. These shaggy dogs gave little notice when Merlin spent a few pre-dawn hours at the cook's table. There he would scribble in silence, while his flickering clay lamp reflected off the shiny bronze pots that hung from the walls.

"I see you are up then," said Sir Gawain from the doorway that led to the dining hall. "There is a visitor in the foyer who wishes to see you. It is Lord Pollox's assistant. His name is Cassius"

"He is here, now?"

"He told me he has urgent news about King Clovis."

Merlin noticed an uneaten dinner roll from last night's meal resting over by the butcher's block. "If you would be so kind," he said, "could you hand me that?" He poured some water into his bowl. "And then bring Mister Cassius in here, but stay close by. I am none too keen on being assassinated. It would ruin my breakfast."

"Aye, Sir." Gawain tossed over the bread and left the room.

Merlin chomped into his half-stale snack. It crunched loud enough to raise the interest of the dogs. They stared at Merlin with sad-eyes.

"You cannot fool me," he said to them. "You curs eat better that most the people I know. This tasty morsel is mine, understand?"

Gawain returned accompanied by Cassius, and said, "Lord Chamberlain Merlin, may I present Cassius of Brittany."

Cassius bowed like a proper Roman. He spoke in Latin like an educated Frank. "*Salve* Your Excellency. I am grateful that you agreed to an audience at this hour."

"Do sit," said Merlin. "It has come to my attention that you have pressing news?"

Cassius glanced at Gawain. "Is it possible that I might speak with you alone?"

"I cannot grant you that. There are certain security measures I am required to maintain. However, my bodyguard does not understand Latin. You can speak freely."

Cassius bowed to Gawain, then told his tale. "I have spent most of my life in Paris. As a boy, I was employed in the household of Governor Syagrius. Since I am not of Roman stock, I managed to survive Clovis's coup. Nonetheless, after Clovis was coronated, I took the precaution of changing my name and moving to Brittany."

Merlin bit into the bread. "A practical course of action."

"It was there that I became acquainted with a lady named *Morgan*. She informed me that she was the half sister of your field marshall, Duke Arthur."

Merlin nearly spit out his snack. "Arthur's sister! That woman is a charlatan. She has been spreading lies about me for ages."

"In Gaul she is widely known to be Arthur's sister. The tribes of the Rhineland also believe this. Is that incorrect?"

Merlin harrumphed. "Arthur is not Morgan's brother, and neither am I. She is simply feigning a relation to Arthur because he has become famous. You should always be wary of people who claim to be lost relatives of great men. It is a common form of deception."

"Oh." Cassius folded his hands. "Wizard Merlin, I am afraid that I must inform you that... How should I say this? I have reason to believe that I that I am Duke Arthur's brother. I hope you will not think me a fraud."

"What?"

"I recently met a gentleman from Anjou named Oderic. He told me he had visited Carmarthen many times to sell the fruits of his orchard. When I told him I was born there, he said I had a striking resemblance to Sir Arthur."

"Yes, I know Oderic," said Merlin. "So, I take it you are a Briton?"

"My mother was a Briton. Her name was Ygerna. My father was a Cornishmen named Gorlius. He served as a steward for a wealthy Roman named Demetrius of Carmarthen. Lord Demetrius helped some Romans escape King Vortiger's persecution. For this reason, the king sent his knights to arrest him. There was a scuffle and my father was killed."

"That was how Vortiger operated."

"After Lord Demetrius was tortured," said Cassius, "he lost the use of his arms and I became his servant. He needed someone to lift things."

"How did you get to Europe?"

"With no husband, my mother Ygerna was easy prey. One of King Vortiger's knights, a man called Uther Pendragon, forced her to be his mistress. By that time Lord Demetrius was deathly ill. His wife, Lady Papanilla feared her family would be sold as slaves. One night, she gathered her household and fled to Gaul."

"And you traveled with her?"

"My mother was pregnant with Pendragon's child at the time. She could not travel, so she asked Lady Papanilla to take me along. I sailed to Brittany and lived with Papanilla's family until she died. After that, I began my service to Governor Syagrius."

"And you believe that Arthur is the son of Pendragon?"

"I never saw my mother again, but some years later Lady Papanilla informed me that Pendragon had been killed and that my mother had died as well. It struck me odd that *Arthur* and *Uther* are such similar names."

"Remarkably so." Merlin poured out a bowl full of water. "And if you are Arthur's half-brother, what of it?"

"As I have explained, I have had the bad luck to work for a man who sought to kill King Clovis. I thought you might have mercy on me and allow me to live here among my native brethren."

"Many people seek asylum here. We cannot accommodate them all."

"I understand. Although I am not a knight, I have many talents that could be useful. Having served under Governor Syagrius, I am fluent in Latin and can read some. I also speak the savage Frankish, and am somewhat proficient in the German languages. I am sure my Briton Celtic will return."

Merlin brushed a few crumbs onto the floor. "Your grammar is indeed excellent." One of the hounds sneaked over and licked up the morsels. "As you know, our court is presently an ally of King Clovis. We are not about to harbor his enemies. Yours is not an easy case, Mister Cassius. I will need to review it with Chancellor Ector."

"Very good, Sir. How long that will take?"

"A few days. I will grant you temporary haven, but only until we have an answer. If the answer is *no*, you will be free to leave. I will not turn you over to the Franks."

"I appreciate your consideration," said Cassius. "And by the way, King Clovis has taken a new name."

"Again? I know the marsh Franks used to call him *Louis*. What is he going by now?"

"*Ludwig*. It is easier for his German subjects to pronounce. Again, Sir, I am grateful for your assistance."

Cassius clicked his heels and bowed. Gawain escorted him out.

Merlin called out, "One last thing lad. You told me that you changed your name after the fall of Syagrius. What did they call you when you lived in Britannia?"

"My name," Cassius replied, "was Mordred." He bowed yet again.

* * *

Merlin listened as Gawain and Mordred's footsteps echoed down the hall, then came to a halt. The fire in the hearth stopped as well. The kitchen door was open. Merlin strolled out into the vegetable patch. He observed a freshly dug burrow down by the base of a fencepost. He banged on it with his knuckles.

"Gopi!" he said. "Wake up."

A groundhog waddled out of her burrow. "What time is it?"

"Nearly dawn. I have a message for you to deliver to the Goddess Aestor."

Gopi sniffed the air. "You woke me up for that?"

"It is the full moon in the month of Mars. You need to get an early start."

Gopi turned around. "I have no idea what you are talking about."

He poked his staff down the hole to block her path. "Today is the cross-quarters. At sunup, the Saxons will crawl from their mud huts and ask you groundhogs to waken the goddess of spring."

"Well, if any Saxons ask, I will be happy to oblige them. Till then, I am going back to sleep."

"I rather like the pagan holidays," said Merlin. "My favorite is Saturnalia, when King Wotan pilots his sleigh through the sky, while his fairy companions throw sugar plums down to the children. Those savages know how to cater an event. When the Pope holds Mass he only serves bread, and refuses to share the wine with anyone but his employees."

The groundhog balanced on her hind legs. "Well, since I am up anyway, what do you think about what Mordred said? Galaru the Rainbow Snake was wondering."

"Mister Mordred," said Merlin, "is what Brother Tinh Tu used to call a *hungry ghost*. Mordred could eat non-stop for a thousand years and still not be satiated. Craving begets more craving."

"What do you intend to do with him?"

"I believe I shall I give him a job as my personal emissary and instruct him to keep his identity hid. We can send him to the court of King Clovis with messages regarding trade or some such. If he is a spy, perhaps he will spy for us as well."

Is he really Arthur's brother?"

"He certainly looks like it. I knew Pendragon. He was the captain of the Dragons. Those goons beat the cash out of Roman families, then slit their throats and sold their children. Every girl in the village had to take a turn in Pendragon's bed, a fair share of the boys too."

"Where is he now?"

"Hell, assuming the system works. One morning they found him with a gridiron in his skull. They never found out who did it. Too many suspects."

"Does Arthur know?"

"I suspect not. Oddly enough, when Uther was a tike he took a shine to one of my rabbits, a white doe I used for breeding. She was always surrounded by her suckling brood. Uther called her *Ygerna*. I never knew why he chose that name. It is not that common."

"It could be coincidence."

Merlin shook his head with dismay. "It just gets worse, Gopi. Uther Pendragon was a bastard. His father was Governor Constans. The Governor had an appetite for blond girls. He would find some winsome Saxon, dress her in silk, and once she was pregnant, it was off to rags and the whorehouse."

"Hold on," said Gopi. "You mean to tell me that Uther Pendragon was the son of a Roman Governor. I though he persecuted the Romans?"

Merlin ran his fingers over his clean shaven scalp. "It boggles the mind."

"That means Arthur is the cousin of King Ambrosius!"

"And one-quarter German. The boy is quite the mongrel."

"Or put another way, his father was sadistic half savage, who brutally persecuted his own people, and raped Arthur's mother. You may want to keep this quiet."

Merlin cradled the groundhog on his arms. "All of humanity is, at some point, descended from concubines and killers. Arthur is just closer to the source."

"You would never know it by looking at him."

"Like they say," said Merlin, "each man is the architect of his own fate. Horace was born to illiterate slaves; Plato's father was not wise; and Joseph was but a carpenter."

BOOK VIII: THE SAGE

Chapter XXXIV: The Mead Moon, AD 503

Colossus magnitudinem suam servabit etiam si steterit in puteo.

A giant will keep his size even when he stands in a well.

* * *

Into the crowded courtyard galloped Field Marshall Arthur. He was running late - which he did not enjoy - but timeliness was a luxury he could no longer afford. Arthur, along with Merlin and Ector, was governing a nation. And whereas he as the youngest of this triumvirate, Arthur was the only one fit enough to travel. Thus, he spent much of his day in the saddle.

Arthur dismounted and tied his steed to a hitching post. He put on his conical straw hat to shade out the noonday sun. Gawain and Tristan saluted. Merlin and Ector sat in the center of the courtyard behind the main kitchen table. It had been hauled outside and placed in front of the stable.

Arthur sat down next to Merlin, dressed in his orange toga, and asked, "Why are meeting outdoors?"

"I directed the staff to whitewash the courtroom this morning. Let us hope it does not rain. It dries so much brighter when there is no humidity."

Ector interrupted. "Did you get anymore m-men?"

"Two ships arrived from Caledonia," said Arthur. "Twenty Scots and a half-dozen Pitcs. Their hair is spiked like a hedgehog, but at least they have no tattoos."

Merlin muttered, "Or at least none you could see." He thumped his staff on the hard packed earth and cried out, "Oh yay, oh yay. The Court of the Knights of Britannia is now in session. Lord Chancellor Ector presiding."

The knights and villagers mulled around, organizing themselves. Ector raised one of his eight remaining fingers. Everyone quieted down, even though Ector was white-haired, nearly blind, and no longer able to walk. On the very day Lancelot's Franks arrived from Gaul, Ector stepped on a nail, which led to an infection that ultimately forced Merlin to amputate his leg at the knee.

Merlin squinted at the notes on his chalkboard and read, "The first order of business is a contract for lard, bacon, and thirty-six hams. It is recommended that the court pay thirty denarii to Maldwyn the Swineherd on the nonas of each month till Dog Days End. All in favor, so indicate."

Ector and Arthur said, "Aye."

"Our second agendum," said Merlin, "is a license request. Mister Talfryn proposes to net elvers in the Severn. That should be good. If he catches any, we can fry them in the bacon fat."

Arthur heard the stomp of a foot behind him. He glanced back in time to see a pale fist wrapped around a highly polished knife slicing toward Ector.

Merlin yelled, "Get down!"

The dagger man slammed into the back of Arthur's chair. Arthur lunged forward. A splurt of blood splashed onto his cheek. Gawain screamed, "Get him!"

In his peripheral vision, Arthur saw the assassin's bare feet planted behind Ector's chair. Arthur grabbed onto Ector's ankle and pushed the old soldier off to the side. Ector hit the dirt with a thud. A woman shrieked. Merlin fell over as well.

Arthur withdrew his sidearm and jumped up. A young man in an off-white smock dashed off. Arthur threw his knife. It hit the fleeing man in the shoulder. An arrow from Tristan's bow whistled through the air. It lodged deep into the assassin's back, and he fell, face down. He had red hair.

Ector curled up in a ball, and held his head. It was bleeding profusely from one side.

Arthur ran over to Ector, nearly slipping on what he thought was a patch of mud. He lifted up his heel. An oval slab of skin was tangled in his spur. It was Ector's ear. Arthur showed it to Merlin.

Merlin called out to Tristan saying, "Go into the kitchen and get me a clean filet knife and a flat metal spoon. Meet me at the blacksmith's."

Tristan sped off.

Arthur asked Merlin, "Are you alright, old man?"

"Yes, boy. Help me carry Ector. Get him to the furnace." Sir Gawain and Arthur hoisted up Ector by the armpits and hauled him off toward the anvil where the horses were shod.

"That bastard!" cried Ector.

Tristan arrived with the kitchen utensils. Merlin wiped off the spoon and stuck the round end of it in the furnace. He cleaned off the knife with the edge of his toga and said, "Tristan, rip the sleeve of your blouse into long rags. Arthur, you and Gawain need to hold his head in place. Ector, you will be fine, but this will hurt. Do you need something to bite on?"

"Your sorry arse!" said Ector. "Just do it."

Gawain wrapped his arm around Ector's neck. Merlin wiped the blood from where Ector's ear once was. A small piece of flesh was still hanging loose. Merlin positioned the knife blade behind it. Arthur noticed Merlin's wrist begin to shake, but only briefly. Then in one smooth move, Merlin sliced it off.

Ector screamed, "Sod it!"

Merlin covered his hand in the end of his toga like a potholder. He retrieved the red hot spoon from the furnace, pushed back Ector's hair, and pressed the bowl of the spoon onto the wound. Ector howled. Steam rose up past his temple. Arthur smelled the scent of cauterized human flesh, an odor much like any other roasting meat. Ector clamped his eye shut and went limp.

Tristan now had some dozen strips of linen in his hands.

Merlin said, "Wrap his head tight. We shall move him later."

Sir Gawain politely shooed away the people gathered round. "Back up and give us some air. Ector has a flesh wound, but the wizard has mended it."

The crowd parted. Through it marched Sir Lancelot, a square-jawed warrior in the Roman mold, albeit with a pale Frankish complexion.

"Duke Arthur," said Lancelot, "I beg your pardon, but I bring you an urgent message from King Clovis. What has happened? Is Ector hurt?"

"Just cut up a bit. Someone tried to stab him." Arthur pointed his thumb toward the corpse. "He looks like a Ten-acre. I wonder how much they paid him."

"I wonder what the druids used to drug him," said Merlin. "My guess is beer laced with bog myrtle and a promise of Valhalla." He leaned over toward Lancelot. "So what does King Clovis have to say? Do you have a letter?"

"No," said Lancelot. "A captain of the Frankish navy relayed the message to me this morning. King Clovis is unable to send any masons. They fear they will be lynched if they come here. You know how guildsmen are. I should also mention that My Liege hopes this will not damage the friendship between our two nations. He would like your response straight away. I have been directed to give it to his captain by sundown."

Merlin rested his haunches on the blacksmith's stool. "I was afraid of this. The Manus Magnus are punishing me." He glanced over at Ector. Tristan had finished bandaging him. Merlin said, "Elevate his head."

Arthur folded his arms. "We need a fort old man. Look at what just happened. We have to get masons. Should we write the Pope? Would he help?"

Merlin removed a stick of slow-burning oak from the furnace timber pile. "What if we build a castle out of wood? The forests of Cambria have not been harvested since the days of Governor Constans. We may not have stone workers, but we do have oaks with bulk enough to withstand a Roman catapult. Surely they could stop a Saxon ax."

"It is not the axes that worry me," said Arthur. "All the Germans need is one lit arrow and your fort will be ashes."

Merlin laid the log back onto the pile. "Not if we build it on an abutment ten rods high, with a nine acre enclosure and a sixty-two yard perimeter. No one can shoot that far."

"That is more like a city than a castle," said Lancelot.

"Then a city it is. We do not have to be confined to a compact space. If the brutes decide to attack us, we will force them to spread themselves thin."

Arthur tugged at his beard. Half of the knights under his command were Franks. Most had Roman grandfathers. These were conservative professionals, proud to stand on walls of granite. A timber fortress would offend their dignity. Wood might be good enough for the savages of Prussia, but not Frenchmen.

Arthur asked, "Do we have any other options? How soon can you build it? We will have to buy saws."

"When I was in the Balkans," said Merlin, "I saw such a structure erected in two months. Granted, the Huns had the benefit of slaves and experienced engineers, of which we have neither."

"Huns?" said Lancelot. "You want to build a Hunnish fort?"

Arthur searched his memory, sifting through every story Merlin ever told. Arthur knew the old man helped construct a castle in Persia. He built another one for King Vortiger, which either fell down or was pulled down. But Merlin never mentioned constructing anything with the Huns. He just sewed saddles.

Arthur said, "Did you ever actually build a fortress? Not as a clerk but as an architect. Can you really do this?"

"Of course. I built Stonehenge, did I not?"

"This is not a magic trick. What will I tell my men? If they think it is not safe, they will sail back to Europe. When you were with the Huns, did you build a fort or did you just carry the lumber? In what capacity did you work?"

"In what capacity?" Merlin planted his hands on his hips. "In the capacity that I had to carry logs like an animal. In the capacity that I had to feed their dogs with butchered human remains. Why are you taking such a tone with me?"

"Someone just tried to kill us! The Germans outnumber us two to one. My spies tell me the Saxons are collecting coins. Why are they doing that, Merlin? Could it be they want to buy horses?"

From below, Ector said, "We will b-build the damn thing out of wood."

Arthur gritted his teeth. "So be it. But this is just temporary. As soon as we can, we are going to build a proper stone wall. That is what I will tell my men, and that is what we will do. I want this in the budget. Agreed?"

Ector gave him a thumbs up.

Lancelot said, "I must give a reply to Clovis. What shall I tell his captain?"

"Inform your king," said Merlin, "that we will be building a fortress at *Camulodanum*, and ask him to provide us with us a dozen pit saws." Merlin knelt down to examine the modest blood stain that had formed in Ector's bandages. "Ptolemy's map of *Europa* shows one city in the middle of Britannia. He called *Camulodanum*. Tell Clovis that our fort will be there."

"Ca-mu-lod..." said Ector. "Where is that?"

"It does not matter. Ptolemy's map is worthless north of the Alps, but every cathedral in Gaul has a copy. If we tell Clovis our capitol is called *Camulodanum*, and he can find it on a map, he will think it is important." Merlin too a swig from the water sack sitting on the blacksmith's table. "We need to continue to build Clovis's confidence, even you Lancelot. Stay mindful of that."

Arthur rapped his knuckles on the top of Merlin's head. "I am ordering you to get some rest old man. Go take a nap. I will clean up here. Ector needs to stop talking. If he moves his jaw he will start bleeding."

Merlin gave Ector a drink from the water sack and said, "If you part with any more appendages, I fear they will bury you in a hat box."

The dead German was surrounded by six-foot wide circle of soil, sopping with sticky blood. Arthur dislodged his dagger and flipped over the attacker, a lad with nary a whisker on his chin. The German's hair had been cut short to look like a Briton's. His still-open eyes had wildly dilated pupils. Merlin was right, the Saxon witch doctors had drugged him.

Arthur closed the dead man's eyes and whispered, "Why did you let them poison your mind?"

Chapter XXXV: The Snow Moon, AD 503

Uri sermonis amator.

A lover of pure speech.

* * *

There were no snow storms on earth like the white dragons that buried the steppes of the Hunnish homeland. These central Asian monsters spit out vertical gusts of wind that transformed your cheeks into a pallet of red. By comparison, the inch-worth of snow that occasionally dusted Carmarthen was only a slippery annoyance. Indeed, there were worse things that could descend upon Britannia.

Merlin entered the foyer of the knight's hall and shook the snow off his boots. A sister was warming herself by a brazier. She had arranged a few twigs of holly in a cup. At first, it stuck Merlin as frivolous. But when he looked around at the rows of sick and dying people sleeping on the floor, he realized the sister was right. The place needed a sprig of humanity.

"I need to speak with Mother Scholastica," he said. "Where is she?"

"In her chambers," said the sister. "She fell ill this morning."

Merlin hung his head. "Her too? Who is in charge?"

"I believe I am." The sister curtsied. "Lady Guinevere Aurelianus, at your service."

He motioned the beak of his staff at her. "Are you the girl who came to court with Thumbs? What are you still doing here? You should be back in Paris?"

"I got delayed. Pollox got a good deal on some tin. They had to jettison some ballast, so I volunteered to stay. The Mother Superior agreed to take me. It is not often that a maiden gets to travel."

"You chose an interesting venue to go on holiday." Merlin peered out into the main room, whose tables and chairs had been replaced with cots and bedrolls. It was a makeshift hostel with two aisles worth of sweaty, shivering patients. The air reeked of diarrhea. "How many did we lose today? Are you are still feeding them willow water?"

"Fourteen. We ran out of willow bark. I sent some boys to strip some more. They should be back by sundown."

"How are you doing? You look pale?"

"I spent two days in the outhouse, but I never had the fever." She handed Merlin a piece of parchment folded into a box. "Sir Percival gave me this. Should I use it?"

Merlin opened it up. Inside it was a leech. "This will do you no good. Leeches reduce swelling due to injury. They are not a cure-all."

Merlin scanned the ad hoc infirmary. It reminded him of his childhood in Constantinople, where epidemics were a regular event. Some were lethal, some not. They tended to cull out infants and the elderly. For some reason, each plague was selective as to who it would kill, based on its own unforgiving criteria.

He said, "This blight seems to be striking the county folk worst of all. Urbanites are faring better."

From across the room someone called out, "Sister, can we get more rags over here?"

Guinevere marched off, and glancing back at Merlin said, "We need more straw as well. Can you get that?"

He pulled out his slate and chalk. "I will add it to the list." While writing, he caught a glimpse of Arthur's cot. It was empty. "Where is Arthur?" he said. He stepped over bodies wrapped in blankets. "Where is he? Uther?"

From the far entrance Arthur reply, "Over here, old man."

Merlin pressed his palm to his chest. Arthur wore a short nightshirt that exposed his legs, with their spotty thighs and pigment free knees and ankles. His feet were covered by a pair of Frankish wooden shoes, no stockings. He tiptoed over a pool of watery brown fluid.

"Where have you been?" said Merlin. "Where is your coat?"

"I was out taking a dump. My fever broke."

"Did you have solid stools?"

"Like a link of sausages. Is Ector all right? How are you? How is Guinevere?"

"Ector is fine. He could stroll through Armageddon and with nary a rash. Myself, I had only dyspepsia and a blast of demonically bad wind."

"How many people have been killed? Is this hitting the livestock?"

"Four hundred of our people have died. They say whole Saxon villages are wiped out. The pigs have it as well. I ordered them to be culled and burned. For the next five days you are to eat nothing but fresh bread, you hear me, boy? I am none to keen on hiring a new domesticus."

Arthur crawled back onto his cot. "Did you see Widow Blodwen yet?"

"Is she here?"

"Her sons brought her in. She forced them do it. A couple of her grandkids died, and she said they had to get her out of the house." Arthur paused. "When they carried her in, she could barely move, but she was still barking out orders. I think she is failing."

"*Spero melior*. Still, I am glad you are well." Merlin patted him on the knee. "I shall go see her straightaway. Do not slay any giants while I am gone."

Arthur closed his eyes and stuck out his tongue. Bishop Thomasius passed by carrying two buckets of water. Because of his gall stones, Thomasius always had to pee with increasing frequency, but aside from that, he kept fit for a man his age.

"Father," said Merlin, "you should not be doing manual labor. That is what acolytes are for. Let me take one."

Thomasius refused the offer. "I need to work. I am taking these to those Iberian sailors over there. I can make it that far."

"You look pale," said Merlin. "Are you all right? How is your wife?"

Thomasius bit his lower lip. He struggled to generate his bucked-toothed optimistic smile. "Kind of you to ask. As it happens, the Lord called her away last night. She had been ill long before this sickness came. At least I have my daughters."

Merlin placed his hand on Thomasius's shoulder. "I am sorry. She was a good woman, Thom. I always liked her. You were lucky."

Thomasius straightened his posture a bit. "Thank you, Merthen. You know, on Sunday afternoon, I am giving a recitation on Saint Origen's Homily regarding the *Book of Ezekiel*. If you are interested, you should stop by. You would not need to attend Mass."

"Yes, Father," said Merlin, "I will do that. Do you know where I could find Widow Blodwen? I would like to visit with her."

"Down the hall and to the left."

Merlin patted the Bishop on the back and made his way to Widow Blodwen's side. She was curled up on a pile of straw, wrapped in a quilt, and much thinner than she ought to be.

"Missus B," he said to her, "what are you doing lying on your arse?"

"Just taking a breather," she replied. "Father Thomasius gave me the last rites. I told him to blow off. He did it anyway."

Merlin knelt down. "Are you thirsty?"

"No, just sweaty."

With a rag, he wiped the perspiration off her face and neck.

"Did you ever meet my first husband?" she said.

"No, only the third and fourth."

"He was pretty much worthless. Drunk all the time. I had to take in a renter to make ends meet."

"You have always been resourceful."

She coughed. "I let out the barn to a Scotsman. He was working as the bishop's clerk. Kind of chubby for a Scot. We called him Porky. Not much to look at, but oh, how he could talk. Sometimes when you blather on, I feel like I am still beside him."

"Well in that case, his arguments must have been well-reasoned and insightful."

She chuckled, then winced. "My son, Rhienalt," she said, "Porky was his father. I never told anyone, not even Rhienalt."

Merlin wrung out the rag. "Would you like me to tell him?"

"No. There would be in trouble if you did. Turns out Porky got himself excommunicated. His Christian name was Pelagius. I heard you mention him a few times. Whatever happened to him?"

"I know very little. He was intelligent. Quite well-read. He became a professor of some sort in Ravenna. He wrote something that upset the Pope, and the cardinals ran him out of town. King Vortiger offered him a job as his chaplain, but it was all a sham. When Pelagius figured out that Vortiger was nothing but a semi-pagan high chief with a second-hand crown, he sailed back to Italy."

"None of my husbands treated me as good as Porky did. I rather like it that he knocked me up. That showed them, eh? How did he die? Did they kill him?"

"He ended up in Africa. Apparently he published some rather nasty articles about Augustine of Hippo. That was a mistake. Everybody liked Augustine, and they loved his mother. The Pope declared Pelagius a heretic, and the world pretty much ignored him. He stopped writing. Either he died, or he just gave up."

"I figure," she said, "with me getting the last rites, I can get into heaven now. I was always hoping to meet up with Porky. If he never got there, I am not sure I want to go."

Merlin brushed aside a lock of her white hair. "In Chapter Twelve of the *Book of Mark*, a Jew asked Jesus which commandment was most important. Jesus told the Jew that if he loved God and treated his neighbor well, he would achieve the kingdom of heaven. He never told the Jew that God required him to join a church. You have nothing to worry about, dear lady. Pelagius is waiting for you."

"I never understood it. What did Porky do that was all so wrong?"

"He said the priesthood had grown corrupt. No one wanted to hear that. Then he refuted the doctrine of original sin. According to Pelagius, the good Lord created human kind - and since the Lord was good - every person he created was good. As long as we stayed in God's light, the Lord would accept us into his paradise."

Widow Blodwen smiled. "That was my Porky, all right. Always on the sunny side."

Merlin took the rag off her forehead. "If there was no original sin, then Jesus died a common man, instead of a sacrifice cleansing humanity of Eve's transgression. The bishops would not stand for it. Myself, I rather like the idea. Jesus spent his days breaking bread with us pathetic blokes. I think he would have preferred to go out that way."

She said nothing.

Merlin reached out his hand. He closed her eyes. Then he joined his palms together and chanted, "*Namo valo ki-teshvariya. Namo valo ki-teshvariya. Namo valo ki-teshvariya.*"

* * *

No one on the room coughed, or moaned, or generated any sound of any kind.

The leech in the box said, "I am sorry for your loss."

"It is an interesting study," said Merlin. He covered up his old friend's serene freckled face. "As soon as Blodwen heard she had a chance of reuniting with Pelagius, she let go."

"When she died," said Gopi, "why did you sing the healing chant? The God Manitou wishes to know."

Merlin set the leech on his knee.

"Brother Tinh Tu use to say that death was a transition, like a river flowing into the sea. It is appropriate to sing the healing chant when a soul passes on.

The recently departed are accustomed to this life, and may feel some trepidation as they rejoin with the universal consciousness. Like a child who has fallen, they need compassion more than a cure."

"And you believe in a universal consciousness?"

"I witness it each spring. When the apple tree blooms, it produces bright flowers, and thus communicates a message as clear as the spoken word."

"What does it say?"

"The tree says, *Help me*. You see, Gopi, most fragrant flowers can only produce a seed if they are disturbed by an insect. This is why apple growers keep bees. The apple blossom is the means by which the tree expresses that it is ready for the bee's assistance. If the flower's message is received, the bee will visit the flower. Only then can the tree produce an apple, which is really just a vessel for a seed."

"I see," said Gopi. "The tree says one word, once a year."

"As does every tree in the forest, in every forest in the world. And just consider how many plants there are, not to mention bugs and fish… and leeches. Each of nature's elements may have scant intelligence on its own, but collectively they engage in a conversation more complex than any human mind could fathom. That is the universal consciousness."

"The voice of God, perhaps?"

"I will leave that to the theologians." Merlin straightened up the blanket swaddled around the Widow Blodwen. "Pelagius would have been better off if he had stayed with Missus B. She would have kept him in line. Damn right she would." Merlin wiped away the tear running down his cheek.

"I will leave you be," said Gopi. "You probably need some time alone."

"No," he said, "stay with me a while."

Chapter XXXVI: The Storm Moon, AD 504

Mus uni non fidit antro.

A mouse does not rely on just one hole.

* * *

What distinguished Mount Baden from Cambria's other high points was its emptiness. No trees grew there. There were two popular explanations as to why: one involving fairy tears the other, dragon breath. Merlin assumed the Romans stripped it bare and built a tower on its ridgeline to watch the muddy river below. Generations of sheep kept it cropped from then on.

Etched into the south slope of Mount Baden was the remnant of a road that had previously crossed west into Saxon territory. There had even been a bridge across the river, but that was torched after King Vortiger was killed. Now, all that remained were two parallel grooves in the soil. Merlin's wagon climbed this cart-way up toward the peak, from where he hoped to view the battlefield.

"We need to be a bit farther east," he said to his driver, Sir Tristan. "Take us there."

"No, Sir. That is across the lines. Field Marshall Arthur ordered us to stay clear of the field."

Merlin waved his fingers dismissively. "That was just a suggestion, boy. Get this chariot moving."

"I am not a boy, Sir. I am a knight who has been given very clear instructions. This cart is not going to move an inch."

"Very well, then." Merlin flung off his brown wool cloak. "Dangers await!" He hopped off his seat and jogged away, his only armor, an orange toga.

Tristan snapped the reigns. "Get back here!" The horses sped off. With a sudden crack, the front left wheel lodged into a foxhole. Tristan was hurled into the air. He landed on the soft turf.

Merlin paused. "Are you all right, lad?"

Tristan dusted himself off and surveyed the vehicle. "Aye. The axle is broken."

"Alas, I am no carter. Good day."

Tristan stomped through the brambles. "Stop damn it! The Germans are coming. Have you lost your mind?"

"Quite a few times. That is why I always tether it to the sleeve of my overcoat. It makes it so much easier to retrieve."

* * *

Something was rustling in the meadow. It was a chicken.

"Gopi!" said Merlin. "It is I. You need not be afraid."

She extended her beak over the tall grass. "Why would I be afraid?"

"It seemed a fair assumption. This is a war zone and you are, after all, a chicken."

She clucked. "I have sired a few gamecocks in my time. You would not call them cowards."

Merlin said, "In Brother Tinh Tu's homeland, chickens lived as wild beasts, high in the jungle canopy. Because of the dense vegetation, they lack the ability to fly long distances."

"Are they large and ferocious?"

"Not especially."

"I have a question," she said. "Marduk, the Storm God wishes to know how you view war?"

"I can state unwaveringly that I view it with contempt."

"And yet, Arthur seems adept at the martial arts. Does that trouble you? You have spent so much time training him for the monastic life."

"Arthur is a knight," said Merlin. "When he kills a German, I am upset. But is he any more responsible than the smithy who manufactured his sword? The farmer that feeds an army is a killer as well. And I gather the taxes that buy the arrows. Who is innocent?"

"Does that mean you accept war? Did the Buddha accept war?"

"War is the result of mindlessness. If we can overcome mindlessness, there will be fewer wars, and perhaps someday we can transform them into something positive. In the meantime, we can only wage peace and hope for the best."

"So the soldier is not to blame? It sounds like you are making excuses for Arthur."

"When I was at Nalanda University, there were quite a few monastics who came from the military. They knew what it meant to suffer ill-being. Those men were wise because when they finally perfected the craft of war, they chose not to become overlords or kings. Instead they followed the Middle Path and gave up their arms. With time, I am certain Arthur will reach the same conclusion."

"That would be consistent with what you taught him," said the chicken. She flapped her wings, flying but a short distance over to the edge of the woods.

* * *

Tristan yelled, "Stop! You are unarmed." He broke into a sprint and caught up with the old man. "I have been ordered to keep you alive."

"I cannot see across the valley," said Merlin. "What is going on?"

"The Saxons are gathering. It looks like four columns, and some Ten-acres. Angles and Jutes are in the rear. We must leave."

"Any horses?"

"Aye. Their horses have armor. Where did they get that?"

"They become more like us every day."

Merlin, with his failing eyesight, could barely see the commotion up stream. "Here comes Arthur! Where is Lancelot?"

Tristan searched the landscape. "I do not see him. We need to go."

A chorus of German attack yodels sprang up from below. The air resounded with the blare of their wooden war horns. In response, Arthur's Celts erupted with the drumming of bodhrans and the wailing of bagpipes.

"The Irish," said Merlin, "they must be behind Arthur. What is happening now?"

"I see the Scots and the Picts," said Tristan. "They are behind the cavalry. Arthur is fording the river. Wait, no, he is turning around mid-stream. He is… he has gone back to the far side."

"What about the Hibernians?"

Tristan squinted. "They seem to be stuck in the mud. The Germans are crossing the river. The Jutes are diving in."

"Where is Arthur?"

"The cavalry has broken apart. They are retreating."

"Well, where in Hades are the Franks? Lancelot is supposed to be here. Where are the Visigoths? This is all bollixed up!"

Tristan withdrew his sword. "Sir, the Picts and the Scots are retreating. We must get away from here."

"How can they be retreating? Who are those men coming towards us?"

"Those *are* the Picts. We need to leave. The Jutes are right behind them."

"Have they gone potty? One cannot retreat up hill. This is nonsense." Merlin ran toward them. "You tattooed morons!" He raised his staff above his head. "The battle is down there!"

A few of the retreating soldiers stopped. A volley of arrows whizzed by. Merlin swung his walking stick like a sword, flailing at his own men.

"Stop!" yelled Tristan.

Merlin berated a Scottish piper boy. "Blow your bloody noisemaker and turn the other way!" He tried to wrestle the instrument from its owner. It generated a low, goat-like moan. He shouted at a company of charging Jutes. "*Ich bin von Etzel!*" He cried at the top of his lungs, "*Etzel, Etzel!*" The wind blew through his toga. It filled like a sail. A few of the Jutes froze in their tracks.

Tristan grabbed Merlin by the shoulders and spun him around. On the top of the ridge, Merlin could see the Frankish cavalry led by Sir Lancelot. Off to his left was an army of Visigoths, with pikes aimed at chest height. The Jutes ran off.

"We must flee!" said Tristan. A line of Frankish war-horses was descending on them.

"Just what is going on here?" said Merlin. The Angles and Saxons were crossing the river. The hooves of their heavy armored horses were pounding the banks on either side into a thick gooey morass. The water turned deep brown.

Tristan leveled his sword at Merlin. "Listen, you miserable old crank. Get your boney arse off this hill or so help me, I will cut it off!"

Merlin observed a massing of soldiers by the water's edge. It was the Germans trying to retreat. They were stuck knee deep the mud. Lancelot's horsemen were aimed directly at them. The Saxons stopped yodeling.

"Point taken," said Merlin.

Tristan reached his arms around Merlin's waist and hoisted the old man over his shoulder. Once again the bagpipes began to sing. The Irish scampered off to a stand of evergreens, and began to climb. The men who reached the top called out to their mates in Hibernian Celtic. The ones still on the ground tossed up their quivers and bows.

The forest edge filled with Irish snipers. They picked off the Germans mired in the flood plain. The brown water flowed red.

Two spike-haired Scots tackled Tristan and Merlin. They lifted up their shields and placed their helmets high upon their pikes. The herd of charging war horses parted to avoid this obstacle. Merlin, Tristan, and their two kilted comrades huddled together. Knight after knight galloped by.

Lancelot's Franks hit the Germans with a crash. Saxons war chiefs tumbled from their saddles, while Visigoth pikes punctured their bowels and intestines. Blood and half-digested food saturated the soil. On the far side of the river, Arthur reappeared with four horsemen. They chased down the Ten-acre Britons.

Those who could run, got away. Those who were slow, screamed as their vertebras and pelvises were trampled under sixteen iron clad hooves.

Merlin stood and observed. Before him he saw Frenchmen, Germans, Spaniards, and Irishmen embroiled en masse in the eastern shore. Roman swords clanked against Saxon axes. Irish arrows sliced through esophaguses and shoulder blades.

A Frankish throwing hatchet gashed open a stallion's bladder. Horse urine splurted everywhere. A Visigoth, who had lost his ax, knocked down an Angle with the flat of his iron shield, and with both feet, stomped on his skull. It cracked open with a pop.

Across the water, two breeds of Britons sliced into each other's tendons. One of Arthur's officers clung onto his partially severed arm, but was unable to keep it in place due to the warm slippery blood that flowed from its stump. A Ten-acre tried to pull an arrow from his neck. A headless German ran ten paces, then stumbled and fell.

A terrified horse attempted to dislodge an eviscerated Frank, whose twisted leg was stuck in the stirrup. The dead Frank's flattened intestines trailed behind like a dirty pink ribbon. It was war without boundaries, the triumph of mindlessness.

Merlin felt the splash of some unknown semi-fluid spurt into his face. He began to chat to himself, "*Gah-tay, gah-tay, para gah-tay, parasam gah-tay bodhi svaha.*" To his left, he heard the thud of a wounded Jute falling down. Sir Lancelot was about to finish the savage off. Merlin stuck his walking stick between them.

Sir Lancelot, who appeared to have excrement dripping from his scalp, lowered his sword. "Have we won?"

"The day is ours," said Merlin. "Start taking prisoners. Tend the wounded."

Merlin glanced up and became aware of Arthur, who had paused in his pursuit, and was now watching the old man. Down by the river's edge, Merlin was tapping men from both sides on the shoulder. "*Mach stille,*" he said. "*Insistere.* Stop."

Across the river, the Ten-acre Britons threw down their arms, then put up their hands. They dragged their German commanders off their horses.

"Take them! Take them!" they cried.

Arthur replied, "You want to leave? Off with your clothes! Leave your weapons."

The Ten-acre Britons stripped naked, and darted off though the woods. The Angles and Saxons had to be prodded a bit, but soon even the older ones complied.

In the end, only two German war chiefs were left, a Saxon and an Angle. They bared their hairy chests, confident and unflinching. They closed their eyes.

Arthur said to them, "*Wenn Ich Sie schlacten, man mag Sie mit Manner dass Ich nicht toeten kann wieder einsteigen.* I think I am better off with you alive." Brandishing Ex Calibur, he sliced them both across the cheek.

The Saxon war chief bowed. He pointed at the pile of armor he had just removed. "You wear the same chain mail we do. *Ihren Ruestung nicht besser ist wie unsere.*"

Arthur gave the garments a glance. "Good day, *Deutchmann*. Go home."

"*Guten Tag, Welschmann.*"

The Angle and the Saxon walked away.

Upon the other shore, the Franks, Visigoths, Irish, Scots, and Britons cheered. They chanted, "Arthur, Arthur, Arthur!"

Duke Arthur waded across the river, and was hoisted onto the shoulders of his victorious army. Pipes and drums blared in celebration.

Merlin forced himself into the crowd, whacking his way through with the head of his staff. "What is wrong with you, boy! You aimed those Jutes straight at me."

"*Salve* and good day to you as well," said Arthur. "I guess no one told the Germans an armored horse cannot swim. They had to learn it sometime, eh?"

"You used me! What if I had been struck down? I could have been killed."

"And what if we had lost? They would have roasted your heart on the same stick as mine."

Sir Lancelot appeared behind Merlin and slapped him on the back, nearly toppling him over. "Old man, you fought back an army of savages armed with just wooden stick. I tell you, Sir, do not challenge me to a duel, for I shall surely lose."

The rest of the soldiers roared with laughter.

"I think it is long overdue that this warrior be dubbed a knight," said Lancelot.

"No thank you," Merlin replied. "My long standing policy is to remain on the blunt end of a sword, regardless of who wields it."

"Merthen," said Arthur, "once things calm down a bit, could we play a round of Chaturga? I still remember all the moves you taught me. I think it might be a good game."

"Come now, boy," said Merlin, "do you actually think I taught you *all* the moves?"

Chapter XXXVII: The Hay Moon, AD 504

Amare et sapere vix deo conceditur.

Even a god finds it hard to love and be wise at the same time.

* * *

The grey slate tiles atop the chapel did not shine in the sun. They did not glimmer like the domes of Constantinople. And yet, Merlin found it easy to stare at them with pride. It was he who found the abandoned slate mine, and he who directed the blacksmith to hammer out the roofing nails. He even designed the stone-bit auger used to drill the nail holes.

Merlin detected an aromatic scent wafting up from beneath his heel. He had inadvertently crushed the stem of a mint plant growing among the high grass that surrounded the bishop's turnip patch. The leaves of this herb were much larger than the native stock. Perhaps it was a variety shipped over from Gaul?

Using the swan-beak carved at the end of his staff, he dug the plant up by the root. He discreetly wrapped it in a couple of oak leaves and deposited it in his purse. Surely, no one would miss it.

"Good morning!" said Bishop Thomasius, busily securing the latch pin of his cassock. "Lovely day. I hear you will be attending the Mass."

Merlin hid his dirt-covered staff behind his back. "I have been scheduled to attend."

"Then I shall have to use my best Latin. Feel free to critique me. I would value your comments. Love to chat, but I am a bit behind. See you soon."

Merlin waved goodbye. The bishop disappeared through the side door of the sanctuary. A black-eyed dove cooed on the roof. It circled twice around above his head, then disappeared.

From behind him, Merlin heard a woman's voice. It was not Gopi's.

"What are you doing here?" said Guinevere, dressed in silk and white lace.

"I believe," he replied, "you meant to say, what are you doing here, *Sir*?"

"Forgive me, Your Excellency. But my interrogatory still stands."

He cleaned off his walking stick. "I am observing the progress of Bishop Thomasus's agricultural plot. His daughters do a fine job with it."

"That is not what I meant? Why are you not in church?"

"I could ask you the same question."

The lady peered up toward the passing clouds. "I needed a diversion. Shall you be at the ceremony?"

"Alas, I cannot. My oars are unwelcome in the Holy See."

She set her hands securely on her hips. "Well, I know you are not a druid. You are too populist to be a Gnostic, too ecumenical to be a Donatist. Could you be an Arian? No, too pragmatic. Are you a Pelagian?"

"Pelagius! That naïve stooge. He soiled the reputation of free thinkers everywhere. As it so happens, I was baptized in Constantinople. My native diocese has been excommunicated. If the Archbishop of Paris found out I attended Mass, Bishop Thomasius might get the sack."

She folded her arms. "I never approved of the schism."

Merlin adjusted his toga. "Young lady, your vocabulary never ceases to amaze me. Why on earth are you staying here in Britannia?"

"This is where my love is, Sir."

He dusted the last bit of grime from his fingers. "I have always been a proponent of arranged marriages. A fellow who pays for a donkey treats it better than the chap who gets it for free."

"So brides are chattel then? That is not very complimentary."

"It is all a matter of perspective. I would pose that my statement is not so much a slander of women, as an endorsement of the ass."

She batted her dark Mediterranean eyelashes. "A tepid rejoinder. Polemics were never your strong suit."

"In that you are correct. My forte is either unmitigated honesty, or monumental fabrication. When it comes to verbalization, I fail to tread the middle path most miserably."

"Is there anything I can say to persuade you to attend my wedding? Everyone would love to have you there. It would be so nice to have another student of Greek."

"If you wish to recite Philemon and Sappho, I am certain Arthur would listen. He speaks Greek."

"Not like you."

"Dear girl, you are going to have become accustomed to living a somewhat less rarefied lifestyle. We Britons are not as urbane as your neighbors in Paris. Even Arthur with all his education, has more in common with the Saxons than the Romans."

"Venerable Sir, on this, I must protest. Duke Arthur may be tasked by Homer, but his Latin could charm the ear of Tacitus."

"Just words." Merlin scratched the stubble on his chin. "Observe Arthur in the wild, and you will find him quite the animal. With the chirp of a nestling or the snap of a twig, his ears perk up, almost canine. When in battle, he fights as if possessed by the bear within his moniker. It is a very sloppy affair."

"How did he get that name? Whenever I ask, he dances around it."

"There was a bit of a mix up when he was impressed into King Ambrosius's army. When I first hired the boy, his name was *U-ther*, but somehow it got twisted into *Ar-thur*. Now all his soldiers call him *the Bear*, on account of his military prowess."

"Did you know his parents?"

"We never met. For all practical purposes, they were the same as mine, *Mister and Missus Unknown*, although Mister and *Miss* might be more appropriate. If you wish to seek out Arthur's lineage, I suggest you look to Sir Ector."

"Duke Ector is quite beloved of you," said Guinevere. "Why is that?"

Merlin felt a thistle stuck to his sandal. He shook it off. "Back when Ector was one of King Vortiger's horsemen, I gave him a pastry laced with digitalis."

"You poisoned Ector? Whatever for? Were you plotting against Vortiger?"

"That bungler. I had no need to dispatch him. Vortiger was more than capable of digging his own grave. What kind of jackass meets with the savages who just stole half his kingdom?"

Guinevere held onto his sleeve. "You drugged Ector so that he would not be able to attend the peace conference with the Germans!"

"You mean the trap? Chief Hengst was notoriously devious. We knew the Jutes had landed in Kent. Governor Syagrius even sent out a letter warning us that Chief Horst was rowing west with Angles, twenty keels worth! After the Germans killed King Vortiger, they roasted his heart and fed it to their pigs."

"You saved Ector from the Kent Council Massacre."

"But Britannia was lost. A monarch should never trust his mercenaries."

"How did you know?" she said. "How did you know the Saxons would kill the King Vortiger?"

"I knew nothing. However, fortune sometimes favors my assumptions."

The way this bride-to be was questioning Merlin reminded him of his oral exams back at University. Miss Guinevere was giving him a grilling as if she were a disciple of old Professor Kumarajiva.

Merlin said, "You certainly are the inquisitive one."

Undaunted, Guinevere asked, "Why did you save Ector? What had he done for you?"

"His wife was blind from birth. I used to read to her."

"She could not see Ector's deformity."

"Nor anyone else's," said Merlin. "Ector always kept to his wedding vows. Even with her passing, he has found no other."

"Celtic knights are not usually known for their fidelity."

"And Roman girls are?"

Guinevere's deep brown eyes sunk to the ground.

It was not often that Merlin spoke to young women, especially ones from Paris. He was mindful that he had the capacity to be overly blunt. He was also aware that when he got into a verbal sparring match, he could sometimes get lost in habit energy and take the friendly competition a bit too far. Above all, he knew he had no justifiable reason for insulting Guinevere the way he just did.

He extended his wrinkled old hand. He grasped hers with its smooth porcelain skin.

"I have only kissed three women in my life," he announced, touching his lips to her palm. "Now it is four."

She blushed.

"And in all my six score years," he said, "you are the only female I have ever encountered who was fluent in the dramas of Seneca, and even more literate than I. Were I to search the world for a maid to match wits with Athena, I scarce believe I could find one more qualified than you."

Chapter XXXVIII: The Corn Moon, AD 505

Dis aliter visum.

It seemed otherwise to the gods.

* * *

Merlin opened one eye. A beam of late afternoon sunlight was striking him in the face. It had broken through the leafy branches of the beech tree beneath which he had intended to make up for some sleep lost the night before. For some reason, the universe was intent on waking him up.

Sir Galahad approached and saluted. "Are you awake, Your Excellency?"

Merlin reached out his hand. "Unfortunately, yes. I was hoping for more than a cat nap."

Galahad lifted the old man his feet and said, "You have been asleep since noon, Sir."

"Well then, I must have had a large cat nap; a tiger's slumber, as it were. Tigers are lovely beasts you know, much like a lion but orange and striped. They can take down a man with just one swipe. And they swim quite well."

"I will do my best to avoid them," said Galahad. "Chancellor Ector has requested that you join him at the stone. He needs you straight away."

"Well, he better be using his crutch." Merlin strolled off toward the lakeside. "He thinks he can walk with that peg leg. I told him, it puts too much pressure on his stump."

A sizable crowd had collected by the lake. Most were Britons and Franks, but there were Scots and Visigoths as well.

"The wizard is coming," said Gawain to Ector, who sat on a field chair and gazed out with his mostly blind eye.

Merlin waved. "*Vale* and good afternoon. Who is our contestant today?"

Tristan stepped forward.

Merlin patted him on his chest with his staff. "An excellent choice."

Tristan spoke. "I would like to nominate Field Marshall Arthur."

Merlin tripped in his sandal. "Come again?"

"You h-heard him," said Ector.

Merlin forced a smile. "Ector my friend, I could never let Arthur take a try. If he succeeded, everyone would assume it was brazen patronage."

Sir Lancelot chimed in. "Venerable Merlin, I think I can speak for all of the officers here when I say there is no one of character who would ever propose that a gentleman of your caliber would ever stoop to such favoritism. And let me make it clear that I will take it as a personal affront if anyone should claim otherwise."

Merlin faced Arthur. "So, you wish to be a king, eh? On what model shall you pattern your government: Vortiger or Attila?"

"We n-need a king," said Ector. "It cannot wait."

Merlin clapped his palms together. "Very well then," he said, "have at it, boy."

Everyone made room for Arthur, who positioned himself in front of the stone. He readied his stance, as if he was about to chop wood. He pulled off his gloves and attempted to take hold of the sword with both hands. But before he managed to actually make contact with it, a flash of miniature blue lighting shot out from the handle. It jolted him backward onto the grass.

One of the Scots whispered, "*He will ne'er gie us a king.*" A Visigoth commented, "*Esta brujo teine parajos en la cabeza.*"

Arthur propped himself up on his elbows and whispered, "Aturpat's jar." A boyish grin spread across his face. "It appears that I have fallen on my arse. I must have tripped. Is there a molehill down there? I should be more careful."

Some of the knights let out a muffled laugh. Arthur hopped to his feet and extended just one white finger. He wrapped it around the handle of Ex Calibur, touching only the leather binding, not the metal. There was a loud pop of aquamarine light, and his hair stood on end, but Ex Calibur was free.

Arthur picked up the copper treads that were twisted around the tip of the sword and said, "Where did you hide the lightning pot? Is it behind the stone?"

Under his breath Merlin blurted out, *"Caco santi!"*

With all the excitement of the young boy he used to be, Arthur said, "I should have figured this out ages ago. I knew you were up to something!" He pivoted around. Every man was down on his knees.

Merlin lunged forward and latched onto his ward by the collar. "What have you done?"

Sir Lancelot dashed to Arthur's defense.

"Stand down," said Arthur. "The wizard and I need to speak."

Merlin let go. Arthur walked off into the woods and motioned for Merlin to accompany him. Merlin, still fuming, complied.

"Why did you rig that?" said Arthur. "What is going on here?"

"It was not supposed to be this way. We needed knights. Now you have mucked the whole thing up."

"Me? You cooked up this scam. What were you thinking? You promised these people they would get a ruler."

"You cannot be the king. What if you fail? You will be killed."

Arthur closed his eyes. He breathed in and he breathed out. "What if I become the leader that these people have already created? Emperors and warlords have done them no good. Now they know how survive without them. What if we make a nation of citizens?"

"Will you listen to yourself! First you fancy a coronation, and then you call for a republic. You cannot have it both ways, boy. Britannia can not have a monarchy and cast votes."

"Why not? That is what Pericles did. He showed the Athenians they could govern themselves. My men may be a pack of mercenaries, but did anyone force them to come here? No, they came by choice. They voted with their feet. The way I see it, we can be another Athens. After all, we already have a Pericles."

Merlin shook his staff in the air. "And you see yourself as him? When did you become so arrogant?"

"I am not referring to myself. I am speaking about you."

Merlin caught his breath. "Me?"

"Aye, Merlin. It is you who planted a seed on this rainy little island. Could it grow? Do you think Britannia could harbor a δεμοκρατια? How long would that take?"

"Boy, you should be asking yourself how long it will take for the Germans to overrun Britannia. Even if King Clovis were to send us every knight in his stable, we would never be able to push them out. If we make but one error, Cambria will be little more than a Celtic plantation ruled over by Angles and Saxons. We shall be vanquished."

"So that means we should not try? And if we lose, what of it? At least our children will be able to say that once upon a time in Britannia, there was a ruler who was fair and just. Maybe I cannot be a proper στρατεγοσ. Maybe this nation is not ready for that. But what if we are?"

"All tyrants start as reformers."

"What about Ashoka? He was a king. Was he not an enlightened man?"

Merlin folded his arms. "He was the exception that proves the rule."

"Well then, I will have to be an exception too. After all, you taught me to read like a Roman and hunt like Jute. I can shoot like a Hun, and just as easily form the lotus blessing. It is all your doing, father. You trained me for this."

Merlin opened his mouth, but no words came out. Did Arthur just call him *father*? The old man dropped his walking stick and began to stagger. "No. " His heart began to pound. His wrist began to shake. "This was not what he wanted."

Arthur gripped Merthen by the shoulders. "What are you talking about?"

"The Buddha. He sent me a vision. I saw you on a slave ship. I was directed to save you. You were supposed to become a monastic. And now, I have failed."

"A vision? You told me you never had visions. When was this?"

"You were a boy. I saw you, your blue eyes. I saw your bleeding feet." Merlin hung his head. "I was trapped, and now I am doomed."

Arthur leaned in close, forcing Merlin to look into his face.

"My eyes," said Arthur, "they are brown, not blue. I have never been on a slave ship, but you have. The boy you saw in your vision was not me. That boy was you, Merlin. Think about it. The Buddha would never tell you that your salvation rested with someone else. That is not the Buddha's way."

Merlin recalled his vision in unusually vivid detail. The boy on the slave ship was bathed in moonlight. The sweet figgy fragrance of blossoming bo trees wafted through the air. What was the color of the ragged urchin's eyes? Yes, they were blue. Arthur was right. The boy was Merlin.

And then, a lost memory bubbled up from Merlin's store consciousness. He was a toddler living with his mother in the brothel. The sailors in the alley were gambling with goat's knuckles. One of them was whittling a stick with his dagger. A rat scurried out onto the cobblestones. Merlin waved to it and it stopped. With a flick of his wrist, the wood carver tossed his knife, skewering the rat in the belly.

Merlin felt sorry for the rat. He did not want to see it die. When it looked right at him, he assumed it wanted to be his friend. He cried and ran off to his mother. She was sitting on the bed where men came to visit her. He jumped into her arms and she rocked him back and forth. And then he remembered what his mother looked like. Her eyes were blue.

"There is no path," said Arthur. "No attainment. One cannot follow the Buddha to Nirvana. You must find your own way. That is what you taught me."

"I have done terrible things," said Merlin. "I killed a man. I deflowered an unmarried woman."

"You brought joy to your brothers at Nalanda, did you not? You brought happiness to the Britons by feeding them, and holding back the Saxons. It was you who helped defeat the Huns. Were it not for you, there may have been no end to Attila's cruelty."

Merlin wept. "I gave him the stirrup. It murdered millions."

"You permitted knights from all over Europe to come to Britannia and live in equanimity, an achievement unequaled since the Republic. You honor Brother Tinh Tu by wearing his robes. You have always lived simply, without too much aversion or attachment, even though you had access to wealth and power. Can you not see this?"

Merlin hid his face. "Were it not for me, Tinh Tu would have lived. He taught me everything. I gave him death."

"You have lived the Practice. You have transformed the suffering of a slave boy into the liberation of a nation. Be mindful, old man. Be mindful."

Merlin wiped the perspiration from his brow. Everything before became shrouded in darkness, as if the sun had gone down in an instant.

"Merlin?" said Arthur. "Answer me? Merthen? Ambrosius? Say something?"

* * *

All Merlin could hear was the creaking of a slave ship. He opened his eyes. The lone flame of a clay lamp was all that lit the galley. He tried to move his legs, but the cage surrounding him was too small. Then a rat appeared in the corner. More followed. They were black and filthy.

He was terrified, as terrified as he had ever been. But, instead of crying out he said, "Do what you must. You are as much as a slave as I."

The rats formed into a circle and began to walk in meditation. They chanted, "Namo Tassa Bhagavato Arahato Samma Sambhudasa." It was the very first chant Brother Tinh Tu taught to Merlin.

The darkness dissipated.

* * *

Arthur was taking off his boot. Around his ankle was a bracelet of eighteen rosewood beads. He untied it. "I think you need this."

Merlin could hardly see for the tears in his eyes. "It is not mine. I am holding it for Brother Tinh Tu. I must return it. I gave him my word."

"Is everything all right?"

Merlin caught his breath. Not only that, he became aware of it. Merlin had always wondered if Arthur was the reincarnation of Ashoka the Great. But perhaps Arthur was actually the reincarnation of Brother Tinh Tu. Or then again, maybe Arthur was just Arthur.

"Yes," said Merlin, "the bracelet is yours."

Arthur jiggled the beads in his hands.

Merlin breathed in and then he breathed out. He straightened his posture, and felt his feet touching the earth. "I would be appalled," he said, "if I saw a father abandon his son."

Merlin tugged on the orange kerchief around his neck. Was he still a Buddhist? Should he crown Arthur as king? What would a thought-worthy monastic do? Instead of answering these questions, Merlin simply chose to observe them. No understanding. No attainment. No obstacles.

He ambled his knobby knees toward the stone and called out, "Son! Come hither. I am about to do something that is monumentally daft."

Merlin marched out within ear-shot of the crowd and yelled, "Stand up you mangy rabble! I have something to enunciate, so batten down your traps."

Merlin eyeballed everyone, moving from one face to the next. It was a technique he learned from James the cithara player. As James was fond of saying, *You should never play to the audience; you should play to each person.*

James also said that magic did not occur when the magician's coin disappeared; it occurred when people felt compelled to watch, even though they knew it was not really magic. And this from a man who never studied the Buddha's Precepts.

Arthur made his way over to Merlin's side.

"Putty in my formidable digits," said Merlin. "Now, get on one knee, son. It is time for us to stir things up."

Arthur knelt down.

Yet again, Merlin began to perspire. His heart pounded, a deafening noise.

* * *

The distant strum of cithara strings rang out. It was James playing on some unseen street corner. The violet blue of the early evening sky was spotted with pink clouds, and stars that burned not white, but orange. In the woods there grew a German oak, an Indian rosewood, and a Himalayan rhododendron. Merlin grabbed onto his staff, but it was not wooden. It was a duck.

Out through the forest came Sir Ector, riding on his Percheron. Young Sir Kay was beside him. Behind them, Morgan and Thumbs were chatting, while young Father Thomasius tried to convince High Chief Aella to attend the festival of St Austremonius. Next to Gawain were Sir Pashent and the Centurion Aethiops, dressed in his finest presentation uniform. His hand was holding that of Scottas's Chinese slave girl. She seemed glad to have his protection.

In her apron, Judith the Jew carried a fresh-baked flat bread slathered with fermented fish paste you could smell a mile away. Over by Sir Tristan, Speck the Negro stood on his hands, while Scottas brushed his favorite ponies. Mister Brynmor's daughter, Delyth, wanted to ride it, but Widow Blodwen told her not to. And in front of them, sat the prostitute Merlin had burned as a witch. Her little babies were cradled in her arms. She rocked them off to sleep.

Under the shade of an apple tree, little Uther sat cross legged holding a scroll. His finger was up his nose. He unrolled the parchment, revealing one word written in the hand of Brother Tinh Tu. All it said was, "svaha," an ancient Sanskrit term, the meaning of which Buddhist scholars never fully understood. Tinh Tu used to translate it as, "Horray!"

* * *

Merlin closed his eyes. When he re-opened them, all he could see was Ex Calibur above in his hands. How it got there, he had no idea. He gently lowered the weapon to touch Arthur's shoulders and whispered. "*Gah-tay, gah-tay, para gah-tay, parasam gah-tay, bodhi svaha.*" With that, Merlin cried out, "*Viva Arturus, Rex Britannia!*"

Everyone cheered except for Merlin. He inhaled and swung his body around. With one graceful motion, he hurled Ex Calibur high into the air. The black oxidized blade spiraled over the heads of Sir Ector and his knights. When it descended, it sliced into the center of the lake, leaving behind only a widening train of ripples.

* * *

A songbird landed on Merlin's shoulder. It was a Kashmir flycatcher.

"You tricked me," he said.

She flitted off, back into the woods. He followed after her.

"No," said Gopi, "if you recall, I asked you to tell me about the boy. I never said the boy was Arthur."

"And the fact that Uther ran into me just after you asked, was that mere coincidence?"

"I prefer to think of it as karma. I have a question."

"And who is asking it?"

"I am. What did you see before you crowned King Arthur? You had a vision, I could tell."

"I did see something," he said. "I saw the Buddha's Thunderbolt."

"Ex Calibur? You mean the sword really is Buddha's Thunderbolt?"

"Of course not." He stroked her head. "It is just a chunk of metal. What was important was the way that I saw it, mindfully, in the present moment, with no regrets from the past, no fears for the future. The very act of seeing, openly and unfettered by delusion, that is Buddha's Thunderbolt. It does not strike you down; it wakes you up."

The bird fluttered her wings. "You achieved interbeing?"

"I would not go that far. But at least I became aware of what it means to be aware. How odd that it took a tool of violence to teach me the way of the Buddha."

"And yet, how apt. Where better to discover it than the last place it should be? Still, it would have been more fun if the sword really had been Buddha's Thunderbolt."

Merlin shrugged his shoulders. "If it is a fairy tale you want, go ask a druid or some other smelly priest. Myself, I need not indulge in fantasy. Reality is strange enough."

"One last question," said Gopi. "Why did you throw the sword in the lake?"

"I bought it to pick apples, not to kill Germans. When the people of Britannia elected I give them a leader, I obliged them. But I was not about to bless the bloodshed they would commit holding back the Saxons. So, I threw away their magic sword. Pericles never needed one. Neither did Ashoka. I reckoned Arthur would be better off without it."

"That was quite mindful of you. One could almost argue... the stuff of legend."

"By the way," said Merlin, "did I ever show you the table Arthur and I cobbled together? It has eighteen legs, one for each bead."

"I have already heard about it. Every poet in Europe tells the tale of brave Arthur and his Round Table."

"Poets? Those lazy drunks should never be believed. That Morgan has been spreading nothing but lies about the boy. If we are not careful, her slander will be accepted as truth, and generations will regard me as nothing but a sharp-toothed cavorting warlock."

"No," said the black-eyed bird. "They will think better of you. The gods have deemed it so."

"The gods: what balderdash. You still persist in trying to persuade me that my fate is governed by a clique of make-believe immortals. I am willing to consider the possibility that you, dear Gopi, may be some kind of genuine spirit, but the gods are simply a fiction. You will never convince me otherwise."

"Or perhaps, it is just the other way around. What if I am real and you are my delusion? What is your name? Merlin, Merthen, Ambrosius? Where were you born? Where is Arthur's castle? Could it be that this is all the musing of a song bird? Was Lao Tsu but a butterfly's dream?"

Merlin raised a finger. "But if, as you suggest, I am one of your mental formations, then all the events of my life say nothing about me." He almost smiled. "Rather, they are the reflections of *your* consciousness. This begs the question, who are you?"

"I am Lady Gopi," she said, "a woman of noble birth who lived in a grand palace by a salt lake brimming with pink flamingos. I once fell in love with a foreign monastic, whom I was forbidden to marry. When he left me, I was so distraught that I gave up on life. As my punishment, the gods cast me into a cycle of reincarnation."

"Did you," Merlin stuttered, "die by your own hand?"

"My crime was even worse. For you see, I lived a long and pointless life, grieving for what I had lost rather than appreciating what I possessed. I became a hermit, speaking to no one. Were it not for the charity of others, I would have starved to death."

"There is no sin in being weak. We are born, not asked."

"In a world of powerless peasants and ignorant savages, I was granted intelligence and a comfortable existence serving a kind and caring princess. I should have used my position to reduce the suffering of others, but instead I wasted it all."

"I am so sorry." He gently stroked the bird's black feathers. "You must have loved him dearly."

"Sometimes I wonder if it was the only thing I did right. But that was then. Now I am on to other things." She flew away, saying, "I must ask you to come with me."

"Where are you going?"

A shaft of light pierced through the high tree canopy. There was a potter's wheel resting on the forest floor. Behind it sat Khnemy, the Egyptian ram-headed god, dressed in the white gown and golden collar of a Pharaoh. He centered a mound of red clay onto his wheel. Water sprung forth from his fingers, and he sculpted a figure of a man. It was Merlin.

The Goddess Athena tapped Merlin on the shoulder. "The jury has come to a decision," she said. "You are to be reincarnated as a rat."

Khnemy, focusing diligently on his work, crushed the statuette of Merlin, then reformed it into a rat.

"I think not," said Merlin. "We Buddhists believe in rebirth, not the transmigration of souls. When I die, I shall rejoin the universe like a raindrop falling into the sea. I will not be reincarnated."

Ganesha trumpeted. "A maggot is what you should be. That would be just. A rat is too good for him. As a rodent, he will still be able to wreak havoc with liberty. What kind of punishment is that?"

"Come now," said Athena, "I think we are all in agreement that my client has had a fair trial. Of course, if you are dissatisfied, I would be more than happy to file an appeal. Who knows, maybe with a different jury, I could get him reincarnated as an ape?"

Lady Gopi swooped down and said, "If I may be so bold Your Graces, may I suggest an alternative sentence. What if Merlin were to become a bird like me? We fly-catchers mate for life. If he became my husband, he would be bound to me forever. I could watch over him, keeping him from pursuing his un-mindful habit energies."

Ganesha swirled the Brahma milk in his golden bowl. "You propose to serve as his court-appointed guardian. Why would you do that?"

"I am in need of good merits," she said. "If I am ever to reach a higher form, I need to burn some karma in this one."

Athena plucked the string of her bow like a harp. "That would be acceptable to the defense. What says the prosecution?"

Ganesha batted his long black eyelashes. "Very well, but if Gopi expires before he does, I reserve the right to strike him dead. He must be supervised at all times."

Khnemy flattened the statue of the rat. "So be it," he said, "when Merlin's life comes to an end, this is how he shall be reborn." The ram-headed god pressed his deft fingers into the clay and created a bird. He sat back and admired his work. And then, with the ever critical eye of the fine artist, added one final touch.

Gopi flew over to the newly formed bird and chirped, "There is a wonderful simsapa tree in the forest of Kosambi. You and I can build a nest there."

Merlin brought his hand up to his face. He saw only feathers. "I am dead then?"

"Death is as much an illusion as life," said Gopi. "Surely Brother Tinh Tu would agree."

"That he would," said Merlin. He flicked his tail. "But are you certain you want me? The solitary life is all I have ever known. I am woefully unaccustomed to domestic relations. Being alone is all I know."

"I will help you," she said. "That is what I am here for. The spring will come, our eggs will hatch, and we will gather food for the chicks. In time, you will help me too."

"But what if you are mistaken? I would not wish for my ignorance to injure you... not again. If I had been aware of how fervently you loved me when we were in India, I would never have left you. I swear Gopi, I never wanted to hurt you."

"I know. Do not worry. We were both very young. There are many things we should have told each other."

"But what will Arthur do without me?" said the blue-eyed bird. "I do not want for him to be like me. I cannot abandon him."

"Fear not, my love. You will be with him always. Whenever they speak his name, they will speak yours a well. For as long as troubadours gather to sing, you will be inextricably bound to him. *Patris est filius.* He is his father's son."

With that the black-eyed bird spread her wings. She flew up towards the clouds. "It is time we go," she said. "We have quite a long way to go. If you like, we can fly past the bo tree where Prince Siddhartha achieved interbeing. Would you like to see that?"

"And how!" chirped the blue-eyed bird. "Now please, teach me how to fly."

"You are a bird. You do not need to be taught." She flew off toward the River Ganges.

He flapped his wings a few times and found himself aloft. Below was the Celtic Sea, the port of Carmarthen, and all of the people who lived there, puttering around like grubs. He heard black-eyed Gopi sing, "*Sita Ram Ram Ram. Jay Jay, Sita Ram Ram Ram.*"

He spiraled around in a circle. "The theory of reincarnation," he said, "holds that an animal of noble character would progress into a higher station, and ultimately arrive at the human form."

His mate did not reply.

"But then again," he concluded, "given the woeful condition of humankind's existence, spending eternity recycling as one of nature's beasts might actually have some meritorious benefits. Perhaps such an existence is as close to interbeing as a beleaguered soul can hope to get."

He glided off to the east, aware of his breathing, and became mindful of the sky, immeasurable in all directions.

Afterword

Ridentem dicere verum quid vetat?

What forbids a laughing man from telling the truth?

* * *

410 CE: The Goths sacked the City of Rome, setting ablaze the Basilica Aemilia and the Roman Forum. They were led by Alaric, a German chieftain from Bulgaria. He was likely familiar with the geography and defenses of Rome having led Germanic mercenaries fighting in the Alps on behalf of the Roman Byzantine Emperor. Ten years earlier, Alaric nearly took Rome, but was paid off with a ransom of silk garments and thousands of pounds of gold and pepper.

415 CE: Kumaragupta, a Hindu, became the king of Northern India. He ruled until 455 CE as part of the Gupta Dynasty, known as the Elephant Kings. He endowed a college of the arts at the Buddhist University of Nalanda, which continued to operate until 1193 CE. Nalanda hosted up to ten thousand students from India and abroad, including China. It is regarded as the world's first international university.

418 CE: In Africa, the Council of Carthage refuted the teachings of Pelagius. He was an ascetic scholar, literate in Greek and Latin, born somewhere in the British Isles. A reformer troubled by the moral laxity of society, Pelagius was a critic of Saint Augustine, Bishop of Hippo. Because of Pelagius's writings advancing free will and denying the doctrine of original sin, he was deemed a heretic. He fled to North Africa, and disappeared from the historic record.

421 CE: Bahran Gur, a Zoroastrian, became the king of Persia. He ruled until 438 CE as part of the Sassanian Dynasty. He is still celebrated in Iranian

culture for his victories over the Byzantine Romans and the Ephtalites, also know as the White Huns. In general, most of the Sassanian Kings maintained non-adversarial relations with Roman Byzantium.

423 CE: Kou Chien Chi, a court physician and Taoist leader, initiated a brief but brutal persecution of Buddhists in Northern China. Although he was only a royal advisor, he was an influential figure in the court of the Wei Dynasty, which ruled Northern China from 386 to 543 CE. Throughout most of their two hundred-year reign, the Wei rulers accepted Buddhism. After Kou died, the repression ceased.

431 CE: The Northern Chinese conquered the Xia state of Inner Mongolia. This territory was inhabited by nomadic horsemen known as the Xiongnu. Following their defeat, the Xiongnu migrated west. Although there is no definitive evidence to indicate that the Xiongnu were in fact the Huns, the Xoingnus' disappearance from western China appears to coincide with Huns' invasion of Eastern Europe.

Circa 450 CE: Patricolus (Saint Patrick) wrote a *Letter to the Soldiers of Coroticus*. In it, he denounced a Christian Welsh chieftain who raided a Christian community on the Irish coast, then sold his captives as slaves to pagan nations, including the Franks. Born in Britain to ethnic Roman parents, Patricolus spent his teenage years in Ireland as an abducted slave. Knowing the culture and language of the Irish pagans, he was uniquely qualified to convert them.

451 CE: At Catalonian Fields south of Orleans - a city named for the influential Aurelianus family - a combined Roman and Visigoth army foiled Attila's attempted conquest of Western Europe. In 474 CE, the Greek historian Priscus visited Attila's camp. He described Attila as a man whose clothing was unadorned, and who ate from a wooden bowl while his guests used plates of silver and gold. Priscus reported that Attila had many wives, a Scythian fool, and a Moorish dwarf.

486 CE: Clovis, a Salian Frank from the coastal lowlands, defeated Syagrius, the last Roman official still governing in Northwest Europe. Clovis was also known as *Choldowech*, *Lodewijk*, *Louis*, and *Ludwig*. He converted to Roman Christianity in 496 CE, allying himself with the Vatican, unlike the other

Germanic nations of Europe, who were largely Arian Christians. King Clovis established his capitol in Paris, thus founding the nation of France.

1938 CE: Archaeologist Wilhelm Konig described a 2,000 year old jar containing an iron bar, a copper cylinder, and an asphalt stopper, found just outside of Baghdad. Decades later, William Gray built a reproduction at a General Electric laboratory. When filled with an electrolyte, such as grape juice, it generated a charge of about two volts of electricity. Now housed in the National Museum of Iraq, it is known as the Baghdad Battery.

116 confusion - cart follow horse